"Phoebe needs us now," Charles said directly, walking over to the dressing table where Nina was sitting. "I don't want us to fight." Suddenly the rage and guilt and fear welled up within Nina, and she blared, "You had to say that bit about us loving her child, didn't you!" She glowered up at him in the mirror over the table.

"I should think you'd be worrying about Phoebe. She almost died, you know."

"She almost killed herself!" Nina bellowed in reply. Clenching her fists, she gave a dramatic sigh. "Maybe it would have been for the best."

"Don't ever say that!" Charles shouted, gripping her shoulder.

"Don't you see?" she said, her eyes betraying her agony as she turned to look up at him. "It's happening all over again. Our marriage began with a curse, and now the Devil's come to collect his due!"

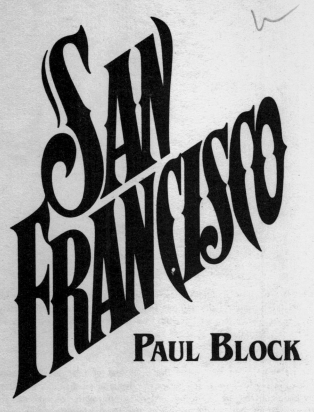

SAN FRANCISCO

PAUL BLOCK

TM

BCI

Created by the producers of
**Wagons West, Stagecoach,
Badge,** and **White Indian.**

Book Creations Inc., Canaan, NY · Lyle Kenyon Engel, Founder

LYNX BOOKS
New York

SAN FRANCISCO

ISBN: 1-55802-187-6

First Printing/August 1988

Produced by Book Creations, Inc.
Founder: Lyle Kenyon Engel

This book is published by Lynx Books, a division of Lynx Communications, Inc., 41 Madison Avenue, New York, New York, 10010. The name ''Lynx'' together with the logotype consisting of a stylized head of a lynx is a trademark of Lynx Communications, Inc.

Printed in the United States of America

0 9 8 7 6 5 4 3 2 1

To San Francisco,
a city that belongs to all America.

And to my children, Kiva and Ueyn,
who are privileged to be able to call themselves
native San Franciscans.

SALOMON'S

SAN F

EMPORIUM

SAN FRANCISCO

RON TOELKE '88

ONE

THE OPEN-TOPPED LANDAU HIT A RUT IN THE MACADAM and lurched, forcing Aidan McAuliffe to grab the side panel with both hands. The inch-wide wrist irons bit into his flesh, but when he glanced at the gaoler beside him, the man merely sneered, giving no indication that he was in any way concerned that the manacles might be too tight. Having previously requested that they be removed or at least loosened, Aidan knew it would serve no purpose to ask again.

Lowering his hands to his lap, Aidan saw that the top layer of skin had peeled slightly where the manacles had been chafing, and he found himself mentally reciting the five layers of the epidermis: *Strata corneum, lucidum, granulosum, mucosum, germinativum.* He imagined each layer being rolled back, revealing the papillary and reticular layers of the dermis beneath.

The coach jounced again, shaking the young physician from his reverie. Clasping his hands, he considered praying, but of late he had been unable to summon the faith. Indeed, it took a supreme effort to keep from blaspheming—from cursing his accusers, his fate, even his God. Had not that

1

very God looked down and done nothing when Aidan had been so cruelly destroyed? Was He not standing by idly while an innocent man was being transported to his death?

Aidan McAuliffe rested his head against the upholstered backrest and watched the buildings passing by. The London streets were darkening, and streetlamps had already been lit. Fleet Street was busy with pedestrians, private coaches, and an abundance of cabs, both the four-wheelers, with seats for up to six passengers, and the faster and more comfortable two-wheeled hansoms, fitted out for two or three. No one appeared to be paying any attention to the landau as it made its way toward Whitehall Street. To them, the vehicle and its two passengers were quite unremarkable, since the gaoler's uniform was hidden by a wool coat and his prisoner had been allowed to make the journey in the suit he had worn during his trial. No one would have imagined that only a few minutes earlier the landau had left the walls of Newgate, the detentional prison where Aidan had been held throughout the duration of his trial. Neither would they have believed that the tall, respectable-looking passenger with the firm yet pleasant features, brown hair and mustache, and penetrating pale-blue eyes had that very morning been convicted of murder.

Aidan felt an involuntary shudder course through him as he remembered the thoroughly demoralizing state of the accommodations—if one could call them that—at Newgate, which more closely resembled a lunatic asylum than a prison. He had been kept in an overcrowded cell with a dozen other unfortunates awaiting trial, and the stench of alcohol, sewage, and unwashed bodies had made his long, grueling hours in the courtroom seem a pleasant relief.

Aidan looked up as the driver pulled the reins, turning the prison landau onto Whitehall, and continued along the Thames toward Millbank Penitentiary, where in two weeks the sentence of the court would be carried out. There at sunset on May 27, 1896, Aidan McAuliffe would be hanged inside the prison walls before a select committee of prison officials and members of the press.

Closing his eyes, Aidan listened to the steady clop of the

2

dray horse's hooves as he recalled the events that had led him, quite literally, to the end of his rope.

Four years earlier, at the age of twenty-four, Aidan completed his medical training in his hometown of Edinburgh, Scotland, and accepted a position with a Glasgow physician, an Englishman named Basil Finn, who shared his practice with his son, Michael. Aidan got along well with the elderly doctor but had no such rapport with his son, a dissolute man in his midforties who took after his overbearing and obsessively frugal mother, Sybil. It was she who really ran the practice, keeping charge of the accounts and preparing the medications, making sure they were as dilute as possible—particularly those intended for patients who were behind in their payments. On more than one occasion Aidan had found her substituting medically worthless foodstuffs for the more expensive ingredients called for in the *British Pharmacopoeia*. But whenever he raised the issue with his employer, the elderly physician shrugged his shoulders helplessly and merely promised to see what he could do.

Basil Finn died of a heart attack two years later, with the practice devolving to his son. In less than a week, Aidan found himself without a job. The end was precipitated by a furious argument between Aidan and the widow Finn that had begun when she took exception to his treating the daughter of a coal miner whose account was in arrears by a few shillings. What really sealed his doom was when he wondered aloud whether her beloved husband's departure might have been hurried along by the untimely substitution of some ordinary garden herbs for the foxglove leaves called for in the preparation of the digitalis used to regulate his heart.

Aidan had not been sorry to leave the Finns or Glasgow behind, and after trying unsuccessfully to find employment in his hometown of Edinburgh, he set his sights on London. His parents had died soon after his graduation from medical school, so he sold the small family home on the outskirts of the city and set out for London with a little over five hundred pounds in his pocket.

Aidan recalled his arrival in London and how a former

medical school classmate had arranged for him to take over the Lewisham office of the deceased Dr. Dennis Kasindorf. For the next year and a half, Aidan had painstakingly rebuilt the practice, steadily winning the confidence of Kasindorf's former patients with his professional yet compassionate manner and by working long hours, so that residents of the district knew they could call on him any time of day. That was why he had been at the office late that second night of March when the Mayhew woman had been brought to see him, precipitating a chain of events that eventually led to this carriage ride to the gallows.

Just then the prison landau veered around a turn, and Aidan grabbed hold of the front edge of the seat to keep from falling against the gaoler beside him. They were passing the House of Commons and would soon be at Millbank Penitentiary; the next time he would see the streets of London would be when he emerged from his cellblock and took a final walk across the prison grounds and past the front gate to the small brick building that housed the gallows.

Reaching up with his manacled hands, Aidan absently stroked his trim mustache, then felt the faint stubble that had begun to form on his chin. He found himself musing whether he should avail himself of the razor that would be provided him on the morning of his hanging—and if he did, whether he should use it to shave his whiskers or to slit his throat. He was a physician, and he knew how to make a cut so that even the best London surgeon would not be able to save him for the gallows. But being a physician, he had taken an oath to save lives, not take them; he knew he would not be able to cheat the hangman of his appointed task.

Aidan watched the streetlamps passing overhead, and they began to lull him, much as if a candle were being passed in front of his eyes by a hypnotist. But he did not fall into a trance or even drift into sleep; instead he found himself reliving that fateful evening in March when the final wheels were set in motion, carrying him inexorably toward this final journey to Millbank Penitentiary. . . .

* * *

Aidan McAuliffe looked up at the clock over the dispensary cabinet. It was ten past nine—two hours after he should have closed the office and returned to his boardinghouse room several blocks away. But he was stumped by some of the symptoms shown by the young Duffy boy and was determined to come up with a diagnosis before morning.

Standing away from the desk, Aidan stretched his stiff muscles, then reached over and turned up the wick of the kerosene floor lamp. He walked to the row of shelves beside the dispensary counter and ran a forefinger along the spines of the medical books as he tried to choose the appropriate volume. Just as he was about to settle on one, there was a loud knocking on the front door of the adjacent waiting room. Aidan glanced again at the clock, then crossed the dispensary and entered the darkened waiting room.

Through the frosted glass of the door, he could make out two figures, one somewhat taller than the other, in the lighted entryway beyond. The taller one began to knock again, more sharply and impatiently, and Aidan hurried over, turned the key in the lock, and swung open the door. He was nearly bowled over as a man staggered into the room with a woman propped up in his arms. The man was gaunt and balding, with thin, severe lips and sunken brown eyes, and he fairly swam in his gray, threadbare suit. Barely conscious in his arms was a well-dressed young woman with long, disheveled brown hair and exceedingly pale skin. She could barely keep her feet, and her eyes kept rolling upward and closing, then fluttering open again.

"Bring her in here," Aidan told the man as he took hold of the woman's other arm and led the way across the waiting room to the examining room beside the dispensary.

"What's her name?" Aidan asked as they entered the dark room, which was dominated by a large examining table with metal stirrups and several supply cabinets along the walls.

"D'know," the man grunted in reply.

The two men turned her around and lifted her up onto the table. Then Aidan eased her back into a lying position, with her legs dangling over the edge of the table. "Wait here," he told the man as he rushed from the room and returned with a lighted lantern from the dispensary. Placing it on one of the cabinets, he looked at the man and asked, "What happened?"

The fellow shrugged. "Found 'er on me stoop. Was swoonin' 'n' such, so I bring 'er 'ere." He raised his hands and began to rub them together; they were smeared with blood. When he realized that the young physician had noticed, he lowered them nervously. "It's from 'er," he said, nodding toward the woman.

Aidan walked over to the semi-conscious young woman, who was moaning slightly, her head lolling back and forth on the examining table. Glancing down, he saw that the hem of her white petticoat was blotched with red and that a small pool of blood was forming on the floor below her feet.

"My God!" he blurted. He quickly pulled off his suit jacket and rolled up his sleeves, then donned a long white apron that was hanging on a wall hook. As he turned toward the table, he saw that the man had backed through the doorway and was watching from partway into the waiting room.

"I have to examine her," Aidan said, walking over to the door. "You wait in there." The man nodded, and Aidan closed the door and returned to where the woman was lying.

After lighting a floor lantern and bringing it closer to the examining table, Aidan raised the young woman's brown wool overskirt, removed the petticoat, and used it to wipe the blood that was smeared all over her stockings and thighs. The woman was sinking deeper into unconsciousness, and as he carefully pressed against her abdomen, she seemed oblivious to what was happening. It took but a few moments for him to diagnose the cause of her bleeding. Apparently she had given birth, though he had no idea what had become of the baby, and she was continuing to bleed because not all of the placenta had been delivered.

Realizing he would have to intervene at once, Aidan quickly assembled the necessary instruments from the nearby surgical cabinet. He pulled the woman higher on the table and lifted her legs into the stirrups, all the while whispering soothingly to her, assuring her that everything would be fine. Then he adjusted the lamp, picked up the speculum, and began a more thorough internal examination.

A few minutes later, he realized things would not be all right. Indeed the woman had given birth, but far ahead of the appointed time—perhaps only four or five months into her pregnancy. And there had been no trouble with the afterbirth. Rather she was bleeding from internal wounds so massive that she could not possibly have inflicted them herself. He had no doubt as to the cause: a botched abortion performed for a few shillings in some squalid room by someone with as much knowledge of medicine as a butcher.

Aidan set to work trying to stop the bleeding and repair the damage—a race he soon realized he had little chance of winning. The woman already had lost so much blood that she was in shock, and the puncture wounds to her uterus were so numerous that it would be like trying to patch a shredding piece of cloth. His only hope was to pack the uterus with absorbent wool and hope that, as the organ continued to contract following the abortion, it would sufficiently constrict the punctures and stop the bleeding. The ragged tear to her cervix would have to be sutured.

While dilating the cervix with a pair of retractors that were highly polished to reflect light into the body, Aidan packed the uterus with the gauze. Then he threaded a Hagedorn needle with a catgut ligature and clamped the needle in a pair of long-nosed needle holders. Repositioning the retractors, he set to work suturing the cervix. Before he had completed the first suture, the bleeding slowed and then stopped. He knew at once that it was not due to his intervention; rather, the woman's heart had stopped pumping blood through her system.

Aidan forced himself to draw in a deep, calming breath as he removed the needle holder and retractors and gave the woman a final examination to confirm that she had died. Having a chance to look at her features closely for the first time, he realized that she was quite attractive and far younger than he had thought—probably still in her teens. Even in death her soft-brown eyes, which remained open, spoke of intelligence and a lively spirit, while her hand-tailored clothing suggested she was from a well-to-do family.

After removing the young woman's legs from the stirrups, Aidan lowered her dress and closed her eyes. He took off his apron, washed at a basin on one of the cabinets, then walked over and opened the door to the waiting room. He glanced around the darkened room and was not too surprised to see that the gaunt man had gone, leaving open the door to the entryway. Perhaps he had been telling the truth about having found the woman on his stoop. Or else he had been the one who had taken her to the abortionist—or more likely was the abortionist himself.

Those questions would have to wait. Back in the examining room, the body of a young woman had to be dealt with. Her family needed to be notified, and an official report had to be made. . . .

"Won't be long 'afore we get to Millbank," the driver of the prison landau called behind him as he turned the coach onto Victoria Street.

"Soon enough f'me," the gaoler muttered with a sidelong glance at his prisoner. He seemed on the verge of saying something further, but apparently he thought better of it, for he turned his head and again stared straight ahead.

Aidan McAuliffe gave a short sigh. He thought of the single time he had been at Millbank Penitentiary, to confirm the death of one of Dennis Kasindorf's former patients, who had received a five-year sentence for embezzling but had died two months short of finishing his term. He remembered Millbank as a labyrinth of long buildings that from above looked like a daisy, the buildings connected to form six pentagon-shaped courtyards around a central hexagon, with a high stone wall surrounding the entire complex. Each prisoner was given his own cell, where he was kept largely in solitude to reflect upon his sins.

Aidan grinned ruefully. Though he would not be staying at Millbank long enough for any meaningful reflection, at least the next two weeks would provide a bit of solitude— something unobtainable at Newgate, where prisoners were herded into large cells while awaiting trial at the nearby Central Criminal Court, popularly known as Old Bailey.

Aidan's grin faded as he recalled the other events leading up to his arrest and conviction. After the young woman had died on his examining table, Aidan searched the pockets of her coat and discovered a letter to her father in which she concocted a story as to why she had left home for a few days without prior warning. The never-posted letter gave her name as Cheryl Mayhew and bore an address in nearby Greenwich, so Aidan paid a local boy to send for the woman's father, Gordon Mayhew.

When the elderly gentleman arrived an hour later, accompanied by a son in his early thirties, Aidan broke the news as gently as possible. Mayhew was shocked to learn of Cheryl's death but was even more horrified upon discovering that she had died as a result of an abortion. Mayhew was a prominent financier whose fear of scandal seemed to outweigh the sorrow of his loss, and he begged Aidan to list some other cause of death on the official documents. When Aidan refused, explaining that such an action was illegal and unethical while assuring him that he would see to it the report was kept confidential, the man went into a rage, accusing the young physician of being the abortionist who butchered his daughter. Aidan tried to reason with the man, arguing that were he the abortionist, he would not have sent for Mayhew and would have no compunction about signing a false report. But Mayhew grew even more livid, saying that he would have Aidan arrested for murder would it not bring scandal to his own family. With that he stormed out of the office, swearing to avenge his daughter's death.

As Aidan had expected, the police kept the true details of Cheryl Mayhew's death from the press, and there was no scandal. Assuming the affair to be over, Aidan paid little attention when a month later another woman was found dead in a London alley, an aborted fetus at her side. He was thoroughly stunned when two days later the police presented themselves at his office and arrested him for murder.

In the ensuing trial, the woman was identified as a prostitute who had sought Aidan McAuliffe's services when she became pregnant. Aidan's shock was complete when a parade of half a dozen prostitutes was called to the stand to testify that his office was a well-known refuge for women in their profession—a place where they could seek medical assistance for some of the ills peculiar to their trade or to end an untimely pregnancy.

Aidan's barrister was unconcerned about the testimony of prostitutes, no matter the number, but even his usually impassive expression changed when the final witness was called. ''Dr. Michael Finn,'' the prosecutor proclaimed, ''who at my entreaty has been so kind as to leave his practice in Glasgow and make the long journey to London so that the court may be better informed as to the true nature of Dr. Aidan McAuliffe.''

Once sworn in before the bench, Finn did not need much prompting to divulge his sordid tale of Aidan's days working for the Finn family, spun in such imaginative detail that even Aidan would have believed the story, were it not about himself. According to Finn, Aidan had taken up with a sorry class of people during his years in Glasgow and had frequented various establishments of ill repute. Finn himself had counseled Aidan on numerous occasions, but the young physician would not change his ways. It was upon discovering that Aidan had performed an abortion on one of the local prostitutes that Finn had been forced to let him go. Afterward he had learned that Aidan had moved to London, but that was the last he had heard of him until being contacted by the prosecutor's office.

Aidan's barrister did his best to refute the testimony of the Glasgow physician and further tried to establish a link between him and a certain Gordon Mayhew. But Finn stuck to his story and denied knowledge of anyone by that name. The barrister did not pursue the line of questioning, since any testimony regarding the young Mayhew woman's death—which so far had not come up at the trial—probably would only work against his client.

Aidan was certain that Gordon Mayhew had paid the prostitutes and Michael Finn for their perjured testimony, his suspicions intensified by Mayhew's son, Jeremy, having attended the trial daily. But with no proof and with his irreversibly damaged, the final judgment was simply a formality. Being found guilty of murdering a young prostitute and her unborn fetus and leaving their bodies lying in a London alley, Aidan McAuliffe would face execution by hanging.

That hanging was two weeks and a mere two blocks away, Aidan realized as the prison landau turned off Victoria Street onto the road leading to Millbank Penitentiary.

Peering into the darkness ahead, he tried to make out the prison wall. All he could see was a hansom cab parked halfway up the street, its horse in harness, the driver seated at the reins in the raised seat behind the closed passenger compartment. As the landau approached, the cabbie slapped the reins and pulled away from the curb just in front of the landau. Almost immediately there was a jarring crunch as the left wheel of the hansom spun off the axle and the vehicle came crashing down on the chassis, almost knocking the driver from his perch. The horse was pulled to the left, and the cab came to a skidding halt sideways across the road, blocking the way.

The driver of the landau fought the reins to steady his own horse, which had reared up as it almost careened into the hansom. Aidan started to stand in his seat, but the gaoler held his arm. Meanwhile, the landau driver pulled back on the brake and climbed down to see if he could help.

"S-sorry, mate," the cabbie called to the landau driver as he stumbled down from his seat and began to stagger toward the passenger compartment. The other driver was already there, and as he yanked open the passenger door, a man in a long black cape and slightly askew top hat climbed out unsteadily, gratefully taking hold of the landau driver's arm as he nodded that he was all right.

Seeing that his own passenger was already being attended, the cabbie changed direction and headed toward the open-topped landau, proclaiming to its occupants, "I'll get 'er out o' yer way in no time. Just un'itch me mare, and ye can go 'round." He came up to the side of the vehicle and gave a gap-toothed smile, his face largely concealed in the shadows cast by his high collar and slouch hat.

Suddenly it struck Aidan that the fellow was not wearing the usual livery of a hansom cab driver; apparently the gaoler was having the same thought, for just then Aidan saw him reach for the pistol under his coat. But before he had pulled aside the lapel, the cabbie said, "Easy, mate," and raised a revolver above the side of the landau.

"What's the meaning—?"

"None o' yer concern," the cabbie cut him off, waggling the revolver. "Up wi' yer 'ands," he demanded gruffly, and when the two passengers complied, he leaned into the coach and reached under the gaoler's coat, pulling out the pistol.

If Aidan and the gaoler were wondering what had become of their own driver, their questions were answered when they saw him being herded back to the landau under the barrel of a gun wielded by the passenger of the hansom cab. When the driver reached the landau, the cabbie directed him into the open coach and climbed in as well, the two men taking the backward-facing seat across from Aidan and the gaoler.

"Put 'em down nice 'n' slow," the cabbie directed the men, motioning them to lower their hands as he closed the door of the coach. Meanwhile his partner climbed into the driver's seat at the front and released the brakes. He slapped the reins and expertly turned the landau around, then started away to the northwest.

The cabbie took care to conceal his identity further, pulling a gray scarf over his face. He did not allow anyone to speak and made no effort to explain where they were headed. He just sat back in the corner of the coach and watched from behind the barrel of his revolver. All that the others could do was stare silently at one another—and it was clear to Aidan from the expressions of the other two men that each thought he was involved in the kidnapping. Yet he was certain he had never seen this cabbie before, though he had to admit that his current fate, despite being unknown, was preferable to the one awaiting him at Millbank.

For more than an hour the landau sped northwest out of

London. After leaving the more populated area behind, the driver pulled the coach off the road into a stand of trees and brought it to a halt.

"Y'stay put," the cabbie ordered Aidan as he opened the door and motioned the other two men to get out.

The driver, his face also masked with a scarf, climbed down and helped herd the two men over to a nearby tree. In the thin moonlight, Aidan could see that this second man had produced some rope from under his coat, and he and the cabbie were tying the two men to the tree. Aidan considered slipping out of the landau and trying to make his escape on foot, despite being heavily manacled, but the two strangers were armed and only about fifteen feet away, and as they worked at tying and gagging the gaoler and landau driver, they continually glanced over at Aidan. Furthermore, Aidan did not believe his life was at risk with these strangers. They seemed to be taking care not to injure anyone, and if they meant Aidan harm, there would be no point in rescuing him from the gallows.

A few minutes later the two men returned to the landau. This time the cabbie climbed into the driver's seat and took the reins, while the second man took the seat across from Aidan. It was not until they had pulled away from the trees and were well down the road that this man put away his revolver and lifted his hands to remove his scarf.

"Robert!" Aidan exclaimed as the scarf dropped away to reveal a young, clean-shaven man with reddish hair and an abundance of freckles. It was Aidan's medical school friend, Robert Gladstone, who had helped set him up in practice in London.

"You didn't think I'd have let them lock you away in Millbank, did you?" Gladstone asked his incredulous friend. He went on to explain that he had hatched up this rescue plan earlier that same day following Aidan's sentencing, realizing that there would be no hope for Aidan once he was transferred to Millbank. The cabbie was one of Gladstone's patients—a man of dubious reputation who was devoted to Gladstone for having saved the life of his son.

13

The man had appropriated the hansom cab for the evening; Gladstone had not questioned how.

Gladstone reached into his pocket and produced a large key on a brass ring. "Courtesy of the gaoler," he declared with a smile as he reached over and unlocked the manacles.

As the iron cuffs fell to the floor of the landau, Aidan rubbed his chafed wrists and breathed a sigh of relief. Gladstone, meanwhile, twisted around on the seat and conferred with the driver, and a moment later the man turned the landau onto a crossing road and headed southwest.

"We went northwest to throw off any pursuers," Gladstone explained. "Our real destination is Portsmouth."

"Portsmouth?" Aidan asked.

"We've got to get you out of the country. I've a brother in Ireland." He reached into his pocket and produced a letter, which he handed to Aidan. "This will explain everything to him. I'm certain he'll put you up until things settle down. Unfortunately, I put this escape plan together so quickly that I didn't have time to obtain the name of an Ireland-bound ship, but we're certain to come up with at least one in Portsmouth."

Aidan nodded and stuffed the envelope into his own pocket, then accepted a second envelope Gladstone held out.

"It's one hundred pounds—all I could come up with," Gladstone told him.

"I can't—"

"Of course you can. Consider it a loan; I know you are good for it."

Aidan felt his eyes misting. "Somehow I'll pay you back. But I'll never be able to repay you for—"

"Nonsense." Gladstone waved away the remark. "I know you'd do as much for me."

The landau continued through the night, steadily bearing southwest toward Portsmouth. After stopping briefly at dawn at a small tavern in Guildford to change horses and have breakfast, the travelers took back to the road. It was nearly dusk when they pulled into the bustling seaport town of

Portsmouth. The cabbie dropped them off in a small business district near the waterfront and then took his leave, with Gladstone explaining to Aidan that the landau would be abandoned in Portsmouth and that he and the cabbie would return separately to London.

Aidan and his friend first visited several of the shops so that they could obtain some needed travel supplies before closing time. They purchased a large carpetbag, changes of clothing, and enough food to last the journey to Ireland. Then they headed toward the piers, where they hoped to book passage on a ship leaving Portsmouth that very night.

As they passed the window of a closed grocer's shop, Aidan grabbed his friend's arm and pulled up short. "Look," he whispered, pointing at that afternoon's edition of the *Portsmouth Mercury*, on display in the window.

Above the mast was a bulletin detailing the daring escape of condemned prisoner Dr. Aidan McAuliffe while being transported to Millbank Penitentiary the evening before. Apparently word had been sent out by telegraph, with local constables being alerted to be on the lookout—particularly in the coastal communities, from where the convict might attempt to flee the country. Though the brief article did not give a description of Aidan, it explained that local authorities had been telegraphed a more complete report.

"We'd best not chance buying a ticket," Gladstone said glumly. "Even if you use an alias, they're liable to check the ship's papers of outgoing vessels and interrogate all passengers who bought tickets in the past day."

Aidan nodded in agreement, but when Gladstone went on to suggest they head by land to Scotland, Aidan cut in, "No, it would be far too risky. I believe we should keep to your original plan—but without the benefit of booking a passage. It's only a short journey to Ireland. I should have no trouble finding a place to hide aboard ship."

"You don't suggest becoming a stowaway—?"

"Precisely."

"It's quite dangerous," Gladstone pointed out.

"Not as much as tramping around the countryside. And if they find me after we've set sail, I can pay my passage.

Thanks to you, I've plenty of funds with which to purchase their silence.''

Thus decided, the two men proceeded cautiously to the waterfront, where they sought out a likely haunt for seamen in which to inquire about upcoming ship departures. They chose the Square Rigger, a combined drinking establishment, restaurant, and inn that faced the piers. After looking through one of the windows and determining that there were no members of the constabulary on the premises, they entered and took a table toward the back of the large room that served as both a dining and drinking area. The walls recently had been painted a white as chalky as the cliffs of Dover, but already an elongated smear of mottled gray soot was forming behind each of the dozen wall lanterns that ringed the room. Four round pillars rose from the wide-plank floor to the intersections of four crisscrossing wood beams that broke the ceiling into nine equal squares. Other than a sketch of a ship that had been painted on each of the pillars, the room was devoid of decoration, save for a pair of anchors hanging on the far wall above a long open window that led into the kitchen.

While Gladstone went up to the window and ordered beer and two plates of mutton stew, Aidan surveyed the tavern patrons. Of the dozen customers, ten were dressed in the rough homespun clothes of merchant seamen. They sat on benches at two long deal tables that dominated the center of the room, enjoying tall mugs of ale as they traded stories of their latest voyages. The remaining patrons were a young couple at a small table near the door. As the Square Rigger seemed a relatively clean and respectable establishment, Aidan took them for lodgers who either were awaiting someone's arrival on an incoming vessel or were themselves due to ship out. They were talking quietly to each other and seemed oblivious to everyone else in the room, though on one occasion Aidan noticed the attractive, copper-haired woman glance over at him.

Robert Gladstone returned with two pewter mugs of ale, which he thudded down onto the table. "Supper will be ready directly," he said, taking the seat across from Aidan.

The food appeared in short order, brought forth by a portly woman with a round, pleasant face and noticeably muscular forearms, no doubt the result of years spent ferrying overloaded trays back and forth from the kitchen. She seemed to know all the seamen, for she traded light banter with several of them as she made her way past their table, and over to the two men at the back of the room.

"There ye go," she said, smiling broadly as she lowered the tray and placed a plate in front of each man.

"Mmmm," Gladstone murmured, closing his eyes as he leaned forward and breathed in the aroma of the stew.

"Made fresh this evenin'. I'm certain both ye gents'll find it to your likin'. But next time ye must try our finnan haddie—a Square Rigger specialty."

"We'd love to, wouldn't we?" Gladstone asked his companion, who nodded in agreement while trying to cover his nervousness. Gladstone looked back at the woman and added, "Perhaps you can have some wrapped for us to take on board."

"Then ye'll be shippin' out soon?" she asked, and when Gladstone nodded, she examined the two men a bit closer. "Passengers, no doubt. Ye haven't the look of the sea."

"Yes," Gladstone admitted. "We're seeking passage to Ireland. Do you know of any ships ready to depart?"

The woman tucked the empty tray under her arm and stood thinking for a moment. "There's the *Hanover*, but she's not settin' sail for another three days. Then there's the *Vigilant*, leavin' at dawn. She's America bound, but she'll first be puttin' in at Cork."

After learning that the *Vigilant* was docked just down the street, Gladstone thanked the woman for her assistance. She took her leave and disappeared into the kitchen, returning a few minutes later with a wrapped piece of the smoked haddock she had promised them. Gladstone and Aidan McAuliffe quickly consumed the hot, satisfying mutton stew, then paid their bill and headed out into the night.

From her seat near the door of the Square Rigger, Rachel Salomon nodded absently toward her companion as he droned on about arrangements for her journey. Her real attention was focused upon the two men who had hurriedly eaten their supper and now were leaving the establishment. She could not be entirely sure, but she was convinced she had seen one of the men before—the quieter, handsome one with the brown hair and mustache who was carrying the carpetbag. *It must have been in London*, she thought, *perhaps at one of the parties held by Lady Malinda Leach.* But then again, she had seen so many young, attractive men that they were beginning to run together in her mind.

Still, there was something intriguing about this particular man—a nervous edge to what was undoubtedly a normally confident demeanor. The man carried an aura of mystery, and Rachel had found it hard to keep from glancing over at him all during the time he was in the room.

As soon as the two men had departed the Square Rigger, Rachel returned her attention to the young man seated across the table from her. He was going on about the imminent journey, oblivious to what had been transpiring around him. "The goods that you purchased for your emporium came down from London yesterday and are already in the hold," he was saying. "Your own cabin will be on the forward—"

She cut him off with a slight wave of the hand. "I'm certain the accommodations will be sufficient for my needs." She gave a slight sigh. "It was such a tiring journey from London, and I really would like a few minutes alone, Isaac. If you would be so kind as to check my room and see that it has been readied, I'll rest here a few minutes longer. I'll be along presently."

The young man named Isaac glanced around somewhat uncomfortably, taking in the rough-looking seamen at the center tables. "Are you certain you wish to remain here unaccompanied?" he asked.

"These sailors seem tame enough to me. I'm certain they wouldn't molest a young woman who is wearing a wedding band." She raised her left hand slightly to display the gold band around her fourth finger and gave a sly grin. "And if they find out I only wear it as a precaution while traveling, there's always Mrs. Foxworth to keep them in line." She looked over at the innkeeper's wife, who had just brought out more ale and was engaging several of the seamen in conversation. When Mrs. Foxworth saw the young woman smiling at her, she nodded and smiled in reply.

"If you're entirely certain," Isaac said, standing from the table. "But Father told me to be sure—"

"Henry worries too much about his *little* American niece. Why, Isaac, I'm almost twenty-five. Surely I'm old enough to be left without a chaperon for a few minutes."

Isaac gave a sheepish smile. "Perhaps I have been keeping too close an eye—"

"You're the perfect escort." She reached up and took her cousin's hand. "But tomorrow I begin the long journey to San Francisco, and I have to make it alone. I may as well start getting used to it now." She patted his hand and then let go of it. "Now run along. I'll be up shortly."

Isaac gave a slightly awkward nod, then turned and started across the room, taking care to give the sailors a wide berth. As soon as he was gone, Rachel turned to Mrs. Foxworth and, catching her eye, motioned her to the table.

"How can I be of service?" the middle-aged woman asked as she came over.

"Those two gentlemen who just left . . . Are you acquainted with them?"

Mrs. Foxworth shook her head. "Tonight's the first I've seen them."

"I hope I'm not being too presumptuous," Rachel said hesitantly, "but I heard you mention the *Vigilant* to them, and I was wondering if they might be fellow passengers to America."

"No, they're Ireland bound. Inquirin' as to a ship, and I told them the *Vigilant* was puttin' in at Cork."

With a look of concern, Rachel said, "I'm afraid that is no longer the case, Mrs. Foxworth."

"But I'm certain it's listed for Ireland tomorrow."

"Yes, we leave at dawn, but the route has been changed. The *Vigilant* has been sold full—both goods and passengers. There'll be no stop at Ireland this journey." She did not add that it was her own shipment of goods for her family's store that was largely responsible.

"Oh, dear," the woman muttered, then shrugged her shoulders. "No harm. They'll be told when they try to book passage . . . and probably will be comin' back here to tell me, as well." She smiled again. "Is there anythin' else I can do for ye, Miss Salomon?"

"No, nothing. Thank you, Mrs. Foxworth."

The older woman turned and headed back toward the kitchen. After she disappeared inside, Rachel stood and donned the shawl that was draped over the back of her chair. She was a tall woman and extremely attractive, with long copper hair that just now she wore pulled up in a sweep. Her lips were full and rested in a natural smile, while her high cheekbones accentuated the eager light that shone in her large, emerald eyes. Everything about her, from her bold yet unpretentious green dress to the confident way she held herself, betrayed the restless, passionate spirit that dwelled within her.

As Rachel walked to the nearby door, she gave a final glance back at the sailors, whose banter grew more boisterous in direct proportion to the number of mugs of ale they had downed. Then she opened the door and stepped into the cool evening air. Pulling her shawl tighter, she stood beside the Square Rigger and let her eyes grow accustomed to the mix of moonlight and lantern light from the piers. Three ships were docked within sight with their bows pointed to sea, the *Vigilant* being farthest to the left. Looking up and down the street to confirm it was deserted, she headed left until she came abreast of the gangplank that led from the pier to the *Vigilant*'s upper deck. She cautiously crossed the street, concealing herself in the shadows of a small shed near the foot of the pier.

It took but a moment for her to pick out the two men from the tavern. They were standing near the gangplank, huddled together seemingly in conversation. As she watched, the man with the carpetbag walked farther out along the dock toward some round objects—coils of rope, Rachel suspected. He sat down on one of them. Then he disappeared from view entirely, as if he was hiding behind it.

A moment later, the second man started up the gangplank at a slow walk. Rachel could faintly hear him calling a salutation as he approached the upper deck, and before he had made it halfway, a sailor appeared at the top and started down. The two men met in the middle, where they conversed for a few minutes. Then they walked together down the gangplank and headed along the pier toward the street.

Rachel quickly pulled back into the shadows as the two men approached. She held her breath, almost afraid to listen as they passed only a few feet away and started along the street in the direction of the Square Rigger. She had seen enough of their faces to know that one of them was the red-haired man from the tavern. And from the little bit she had been able to hear, she guessed that he had made up a story about one of the ship's mates being a bit too drunk and needing assistance at a nearby tavern.

Once they had passed beyond the shed, Rachel ventured out slightly and again surveyed the pier, wondering why the red-haired man had concocted such a story to draw away the sailor on watch. There could be only one explanation, and her suspicion was confirmed when the man with the carpetbag emerged from his place of hiding and scurried back along the pier. He paused only briefly at the foot of the gangplank, then he clutched the bag against his chest and started toward the upper deck.

Transfixed, Rachel watched as the man stepped up onto the deck, looked back down once, then headed along the rail toward the rear of the ship. Four quarter boats were hanging on davits out over the rail near the aft deck, and when the man reached the first, he stepped up to the rail and lifted the tarpaulin covering the boat. As the man stood gazing into it, Rachel found herself wondering about the number of people who could hope to be rescued should it ever become necessary to use these tiny, flimsy-looking lifeboats—and with only eight on the entire ship.

The man seemed to make up his mind, because he hoisted his carpetbag into the belly of the small boat, took a last furtive glance around the deck, and then climbed in, pulling the tarpaulin back in place above him.

Rachel stood pondering whether she should turn in the man to the authorities or instead warn his red-haired friend that he had stowed away aboard a ship bound not for Ireland but America. Suddenly she heard voices and jumped back into the shadows just as the man and the sailor reappeared. The sailor was grumbling, and Rachel heard the red-haired man saying, "I tell you he was there, falling in his ale and begging someone to summon the watch from the *Armistead*."

"*Arm'stead*?" the sailor asked. "This is the *Vigilant*, man. The *Arm'stead*'s two berths down."

"But I thought—"

"Damme, man, you should o' said it 'afore," the sailor declared, pushing ahead and leaving the other fellow standing alone at the foot of the pier.

Rachel moved even deeper into the shadows as the red-haired man watched the sailor trounce up the gangplank and disappear on the upper deck. The man turned then and started back toward the street, and Rachel could see that he was smiling—but it was a smile edged with concern, for surely he knew that while his own part in the drama was complete, his friend's journey was only just beginning.

Rachel considered confronting the man and telling him what she knew, but something made her hold back. After all, she had no idea what the two men were up to and whether her news would be received with kindness or would put her in danger herself. And so she let the red-haired man pass, waiting until long after his footsteps had faded before venturing out from her own hiding place and making her way back to the safety of her tavern lodgings.

The eastern sky was a thin wash of pink and orange as seagulls screaked and people jabbered at one another while awaiting the departure of the *Vigilant*. Rachel Salomon gave her cousin Isaac a final embrace, leaving him among the gathered throng along the shore as she headed out along the pier. The morning air was chill, but she was wearing her brown shawl loose around her shoulders and hardly noticed. Instead she felt a warming surge of excitement as she remembered the events of the previous night and reflected on the adventure still to come.

With the sky lightening, Rachel was afforded her first good look at the *Vigilant* since arriving in Portsmouth the evening before. The vessel was a three-masted clipper, two-hundred-feet long and nearly thirty years old, but looking newly built courtesy of a recent overhaul at the shipyards in Liverpool. Launched in 1868, it was one of the early composite clippers, its decking and outer shell constructed from teak planks that were bolted to an iron skeleton, with rubber sheets separating the two layers to keep the metal from corroding. Her sides had been painstakingly scraped and repainted a rich royal blue, with gold scrolls and tendrils adorning the raked sides of the bow. The brass portholes and fittings gleamed like gold, even in the thin morning light, and the sword-wielding maiden that graced the bow was carved and painted with such realism that she seemed fully capable of cutting a path through even the heaviest fog or storm, a protectress worthy of the words along the blade of her sword: Ever Vigilant.

Rachel's family had urged her to book passage aboard one of the sleek new steamships that ferried passengers between America and the Continent, even though the goods she had purchased for Salomon's Emporium would be making the trip around Cape Horn in a less-expensive clipper ship. But Rachel found it far more thrilling to be on a ship under full canvas, such as the *Vigilant,* and so she had decided to accompany the goods, at least as far as New York, where she would catch a train to San Francisco.

Rachel mounted the gangplank and headed toward the quarterdeck at the stern of the ship, where passengers and crew were gathering along the rails to wave at relatives and friends who lined the shore. Stopping just short of the quarterdeck at an empty place along the rail near the most forward of the starboard lifeboats, she fought the temptation to lift the tarpaulin cover and introduce herself to the handsome man from the tavern.

It was just as Captain August Toomey was giving the order for the gangplank to be removed that a commotion on the pier caught Rachel's attention. Three men had separated from the crowd and were running toward the ship, signaling their intention to board.

As the men drew abreast of the gangplank and started up, Rachel saw their badges and realized they were members of the local constabulary. A moment later they gained the upper deck and were met by Captain Toomey, who had come forward with several of his men to ascertain the nature of the problem. While the captain and the oldest of the constables were conversing, Rachel moved casually along the deck, positioning herself so that she could better hear what was being discussed. Soon other passengers drifted over and joined her at the rail.

". . . and I'm sorry t'cause you this delay," the constable was saying, "but the rogue must be seized 'afore he beetles off completely."

"As I said," Captain Toomey responded, "we have kept track of all passengers boarding the vessel. We've sold no new bookings during the past day, and the *Vigilant* was under watch the entire night."

"Then you're sure he kinna be aboard?" the constable pressed, and when Toomey replied that he was entirely certain, the man added, "For 'tis a terrible thing he's done—murder 'n' such. And a doctor, no less. Then to do a midnight flit off the streets of London—a fortnight short o' the gallows, no less. But we'll catch him, be sure, though he's likely on the Scotland road even as we speak."

It came back to Rachel then—the numerous newspaper articles and all the gossip about the young physician named Aidan McAuliffe who was being tried for murder. She had departed London before the verdict had been announced, but apparently the man had been convicted and sentenced to hang, only to cheat the hangman by managing somehow to escape.

Rachel noticed that the constable had handed a photograph to Captain Toomey, who was holding it to the morning light so as to see the image better. She slipped away from the other passengers at the rail and walked closer, trying to get a view over the captain's shoulder.

"The likeness was taken at Newgate," the constable explained. "Just in from London this mornin'."

Craning her neck, Rachel caught a glimpse of the image on the photograph: a handsome, pleasant-looking man with dark hair and a trim mustache. She gave a sharp gasp, then hurriedly backed away, her pulse quickening as she realized that Dr. Aidan McAuliffe and the man from the tavern were one and the same—and that he was hiding in a lifeboat but a few yards away. She knew now why he had seemed so familiar, since the newspapers had printed numerous sketches of him sitting in the dock at Old Bailey.

Rachel started easing toward the small boat that hung out over the rail on the nearest davit, all the while looking back toward the gangplank. It was when the captain was returning the photograph, shaking his head to indicate he had not seen the man in question, that she realized the two younger constables were no longer on hand, and in a panic she spun around, her eyes searching the deck.

One of the constables was moving among the passengers near the stern rail. He had a duplicate photograph of the escaped convict, and he was showing it to the assembly, apparently without result. It took Rachel a few moments to find the other constable, and when she did, her breath caught in her throat. He was leaning over the rail, peering under the tarpaulin of the farthest of the four starboard lifeboats.

The constable replaced the cover and looked around, as if wondering what he should be doing, and then almost as an afterthought he approached the third boat in line. As the man lifted the edge of the tarpaulin and looked inside, Rachel hurried the rest of the way to the near lifeboat, her mind racing as she debated what to do. This Aidan McAuliffe was a convicted murderer, she reminded herself, and she had no reason to interfere with his apprehension. Yet something about him did not jibe with the crime for which he was accused—something that made his reported protestations of innocence ring all the more true. And if by any chance he *was* innocent—

There was no more time for debate, for now the constable had moved to the second boat, completed his inspection, and was approaching the remaining one. Rachel's mind raced, searching for the appropriate words and action. And then, just as the constable drew near to where she was standing, she spun toward the lifeboat, grabbed hold of the tarpaulin, and unhooked the grommets. Flinging back the corner of the cover, she swung toward the constable and proclaimed, "So we're looking for stowaways, are we?" She gave a mischievous grin. "Surely you'll be wanting to check in here. And you mustn't forget the cook's galley and the captain's sea chest."

The constable, a young man barely out of his teens, was noticeably nervous at being confronted by such an attractive and well-dressed American woman. Not knowing what to make of her bold behavior, he shifted on his feet and looked over her shoulder toward the lifeboat as he stammered, "Well, um, it's just that we've a convict escaped, and we're needin' to make sure he's not aboard—"

"A convict, you say? On board a ship to America?" She giggled. "Since you Englishmen think of us as a nation of thieves and miscreants, I should think you'd be more than delighted to have one of your English scoundrels run off there on his own." The young man's face was flushing red as she continued, "But of course it's your duty, so go on about your business." She waved her hand toward the lifeboat. "And certainly don't take my word that it's empty. You'll be wanting to check for yourself—and the rest of the vessel, to be sure. But you'll have to hurry; I'm told there are a dozen ships departing this very morning."

"O'Donnell!" a gruff voice called, and the young constable glanced toward the gangplank, where his superior, joined now by the third constable, was waving him over. "We've kept 'em long enough!"

The young man looked relieved. With a self-conscious grin, he said, "I'm sure you're right, miss. It'd be a fool's escape to America, that's f'certain.'' Nodding perfunctorily, he turned on his heels, strode away along the deck, and followed his fellow constables down the gangplank.

Rachel stood with her back against the rail and fought to steady her breathing. She was only faintly aware of the captain giving the order to remove the gangplank and set sail, and then she heard the slap of oars against water and felt the ship give a slight roll as it moved away from the pier under the power of several rowboats. At their stations around the deck, the seamen took to their lines, ready to let out sail.

As the buildings and people along the shore began to fall away, Rachel relaxed her grip on the rail behind her and slowly turned around. Trying to be as inconspicuous as possible, she stepped close to the rail, leaned out over the lifeboat, and reached for the open corner flap of the tarpaulin to pull it back into place. She decided to hazard a quick look inside, thinking she would give the undoubtedly terrified stowaway some expression of encouragement.

Enough light spilled into the belly of the small boat that Rachel could clearly make out the interior. Yet what she saw was nothing but a few empty benches. She rolled back the cover even farther and bent over until she had a full view of the entire lifeboat. She had not been mistaken; there was no one inside.

Feeling somewhat dazed, Rachel pulled the tarpaulin over the top of the boat and hooked the grommets in place. She turned and leaned back against the railing, absently watching the milling passengers, the crew working the lines, the topsails unfurling. She knew that she had seen Dr. Aidan McAuliffe sneak on board and stow away in the front starboard lifeboat, but now he was gone. Either he had discovered that the *Vigilant* was not bound for Ireland and had disembarked during the night, or else he was now hiding in some other part of the ship.

The mainsail caught the faint breeze. Then the smaller sails filled, pulling against the masts as the rowboats dropped away and the *Vigilant* started out of Portsmouth under her own power. Rachel heard the waves slapping against the bow and felt the deck begin to creak. She wrapped her shawl more tightly around her, the morning breeze suddenly far more bracing and chill.

TWO

THOUGH IT WAS STILL AN HOUR BEFORE SUNSET, THE STREET-lamps had all been lit, so thick was the fog that had settled over London. As Jeremy Mayhew walked west along Oxford Street, he felt the cold, gray mist clawing at him, heavy and oppressive. He ran his hand across his forehead, then rubbed his wet palm on his black greatcoat to wipe away the mixture of mist and nervous sweat.

As Jeremy crossed Park Lane, a dark figure loomed out of the fog on the opposite corner. Jeremy saw the glow of a cigar being inhaled, and as he came up onto the sidewalk he recognized the burly shape of Nate Gilchrist. It was not until he was within a few feet, at the very edge of Hyde Park, that he could make out Gilchrist's features. At six foot four, Gilchrist was half a foot taller than Jeremy and outweighed him by at least fifty muscular pounds. And at forty-two, he was ten years older and a good twice that many years wiser in the seamier ways of the London underworld.

'' 'Ave y'got the address?'' Gilchrist asked as Jeremy came to a halt in front of him. When Jeremy nodded, Gilchrist added, ''Then we best get a move on.''

"It's just north of here," Jeremy said with a slight note of trepidation. "Off Edgeware Road, I'm afraid."

"I figured as much," Gilchrist grumbled, frowning disapprovingly. "But don't y'worry none. There's few that'll mess with Nate Gilchrist—even in *that* sorry district." He patted the bulge at his left side, where he kept a short-barreled Deane-Adams revolver in a shoulder holster. Jeremy knew that his companion also kept a six-inch dagger sheathed on the right side of his belt.

"I'm not worried," Jeremy said brusquely as he took out a thin cigar and rubbed it between his fingers. "I just don't like this business—none of it."

"Y'want to see yer sister's murderer 'ang, don't you?"

"Of course, but this skulking around—"

"We ain't skulkin' or such. We're just goin' t'meet a man who may've 'elped a condemned killer escape."

"This should be left to Scotland Yard," Jeremy put in.

"Yer father's 'ad enough with waitin' on their kind, and I can't say as I blame 'im. Now if y'don't 'ave the stomach to face this man and—"

"Let's get going," Jeremy cut him off. Without ever lighting his cigar, Jeremy tossed it down and ground it into the pavement with the toe of his black shoe. Pulling his greatcoat higher on his neck, he stepped off the curb and started across the street.

Nate Gilchrist took another puff on his own cigar and smiled. "You'll do just fine," he drawled to himself. "Stick with Nate Gilchrist and you'll do just fine."

Jeremy Mayhew stood in front of the dark entranceway of an even darker little rooming house, which was so covered with coal soot that it was difficult to discern the lamplight that filtered through the grimy windows. Jeremy hesitated, as if afraid that some beast might be lurking in the black mouth of the entranceway. He glanced up and down the street, a bleak landscape of gray fog, coal smoke, and dilapidated buildings. The only movement was under the lamppost at the corner, where a corpulent young trollop was allowing an equally rotund man to sample her neck before leading him to an unoccupied doorway for a more thorough examination of her charms. As the man nibbled at her ear, she motioned toward Jeremy and winked, as if signaling that she would soon be available, should Jeremy be so inclined.

Jeremy turned away from the woman, suddenly finding the courage to approach the doorway and knock. At his side, Nate Gilchrist suppressed a smile.

A few moments later, the door creaked open and an exceedingly wrinkled old man stuck out his bony head. "Wha' d'ye blokes want?" he asked in a raspy voice.

"We've come to see Peter Aronson," Jeremy explained. When the man raised an eyebrow distrustfully, Jeremy added, "We're with the cab company."

"Pete do somethin' wrong?" the man asked. "If the lad's lost another job, I'll 'ave t'put 'im out. This ain't no charity ward I'm runnin'."

"It's nothing like that," Jeremy assured him. "We just need to speak with him for a moment."

"In tha' case, it's right upstairs—number three on the left." The old man backed into the hall to let the two men enter. "He should be 'ome. I 'eard 'im stumblin' about not two minutes ago."

Jeremy nodded and led the way up the rickety staircase. There was one dim lamp burning in the hall, and Nate Gilchrist turned up the wick so that they could see the numbers on the doors. On the left side were three peeling brown doors, and the one closest to the front of the building bore a flaking numeral three, apparently painted years before in a chalky white.

"That's the one," Gilchrist said, and Jeremy walked over to it and knocked. Shuffling footsteps could be heard inside the room, and then the door swung open and a short, middle-aged man peered out.

"Are you Peter Aronson?" Jeremy asked.

"Who wants t'know?" the man replied cautiously as he closely eyed the well-dressed young man with the black hair and trim mustache and his older, burly companion.

"My name's Mayhew, and I've come for some information."

"What about?"

"Your cab was stolen three days ago—on Wednesday—was it not?"

"You with the police?" the man asked. "I already told 'em all about it."

"Then you *are* Peter Aronson?" Jeremy pressed.

"What if I am? I had nothin' t'do with what happened with that cab. Like I told the bobbies, I parked it in front of Gaffney's and was inside havin' me dinner when some bloke made off with it. Next thing I find out, it's been in some kind of accident over near Millbank and some poor sot's escaped and cheated the hangman of havin' his day. But I had nothin' to do with that. I've got witnesses—they seen me in Gaffney's that whole time."

Nate Gilchrist pushed forward into the doorway and said, "We know all about yer alibi, and it don't amount to a fart in a dung'eap." As Aronson backed into the single room, Gilchrist continued, "A well-executed escape like the one the other night don't rely on the perpetrators gettin' lucky and findin' a hansom parked in front o' Gaffney's with the cabbie inside eatin' dinner all nice as y'please." Gilchrist circled the shabby room until he was behind Aronson, who turned nervously to face him. "And from the looks o' this place, it ain't likely y'be the kind o' chap t'take 'is dinner at a fine place like Gaffney's."

"Now just a minute," Aronson said. "If you think—"

"I'll tell y'what I think," Gilchrist cut in, stepping close to the man and jabbing a thumb against his chest. "I think someone paid you t'leave yer cab in front o' Gaffney's—and paid f'yer dinner, as well. And we want t'know who that fellow was."

"I eat there all the time," the man argued. "At least whenever I get a big enough tip. Ask the proprietors."

"And who gave you the tip that night?" Gilchrist pressed. "Who paid f'yer dinner?"

"I think you fellows had better show me your badges," the man said, his voice cracking with trepidation as he backed away from Gilchrist.

"We're not with the police," Jeremy Mayhew interjected,

moving in front of his partner. "Let's just say that we have an interest in this case—an interest that could be quite lucrative to a man like yourself." He reached into the pocket of his coat and produced a wallet. Opening it, he removed a folded wad of bank notes. "What do you say, Mr. Aronson?" One at a time, he folded back the notes.

Peter Aronson's mouth fairly drooled. His hand lifted ever so slightly toward the offered money, but then he pulled it back and stood wringing his hands together, his face the picture of agony.

"There's nothin' t'tell," the man insisted. "Me cab was stolen, plain and simple. I'd like t'help you, but—"

Gilchrist started forward menacingly, but Jeremy raised his hand to signal him back. "Are you certain your misplaced loyalty is worth—let's say, twenty pounds? After all, we're only asking you to speak the truth."

The little man could hardly contain himself. His hands were shaking, and his lips quivered as he replied, "Like I said, there's nothin' more to the story. I'd surely like t'help, but you wouldn't want me t'lie."

Gilchrist took a step forward and said, "Mr. Mayhew's makin' you a generous offer—one you'd do well t'take."

Aronson looked back and forth at the two men. "I can't. I'd like to . . . but I can't. There's nothin' more t'tell," he concluded without conviction.

"Let's get out of here," Jeremy told his partner, who did not seem eager to leave. But when Jeremy walked out into the hall, Gilchrist followed, pausing for a moment in front of Aronson and giving him a menacing scowl. Then the two men descended the stairs and a moment later were back on the street.

"What do you think?" Jeremy asked as they crossed the road and looked back at Aronson's rooming house.

"He's a liar, pure and simple."

"How do we get him to talk?"

"Maybe there's no need," Gilchrist replied, nodding up toward the second floor of the building, where the light had just gone out in the front left room. Taking hold of Jeremy's arm, Gilchrist pulled him into a shadowed doorway nearby.

"Looks like he's leavin'. My guess is he'll lead us straight to the man who borrowed 'is cab that night."

A minute later, the front door of the rooming house opened, and the little man from room three stepped out and cautiously looked up and down the foggy street. After deciding that his visitors had departed, Peter Aronson stepped down onto the sidewalk, turned right, and headed up the street. When a plump woman moved out of the shadows near the corner lamppost, Aronson merely waved her away and continued across the road.

"C'mon," Gilchrist said, moving out of the doorway.

Jeremy Mayhew hurried after Gilchrist, pausing only momentarily at the corner as the woman leered at him and called, "Two shillings a throw—three for the two o' you."

"Uh, not tonight," he mumbled, hurrying across the street after Gilchrist.

"What's the matter?" she called. "You like boys?"

Jeremy glanced over his shoulder and saw the woman standing under the light, her hands on her ample hips as she threw back her head and laughed.

Turning back around, Jeremy quickened his pace and caught up to Gilchrist, who cautioned him to walk quietly. For fifteen minutes they followed Peter Aronson through some of the shabbier districts of London, until at last the man came to a halt in front of a single-story house that was only in slightly better repair than Aronson's rooming house. Gilchrist pulled Jeremy into the shadows of a building just in time, for Aronson turned in their direction to make sure no one was following. Apparently satisfied that he was alone, Aronson stepped up to the door and knocked soundly.

Gilchrist waited until someone answered the door and Aronson was let inside. Then he signaled Jeremy to follow as he cautiously approached what appeared to be a tiny single-family home jammed between larger apartment buildings. There was no light coming from the front room, but a lamp could be seen burning at the back, and so Gilchrist led the way around the corner and down a narrow, garbage-strewn alley that ran behind the buildings.

"That's the one," Gilchrist said, pointing at a lit window at the rear of the house Aronson had entered.

The two men picked their way through the rubble until they were directly underneath the window in question. Looking around in the thin light that spilled into the alley, Gilchrist spied a wooden crate, which he placed against the wall under the window. Standing on the crate, he could just see into the room, and he lowered his head quickly and signaled that Aronson was inside. Ever so cautiously, Gilchrist grabbed hold of the bottom of the window and pushed upward, forcing it open about half an inch. Then he tilted his head and held his ear as close as possible to the opening without being seen. He listened for several minutes, his head nodding every once in a while. At last he climbed down from the crate and led Jeremy back down the alley.

"What did he say?" Jeremy asked as soon as they were far enough away from the building.

"He was talkin' to 'is sister's 'usband—tellin' 'im all about our little visit. The brother-in-law's the one who took the cab and drove it durin' McAuliffe's escape."

"Where was he taken?" Jeremy asked eagerly.

"McAuliffe? He didn't say. But he knows, all right."

"Then he's the one we've got to speak with."

"Might as well do it now," Gilchrist said, explaining that he heard the man say that his wife was away, which meant he would be alone once Aronson left.

The two men headed back to the corner, where they stood looking down the street until Peter Aronson emerged from his brother-in-law's house. Turning quickly, they pretended to be walking away on the side road, giving Aronson plenty of time to disappear down the main road. Then they doubled back and proceeded to the house.

"I'll do the talkin' this time," Gilchrist announced as he mounted the stoop and rapped loudly on the door.

Soon the door opened, and the man inside, thinking his brother-in-law had returned, started to say, "Pete—?" He was cut off by Nate Gilchrist pushing into the foyer. Jeremy Mayhew seemed taken aback by Gilchrist's action, and he hurried inside and shut the door behind him.

The man glowered at the two intruders. "What the hell are you—?"

This time Gilchrist cut him off by ramming him against the foyer wall. "Shut up!" he demanded, holding the man in place with one huge hand. "You'll talk when I say to!"

The man was only Jeremy's size and several years older than Gilchrist. He could see that he did not stand a chance if it came to a fight, so he made no attempt to move, though his eyes searched for something to balance the odds. "What d'you want?" he finally asked, trying to calm his voice.

"Me friend 'as a few questions f'you," Gilchrist grunted, moving to the side and motioning Jeremy closer.

With some trepidation, Jeremy stepped up beside the man and asked, "What's your name?"

"Who wants t'know?" the man retorted. By way of reply, Nate Gilchrist swung a sudden left hook, catching the man on the jaw and dropping him to his knees.

"Get up!" Gilchrist blared, grabbing the man's collar and yanking him to his feet. "Now answer the question!"

"M-Murchison," the man slurred, rubbing his jaw. "Mick Murchison."

"That's better," Gilchrist declared. He turned to Jeremy and nodded. "Go ahead."

"All we want is some information," Jeremy hesitantly continued. "Just tell us what's become of Aidan McAuliffe, and we'll be on our way."

Murchison looked at them in surprise. "What're you talking about?" he asked, to which Gilchrist grabbed his collar and twisted violently, causing the man to gag.

"Make it easy on yerself," Gilchrist said, forcing the man to his knees. "Just tell me friend what he wants t'know, and no one need get hurt." He eased up on the man's collar, then hoisted him back to his feet.

"I . . . I d-don't know any Aidan Mc—McAuliffe," the man stammered.

With a curse, Gilchrist drew back his right arm and sank his fist in Murchison's stomach, doubling him over. "Y'don't, d'you? We'll just 'ave t'see how quick y'can remember!"

Murchison choked and grabbed at his belly as Gilchrist

hauled him upright, backhanded him across the face, and threw him across the foyer against the opposite wall. He lost his footing and fell to the side, his head striking the edge of a small table as he tumbled to the floor.

"Enough!" Jeremy shouted, horrified at what he had just witnessed. Pushing past Gilchrist, he knelt and eased Murchison onto his back, saying, "It's all right. No one's going to hurt you anymore. We just want to know where Aidan McAuliffe . . ." His words trailed off as he looked more closely at Murchison. There was a deep gash where his head had struck the table, and blood was seeping from the corner of his mouth. He did not appear to be breathing. "Are you all right?" Jeremy asked cautiously. "Mr. Murchison! Are you all right?"

Nate Gilchrist pushed Jeremy aside and grabbed hold of the man on the floor. Shaking him roughly, he called his name several times, then let him drop back against the floor. Standing, Gilchrist slowly shook his head. "Poor bloke's dead," he said matter-of-factly.

"Dead?" the stunned younger man repeated. "You killed him? That can't be."

"It sure as 'ell can. Look f'yerself."

Jeremy shook his head and backed away from the body. "You shouldn't have. . . . I mean, he's dead. How're we gonna find out . . . ?"

"Not from 'im, that's f'damn sure." Gilchrist pulled Jeremy by the sleeve toward the front door. "C'mon. Let's get out o' here."

"What're we gonna do?" Jeremy muttered as Gilchrist pulled him over to the door.

"Let's go," was all Gilchrist replied. He turned and yanked open the door, only to find Peter Aronson standing on the stoop, his hand raised to knock as the door swung wide.

Aronson's eyes widened as he recognized the big man in the foyer. Suddenly his reason for returning did not seem at all important, and he turned to beat a hasty retreat. But before he made it down the first step, a pair of hands hauled him backward through the doorway and spun him around.

"What're you doin' 'ere?" Gilchrist demanded as he kicked the door shut.

"I . . . I j-just—" Aronson stammered, his voice breaking when he saw his brother-in-law's body lying faceup on the floor. With a shock of recognition, he gasped and leaped past Gilchrist at the front door.

Gilchrist dove at Aronson from behind, slamming him into the door, then grabbing him by the hair and smashing his head against the door several times, until the bone cracked and blood spurted from the nostrils. Pinning Aronson's arms behind his back with one hand, Gilchrist wrapped his right arm around Aronson's neck. Squeezing cruelly, he spun the little man toward Jeremy, who stood immobile with shock, his hand trembling as he raised it toward Gilchrist as if urging him not to kill the man.

"We 'ave to, don't y'see?" Gilchrist proclaimed. "You told 'im yer name. He knows who you are."

Jeremy continued to shake his head, unwilling to accept the truth of what his partner said. Aronson, meanwhile, could do nothing but gasp for breath, his face turning increasingly purple by the second.

"It's got t'be done," Gilchrist insisted, tightening his arm around Aronson's neck and lifting him slightly off his feet. "And you're gonna do it!"

"Me?" Jeremy gasped incredulously. "I couldn't."

"We're in this together, lad, or not at all. I'll not be takin' the fall alone." As he gave Jeremy a moment to consider what he had said, Gilchrist eased up on his choke hold just enough to allow the terrified older man to take in a breath. "We've got t'hurry—'afore the wife gets home," Gilchrist went on, tightening his hold again. "Now do as I say and come over 'ere."

Jeremy hesitated, then slowly approached. He reached up, as if to smother the man, and then he pulled his hands back and mumbled, "I can't."

"Under me coat," Gilchrist barked. "The knife. Take me knife."

Jeremy looked at him curiously. When Gilchrist again ordered him to take the knife, Jeremy reached past Aronson, slipped his hand under the right side of Gilchrist's coat, and drew the six-inch dagger from its sheath.

"Use it!" Gilchrist ordered, nodding down toward the man's chest.

Jeremy stared at the knife, then up into Aronson's bulging eyes as the man tried in vain to speak.

"Do it now!"

Jeremy held forth the knife, moved it to within inches of the man's midsection, then backed away, shaking his head. "I c-can't," he whimpered, tears welling up in his eyes as he held the quivering knife pointed at Aronson's belly.

"Damn you!" Gilchrist shouted. All at once he shoved Aronson forward at Jeremy's hand.

Jeremy felt the blade sink into the man's flesh, felt the warm rush of blood on his hand as he yanked the blade free. He looked up in shock, saw the man's eyes widen further, heard his garbled scream.

"Do it!" Gilchrist bellowed. "Now!"

Jeremy could feel himself sobbing as he drew his arm back and drove the knife full-hilt into Aronson's belly. His tears were as hot as the blood that flooded his hand as he withdrew the knife and plunged it again and again into the poor man's stomach and chest. The next thing he knew, Gilchrist was pulling him away from the body, which lay motionless on the floor. Jeremy looked up into the bigger man's hard gray eyes, then suddenly felt the cold steel in his hand. He dropped the knife to the floor and backed away, his tears drying, his eyes growing cold and hard.

"You did just fine," Gilchrist remarked, slapping him on the back. "Now let's get out o' here."

"Yes," Jeremy muttered as Gilchrist pulled him over to the front door and led him out into the night.

The second evening out of Portsmouth, Rachel Salomon made her way to her cabin on the forward deck following dinner at the captain's table as a guest of Captain August Toomey. The night was cloudless and brisk, and she pulled her woolen shawl tighter over the shoulders of the burnished-gold gown she had worn for the occasion.

As Rachel passed the forward starboard lifeboat, she thought of the mysterious stowaway who had seemingly vanished from inside it. Although she had not forgotten Dr. Aidan McAuliffe, she had all but come to the conclusion that somehow he had learned the *Vigilant* was not stopping in Ireland and had disembarked during the night before it sailed. Certainly he had not turned up among the two hundred passengers, nor had Rachel been able to find him anywhere else aboard ship, despite having searched surreptitiously during the past two days at sea.

Reaching her cabin, Rachel entered and closed the door behind her. She lit the hanging lantern near the door, then jumped slightly as a gentle voice said, "Please, don't be alarmed." She did not have to turn around to know that the voice belonged to Aidan McAuliffe.

"How did you get in here?" she asked calmly as she went about adjusting the wick and finally turned toward the handsome young physician, who was seated in a chair by the dressing table. As he stood, she noted that he had shaved off his mustache.

"You left your cabin unlocked," he explained.

"Yes, of course. After all, there's not much risk of theft on a ship. There's no way for a criminal to escape." She emphasized the final comment and gave a knowing smile.

"Then you know who I am?"

"You're Dr. Aidan McAuliffe, late of London, most recently an honored though much-maligned guest at Newgate."

"If you knew all that, why did you try to help me yesterday morning when the constable was searching the lifeboats?"

Rachel crossed the small room and placed her shawl on the bed. With an amused grin, she turned to Aidan and asked, "Did you like my performance?"

"It was inspired. And when that red-faced young man turned tail and ran, it was all I could do not to applaud."

"But where were you?"

"In the last place I thought they'd look—milling among the passengers."

"But I saw you get into the lifeboat."

"I figured as much. You're the young woman who was in the tavern the other night, aren't you?"

"Rachel Salomon," she replied with a nod, then raised one eyebrow and added pointedly, "I'd offer my hand, but they say you murder young women like myself."

Aidan's expression darkened. "I've never killed anyone," he denied flatly.

"I thought so. Which is why I helped you."

"But I was convicted."

"I read the news accounts, and it was a sorry affair indeed. It never would have been tolerated in America, where a man is presumed innocent until proven guilty."

"They had witnesses," Aidan reminded her, as if arguing the case for the prosecution.

"Witnesses can be bought—especially ones of the sort that prosecutor trotted out."

"But what convinced you otherwise?" Aidan asked.

"I only read the newspaper accounts, of course, and couldn't be sure, but I found myself believing the many men and women who came forth to attest to your good character. And there was another thing."

"Yes?" he asked when she paused.

Rachel waved her hand, indicating the chair by the dressing table. "Please, sit down." She pulled over a second chair from across the room. When they were both seated, she continued, "You are a physician and a surgeon, Dr. McAuliffe—"

"Aidan," he insisted.

"Yes, Aidan," she repeated. "As I was saying, you are a physician and a surgeon, and from all accounts you are a damn good one." Realizing the word she had used, she said, "Excuse my bluntness. I'm afraid it's a sign of my San Francisco breeding."

"I like a woman to speak directly," he assured her.

"Then I will. From everything I read, you are certainly skilled enough to terminate a pregnancy—which is precisely why I believe you to be innocent."

"I don't understand."

"That prostitute who died with her aborted infant at her

side—the one they say you murdered—she was dreadfully mutilated, was she not?''

Aidan frowned and nodded.

"Obviously the work of a back-alley butcher, not a surgeon. If you had set about to end her pregnancy, the woman would never have died—especially not in so piteous a manner. Am I not correct?''

Aidan smiled. ''You should have been my barrister.''

"I'm afraid it would not have helped in a country where a man is guilty until proven otherwise. Now as to your current fate, I presume that by now you realize we're not putting in at Cork.''

"I figured as much when I saw the coast of Ireland recede into the distance off the starboard side. That's when I decided to risk throwing myself on your mercy.''

"Where have you been hiding until now?''

"After you saw me get into the lifeboat, I decided it was too obvious a hiding place—the first spot they'd search. During the night I slipped out and took up quarters in a closet of sorts, used to store canvas, mops, and the like. Enough light filtered through at dawn to allow me a pleasant shave—'' he rubbed his clean-shaven upper lip ''—thanks to the toiletries provided by a good friend.''

"The man with the red hair?'' she asked.

"Precisely,'' he admitted with a nod. ''When the passengers began boarding, I hid my carpetbag among the canvas and stole from my cabin, figuring I'd do best to hide right out in the open where I could keep an eye on things, should trouble arise.''

"And you've stayed in that closet ever since?''

"During the night. But I found it a simple matter to mill among the passengers during the day. It's surprising what little notice anyone takes of someone who acts as though he belongs where he is.''

"But I haven't seen you.''

"Ah, but I've kept my eye on you—from afar. I would have introduced myself and thanked you for what you did, but I didn't want you to get caught up in my troubles. I thought I'd soon slip ashore in Ireland, and that would be the end of it.''

''And now you're bound for New York.''

''If that's where this ship is headed.''

''It is. Then it'll circle the Horn to San Francisco.''

''And your destination . . . ?'' he inquired politely.

''New York by sea. Then on to San Francisco by rail.''

There was an awkward pause as Aidan tried to phrase what was on his mind. Rachel sensed his struggle, and finally she suggested, ''Why not speak plainly, Dr. McAuliffe—I mean Aidan.''

After drawing in a breath, Aidan plunged ahead, saying, ''I need your help. But if you refuse—even if you turn me in to the captain—I will not think you the worse for it.''

Rachel gave a slight pout. ''Do you think I would have gone to all that trouble yesterday morning just to turn you in tonight?''

''Well, no, but still it's not right for me to presume upon a woman's kindness. Yet I'm afraid I must. You see, I don't think the closet will stand the test of time during such a long voyage. And then there's the problem of getting ashore. An English ship is rarely questioned in Ireland, and had we docked there I might have simply walked ashore. But in America, I'm afraid the customs procedure is far more rigorous.''

''Yes, it is,'' Rachel acknowledged. ''In fact, the ship will be boarded and searched well out in the harbor, and every passenger will be checked for papers.''

''I was afraid of that.''

''But let's not lose all hope,'' Rachel quickly added. ''After all, it's a long journey, and surely we can devise some plan before we get there.''

''Then you'll help me?'' Aidan asked eagerly.

''Of course. That is, if you want me to. After all, you've heard no one attest to *my* character.''

''I know enough about you. You're kind to a fault, and you have the courage to do what you think is right, regardless of the consequences.''

''Thank you,'' she replied. ''If you'd like to know a bit

more about me, my true age is twenty-four—I don't believe in shaving years for the sake of convention—and I am the eldest daughter of Charles and Nina Salomon. My father is a dear man—the source of any kind streaks in his children. And Nina . . . well, let's just say that Nina gave me the backbone to stand by my convictions—and the curse of always saying what I think.''

"Both admirable traits.''

"Perhaps—when tempered with my father's kindness.'' She grinned, as if from some private thought. "Perhaps some day you will meet Nina and can judge for yourself.''

"Do you always call your mother by her Christian name? That seems quite progressive.''

"It has nothing to do with being progressive,'' Rachel replied with a slight laugh. "Father is fifty-five, and from the moment his first child was born, he wanted nothing more than to be a father and someday a grandfather. Nina, on the other hand, is ten years his junior, and she has spent her life denying that she is old enough to be a mother. From the start she insisted we call her Nina, as if she were some kind of big sister. God forbid the day she has a grandchild. If the little tot ever calls her Grandma, I think she'll die of mortification.''

"Then you and your husband have no children?''

Rachel seemed taken aback for a moment, but then she realized that she was still wearing the wedding ring. Deciding that it might be best—for both of them—if she did not yet admit to being unattached, she chose not to correct him but merely said, "No, not as yet.''

Aidan looked at her curiously, then asked, "Didn't you say your name is Salomon?''

"Yes, I did. Why?''

"But if you're married—''

"I find it more convenient to use our family name,'' she quickly interjected. "You see, my parents own a mercantile establishment in San Francisco—Salomon's Emporium—and I often travel on business for the company. My father's health is not as it should be, so I made the journey to London to

44

purchase goods for the store. My older brother, Jacob, is on a similar trip to the Orient right now.''

''There are just the two of you?''

''No. I've a younger brother named Maurice, who will meet me in New York and escort me the rest of the way home. And there's Phoebe, who's only nineteen. I assume she's spending her time trying to avoid Nina's latest schemes to match her up with the proper man.''

''Did she succeed in your case?'' Aidan inquired somewhat cautiously.

''Mother gave up on me long ago. She knew that when the time came I would make my own choice.''

''I trust it was a satisfying one, Mrs. Salomon.''

''You must call me Rachel,'' she said quickly, wishing to change the subject before he inquired further about her husband. ''And now I think we'd do well to retrieve that carpetbag of yours. For the rest of the journey, you'll be staying right here in this cabin.''

Aidan looked a bit perturbed. ''But it wouldn't be right. After all, you are a—''

''Lady,'' she completed. ''Yes, I am a lady, and you are not only a physician but a gentleman—am I not right?''

He smiled sheepishly and nodded.

''Then I've nothing to worry about, and it's settled,'' she proclaimed.

''Thank you, Rachel.'' Standing, he approached her seat and held out his hand. ''May I?''

With a cautious smile, she raised her hand, and he lifted it to his lips.

THREE

"PHOEBE? ARE YOU READY YET?" A SOMEWHAT THROATY female voice called, and then without even a knock the bedroom door was thrust open and a tall, elegantly dressed woman entered. She was wearing an ankle-length gown of shimmering burnt-copper silk, embroidered in royal blue with a Chinese floral motif. The dress was quite modern, with only the hint of a bustle, which accentuated a firm, youthful figure that belied the woman's forty-five years.

"Oh, Phoebe Salomon! Look at you!" the woman chided as she crossed to where a young woman in a dressing gown was seated at an ornately carved French writing table, which stood beside an equally elegant Louis Quatorze canopy bed. "You haven't even begun to dress!"

"I'm just finishing, Nina," Phoebe said somewhat distractedly as she jotted a few more words into the book in front of her, open to the heading marked Saturday, May 30, 1896.

"That diary again," Nina lamented, voicing a sigh. "Isn't it time you put such childish fancies aside? You're nineteen. You should have other things on your mind."

"Yes, Nina," Phoebe replied, not listening. She scrawled a final word, put down her pencil, and closed the book. Snapping shut the locking clasp, she pressed her palms against the top of the book and closed her eyes, as if gathering courage.

"Here, let me look at you," Nina said, grasping her daughter's shoulders and spinning the swivel chair around. She frowned and clucked her tongue in despair. "Dear me. You always look so pale—just like your father. It's a shame you didn't get my coloring."

Nina raised one hand and tucked a few strands of Phoebe's blond hair into place, slightly shifting the cloisonne comb that held it up in a bun. "That's better," she pronounced, stepping back to admire her work. "But you need more rouge on your cheeks—and powder to cover those lines." She waved a hand at Phoebe's somewhat plump neck and shook her head. "I don't know why so many people think those lines are flattering. To me a sleek figure is the sign of proper breeding. You're only nineteen—far too young to be putting on weight."

Phoebe lowered her head and stared down at the floor.

"Now don't go pouting; it's bad for your complexion. I want you to make a good impression on our guests."

"Yes, Nina."

Circling the bed, Nina opened the large walk-in closet and rummaged through the dresses on the rack. Choosing a deep-blue satin gown, she brought it out and laid it across the bed. "This will be perfect," she said. "It highlights your strong point—those soft-blue eyes of yours. And it has a lovely gather at the waist; if you've added a few pounds, no one will be the wiser. Just don't overeat. It will draw attention to your flaws."

Nina stood for a few moments watching her daughter, who continued to sit looking at the floor. "You're sulking now, aren't you?" Nina asked. "Is it the dress? Do you want to wear a different one?"

Phoebe glanced up. "No, it's just . . . ." Her voice trailed off, and she looked back down.

"You're not going to be in one of your moods tonight, are

47

you, Phoebe? I must say, you have been moping around the house long enough. Some of our best friends are going to be here tonight, and I want you to make a good impression. Isn't that what you want?''

"Yes, but—"

"Then let's have a smile."

Nina stepped closer and took her daughter's hand. Phoebe looked as if she was about to burst into tears, but then she raised her head and forced a smile.

"There, that's better. Now get dressed; I want you to bring your father down as soon as the Emrichs arrive." Seeing Phoebe's sudden look of concern, she added, "Yes, Carl Emrich has been invited, as well. I don't see why you avoid that young man. He is handsome and the perfect gentleman. And if that were not enough, he will one day head Emrich Shipping and come into a sizable fortune."

"I don't like Carl," Phoebe said flatly.

"You don't even give him a chance. It's obvious that he likes you. I only ask that you make an effort to be friendly. Is that so hard?"

Phoebe stood and started to pace in front of the bed, rubbing her hands nervously. "I'm just not interested in Carl. And he doesn't really like me. He's just trying to promote a business deal between our two—"

"And what's so wrong if Salomon's benefits by your marriage? If you had any idea what shipping costs do to our profits, you'd see how beneficial a union with Carl Emrich might be."

"Is that all you want?" Phoebe asked abruptly, spinning to face her mother. "Don't you care at all what I want?"

"But of course, dear," Nina soothed, coming forward and touching her daughter's arm. "I would never force anyone on you—even for the sake of your family. I just want you to give Carl a fair chance. It's for your own good."

Phoebe turned away, folding her arms across her belly. Her voice was exceedingly thin and distant as she said, "There are other well-to-do young men out there—other equally good matches for Salomon's Emporium."

48

With a petulant frown, Nina snapped, "If you're referring to Eaton Hallinger—"

"What's wrong with Eaton?" Phoebe demanded, turning toward Nina. "His house is just as large as ours, and his father practically owns his own bank."

"You'll not mention Abraham Hallinger in this house, young lady! And as for that wastrel son of his, you know that I've forbidden any of my children to associate with him or his kind."

"Eaton is not—"

"The hell he isn't!" Nina roared, her bitter tone stunning Phoebe into silence. "He's no good, just like his father. And he wants only one thing from you—the same thing every man of his sort wants. When he gets it, he'll turn his back on you and go after some new conquest."

"That's not true!" Phoebe exclaimed. "He'd never do that!"

"How do you know?" Nina asked pointedly. "You're not speaking from experience, are you?"

Phoebe's jaw dropped, and her lips quivered as she stammered, "We're just . . . g-good friends. That's all."

Adopting a friendlier tone, Nina suggested, "Then prove it by being courteous to Carl Emrich this evening." When Phoebe looked away without responding, Nina cupped the young woman's chin and raised her head, saying, "I don't mean to be harsh, dear, but I know the Hallingers. I was there when Abraham betrayed your grandfather and nearly destroyed our business. And his son is cut from the same cloth. In time you'll see I'm right; he's no good for you." Gently patting Phoebe's chin, she added, "Now hurry up and get dressed. And remember what I said about not overeating. It's bad for your figure and will make a poor impression on Carl."

As Nina lowered her hand to leave, Phoebe suddenly grabbed it, pulled it to her cheek, and started to cry.

"There, there," Nina purred, stepping closer and embracing her daughter. "Have I upset you?"

Phoebe shook her head but continued to sob.

"Then what's the matter? Is it because I said you've gained

weight? I'm a foolish woman; pay no attention to me.'' She patted Phoebe on the back. ''Men like a woman with a robust figure—someone who fills out her clothing. Just look at Lily Langtry and Lillian Russell. You're every bit as beautiful as they are. You'll see—the skinny Sarah Bernhardts will have their day and be gone. And then you'll be glad you paid your Nina no mind.''

When Phoebe did not stop crying, Nina pushed her away slightly and again raised her chin. ''Enough of this,'' she lightheartedly scolded. ''I apologized, didn't I? It's not as if the world is coming to an end.''

Suddenly Phoebe stopped crying—but only for an instant. Her face tightened, her eyes opening wide. And then she wailed, ''Oh, no!'' and threw herself on the bed—right on top of the gown Nina had laid out for her.

''Heavens! What's the matter?'' Nina implored as her daughter sobbed uncontrollably. Nina circled the bed to sit beside Phoebe, but then she halted abruptly, her features darkening. When she spoke, her voice was harsh and unwavering. ''It's Eaton Hallinger. He's taken advantage of you, hasn't he?'' When Phoebe cried all the louder, Nina blared, ''He has! I knew it!''

Nina reached down and shook her daughter's shoulder. ''You will never see him again. Is that understood? And if he tries anything more, I'll see him in hell!'' She forced Phoebe onto her side so that Phoebe would see her as she ordered, ''You'll put an end to this before something worse happens. Before you become . . .''

Nina's words died on her lips as Phoebe pushed away and buried her face in the satin gown, choking on her tears.

''Oh, my God, no!'' Nina suddenly shrieked, backing away from the bed. ''You aren't! Dear Lord, tell me that you aren't!''

For a long while Nina just stood there, shivering with anger and fear as her daughter continued to sob into the dress. ''You fool,'' she finally hissed, almost too softly for Phoebe to hear. ''You stupid fool. What have you done?'' She raised her hand to her mouth and bit back the tears that welled up in her eyes. ''Oh, you foolish child,'' she exclaimed more loudly as she staggered back to the bed and sat beside Phoebe, holding her in her arms. "You foolish, foolish child."

"I . . . I'm s-sorry," Phoebe weeped in a piteously weak voice.

"I know you are. I know."

Phoebe rolled over and wrapped her arms around her mother's waist, gripping her tightly. "H-Help me," she begged, her body racking with sobs.

"I will, Phoebe. Don't worry. Nina will make things right again," she promised as she rocked Phoebe in her arms.

After several minutes, the young woman began to calm down, and Nina stood and helped her under the covers. "You stay up here tonight," Nina told her. "I'll explain to the guests that you aren't feeling well."

"What about—?"

"We'll worry about it tomorrow. For now, don't tell anyone about your . . . condition." Just then a thought came to her, and she asked with trepidation, "Does Eaton know?" When Phoebe shook her head, Nina sighed. "Good. He must never know. That goes for Charles, as well."

Phoebe looked up at her mother, her eyes beseeching. "But Father—"

"You mustn't tell him," Nina sternly commanded. "You know his heart is weak. I fear he couldn't stand the shock—the shame that would fall upon our family."

Phoebe began to cry again, but more softly.

"You must get hold of yourself," Nina insisted. "You have to trust me in this; I told you I'd make things right."

Choking back her tears and pulling the blanket higher, Phoebe closed her eyes and gave a faint nod.

"That's better. Now, the important thing is to let no one know of your condition. If word were ever to get out, you'd be ruined, and our family would be the laughingstock of San Francisco."

"But Eaton might—"

"He'd never marry you—and I'd never let him. Don't you

see? He's trying to ruin you, like his father tried to ruin my father. No . . . he mustn't know. You must never tell him. Is that clear?''

With a look of resignation, Phoebe nodded and curled up on her side, as if going to sleep.

''That's it. You rest. I'll see you in the morning, and then we'll sort out this mess.'' Leaning over the bed, she lightly kissed her daughter's forehead. Picking up the blue dress, she smoothed it out and draped it over the foot of the bed. Then she turned and walked from the room.

As the door closed, Phoebe rolled over and stared at the lamp still burning on the writing desk beside the bed. She reached toward the light, then dropped her hand and began again to cry.

Nina struggled against a maelstrom of emotions as she headed down from Phoebe's third-floor bedroom to her own room on the second floor. Sitting at her large dressing table, she stared into the gilt-framed mirror and was not at all pleased with what she saw. Her anger had aged her several years, and with a frown she quickly went about repairing the damage, utilizing a pat of powder here and a dab of rouge there.

Picking up her silver brush, she pulled the combs from her hair and let down her long brunette locks. She looked closely for a trace of gray and was pleased to find none. Then she pulled the hair over her left shoulder and began to brush, until it shone enough to bring out the yellow flecks of light in her brown eyes. Piling her hair back up into a sweep, she positioned the combs and patted her creation into place.

Looking at her image in the mirror, Nina at last found herself smiling again. After all, she was only forty-five, and she had the features and figure of a woman ten years younger. Why, just a year ago had not she and her daughter, Rachel, been mistaken for sisters by that divine tenor Jean de Reszke when they saw him perform at the Metropolitan Opera House in New York City? Now, there was a man who could set a woman's heart fluttering with the sweetness of his voice and the mischievous light in his eyes. He was a man for whom it might almost be worth . . .

Nina shook off any such thoughts. She was a married woman—a dignified woman of prominent social standing. She was determined that the Salomons would not suffer scandal of any kind—neither from herself nor from her foolish young daughter. Nina would have to be content with what life had given her. If only it had not given her a husband ten years her senior—and so much older than that in body and spirit.

As if on cue, there came a rapping on the door and, with Nina's permission, Charles entered the room. He walked with a cane, the legacy of a serious heart attack he had suffered the year before. But though his hair and mustache were silver and his movements measured and slow, he was still an extremely handsome, youthful-looking man, with soft, pleasant features.

"I've something for you, my dear," he said in a gentle voice as he came up behind Nina. Leaning his cane against the back of her chair, he rested one hand on her shoulder and brought the other around in front of her, presenting a beautiful white rose. "The first from our garden. I picked it for you this morning."

"It's lovely," Nina remarked, smiling faintly as she took the rose and laid it on top of the dresser. She tilted her head and allowed her husband to kiss her cheek. Then, shifting slightly on the chair, she looked him over. He was still in his gray smoking jacket, though he had on his dress pants and shoes. "You'll wear that silk tie I put out for you, won't you?" she asked, and he nodded. "And can't you make do without that cane? Just for tonight?"

"Of course, dear," he promised.

"I want everything to be perfect," she declared, turning back to the mirror and examining her reflection.

"Your parties are always perfect," he complimented her. "I've heard it said countless times: 'No one knows how to orchestrate a party like Nina Salomon.' "

"Do you think so?" she asked exuberantly as she looked up at him in the mirror.

"But of course. And tonight will be no exception." He picked up the cane and turned to leave, then glanced back and asked, "Is Phoebe ready yet?"

"Uh, no. She says she isn't feeling quite right, but I think it's because she doesn't want to see Carl Emrich."

"Shall I go up and speak with her?"

"No," Nina abruptly replied. "She's resting. She'll be down later if she's up to it. Now, you run along and finish getting ready. And don't forget that silk tie."

"I won't," he assured her.

Nina watched in the mirror as Charles walked to the door and then paused and stood looking at her. "Is something wrong?" she asked self-consciously. "My hair?" She started patting it.

"Good Lord, no. I was just admiring you." He smiled. "Do you know, Nina . . . you are as beautiful today as the day I first met you."

Nina felt herself blushing. Impulsively, she stood and crossed to where he was standing in the doorway. She kissed him tenderly on the cheek, then turned him toward the hall and said, "Now be a good boy and run along. I'll have Cameron fetch you when the guests start arriving."

With a nod, Charles headed down the hall to his own room. Nina watched until he disappeared inside, and then she closed her own door and sighed. *What am I going to do with you?* she thought, then glanced up toward her daughter's third-floor room. *With the both of you.*

Shaking her head, she walked to the bed and picked up a long black shawl, trimmed in mink, which she had set out earlier in the evening. Draping it over her right shoulder and letting the mink drag casually on the floor, she swept along the hall and started down the polished, black marble stairs. The staircase resembled the letter Y, with a wide lower section that led from the foyer to a landing, where the stairs narrowed and branched left and right to the second floor.

"Cameron?" Nina called as she reached the landing. "Cameron," she called a second time, and a moment later a portly, middle-aged man appeared in the foyer, dressed in the black evening jacket of a butler.

"Yes, madam?" he asked from the foot of the stairs.

"Has anyone arrived?"

"Not as yet."

"Good. Is everything ready?"

"As you ordered, madam."

"You may go about your business."

"Thank you." He turned to his left and headed back to the large reception hall just off the foyer.

Nina sat down on the small marble settee that stood against the back wall of the landing, from where she had a full view of the front door, directly across the foyer from the staircase. She seemed distracted as she fluffed the mink trim on her shawl, her concern about her youngest daughter etched plainly on her face. But when the doorbell sounded a few minutes later, Nina's expression immediately transformed. Standing, she struck a suitably dramatic pose and waited as Cameron reappeared and opened the door. She held her pose a bit longer while he took the lady's evening wrap and the gentleman's coat and hat. Then as they came forward into the foyer, Nina began her descent.

"The Claybournes," Cameron announced before turning and disappearing into the cloakroom at the far end of the foyer.

"Robert. Annette. How dear of you to come," Nina gushed as she came gliding down, her fur-trimmed shawl trailing behind her on the stairs. Reaching the bottom, she raised one hand and waited for them to approach.

"You are as beautiful as ever," declared Robert, kissing her hand. He was a balding, rotund fellow with enormous black sideburns that helped draw attention away from his equally enormous nose.

"Your dress is stunning," Annette crowed, her voice a high-pitched warble.

"And don't the two of you look delightful," Nina cluckled. "When the others arrive, you'll simply put them all to shame."

"Oh, dear, are we the first?" Annette asked, sensing a disapproving tone to her hostess's comment.

"Fashionably punctual," Nina proclaimed, taking Robert by the hand and leading him toward the reception hall. At the high-arched entranceway, she stopped and said, "Won't you be a dear, Robert, and amuse yourself for a moment so that we girls can have a little talk?"

"Anything the lady of the house requires," he replied with a low bow. "Excuse me, my dear," he told his wife. Then he spun on his heels and strode into the hall.

Taking Annette's arm, Nina led the short, heavyset woman back into the foyer.

"Do you really like my dress?" Annette asked, looking down dubiously at her somewhat plain black gown with its high-necked collar and oversized bustle. "You know about these things, Nina. Does it . . . compliment my figure?"

"It complements you perfectly," she responded truthfully, suppressing a grin at her play on words. "But I daresay it looks a trifle familiar. You haven't worn it here before, have you?"

"Of course not," Annette replied defensively. "But I bought it at Salomon's Emporium. Perhaps you saw it—"

"Yes, indeed. I purchased it myself on a trip to New York. Let's see, was that last season or the season before? No matter," she said, dismissing the thought with a wave of her hand and taking no notice of Annette's dejected expression. "It was obviously created for you."

"Do you really think so?" Annette asked, brightening up considerably.

"Yes, but . . ." Her hesitation hung heavy with portent.

"What is it? You must tell me."

"It's that shawl," Nina admitted, nodding toward the black lace shawl around the woman's shoulders.

"But this was made by my mother."

"And your mother does lovely work. But I'm certain she would want you to be dressed in the latest style. As a matter of fact, our store recently received a shipment from Paris that included a shawl that would add a dramatic touch to your already stunning outfit. I have one right upstairs, and I'd be honored if you'd wear it for the evening.''

"Really? But I couldn't impose—''

"Nonsense. We're friends. And believe me, while your mother's shawl is . . . a sentimental touch, the one I have in mind will be so much more commented upon.''

"If you really think so . . .''

"Then it's settled,'' Nina declared. Leading the way over to the stairs, Nina called for Cameron and directed him to take Annette's shawl to the cloakroom and then fetch her own French silk shawl from her closet. A few minutes later, Annette was redressed to Nina's approval.

"You're right,'' Annette conceded as she admired herself in a mirror along the foyer wall. "It *is* dramatic.''

"And so are you,'' Nina proclaimed as she led her to the reception hall. "Now go on in and join Robert. Charles and I will be along presently.''

As soon as Annette had disappeared inside, Nina returned to the stairs and headed back up to the landing. She did not have to wait long until the bell rang a second time and the next visitors were announced.

"Ferris. Marjorie,'' Nina greeted them as she floated down the stairs, her mink shawl trailing behind her. "And don't you both look captivating!''

"We do, don't we,'' the dapperly dressed man named Ferris agreed, kissing her hand. "Do you like it?'' he asked, stepping back and showing off his formal cutaway jacket, edged in black silk.

"You've been naughty,'' Nina chided with a mock pout. "That did not come from Salomon's Emporium, did it?''

"Not everything comes from Salomon's, my dear,'' Ferris remarked with a grin.

"He bought it on our trip to Chicago,'' Marjorie explained.

"Yes, I should have known from the tie.''

"The tie?'' Ferris asked in surprise.

"They make the most sporting jackets in Chicago, but they know nothing about ties. Yours should have been of silk, to match the lapels.''

Rubbing his trim brown beard, Ferris gave Nina a suspicious squint. "And I suppose Salomon's Emporium carries just the one?"

"As it happens, I had my personal tailor make Charles just the thing from a bolt of striking black silk that I picked up in New York last year." She led the couple toward the reception hall. "If you'd like, I could have Cameron fetch it from upstairs. It would make such a strong statement with that jacket, and I'm certain Charles wouldn't mind. . . ."

FOUR

JEREMY MAYHEW STOOD ON THE STOOP OF HIS FATHER'S London town house and rubbed his hands together, like Lady MacBeth trying to wipe away imaginary spots of blood. Two weeks had passed since the deaths of the cabbie and his brother-in-law, and Jeremy was about to meet with his father for the second time since then—this time at his father's urgent summoning. Though on their previous visit Gordon Mayhew had accepted Jeremy's story that he had not had a chance to interview Peter Aronson nor been involved in his murder, Jeremy now wondered if his father had come to doubt the story—or worse, if he had evidence proving Jeremy's participation.

It was not that Jeremy feared his father would inform the authorities, but the bungled affair would only confirm Gordon Mayhew's suspicion that, at thirty-two, his son was well on the way to proving himself a failure at everything he attempted, from careers in the military and finance to marriage. Jeremy gave a wry grin as he thought of his beautiful young wife, Irene, and remembered his father's words: "Only you, boy, would choose a wife who'd throw away the Mayhew fortune and run off with a penniless French poet! You must've been a sorry husband indeed.''

Jeremy looked down at his gray suit, as if searching for evidence of the crime he had committed, despite his being clothed in an entirely different outfit. Then he drew in a deep breath, let it out slowly, and knocked on the door. It was opened by Jonathan Mackintosh, his father's dapper, middle-aged secretary, who greeted him and immediately led him back toward Gordon Mayhew's private office.

"Mr. Mayhew is quite excited," Mackintosh said, smiling as they approached the office door.

Feeling a touch of relief, Jeremy asked, "Have they caught Aidan McAuliffe?"

"No, nothing like that. But new evidence has turned up." He opened the door to his own office, which adjoined Mayhew's. "I'll let Mr. Mayhew tell you all about it." He crossed quickly to the connecting door, knocked lightly, opened it a crack, and said, "Sir, your son has arrived."

"Send him in," a voice boomed, and Jonathan Mackintosh pushed the door wide and motioned Jeremy inside.

Jeremy felt like a schoolboy confronting the headmaster as he entered the office and heard the door shut behind him. It was a cavernous room, the walls lined with hundreds of books, which ran the gamut from Shakespeare to medicine to law. At the center of the room was a massive oaken desk, with several leather chairs facing it. But what dominated the room was the man seated in the high-back desk chair, just now smoking a long, fat cigar. The man might have looked like a taller, heftier version of his son but for one striking difference: Gordon Mayhew had no trace of hair on his head—not even facial hair or eyebrows. Mayhew had done much reading about the rare condition, called alopecia, that had caused his hair to start falling out in his school days, though such knowledge did little to erase the other legacy of this mysterious disease—his perpetual scowl.

"Sit down," Mayhew said brusquely, waving a hand at one of the chairs in front of the desk as he continued to examine some papers in front of him. As soon as his son was seated, Mayhew looked up and began to tap the papers.

"Know what I've got here?" he asked. Before Jeremy could open his mouth to reply, Mayhew continued, "A deposition, that's what. We'll have that bastard McAuliffe in custody within days." He allowed himself what passed for a smile. Almost immediately it settled back into a frown.

"Where is he?" Jeremy asked.

"On his way to New York." Picking up the top sheet of paper, Mayhew read, "The *Vigilant*. A chap by the name of Foxworth claims that's the ship McAuliffe used to escape from England."

"Who's this Foxworth fellow?"

"A man who saw our reward notice."

"Do you believe him? Perhaps he's just after the reward."

"Of course he wants the hundred pounds," Mayhew replied with a note of irritation. "But this fellow's different. He found out he won't see a shilling until McAuliffe is in custody, yet he's keeping to his story. And I believe him."

"Can you be sure?"

"He's waiting in the study, ready to repeat his story to the Yard."

"Scotland Yard? I thought you wanted to handle this privately."

"Don't be stupid, boy," Mayhew derided, putting down the paper and glowering at his son. "That boat is due to arrive in New York in a couple of days, and only the Yard has the authority to request that the Americans search the ship and detain Aidan McAuliffe. Meanwhile our lawyers will arrange for extradition." He took a puff on his cigar, then blew the smoke toward the ceiling. "Makes no difference to me, boy, who brings in that scoundrel—so long as he hangs. Then Cheryl can rest in peace."

There was a knock at the door, and it opened enough to reveal Jonathan Mackintosh's face as he announced, "Inspector Sterling Hampshire is here."

"Yes, yes. Show him in," Mayhew said impatiently.

A tall, slim man in a brown vested suit entered and approached the desk. Gordon Mayhew and his son stood, and the three men shook hands, with Mayhew signaling Mackintosh not to leave as yet.

"This is my son, Jeremy," Mayhew said by way of introduction. "Please, take a seat, Inspector Hampshire."

"I was told you've obtained some new evidence," Hampshire said without preliminaries, his tone betraying his disapproval of a private citizen's being involved in a Scotland Yard case.

"A response to the reward notices I placed in newspapers throughout England." Mayhew tapped the papers on his desk. "I've a notarized deposition here, but I thought you'd want to hear the story from Mr. Foxworth directly." He glanced at his secretary. "Bring Mr. Foxworth here."

As Jonathan Mackintosh left to fetch the witness, Inspector Hampshire took out a pad and pencil and began jotting down notes. "Foxworth, you say?" he asked.

"Yes," Mayhew replied, looking down at the deposition. "Hugh Foxworth. He's a Portsmouth innkeeper."

Just then the door reopened, and the man in question was ushered inside, with Mackintosh leaving the room and shutting the door behind him. Hugh Foxworth was an exceedingly gaunt little man, with thinning white hair and a pencil-thin mustache, his sunken brown eyes set above a hooked nose and bony chin. His gray suit was clean but threadbare and of a style that had been only marginally fashionable some thirty years before. He held a gray bowler in his hands and was nervously fingering the brim as he shuffled toward the desk and nodded at the seated men.

"Take that seat over there," Mayhew said, pointing at a narrow sofa that sat a bit removed to the side. Foxworth quickly complied. "I want you to repeat your story for Inspector Hampshire of Scotland Yard. From the beginning."

" 'Tis like I was tellin' Mr. Mayhew," Foxworth began hesitantly. "It was me wife who saw 'im—at me inn, the Square Rigger. The missus waited on a couple o' gents the night 'afore the *Vigilant* set sail. They asked about ships t'Ireland, and she told 'em the *Vigilant*. Of course, that was 'afore she 'eard it wasn't puttin' in at Cork but was sailin' straight through t'New York."

"Why didn't you tell this story before?" the inspector asked.

"Didn't know it. I never seen the gent meself, and the missus thought nothin' of it till she spied that notice in the paper. That's when she told me. Even then she says we shouldn't get involved, but I knew it was me duty."

"You sure it wasn't the reward money?" Hampshire pressed.

"I'd 'ave come forth anyway," Foxworth replied somewhat indignantly. "After all, he's a murderer, ain't he?"

"That he is," Mayhew put in. "And thanks to you, he may soon be brought to justice."

"Mr. Foxworth, would you be willing to come over to our headquarters and sign a statement?" Hampshire asked.

"But Mr. Mayhew already 'ad me sign—"

"Yes, but we'd like our own. You'd be doing us a great service."

Foxworth shifted uncomfortably on the sofa. "I'd like to, but I'm catchin' the evenin' coach to Portsmouth, and—"

"If you'd do the inspector this favor," Mayhew interjected, "I'd be glad to arrange for a room at Mrs. Waite's rooming house over on Grasmere Street—at my expense. And of course I'll reimburse you for your coach ticket."

"But you said I wouldn't see no money until—"

"This is in addition to the reward—with no stipulations attached. It's in way of thanks for making the long journey from Portsmouth."

Hugh Foxworth's eyes brightened, and a smile cracked his thin, dry lips. "Well, if the inspector thinks it necessary—why, yes, I'll be glad to oblige."

Gordon Mayhew rose from his chair and stood with his palms on the desk. "Inspector Hampshire, I'll leave it to you, then, to contact the American authorities and have that ship seized and searched."

Hampshire put away his notebook and stood. "If Mr. Foxworth's story checks out—the dates and such—we'll send a wire at once to New York. We'll also investigate any ships that left Portsmouth for Ireland that day, in case McAuliffe discovered the mistake in time. Meanwhile, if you would be so good as to send a copy of your deposition—"

"I already had one drawn up for you." Mayhew picked up

a couple of the sheets and handed them across the desk. "Good day, Inspector Hampshire . . . Mr. Foxworth." He nodded at the two men. "Mr. Mackintosh will show you gentlemen to the door."

As if on signal, the door opened and Jonathan Mackintosh appeared to usher them out.

As soon as the men were gone, Gordon Mayhew turned to his son and declared, "They better not bungle this affair." He ran a hand over his sweaty bald pate. "If McAuliffe slips through our hands in New York, we may never find him."

"We will," Jeremy assured his father, doing his best to imbue the words with conviction. "Aidan McAuliffe will be brought to justice—if I have to go to America myself and drag him back."

Mayhew gave a slight chuckle, as if the thought amused him. "If it comes to that, boy, you'd best take Nate Gilchrist along. I wouldn't want to have to send the Yard out hunting both McAuliffe *and* you."

Rachel Salomon slipped into her cabin aboard the *Vigilant*, nearly bowling over Aidan McAuliffe, who just then was pacing in front of the door.

"What is it?" he asked. "What was all the commotion?"

"They've sighted Nova Scotia. America is not far beyond."

Aidan sighed with relief. "I thought it was another vessel—maybe the British Navy come to search the ship."

"You've been letting your imagination run wild." Rachel looked around at the small, cramped cabin. "It's no wonder, being cooped up in here for two whole weeks—not even being able to let anyone in to clean up. And you must be so sore from sleeping on those thin little cushions on the floor, what with the way the ship was lurching about last night."

Aidan came forward and took Rachel's hands. "I've been perfectly comfortable," he assured her. "And it's all thanks to you. You've saved my life." He squeezed her hands gently, then reluctantly let them go.

Covering the blush that rose in her cheeks, she turned away, motioned toward the floor, and said, "And broken your back, I'm afraid."

"It's far more comfortable than a lifeboat or a slop closet."

"I suppose so," she admitted. "But as to saving your life, so far it's only a temporary reprieve. There's still the problem of getting you ashore."

"I'll swim," he declared flatly. "Maybe when it gets dark tonight we'll sail close enough to land, and I can slip away before we ever reach New York."

"But it's only the thirtieth of May; the water will be frigid," she pointed out.

"I got used to the cold growing up in Scotland."

"Are you a good swimmer?"

"Well, no," he said sheepishly. "Growing up in Edinburgh, one doesn't get much opportunity."

"But you *can* swim."

"Not exactly. But it can't be very difficult."

Rachel could not help but grin. "Aidan McAuliffe, you are not going to tempt the Atlantic your first time in the water. We'll think of another way."

"I'll just have to take my chances hiding on board when they search the vessel out in the harbor of New York. Then when we dock, I'll figure a way to sneak ashore."

"If only we could get you off before we get to New York," Rachel mused. Suddenly she snapped her fingers. "I've got it," she announced, adding the word, "Halifax."

"Halifax? What do you mean?"

"We'll be passing near Halifax Harbor. I'll convince the captain to put ashore there for a few hours."

"How will you do that?"

"Simple. I'll assume we're scheduled to stop there so that I can transfer some goods to a small export company that our store often does business with. When the captain protests that no such stop was arranged, I'll claim that someone at his shipping office must have lost the order. Don't worry—I'll convince him to stop. After all, most of the hold is loaded with goods being shipped to Salomon's Emporium. He won't want to upset me and jeopardize his

65

contract to sail our goods the rest of the way around the Horn to San Francisco.''

''I hate to see you taking that kind of risk.''

''What risk?'' she said casually. ''I've been to Halifax a number of times and have friends there. Believe me, it will be a simple matter to get you ashore—the Canadians are very informal when it comes to British ships.''

''If you think it's the best—''

''It is. Trust me. Soon you'll be on solid ground again, and you'll be able to put the past behind you.''

''Not all the past, I hope,'' he said softly, and Rachel looked down uncomfortably. ''I'll never forget you—or what you did for me,'' he told her. ''Your husband's a lucky man.''

Turning away, Rachel said, ''You speak as though we'll never see each other again.''

''We may not,'' he said plainly.

Looking back at him, Rachel smiled. ''I'm not so sure about that. But right now we'd better put our attention on getting you off this ship.'' She crossed to the door and reached for the knob.

''Where are you going?'' Aidan asked.

''It's time Captain Toomey and I had our little talk,'' she declared with a wink. Then she opened the door and disappeared down the corridor.

Later that afternoon, the *Vigilant* entered the mouth of Halifax Harbor and sailed toward the docks that lined the western shore at the foot of the city. As Rachel had predicted, the entire customs procedure consisted of a five-minute visit by the harbor master, who spent four of those minutes reminiscing with Captain Toomey about the last time the *Vigilant* put in at Halifax.

While the crew off-loaded several crates of goods picked out by Rachel, one of the seamen carried a message to Cabot Export, a small company occupying a single room in an alley off Barrington Street. Fifteen minutes later, the seaman returned with Scott Cabot, the fair-haired young owner and sole employee of Cabot Export. His brown suit was a bit too loose on his narrow shoulders, and he wore a flat-crowned slouch hat that was far too informal to be worn with a suit. His shirt was buttoned to the neck, but his bowtie hung undone from his collar, as if he had been relaxing at his office and had hurriedly thrown on his coat and hat when the seaman told him of Rachel's arrival.

"Rachel Salomon!" he called as he ran up the gangplank and met her and the captain on the deck. "I didn't expect to see you in Halifax, but it's certainly a pleasure." He shook Rachel's hand, then removed his wire-rimmed glasses to wipe off the steam that had formed from his having run to the dock.

"Surely you received a cable from London," she said in mock surprise.

"No," he replied, putting on his glasses. He took off his hat and rubbed the perspiration from his brow. "I'm certain I'd have remembered such a cable."

"Dear me," Rachel said, turning to the captain. "It seems I owe you and your company an apology. Apparently my own associate in London failed to notify both your company and Mr. Cabot of my intention to stop in Halifax. I'm so sorry. I promise I'll send him a stiff reprimand just as soon as we reach New York."

"No harm has been done," Captain Toomey assured her. "I'm only grateful that we discovered the mistake before we were past Halifax." The captain turned and bowed slightly to Scott Cabot. "I will leave you to your business. But I must request that we sail within two hours—we want to catch the evening tide."

"I need to accompany Mr. Cabot to his office, but I shall return well before then."

"Fine," Toomey said. "If you will excuse me . . ."

As the captain walked away, Rachel turned to Scott Cabot and said, "I'd like you to come to my cabin for a moment. I have some papers for you there."

"Of course," Scott replied, holding out his arm to escort Rachel.

They made their way to the forward deck and headed down the corridor between the starboard cabins. Stopping in front of one of the doors, Rachel rapped three times and then turned the knob, motioning the young man inside. She followed him in and quickly shut the door.

Scott almost jumped with a start upon discovering a man in the cabin. He looked uncomfortably at Rachel, who said, "Scott Cabot, I'd like you to meet a friend of mine—Aidan McAuliffe."

"A pleasure to meet you," Scott said, shaking Aidan's hand.

"Scott runs Cabot Export, which provides many of the fine woolen products sold by Salomon's Emporium," Rachel explained. Then she turned to Scott. "My friend Aidan is a physician, but right now I'm afraid he's got himself in a bit of a bind."

"I'm running from the law," Aidan interjected.

"I . . . I don't understand." Scott looked back and forth between them.

"Scott," Rachel said, taking the young man's hand, "I have to take you into my confidence. Aidan was falsely convicted of murdering a woman in London. There was a wealthy individual who framed Aidan—bought off witnesses, paid others for perjured testimony. It's a long story, but for now you will have to trust me."

"Of course I trust you, Rachel. But I don't see—"

"I need you to help me get Aidan off this ship before we get to New York."

"You don't have to get involved," Aidan cut in. "If you don't want to help, you can leave, and no one will think the worse of you."

"I only ask that you not tell anyone what you just learned," Rachel added.

"Of course not," Scott assured her. "But how can I be of help?"

"You and Aidan are nearly the same age and size. You're a little thinner and your hair is a few shades lighter, but you even have the same blue eyes. You two could exchange coats. Then, wearing your glasses and hat, Aidan could walk off this ship at my side."

"Yes, I see," Scott said as the plan became clear. "But that would leave me on the ship, wouldn't it?"

"Yes," Rachel agreed. "But you're not wanted for murder."

"I know, but that still leaves me on board when the *Vigilant* sets sail."

"Haven't you ever wanted to see New York?" she asked with an impish grin.

"Of course, but—" Scott suddenly fell silent. He looked first at Rachel, then at Aidan. Facing Rachel again, he said, "You don't seriously mean for me . . ." His voice grew smaller and then trailed off, while Rachel's smile grew ever wide.

Rachel pulled her black evening wrap tighter over the shoulders of her gold, ankle-length dress as she stepped out onto the main deck of the *Vigilant*. She took a moment to adjust the large ruby brooch at her neck and to pat her copper-colored hair into place under a velvet hat bearing two enormous ostrich feathers. The ostentatious hat was from her uncle Joseph in London—a present she had sworn never to wear. But this afternoon it seemed the perfect accessory to draw attention away from her escort.

Clutching a small black purse, Rachel took her escort's arm and followed him across the main deck. As they stepped onto the gangplank, she told the seaman on watch, "Please assure Captain Toomey that I will return within the hour."

"Yes, Mrs. Salomon," the sailor replied, taking little notice of the man in the slouch hat and wire-rimmed glasses who had come aboard less than a half hour before and was leaving now with Rachel. In fact, the sailor was not paying attention to the huge hat, either, but to the way the brooch rose and fell with every heave of Rachel's chest. As the couple headed down the gangplank, his focus shifted to the graceful curve of her hips and narrow waist.

At the foot of the gangplank, a pair of sailors was sitting on the crates that had been off-loaded from the ship. They quickly rose, and one asked, "What shall we do with these?"

Without turning toward them, the man with the glasses replied, "I'll send someone around for them shortly."

"Aye, sir." The sailor turned toward his mate. "C'mon. We'd best get on board." The other man nodded, and the two of them started up the gangplank.

Holding her companion's arm, Rachel steered him down Water Street. They turned right on Sackville Street and walked up the hill to Barrington, where they headed left until they came to a small alley.

"Scott's office is down there," Rachel said as Aidan pulled off the glasses and rubbed his eyes from the strain of looking through the lenses. "You can wait there until he gets back," she added, taking the glasses from him and slipping them into her purse.

"I'll bet he's relieved he won't have to go all the way to New York."

"Yes," she agreed. "That was a much better idea to stop the ship as it's pulling out and pretend Scott had slipped back aboard without being seen."

"I just hope the captain believes it."

"I'll take care of Captain Toomey," Rachel assured him.

Aidan glanced around and saw that they were the object of attention to the occasional passersby who came walking along Halifax's main business street. "I suppose we should say good-bye," he said with a slight sigh.

"Not just yet. There's something I want to show you first."

Rachel again took Aidan's arm and led him back along Barrington Street, turning at the next corner and leading him away from the harbor up a narrow, fairly steep road. After climbing several blocks, Aidan found himself at the foot of a broad, grassy hill, which sloped upward to the low stone ramparts of a fort. Near the base of the hill was a wooden clock tower that vaguely resembled a lighthouse.

"That's the Citadel," she announced, pointing to the fort. "And this is the Old Town Clock. Your own Prince Edward commissioned it when he was stationed here around eighteen hundred. They say he was a fanatic about time and had it built so that any soldiers on leave in town wouldn't have an excuse for being late at curfew. As a matter of fact, the fort is still garrisoned by British troops.''

"I guess we'd best not take a tour of it, then,'' Aidan commented with a grin.

"No, but let's go just a bit closer. Just don't look back until I tell you to.''

Aidan did as she requested, keeping his eyes straight ahead as they climbed the hill to a point halfway between the clock and the fort. There Rachel came to a halt and said, "We're high enough. You can look now.''

Aidan turned around to find a breathtaking panorama of the city and harbor of Halifax. To the left of where they stood, the sun was just setting in a cloudless sky, casting long fingers of yellow light and gray shadow upon the stone and brick buildings that sat cheek by jowl along the hills of the city. Carriages moved briskly along the darkening streets, while ships of every size and description sat moored to the docks that lined the shore or sailed slowly in and out of the wide harbor.

"It's beautiful,'' Aidan whispered.

"I wanted to show it to you,'' Rachel replied, moving closer and taking his hand. "It reminds me of home.''

"San Francisco?''

"Yes, though Halifax is smaller and the hills are more gentle. But the feeling is the same.'' She turned from the harbor and looked at Aidan. "I hate when everything is flat. I need movement around me—even from the land.''

Aidan stared into Rachel's emerald eyes for a long moment, then turned away and gazed out over the harbor. "I'm afraid I may have brought you more movement than you ever counted on.''

"Never,'' she insisted, squeezing his hand. "I care what happens to you, Aidan. I . . . I want to see you again.'' Letting go of his hand, she reached up and touched his cheek. He turned toward her, and they stood gazing into each other's eyes. Slowly Aidan's hand came up until he was touching Rachel's cheek, as well. Then they kissed, gently, cautiously.

As their lips parted, Aidan pulled back slightly. "I'm

71

sorry," he breathed. "That was wrong of me. And after you've been so kind."

"Don't apologize. I wanted you to kiss me. After all, we don't know if we'll ever see each other again."

"But you're a married woman, and—"

Rachel touched a finger to his lips. As she looked up at him, she yearned to tell him that she was not married, but she knew that he might put himself at grave risk by following her to America. Here in Nova Scotia he would be able to establish a new identity. Perhaps when enough time had passed, they would find themselves together again.

"There are things I want to tell you," she confided, her voice soft and hesitant. "About myself. About my marriage. But not today. Right now you must put all of your attention on creating a new life for yourself." She paused, then added, "Just promise me one thing, Aidan."

"Anything at all."

"Promise me that if it's ever safe for you to come to America, you'll visit me in San Francisco."

"But your husband—"

"Promise me," she repeated, again holding her finger to his lips.

Rachel felt her eyes fill with tears as Aidan kissed her finger, then the palm of her hand. She slipped both her hands around his neck and pulled him close, her own lips opening and meeting his, her body trembling as he held her in his arms.

The sun had dropped below the horizon, and the lights of the city were beginning to glimmer on the black water of Halifax Harbor as Rachel reboarded the *Vigilant* and, after catching a final glimpse of Aidan standing at the foot of Sackville Street, hurried to her cabin.

"I'll never be able to thank you enough," Rachel told Scott as she entered the room, tossed her hat on the bed, and held out Scott's glasses to him.

"Thank me?" he asked incredulously as he rose from his chair and put on his glasses. "After everything that you and your family have done for me?"

"We've done nothing."

"If it weren't for your loans three years ago, Cabot Export never would've survived its first year in operation."

"That was a business transaction. What you did today went far beyond, and I'll never forget it."

"Just as I won't forget you interceding to get me that loan from your father," Scott avowed. "You took a personal risk back then. I've done nothing more today."

"And I'll be forever grateful."

"Now about getting me off this ship . . ."

"As we decided earlier, we'll wait until we're pulling away from the dock and then pretend that you reboarded when no one was looking to bring me some papers. Captain Toomey will pull back to the dock, and you'll simply walk ashore."

"I gave that quite a bit of thought while you were gone, and I'm afraid it may not work."

"Why not?" Rachel asked.

"I'm afraid he may see through that ruse or at least become suspicious. And if anyone ever learns that your friend stowed away on this ship, it might lead the authorities right to you—and to Halifax."

"What do you suggest?"

Scott nodded toward the porthole. "It's getting dark. I'll wait until the boat is pulling away, and then I'll slip over the side and swim to shore. It will be simple."

"Can you swim?"

"Of course. I grew up right here by the harbor."

"But the water must be so cold."

"As a boy, I went swimming many times in May. The water will be a bit chilly, but it's actually warmer here than along most of the American coast, since we're right in the middle of the Gulf Stream."

"Are you certain you want to do this?" she asked.

"Yes, Rachel, I do."

"You're a dear," she said, stepping up to him and impulsively kissing his cheek. "And what can I do to help?"

"You'll provide the diversion."

"I've had plenty of experience at that," she replied with a smile. Just then the boat gave a lurch and began to creak as it pulled away from the dock. "And there's no time like right now," she added, picking up her hat from the bed. Pinning it back in place, she walked back over to Scott and took his hands. "You be careful now," she told him.

"Don't worry about me," he urged her. "And rest assured I'll have those off-loaded crates on their way to San Francisco on the next boat out."

"Not all of them," Rachel said. "There's one that's smaller than the others; it's for you and your wife."

"I couldn't—"

"You can, and you will. And the next time I come through Halifax, I expect a home-cooked meal served up on it. I hope Cayleigh likes Wedgwood."

"Oh, Rachel, I—I don't know what to say," he stammered.

"Just help Aidan for me. That will be thanks enough. And there's one other thing. . . . Would you give him something from me?"

"Of course. What is it?"

Rachel went over to the bureau and opened a box, from which she removed ten gold coins. "Two hundred dollars," she said, counting them out. "Aidan may not want to take it, but convince him it's a loan." She turned back to the bureau and picked up a velvet bag with a long drawstring. Opening it, she emptied some jewelry, then placed the coins inside and tied the drawstring. "Here, tie this to your belt," she said, handing him the bag.

He quickly tied the bag in place and tucked it into his pocket.

"What about your glasses?" she asked with concern.

"Don't worry; I can hold on to them," he assured her.

"You're ready, then?"

Scott nodded as he removed Aidan's coat so that it would not weigh him down in the water.

"Then let's go," she declared.

Rachel led the way out onto the main deck. The ship was already well away from the dock and was sailing along the shore toward the mouth of Halifax Harbor. Most of the passengers were at the aft quarterdeck, looking back at the city, while a few stood at the bow.

As they moved along the deck, Scott pointed to a place at the starboard rail next to the very lifeboat in which Aidan had first stowed away. "It's dark enough there," he whispered. "Just keep everyone away."

"Thank you again," she said.

"Don't worry, Rachel. My wife and I will take care of Aidan for you."

"I know you will." She gave him a quick embrace. "Now be off with you."

Scott moved away from Rachel and casually sauntered over to the rail, taking up a position in the shadows between the first two lifeboats. He glanced around, then looked back at Rachel and nodded up toward the bridge, where the captain was conversing with a couple of seamen in full view of where Scott was standing.

Rachel looked to where Scott had indicated and saw the captain and his men. With a nod to Scott, she mounted the stairs and approached the group of men. "Captain Toomey," she called, drawing his attention. "May I speak with you a moment?" She stood smiling at him until he dismissed the seaman. When they were alone, save for the first mate at the wheel, she continued, "I want to thank you for altering your course today." She deftly took his arm and led him toward the front of the bridge. "Could you tell me what that light is over there?" she asked, pointing toward a large island that was looming in the distance off the larboard bow.

"Why, that's the lighthouse on McNab's Island," the captain answered. "It's at the mouth of Chebucto Bay, or Halifax Harbor, as this body of water is commonly called."

"You're so knowledgeable of the sea," she remarked. "How long have you been a captain? . . ."

Back on the main deck, Scott had already pulled off his shoes and tied them together. After looking around to make certain no one was in the vicinity, he removed his glasses and stuffed them into one of the shoes. Then he slung the shoes around his neck and climbed over the rail. Crouching on the edge of the deck and holding on to the bottom rung of the rail, he worked his way to the right until he was hidden in the darkness directly under the forward lifeboat, which hung out over the rail. He took several deep breaths, holding the last one. Then he pushed away from the rail, straightening his body and grabbing hold of the shoes as he dropped feet first into the cold, black water.

FIVE

"I'M SORRY. . . ." PHOEBE SALOMON WHISPERED AS SHE lowered her pencil and closed her diary. Without bothering to lock the clasp, she left it on the French writing table and returned to her bed, where she curled up under the blanket. Drawing her arms tight under her chest, she could feel the slight swell of her belly. *Soon people won't think I'm just putting on a little weight,* she told herself. *Soon everyone will know.*

Nina was right: Phoebe had been so very foolish. But she had really cared for Eaton Hallinger. Though he was eight years older than she and quite sophisticated in the ways of the world, there was so much of the little boy in him—so much that reminded Phoebe of her own dear brother, Maurice. Eaton had charmed her, plain and simple. And she had fallen for his charms. "But just that once," she reminded herself, though she knew there was an earlier incident when he had touched her brazenly and she had wanted him to do so much more.

"I should have told you I'm pregnant," she whispered, her eyes filling with tears. But she had not been able to face him again after that evening last fall when she had given herself to him in the back of his cabriolet under the trees of Golden Gate Park. When he had later tried to call on her, Nina had rebuffed him, and then Phoebe herself had sent word through her brother that she desired he not call upon her again. But it was a lie. What she really desired was to see him, to touch him, to feel him touching her. But she was so ashamed—so very frightened and ashamed.

It was several months later that Phoebe had begun to realize that something was wrong and that her body was going through changes she could not understand. But when she had tried to talk with her mother about it, Nina misunderstood and used the opportunity to lecture her youngest daughter on what she called the sins of self-pollution. Even now Phoebe could hear her mother going on about how "young women who indulge in the secret vice of self-abuse invariably find themselves inflicted with stomach cramps, pale complexions, an unnatural craving for food, or no appetite at all. And it can have such an untoward affect on the humors of the brain that one can find the wards of city asylums largely populated with these pitiable, lost souls."

Phoebe had not understood a word of it until she summoned the courage to ask Rachel, and then they had shared a sisterly laugh. But it was a bitter joke for Phoebe, who by then had begun to sense what was really happening to her. Yet she had still been too confused and frightened to confide even in Rachel, and so she had continued to carry the secret alone, even when the truth became too obvious to disbelieve.

I should have told you, Eaton, her mind repeated over and over again. Yet she knew that it was too late now. Not long after breaking off with Eaton, she had learned that he had a new woman in his life, the daughter of one of the directors of the Central Pacific Railroad. Though the two women had never met, Phoebe had been told she was a lovely creature, attractive and well-connected, the kind of woman who could advance the career and status of a man like Eaton Hallinger. Rumor had it that they were secretly engaged and that a formal announcement would be made later that summer.

"No, I can never tell you, Eaton," Phoebe realized aloud.

"You'd do the right thing—and you'd never forgive me for it!" She buried her face in the pillow and sobbed.

For a long time Phoebe just lay there, at times crying, at times feeling as if she might break into hysterical laughter. There was something tragically funny about the whole situation. Phoebe was the cautious one—the family mouse. It was far more likely that bold, self-assured Rachel would find herself in a predicament such as this. And few would be surprised if Jacob or Maurice were dragged to the altar for compromising the virtue of some innocent young woman. But Phoebe? Such a thing was inconceivable. Yet it was true.

Phoebe felt herself growing lightheaded, as if she had just sampled her third or fourth glass of champagne. It was a welcome feeling, and it blended nicely with the faint strains of Strauss's "Tales from the Vienna Woods," which drifted upstairs from the first-floor reception hall, where a small chamber orchestra was providing the entertainment.

How Phoebe loved to dance, and right now she would not even mind if it were in the arms of Carl Emrich. After all, there was nothing wrong with Carl, though his hands and forehead perspired so perpetually that it looked as if he might melt into the floor.

"And why shouldn't I dance?" she asked herself, leaning up on her elbows. She glanced down and saw her blue satin gown draped over the foot of the bed. Though Nina had chosen it, Phoebe had to admit that she looked quite stunning in it. Yet she might never have the opportunity to wear it again. Certainly within a few more weeks she would not be able to fit into it.

"That is, if I *am* pregnant." She wiped the tears from her cheeks with the back of her hand. *What if I'm not?* she wondered for the thousandth time. During the past few months she had read what information she could find—from the obscure, 1839 edition of *Castle's Manual of Surgery*, which had belonged to her father's uncle, to the recently published *Ladies' Guide in Health and Disease*, by Dr. J. H. Kellogg, with its overlay pictures of the human body and its detailed accounts of pregnancy and childbirth. And from all she had read, there was still reason to hope that she was merely gaining weight and that the cessation of her menstrual flow was due to other, perhaps dietary, causes. Yet that did not explain the movements she had been feeling for several weeks within her belly when she lay very still.

Phoebe shook her head; she would not allow any such thoughts—at least not tonight. "Nina will make it right," she reminded herself. Phoebe had confided her deepest fear, and now her mother would take care of her and somehow set things right.

From downstairs, the music shifted to a spirited piece that Phoebe could not quite identify—Mozart's "Eine Kleine Nachtmusik" perhaps. Sitting up on the bed, she swung her feet to the floor and sat perfectly still, listening to the lively music and staring at the gown at the foot of her bed. "Yes, I'll go downstairs," she whispered as she rose on somewhat unsteady legs and picked up the gown, holding it in front of her as she walked over to the full-length mirror that stood against one wall.

Seeing how lovely she looked, despite the streaked makeup on her cheeks, Phoebe proclaimed, "Yes, I will go down to the party . . . if I can still fit into this dress."

"Why, Miss Phoebe, you look marvelous," a voice called as the youngest Salomon daughter came down the wide marble staircase half an hour later.

"Thank you, Cameron," Phoebe replied, turning at the foot of the stairs and smiling at the portly butler, who stood at the arched entrance to the reception hall, where he could be of service if called upon.

"Your mother said you had taken ill. I trust you're feeling better?"

"Much better. And the music sounded so lovely. . . . I simply had to come down."

"Everyone will be delighted." Cameron backed from the doorway so that Phoebe could enter the large hall, where some thirty guests were enjoying music and hors d'oeuvres.

Just then a lilting voice called, "Who's that?" and Nina Salomon appeared in the doorway. "Have the Emrichs finally arrived—?" she asked, her words cutting off when she looked past the butler and saw her daughter standing in front of the staircase. "Why, Phoebe . . . what are you doing down here?" she asked in surprise, her smile fading as she crossed the foyer.

Phoebe suddenly felt extremely guilty. "Why, I thought I'd join the guests. . . ."

"But in your condition? Hadn't we decided—?" She stopped abruptly and glanced back at the butler. "Cameron, please make sure all the guests are being attended to."

Taking the cue, Cameron nodded and disappeared into the reception hall.

Nina turned back to her daughter, her expression betraying both her annoyance and concern. "Now, Phoebe," she began, "I thought we discussed this upstairs."

"But I feel much better, and—"

"It's not how you feel that worries me. It . . . it's how you look." She waved her hand up and down in front of Phoebe. "Someone might notice. There could be talk."

Phoebe glanced down and saw the way her belly was stretching the blue satin material, and her lower lip began to quiver. "I've just gained a little weight," she insisted, as if trying to convince herself.

"Oh, Phoebe, don't be so naive. I told you we'd work this thing out, but you have to give me some time. And certainly you can't go out in public right now—not in your condition. Now run along upstairs. I'll see you in the morning."

"But the party . . ." she implored, forcing a smile as she looked beyond Nina to the bright lights of the reception hall. "And what about Carl?" she added in an attempt to win her mother's approval.

"Don't be stupid!" Nina blurted. "He'd have nothing to do with you now. No decent man would!"

Phoebe raised a hand to her mouth and bit down hard as the tears welled up again.

Nina stood glowering at her daughter, shaking her head as if not knowing what to do. Finally she sighed, then reached up and gently pulled Phoebe's hand from her mouth. Patting it, she cooed, "There, there now. I didn't mean to speak so harshly. But you simply must face reality." She paused until she was certain she had her daughter's full attention. Then she concluded, "I want you to go back to your room and get some sleep. All right?"

Phoebe gave a slight nod and stared down at the floor.

"That's better." Nina let go of her hand. "Now, run along before someone sees you." As Phoebe turned and started up the stairs, Nina called after her, "You do look lovely, Phoebe."

"Thank you," Phoebe murmured without looking back. She continued up a few more steps, then stopped and listened to the swish of her mother's gown as she made her way back to the reception hall. Turning to lean against the marble bannister, Phoebe raised a hand, her lips forming her mother's name. But Nina had already disappeared inside, where she could be heard talking gaily with the guests.

Phoebe stood immobilized halfway up the stairs, afraid to return to her empty room, even more fearful of going back down. She could feel her dress constricting her, until her breath came in short, ragged gasps. Her head swam as flashes of heat coursed through her body. She thought that she would lose her balance, for now the staircase itself began to shift and roll beneath her feet. It was so stifling hot. If only she could have some fresh air—if only she could breathe freely once again.

Gripping the bannister, Phoebe forced herself to turn in place. For a moment she stood teetering on the wide marble step, and then she staggered back down the stairs and rushed across the foyer to the front door. Grabbing the knob with both hands, she opened the massive oak door and slipped out into the cool evening air. Pulling the door shut, she leaned against it and gazed down off Nob Hill, mesmerized by the glimmering city lights below. She took several deep breaths, felt the coolness pouring into her, and then pushed away from the door and headed down the long walkway. Behind her, a near-full moon peaked out from behind the gaudy turrets and gargoyle-tipped spires of the gray stone mansion.

The streets began to blend one into the other as Phoebe wandered into the lower regions of San Francisco—down along Taylor Street into the Uptown Tenderloin, then turning left on O'Farrell toward the dazzling lights of Market Street, which cut the city in half at an angle like New York's famed Broadway. She paid no attention to the men who, upon spying an unescorted woman in a lavish gown but with no coat or shawl, assumed she had just emerged from one of the more reputable sporting houses along O'Farrell Street and made lewd offers as she walked past. Neither did she note the petticoats and garters that hung overhead from the closed shutters of a number of buildings; like three golden balls outside a pawnshop, they were an advertisement of sorts for the wares that could be purchased inside.

Phoebe paused at the corner of Market Street. She looked left and right along the north side of the road—the four-bit side, it was called, where the wealthier, more respectable women strolled. Across the wide thoroughfare from where Phoebe was standing was the two-bit side. It did not lack for women, but they were invariably the kind who did not lack for men. It was there, along the five-block strip known as the Line, that men came to line the corners and stand at the openfront cigar shops and view the passing parade of women.

Almost directly across Market Street, through the passing stream of cable cars, horse-drawn drays, and fringe-topped surreys, Phoebe saw the lights of the Midway Plaisance, where for ten cents patrons could enjoy live, exotic dancers from the Orient, some wearing queer Egyptian headdresses and pantaloons, others dressed in curious Turkish trousers, their midriffs daringly bare. Just beyond the Midway to the west stood the Eden Musée, with its wax figures ''More Lifelike Than Madame Tussaud's in London!'' And farther still was what appeared to be an open field filled with tents and wagons, all ablaze with torches and lanterns, like a gypsy carnival. Among the tents were jugglers and dancers, black minstrels and snake-oil salesmen—something for every conceivable taste.

Phoebe found herself walking across Market Street, oblivious to the passing traffic. The bell of a cable car clanged in warning as it passed within inches of her, while a passing four-wheel hack had to pull up short and blare its horn.

Phoebe seemed neither to notice nor care as she headed south, toward the lights.

Stepping up onto the sidewalk, Phoebe slowly approached the Midway and stood looking through the window at the risqué life-size photographs of the dancers within, while but ten feet away a barker shouted, "Step right this way! A mere ten cents will buy you the mysteries of the Orient. Ten cents to see the infamous whirling dervish herself, Little Egypt, direct from the great Chicago Fair!"

Phoebe suddenly felt very cold, and she crossed her arms in front of her and rubbed her shoulders. She looked down at her own dress, wondering if one day she might end up clad just as provocatively as the poor souls of the Midway, forced to earn a living here somewhere on the two-bit side of the street.

With a shudder, she began to walk east down Market Street. At each corner, at least one of the bolder men would call or whistle at the alluring woman in blue, but she paid them no attention and continued to walk the Line. Faces loomed up in front of her and fell away just as quickly as evening revelers staggered past her down the road. Phoebe saw little of it and heard few of the suggestive comments, her head filled only with the jumbled din of music and laughter.

Just then someone grasped her arm and pulled her to a halt, shaking her from her reverie. "It's all right, Miss Salomon," the man said in a slightly slurred voice.

"Who are you?" she asked, eyeing the young man. His black suit was wrinkled and dusty, his derby slightly askew.

"You shouldn't be down here on your own, y'know."

"Who are you?" she repeated.

"It's me—Garth. I'm friends with Maurice."

Phoebe eyed him more closely but could not recall any such friend. Still, she relaxed slightly at the mention of her brother.

"Y'really shouldn't be walkin' here all alone. Lemme take you home."

"I . . . I don't want to go home," she replied, gently trying to pull her arm free.

"Maurice would want me to see you were taken care of." He leaned closer and smiled, and she smelled the liquor on his breath.

"I'll be all right," she insisted, at last breaking his hold. "Thank you, anyway."

Phoebe walked away without looking back. After another block she began to feel safe again and had almost forgotten the incident when suddenly her arm was grabbed once more and the fellow named Garth started to walk alongside her.

"I ain't gonna hurt you," he drawled. "But somethin' could happen to a nice gal like you down here. Lemme walk you home."

Phoebe felt her body shiver, but she did not try to pull away as Garth led the way to the next corner and then crossed with her to the north side of the street, where he turned up Montgomery Street. It was darker there, and he quickened the pace as they made their way toward the edge of Chinatown, where they would turn left up California Street to Nob Hill. But he continued straight across California, and when she tried to pull up short, he merely gripped her arm all the tighter and dragged her along.

"Where are we going?" she demanded and then began to cry, though she was unsure what she was crying about.

"Right here," Garth muttered as he came to an abrupt halt beside a narrow alley between two buildings. "Right here," he repeated, dragging her into the alley.

"Don't . . ." she pleaded as he dragged her deeper into the darkness. "I can't. . . . I d-don't want to."

"I ain't gonna hurt you," he promised as he pulled her to a halt and turned toward her. "Just give us a kiss."

Garth was still holding her arm with one hand, and now he gripped her neck in his other hand and leaned closer. Phoebe quickly turned away, so that his lips merely grazed her cheek.

"A kiss is all," he insisted. "No one's gonna hurt you. Just give us a kiss."

He pressed her back against the wall of the building and let go of her arm, taking her face in both hands and holding it in place as he kissed her lips. Phoebe pushed against his chest and tried to squirm away, but he held her tight against the wall. She began to sob more loudly, and when he stopped kissing her lips and moved to her neck, she stammered, "Please . . . d-don't hurt me. Oh, God, please."

She broke down completely, and suddenly Garth seemed to realize what he was doing and let her go. She immediately slid down the wall to the ground, where she sat hunched with her arms around her legs, her head buried against her knees.

"Are you all right?" Garth asked, the liquor slurring his words.

"Oh, God, help me!" she whimpered, her voice muffled by her dress.

Garth knelt beside her and placed a hand on her arm. "I'm sorry," he told her. "I didn't mean to hurt you. I thought you was looking—"

Suddenly Phoebe reached out and pulled Garth close, burying her face in his shoulder. "Hold me," she begged. "Just hold me."

"It's okay," he said in surprise. "Just take it easy." He reached up and tried to loosen her grip around his neck.

"I'm sorry," she mumbled over and over as she held him even more tightly, frightened that he would disappear and she would be alone. Then without warning she grabbed his hair and kissed him passionately on the lips.

"Hey, what is this?" he yelled, pushing her away and standing up.

Phoebe jumped to her feet and threw her arms around him. "Hold me," she pleaded. "Don't leave me alone!"

For a second Garth was at a loss as to what to do. He had expected a kiss and had hoped for more, and now here she was clinging to him, pressing her body tightly against his. Deciding that things were going better than he had planned, he wrapped his arms around her waist and started kissing her neck, his hands working their way up along her spine toward the fasteners at the back of her dress.

At first Phoebe acquiesced, pulling him closer and meeting his kisses with her own. But then, just as he was undoing the first of the fasteners at her neck, she seemed to realize what was happening, and she pushed him away. "What are you doing?'' she gasped, backing away a few steps. ''Leave me alone!''

''What is this?'' Garth demanded. ''Are you crazy?'' He reached for her, but she slapped away his hand.

''Get away from me!'' she yelled. ''Leave me alone!''

Garth's face screwed up in anger, and then he lashed out, slapping Phoebe across the cheek and stunning her. Grabbing her by the shoulders, he pulled her to him, then dragged her down to the ground. Phoebe tried to push him away, but he was too strong and heavy as he climbed on top of her and started to yank her dress up over her knees.

Phoebe was moaning, trying to cry out as he pressed his lips against hers and thrust his tongue into her open mouth. Her arms flailed about wildly. She could feel her dress sliding higher up her legs, his hand crudely groping at her thigh. Suddenly her hand struck something cold and hard lying on the ground a couple of feet from her head. Her fingers opened, searched, and grabbed hold of a large rock.

''No!'' she screamed, swinging the rock against the back of Garth's head. She heard a dull thud as it connected with his skull, and she drew her arm back and swung the rock again and again.

With a cry of pain, Garth rolled away from Phoebe and pulled himself up on his hands and knees. He grabbed at the back of his head, and his hand came away wet with blood. ''Damn!'' he cursed, falling over onto his side.

Phoebe managed to scramble to her feet, the rock still clutched in her hand. ''You shouldn't have done it,'' she muttered as she backed down the alley. ''You shouldn't have done that to me.'' She felt the rock slip from her fingers, and then she turned and ran out into the street, racing back toward the lights.

Reaching California Street, Phoebe staggered out into the middle of the road and turned in circles, not knowing which way to go. In her mind she saw the drunken man pawing at her in the alley, then saw Eaton Hallinger lifting her skirt in the back of his carriage. She felt the joy—and the pain—as he entered her and left a growing seed behind.

Suddenly she was able to see with a clarity that was blinding to her. She knew with certainty now that she would never be the same innocent young girl again. The only thing left for her was shame and degradation . . . the two-bit side of the street.

Phoebe stumbled up California Street, watching a blaze of lights draw ever closer. Bells clanged all around her; voices shouted. She glanced down, saw the steel tracks at her feet, and knew she should run somewhere, anywhere, away from those lights. But they were so dazzling, the bells so inviting. Yes, she would run. She would put an end to this nightmare and go to sleep in the light.

With a cry of joy, she raised her arms and ran directly at the approaching cable car. By the time the driver realized what she was doing and yanked the lever to detach the cable and engage the brakes, the beautiful woman in the blue satin gown had already thrown herself under the heavy iron wheels and had disappeared from sight.

SIX

"How is he feeling?" Aidan McAuliffe asked as Scott Cabot's wife returned to the kitchen of their Halifax home with a dinner tray.

"His appetite is off a bit," Cayleigh Cabot replied, unloading the half-finished dishes at the sink.

"It won't be June until tomorrow; that water must have been freezing last night," Aidan commented. "It's no wonder Scott took ill."

Cayleigh scraped what was left of Scott's dinner off the plate, then went over to the kitchen table and sat down across from Aidan. At twenty-nine, she had seen many hard years, and it showed in the lines at the corner of her eyes and in her somewhat thin figure, which just now was not overly enhanced by the rather austere, high-collared brown dress she was wearing. Still she was an attractive, petite brunette with soft-brown eyes and an earthy magnetism that revealed itself on the infrequent occasions when she allowed herself a smile.

Cayleigh picked up a slice of bread, then glanced at Aidan's plate and said, "Is something wrong with the stew?"

89

"Not at all. It's delicious," he assured her. "But after only a day on land, I'm still finding it hard to settle my stomach."

Cayleigh nodded, accepting his explanation. She raised the bread to her lips, then lowered it and asked, "Will you be staying in Halifax long?"

"I'm not sure. But if I'm in the way—"

"No, not at all. Scott says you are to stay with us while you're in Halifax, and I was simply wondering how long that might be."

"I don't wish to impose. Perhaps as soon as your husband is feeling better we can come up with another arrangement."

"Please, not on my account," Cayleigh put in quickly. "I don't want to give you the wrong impression. I'm pleased to have you as a guest. I'm just . . . concerned." She put down the piece of bread and placed her palms on the table on either side of her plate. "I want to be square with you," she said. "Scott and I are married—we try not to keep secrets."

"Then he told you why I'm here?"

"Aye, he did, though I think he would have preferred not to."

"I'm glad he explained the situation. And if you're at all uncomfortable—"

"I'm just concerned. Scott's worked hard to build up his business, and I'd hate to see him do anything that might hurt it."

"You mean by harboring a convict," Aidan added, and Cayleigh nodded. "That's why I won't stay any longer than necessary," he promised.

"It's just that Scott is such a good, gentle man. He'd do anything to help someone in need."

Aidan put down his fork and looked at Cayleigh closely. "You don't like me very much, do you?"

"Goodness sake, why do you think that?"

"Pardon me for speaking plainly, but you seem more than a bit unhappy at my presence."

Cayleigh looked down and slowly shook her head. "It's not what you think. It's just that you . . . bring back memories I'd thought I'd forgotten."

"Me?" Aidan asked incredulously. "But how?"

"For one thing, your name." Cayleigh laughed lightly. "Isn't that silly?"

"My name? What about my name?"

"My first husband was a fisherman who died six years ago in a boating accident. His name was Aidan." She looked up at Aidan and smiled, tears filling her large brown eyes. "We were very much in love."

"I'm sorry. I had no idea."

Cayleigh stood and took her plate over to the sink. With a lilt in her voice, she said, "It's just a foolish notion, is all. You don't even look like Aidan . . . I mean, like *my* Aidan. He was husky, his hair a shade lighter. And he had the silliest grin. He always knew how to make me laugh." She returned to the table and started clearing it off. "Lord, how I miss the way we used to laugh." Suddenly she started to giggle.

"Laughter becomes you," Aidan complimented her, standing and helping clear the dishes.

"I was just thinking of the time my Aidan took me out to Middle Head up on Cape Breton Island and threatened to jump off the cliff if I didn't marry him. Mind you, those cliffs are a good hundred feet high, with nothing but rocks and swirling ocean below. Well, I looked him up and down and said, 'In that case, jump!' And he did! I was so shocked, I ran to the edge of the cliff and looked down. And there he was, lying on his back on a rock shelf no more than six feet below, looking up at me with that silly grin of his and saying, 'Now will you marry me?' And I did—and never regretted a single day."

"Then other than our names, you don't have to worry about me reminding you of him. The closest I ever came to killing myself over a woman was the time in grade school when Barbara Eastmann wouldn't talk to me for a year because I failed to write to her while spending my summer holiday down south in London."

"What did you do?" Cayleigh asked.

"I must've been only thirteen or so, but she was so beautiful—hair the color of wheat and eyes as blue as a highland lake—and I was so in love. Well, I told all of her friends that if she wouldn't forgive me, I was done for this world—I'd swim out into the middle of Loch Ness and let old Nessie put an end to my misery.'' He shook his head and frowned at the memory.

"Well . . . what happened?" Cayleigh pressed. "Did she forgive you?"

"She sent me one of her father's old straight razors with a note that read, 'If you are intent on doing yourself in, do it properly! And when you get to the other side, don't forget to write!'"

Cayleigh burst into laughter, and Aidan joined in. When she finally caught her breath, she asked, "Do you still love her?"

"Eventually she moved away, and I never learned what became of her or how she turned out." He sighed. "They say that the first love is the hardest to get over."

"Aye," Cayleigh agreed, her smile growing bittersweet.

"Thank God, Barbara was the second!" Aidan suddenly blurted. "Now the *first* one—Deborah Ilene," he breathed longingly. "There's a girl I won't get over easily!"

Cayleigh looked at Aidan's earnest expression and burst into laughter again.

"What's all this commotion?" a voice called from the hallway, and Scott Cabot came into the room wearing a blue-plaid dressing robe. "Are you making fun of my wife?" he asked Aidan facetiously.

"Just women in general," Aidan explained, sitting back down at the table.

Cayleigh went over to her husband, her laughter replaced with a look of concern. "You should be in bed," she told him, pulling his robe tighter around him.

"I heard the laughter and had to come down. They say it's the best medicine. Isn't that right, Doctor?" he asked, turning to Aidan.

Nodding in agreement, Aidan replied, "It was Dr. Thomas Sydenham who said, 'The arrival of a good clown exercises a more beneficial influence upon the health of a town than of twenty asses laden with drugs.' "

"There, you see?" Scott proclaimed, looking back at his

wife. "And it seems so long since I've heard you laughing," he added, tenderly touching her cheek. "I like it."

Cayleigh gave a faint smile and headed back to the table. "Aidan was just telling me a funny story."

"Then we should keep him around, don't you think?" Scott walked over to the table and sat between Aidan and Cayleigh. "I'm not very good at funny stories, Aidan. I'm afraid I'm a bit dull, so humor will have to be your specialty. What do you think?" Blocking the words out in the air, he intoned, "Cabot Export—Purveyors of Fine Woolens and Witticisms."

Aidan grinned. "I like that. But I'm afraid I don't quite understand."

"I never was witty, so I'll put it plainly." Scott removed his wire-rimmed glasses and wiped the lenses on the lapel of his robe. "I'd like you to stay on in Halifax—at least for a time. Cabot Export is growing, and I could use another set of hands—someone to handle the office when I'm away on buying trips. In fact, I'll be leaving for Cape Breton in a few days and normally would have to shut down the office. With a little training, I'm certain you could handle the daily routine." He put his glasses back on.

"But do you think that's wise?" Aidan asked.

"You can't spend the rest of your life looking over your shoulder. There's no reason to think anyone will trace you to Nova Scotia, so you might as well get started making a new life for yourself right here."

Aidan shook his head dubiously. "I'm not sure that's a good idea."

"Don't be silly. We wouldn't want to lose someone who can make Cayleigh laugh, now would we, Cayleigh?"

Cayleigh had been staring down at her hands, clasping them together a bit nervously. Now she glanced at Aidan, then turned to her husband and replied, "No, we wouldn't." Looking back at Aidan, she continued, "Scott is right. You'll be much safer making a start for yourself here, among friends."

"You'll need to use a different name, of course," Scott

pointed out. ''But I'm sure we can come up with a believable background for you—perhaps a long-lost cousin of mine.''

''No,'' Aidan declared sharply. ''It's one thing for you to take me in and give me a job. But if anyone ever finds out who I really am, I don't want it to look as though you were knowingly harboring a fugitive. If it comes to it, I'll say that I jumped ship, followed you to your office, and pretended I had just come to town looking for work. That way no one will ever find out that you or Rachel were involved in my escape.''

''Fine,'' Scott agreed, realizing the wisdom of Aidan's words. ''Now, let's figure out what we're going to call you.''

''I think Aidan should keep his first name,'' Cayleigh suggested. ''It would be less confusing, and there would be less chance of him responding to the wrong name.''

''You're right. But what about a surname?'' Scott asked.

Aidan thought a moment, then said, ''I once had a teacher I liked named Aylward.''

''Then Aidan Aylward it will be.'' Scott turned to Cayleigh. ''Why not get some paper and a pencil, and we can start figuring out exactly who this Aidan Aylward is.''

Phoebe Salomon saw the cable car approaching, heard the clang of the bell and screech of the iron wheels upon the track. She stood there with arms outstretched, waiting to embrace it as if it were a lover. The force of the impact knocked her down, pulled her under. The screeching, the moaning, grew louder as they continued to embrace. She felt the pressing weight against her chest and thighs, the incessant pounding deep within her. Her lips opened. She screamed once, sharply, but he pressed his lips against her mouth, stifling her cry. Harder and deeper he plunged, groaning, grinding his hips, his fingers tightening against her breasts. And then the screeching became a prolonged cry, and with a shudder she felt him bursting within her, wave upon wave, melting, slipping through her fingers, until her arms closed around herself and he was gone.

''No,'' she moaned, her arms flailing as she clutched at

the heavy, empty fog, but he was gone. "No! . . . No! No! No!"

Phoebe felt herself bolt upward, but something was gripping her chest, and she fell back. Her eyelids opened, and the sweat poured into her eyes. The world blazed so brightly that she could barely see as she tried again to rise but was pulled back against something soft—a mattress. But this was not her room. It smelled sickly, like death.

She blinked, her eyes growing accustomed to the light. She was in a narrow bed, the room a brilliant white. All around her stood cold metal tables, bottles, towels, and gauze. And everywhere that choking, cloying smell.

Tilting her head, Phoebe glanced down, saw the white sheet that covered her, the wide leather strap that pinned her chest and arms to the bed, the narrower strap across her ankles. She tried to move, struggled against her bindings, and felt a sudden shock of pain shoot up her right arm. She gasped, but the pain would not stop. Louder she screamed, shrieking, her arm swelling, throbbing, aching to explode.

Somewhere behind her a door burst open, and someone came rushing in. "It's all right," a man's voice called, and then a pair of hands grasped her shoulders and pressed her down against the mattress.

Phoebe was still moaning as she opened her eyes and saw the man dressed in white hovering over her. "Everything's going to be all right," he said with a weak smile, and she broke down and cried. "You are in the hospital," he told her. "We want to help you."

"It . . . it hurts," she gasped.

"I know," he said. "But it will pass." He turned toward someone behind him and said, "Morphine."

A moment later, a woman came around Phoebe's left side and lowered the sheet from her shoulder. Phoebe felt the sharp stab of a needle, heard herself crying, her voice growing fainter and more distant until it, too, was gone.

When Phoebe awoke again, a nurse was sitting in a chair on the left side of her bed. The woman, seeing Phoebe's eyes open, leaned over and smiled. "There . . . are you feeling better?"

Phoebe's brow furrowed. She could feel a dull throbbing on her right side, but the terrible pain was gone. She did not respond to the question, but the nurse seemed to sense the answer, because she said, "I thought so." Then the nurse pulled her chair closer and touched Phoebe's left hand through the sheet. "My name is Lola. What is yours?"

Phoebe just stared at the woman.

"That was quite a fright you gave everyone. Do you remember what happened?" When Phoebe merely squinted her eyes slightly, Lola continued, "You were struck by a cable car on California Street. Didn't you see it coming? The operator said you ran right into it."

This time Phoebe turned away and closed her eyes.

"You must have been confused." The nurse patted Phoebe's hand. "Surely you didn't mean to do something like that—not a sweet young woman like you. Not when you have so much to live for." When Phoebe gave no sign of responding, Lola placed her hand on Phoebe's belly and said in a soft, calm voice, "Your baby is fine."

Phoebe turned now to the woman, her eyes opening wide, her lips quivering. Still she did not speak.

"The doctor says that the fetus is doing fine." The nurse cocked her head, then asked in an exceedingly gentle voice, "Is that why you did it?"

Phoebe looked away and began to cry softly.

"There, now," Lola soothed, again patting Phoebe's hand. "Things can't be so bad that you'd want to end it all. You're not wearing a wedding ring, but I can tell you're a respectable woman, aren't you? Not like some of the young women who get themselves in trouble. And it always seems to be the respectable ones who do something like this. The others . . . find more practical solutions."

The nurse stopped speaking but continued to hold Phoebe's hand through the sheet as she hummed a gentle melody. Slowly Phoebe stopped crying. When she turned back and opened her eyes, Lola said, "You must have a family that misses you. You didn't have any identification—we don't even know your name.''

Almost without moving her lips, the young woman whispered, ''Phoebe.''

''Oh, what a lovely name. And what is your last name?''

Clamping her eyes shut, Phoebe stammered, ''S-Salomon.''

''Salomon,'' Lola repeated thoughtfully. ''That sounds familiar. You don't happen to live on Nob Hill, do you?'' When Phoebe nodded, the nurse's eyebrows arched. ''Oh, dear.''

''D-Don't tell them,'' Phoebe blurted, her eyes widening with fear.

''But we must. You will need special care. They simply have to be told.''

''Please don't,'' Phoebe begged. ''I . . . I won't d-do anything like this again. I p-promise.''

''But Phoebe dear, they'll find out anyway—when they see your arm.''

''My . . . m-my arm?'' she asked in growing distress.

''Yes, your arm,'' Lola said plainly. ''Surely you remember . . .'' Her words died off as she saw the confusion in the young woman's eyes. ''Don't you remember? When they brought you in here, you were conscious. The doctor got your permission.''

Phoebe's eyes were wide with fear as she shook her head and said, ''What are you talking about? What's going on?''

''Oh, dear, I'm so sorry.'' The nurse rose and came slowly around the foot of the bed to Phoebe's other side. She placed a calming hand on Phoebe's right upper arm. ''It was terribly mangled; they had to operate. The doctor thinks he saved your arm, but the nerves were so badly damaged, you may never be able to use it again.''

With a gasp, Phoebe looked down at where the woman was touching her arm. She noticed then that the wide leather strap over her chest held her left arm in place but was not covering her right, which was completely wrapped in bandages. She tried to lift the injured arm but was unable to move it even the slightest amount.

''I'm afraid it's paralyzed,'' the woman was saying, but

Phoebe barely heard the words as she struggled to flex her fingers and discovered she could not even feel her hand.

"No!" she shrieked, shaking her head left and right. *"No! No! No!"* She did not hear the nurse race from the room and call for the doctor. And this time she did not even feel the needle breaking her skin, the medication being pumped into her arm. All she was aware of was a scream that filled her head long after her own voice had stilled . . . a scream that rose from within her and blotted out the light.

"Phoebe? Phoebe, dear," a voice called to her through the fog. She tried to open her eyes, but they were so very heavy. And her head was filled with a rushing sound, something like the scream but more like a river filled not with water but with a thousand crying voices. Were they calling her? Did they want her to swim to the other side?

A more incessant cry pierced her consciousness. "Phoebe! Wake up, Phoebe! It's me!"

Phoebe felt her eyelids opening and found herself amid a dusky, swirling fog, with a faint flicker of sunlight somewhere to her right. A face hovered overhead, and for a moment she thought it was God. But could God be a woman? And then a memory of those features surfaced, and her lips formed a name that her voice was unable to say: Nina.

"Phoebe," her mother called again, shaking her. "Wake up, now. We've come to visit you."

The fog began to disperse, and Phoebe realized that she was in the same hospital room, though this time it was night, the flickering sun a kerosene lantern on a nearby table. She looked around but saw only her mother in the room. Her lips tried to form her father's name, but still her voice would not come.

"Charles is with the doctor," Nina explained. "It seems you'll have to spend a few more days here to make sure there's no infection." She sighed, taking a seat on the left side of the bed. "Dear Phoebe, what have you done to yourself?"

Phoebe turned away, unable to face her mother's eyes.

Nina sniffled, then lifted a handkerchief and dabbed at her

eyes. "Do you hate me so much that you would do such a thing?" she asked. "Were you not in your right mind? That's what people will think, I'm afraid."

Phoebe turned back to her mother and opened her mouth, struggling to speak.

"Don't try to talk," Nina said, touching Phoebe's good arm. "The doctor said you should rest."

"I . . . I'm s-sorry," Phoebe managed to whisper.

Nina forced a smile, then waved her hand in the air. "You were always such a foolish child. I never could understand you. And now this. . . ." She choked back a tear. "Couldn't you trust me? Couldn't you give me a chance to help you? What will people say? If they ever learn the truth, they'll think you insane."

"I'm sorry," Phoebe repeated, her voice weak but steadier.

Leaning closer, Nina's eyes brightened as she proclaimed, "You must tell everyone it was an accident. No matter what people say, you must insist it was an accident. Perhaps I can arrange for you to go away for a time—to recuperate. And then in a few months you can come back, and no one need ever know about . . . about that other thing." She glanced down toward Phoebe's belly. "Of course if your arm does not improve, marriage will be out of the question, but you can live with us, and no one need know about anything but the . . . accident."

Phoebe's eyes filled with tears, and she turned away.

"It will be all right," Nina insisted. "You'll see."

Phoebe hardly heard what she was saying. Instead she listened to the din that rose again within her head. She began to take comfort in it, as though it were a river that would carry her away to somewhere safe and alone.

Across the room, the door opened, and Charles Salomon entered. "How is she?" he asked, crossing to the other side of the bed. When he passed in front of Phoebe, she recognized him and looked up, her eyes betraying a smile.

"How do you think she is?" Nina said somewhat irritably. "Just look at her." She turned away and stared toward the dark windows.

"Phoebe? Can you hear me?" Charles asked, leaning his cane against the bed and sitting down on his daughter's right side, near her injured arm.

Phoebe nodded slightly but did not speak.

Smiling, Charles touched her cheek. "We love you," he whispered. "It doesn't matter what happened. We love you, and we want you to come home—just as soon as the doctor says you are ready." He saw tears begin to flow down Phoebe's cheeks. "Don't be upset," he implored her. "Nothing matters but that you get better and come home to us. We love you, and we'll love your child."

Nina gave a startled gasp and shot her husband a bitter look. She was about to speak, but she saw the expression in his eyes as he glared over at her, and she held her tongue.

"We want you to rest and get better," Charles continued, tenderly stroking his daughter's cheek. "Everything will be all right. I promise you. Just rest and get better."

Phoebe smiled as she closed her eyes. She felt her father's warm hand against her cheek and listened to the rushing music that filled her head. Slowly she fell asleep.

Half an hour later, Nina climbed into the family's black phaeton and waited while her husband pulled himself aboard and sat beside her. She could feel her chest heaving and knew that she wanted to lash out at someone—anyone—for the cruel fate that had struck herself and her child.

Charles signaled the coachman to take them home, and the big open-topped phaeton pulled away from the curb. For a few minutes they rode in silence, Nina huddled under a blanket, Charles gazing silently at the passing city lights. Finally he turned to her and said, "The doctor was fairly optimistic, despite the fact that she'll probably never have much use of her hand. He said that there were several deep gashes along her arm but that they should heal quickly, barring infection. And he doesn't expect any complications with the baby."

Nina tried to contain her growing anger. Keeping her voice level, she replied testily, "Maybe we should go out and celebrate." She turned away and stared out of the carriage.

Charles looked at her in anguish. He was about to speak

again, but he seemed to decide that he would do well to let Nina work through her mood in silence, and so he leaned back in the seat and looked straight ahead.

A few minutes later the phaeton pulled up in front of their Nob Hill mansion. Charles stepped down first and held out his hand, but Nina made a point of disregarding it as she climbed down and pushed past him to the house. Cameron already had the front door open, and Nina breezed inside, flinging off her wrap and dropping it at his feet. Charles was left to follow at his slower pace. By the time he made it inside, Nina had already reached the landing on her way upstairs to her room.

Charles handed Cameron his coat and hat, then started up the stairs. It took a couple of minutes to make it to the second floor, by which time he was panting with the exertion. He paused a moment, leaning on his cane and catching his breath, then headed down the hall to Nina's room. Finding the door closed, he knocked, and when there was no response, he turned the knob and entered.

"Phoebe needs us now," he said directly, walking over to the dressing table where Nina was sitting. "I don't want us to fight."

Suddenly the rage and guilt and fear welled up within Nina, and she blared, "You had to say that, didn't you!"

"What are you talking about?" he asked.

"You know exactly what I'm referring to—that bit about us loving her child. You know she can't keep that baby."

"Is that what's upsetting you?"

"What do you expect?" She glowered up at him in the mirror over the table.

"I should think you'd be worrying about her arm. She almost died, you know."

"She almost killed herself!" Nina bellowed in reply. Clenching her fists, she gave a dramatic sigh. "Maybe it would have been for the best."

"Don't ever say that!" Charles shouted, gripping her shoulder.

"Don't you see?" she said, her eyes betraying her agony as she turned to look up at him. "It's happening all over again. Our marriage began with a curse, and now the Devil's come to collect his due!''

''This isn't your fault.''

Nina laughed bitterly. ''Like mother, like daughter.''

Charles eased his grip on her shoulder, his voice growing softer as he told her, ''That wasn't your fault, either. It was just as much mine.''

''But when I became pregnant, we got married. There's no such marriage in store for Phoebe.''

''Perhaps when the father finds out . . .''

''The father? You don't even know, do you?''

''Don't know what?''

''It's Eaton Hallinger! And no child of mine will marry a Hallinger!'' She abruptly stood and strode across the room, coming to a halt at the foot of the bed with her back to her husband.

''But if he's the father . . .''

She spun around and glared at him. ''That makes no difference! And anyway, it no longer matters. Even if I'd allow such a marriage, he wouldn't have her. Not any longer. Not crippled like that.'' She turned away again.

Leaving his cane propped against the chair, Charles came up behind Nina and placed his hands on her shoulders. ''You don't know if that's true,'' he said. ''Maybe if I speak with him and explain what has happened—''

''I suppose you think yourself an expert on how a man reacts when he discovers he's gotten a woman pregnant,'' she taunted over her shoulder. ''Well, you only know what you did, not what a real man would do.''

''You're not being fair,'' Charles said defensively.

''I'm not, am I? You didn't really want to marry me. You only did it because, if you hadn't, Father would have destroyed your career—your future. Remember how frightened you were to tell him I was pregnant?''

''We both were frightened. He was my boss—and you were only seventeen.''

''You never could stand up to him. When he insisted you change your name to Salomon so that the family name would live on, you went right along with him without even the slightest objection.''

''I did that for you,'' Charles protested. ''I thought you wanted me to.''

''You never even asked me.''

''Nina, you're being unreasonable,'' Charles argued, turning her shoulders to face him. ''You're just upset about Phoebe. But don't blame me—and don't blame yourself. This has nothing to do with what happened almost thirty years ago.''

''It has everything to do with it! Our marriage was not born out of love but out of lust—and I've been paying the price ever since!''

''That may be true for you, but I have always loved you. Everything I did back then—marrying you, changing my name—I did out of love.''

''You did it out of guilt . . . for what you did to me!''

''What *I* did?'' he gasped, his voice rising with indignation. ''I seem to remember that *you* were the one who came to *me*. I wanted us to get married first, but you said you couldn't wait any longer. You had to have it right then and there!''

Nina's mouth dropped open, and she pulled away and stared at him in shock, tears welling up in her eyes.

''I . . . I'm sorry,'' Charles apologized, taking a step toward her. ''I didn't mean to say that. I love you.'' He slipped his arms around her shoulders and pulled her to him. ''I have always loved you,'' he whispered into her ear.

Nina leaned her head back, her eyes closing as he began to kiss and caress her neck. Then abruptly she snapped her head forward and pushed him away. ''How can you do that?'' she exclaimed. ''Is that the only thing on your mind . . . and at a time like this?''

''I was only trying to kiss you.'' Charles backed away and stood looking at her, his shoulders slumped, his face crestfallen. Then he shook his head sadly and muttered, ''You didn't used to be so cold—or so cruel.''

''I don't mean to be cruel,'' she insisted, her tone softening. ''But your heart attack . . . The doctor said—''

"You put me out of your bed long before my heart attack. And you've kept me out even after I felt strong enough again."

"It . . . It's just that I . . ." Nina turned away, holding her hands to her mouth.

"I need you, Nina," Charles breathed tenderly, moving up behind her. "Without you I am nothing."

"Oh, Charles, I want you, too!"

Nina spun around and fell into her husband's arms, pulling him close and pressing against him with an urgency that had lain dormant for years. At first Charles did not know how to react, but then he felt her hands reaching for his waistband, unbuttoning his trousers, and he grasped her hair, arched her head back, and kissed her with a passion that for him had never died.

"Yes . . . yes," she panted as he unfastened the top of her dress, his lips searching her neck and shoulders. "I want you. . . ."

Nina leaned back in her husband's arms as he lifted her onto the bed. "Yes," she moaned over and over as he climbed up beside her, his hands deftly undoing her dress and dropping it from her shoulders. She helped him slip the dress off her, and then she reached over and started to remove his trousers. They were still half dressed, but she could not wait any longer, and she pulled him on top of her, lifting up her petticoat as she whispered, "I want you . . . now." She felt his hand groping, yanking aside her panties, and then he was entering her. "Yes," she cried as she gripped his hips and met his thrust.

Charles groaned as he thrust again and again, but then he pulled back slightly, hesitating as he held himself over her. "No," she urged. "Don't stop!" She raised her hips, pulling him down against her, and then she moaned with pleasure as he began to thrust again. Almost immediately his body shuddered, as if he were reaching his climax. But something was horribly wrong. He let out a sharp cry, his body jerking wildly as he fell away from her and lay on his side, clutching his chest and gasping for air.

In terror, Nina slid off the bed and stared down at her

husband. His face was turning purple as he choked and gasped, trying in vain to draw in some air. His eyes seemed to bulge as he stared up at her, and then they rolled back, until all that she could see were the whites.

"Charles!" she cried, reaching toward him, then pulling back her hand as his body suddenly was racked with spasms. She stood there for a moment, immobilized with shock. Then she turned and ran from the room, shrieking hysterically as she raced down the hall in her petticoats and slip.

SEVEN

"MAURICE!" A MAN SHOUTED ABOVE THE DIN OF VOICES
and the sprightly tinkling of piano keys. "Over here!"

Maurice Salomon elbowed his way through the press of
evening revelers that had crowded into the main room of
the Club Parisienne and headed toward a small table at the
back, where a tall, blond-haired man was seated between a
pair of young, attractive women.

"Damien!" Maurice called with a smile, waving as he
approached.

"And don't we look dapper!" Damien gushed, standing
a bit unsteadily as Maurice came up to the table. His faint
French accent betrayed his New Orleans Creole heritage.
"Maurice Salomon, I want you to meet two lovely ladies—
Agnes and Lorraine." He immediately plopped back into
his chair, as if mildly inebriated.

Maurice bowed from the waist, and as he smiled, his
dimples and youthful features made him appear younger than
his twenty-one years. Like Damien, he was slender and well
turned out in a smart black cutaway suit, to which he had
added a narrow white scarf to give himself a touch of the

Bohemian. He sat down across from Damien and looked back and forth at the two women, both appealingly full-figured brunettes wearing the modern, lowered necklines that added a hint of mystery as to their character. They looked him over, as well, and seemed taken by his appearance, with the slightly more robust woman appearing particularly pleased.

"I think Lorraine is in love," Damien proclaimed with a gay laugh. "It's either your dimples or your red hair." He raised his glass and tipped it toward his friend. "Here's to your roguish red hair!" He quickly downed the contents and waved at a passing waiter. "Champagne all around!" he called, and the man nodded and disappeared into the crowd.

The woman named Lorraine was blushing slightly. Her friend Agnes turned to Maurice and said, "Mr. Picard has been telling us all about you. Is it true that you own a great emporium in San Francisco?"

"Well, actually my father—"

"Turned it over to him on his twenty-first birthday," Damien cut in, raising one eyebrow slightly at his friend. "Tell them why you're in New York, Maurice."

"My sister is on a buying trip to England, and I've come to escort her back to San Francisco."

"And his brother is off buying up half of Japan and China," Damien elaborated. "He's got his whole family traveling all over the world just to keep Salomon's Emporium stocked with the latest fashions." Leaning toward Lorraine, he asked, "Have you heard of Salomon's Emporium?"

"I'm not sure," she said softly.

"Well, certainly you've heard of Nob Hill."

"Isn't that where the Stanfords and Huntingtons have those huge homes?" Agnes asked, her eyes widening.

"And the Salomons," Damien pronounced. "Right up there with the great railroad and mining kings."

"Well, it's really just—" Maurice started to say, but Damien cut him off with a laugh.

"Now, don't pretend it's just an ordinary little home." Damien shifted on his seat toward Lorraine. "Maurice and

I met only last week when he arrived in New York, but already I know him like a brother. And believe me, he is the modest type. If the truth be told, that boy lives in a mansion. I haven't seen it yet—and I certainly expect to be invited one day—but I hear tell it's got three floors, thirty-six rooms, and a whole coterie of servants." He leaned back in his chair and smiled. "Yes, Maurice Salomon has done well for himself in this world."

Just then the waiter appeared with an open bottle of champagne and four full glasses, which he served around the table. Damien quickly pulled out his wallet, removed a twenty-dollar bill, and placed it on the tray.

"You may keep the excess," Damien declared magnanimously, accepting the waiter's profuse thanks. "But one favor, please," he added as the man was about to leave. "When the tinkler finishes that tune, see if he knows anything more lively—the 'Mississippi Bayou Rag,' perhaps?"

"Of course, sir," the waiter said, hurrying over to the piano player to pass along the patron's request. Within a matter of moments, the black pianist—or tinkler, as men of his profession were popularly called—launched into a jaunty version of the latest hit of the supposedly sinful new ragtime music, which was just becoming the rage at more risqué clubs like the Parisienne.

"Another champagne, ladies!" Damien exclaimed with enthusiasm, his clear blue eyes sparkling as he tipped the bottle and refilled their glasses.

Agnes picked up her drink and almost downed it in a single gulp, then burst into giggles. Across from her, Lorraine raised her own glass and took a delicate sip, all the while her large brown eyes fastened on Maurice, her cheeks blushing more brightly than rouge.

"Well, ladies, I'd say it's time for a change of scenery. Don't you agree, Maurice?" Damien gave his friend a sly wink. "That is, if Maurice is able to join us." Addressing each lady in turn, he explained, "Maurice has been down at the waterfront seeing about the arrival of his sister's ship." He turned back to his friend. "What did you find out? Will she be docking tonight?"

"No," Maurice replied. "The ship is still out in the harbor and won't be berthing until morning. Apparently the customs search is more rigorous than usual."

"Anarchists!" Damien proclaimed, standing and shaking his fist. "Another shipload of anarchists, no doubt! But don't worry, they'll all be unmasked and sent packing back to wherever they crawled out!" He picked up his glass, tucked the bottle of champagne under his left arm, and held out his right arm for Agnes, who stood and slipped her hand through his. "Come along—and bring your glasses," he urged the others.

Maurice glanced over at Lorraine, who gave him a shy smile. Shrugging his shoulders, Maurice stood and picked up his glass. He held out his arm, and soon Lorraine was at his side, champagne glass in hand as they followed Damien and Agnes through the crowded room. When they drew alongside the long mahogany bar, Damien tossed another twenty-dollar bill onto the bar and called, "For the glasses." The bartender nodded and waved them on.

On the street, the two couples fell in step with the throng of people along Broadway. As they walked, Damien continued to pour champagne and occasionally broke into verses of "The Sidewalks of New York," all the while raising his glass and toasting his companions, pedestrians, light posts, even the occasional passing horseless carriage.

The couples had passed St. Paul's Church and were just approaching City Hall Park when Damien came to an abrupt halt, raised his glass to the imposing five-story edifice across the street, and proclaimed almost religiously, "The Astor House!" He downed the contents of his glass and turned to the women. "Have you women ever seen the rooms in the Astor?" When each shook her head, he continued, "Maurice has a suite on the top floor that would more appropriately be called a king's apartment. Everything velvet and silk, with brass that gleams like gold!"

"It sounds divine," Lorraine said, gripping Maurice's arm a little tighter.

Damien turned to Maurice and gave him a half wink, then nodded his head slightly as if urging him to speak. At last taking the hint, Maurice mumbled, ''Would, uh, you ladies like me to show you—?''

''Oh, Mr. Salomon, would you?'' Lorraine asked eagerly.

''You must call me Maurice,'' he insisted.

''Maurice . . .'' she repeated, looking down shyly.

''Then it's decided?'' Damien asked. Without awaiting an answer, he hurried them across the street and through the four massive Doric columns that held up the Greek-style portico. Nodding politely as the doorman opened the big front door, Damien led them into the lobby. There the women came to an abrupt halt, their eyes widening in wonder at the immense, glittering room, ablaze with kerosene lanterns and lush with exotic plants that hung from ornate iron trellises over the most elegant, plush furniture they had ever seen.

Damien slipped Agnes's hand from his arm and placed it on his friend's other arm. ''If you'll see to the women, I'll have room service send up another bottle or two.'' With a nod, he headed to the service desk.

''This way, ladies,'' Maurice announced, leading the women across the lobby to a pair of gleaming brass elevators. A moment later they were joined by Damien, and the foursome entered one of the elevators and were whisked by the operator to the fifth floor.

Maurice led the way down the carpeted hall and unlocked the door to his suite. He lit the wall lantern in the small front entryway, while Damien removed the women's wraps and hung them in an adjoining closet. Then the gentlemen led their guests into the large parlor.

As Maurice lit several more lamps, the women stood marveling at the opulently furnished room, the likes of which they had only seen in the detailed sketches of *Godey's Lady's Book*. There were two long couches and a pair of matching settees upholstered with rich green velvet. Half a dozen armchairs had a floral motif that picked up the green of the couches, and the champagne-brown carpet and floor-length curtains, edged with gold, provided a pleasant contrast. The fringed lampshades matched the gold curtain tassles, and the sideboards and end tables were of the richest mahogany, polished to a mirrored luster. At the far end of the room, a closed door led to the bedroom.

"Sit down . . . be comfortable," Damien said, leading Agnes to one of the sofas. Lorraine blushed slightly as she followed Maurice to the other couch. They had barely settled in place when someone rapped on the door.

Maurice quickly rose and headed to the entryway, returning a moment later with a tray bearing four fresh glasses and an open bottle in a silver bucket. This time he did the honors, placing the tray on the small tea table between the couches and serving each of them a fresh glass of champagne.

"To the first day of June, eighteen hundred and ninety six!" Damien proclaimed, raising his glass.

As the group drank and then began to toast each other's health, Damien regaled them with stories both humorous and provocative of New Orleans and its naughty ways. Though he was only twenty-five, it was obvious that he had lived those years to the fullest—raised, he claimed, in one of the most respectable bordellos in the French Quarter. Agnes was particularly impressed with the story of how Damien, at the age of fifteen, was challenged to a duel by his mother's lover after Damien had walked in on them flagrante delicto and with his fists had taken objection to the particular position in which the man had placed his mother.

The women might have protested Damien's increasingly bold discourse had it not been for their copious consumption of champagne. It so loosened Agnes's tongue—and inhibitions—that she recounted a story of her own about how her father once came home so in his cups that he mistook fourteen-year-old Agnes for her mother, who had to drag him from Agnes's bed over his profane insistence that he was able to recognize his own wife's derriere when he saw it. Finishing her tale, Agnes burst into a titter of laughter and then gave a burp. "Oh, dear," she said, throwing her hand to her mouth and then breaking into renewed giggles.

Damien must have decided that she had consumed the right amount of spirits, because just then he stood, held

111

out his arm, and suggested, "Perhaps you would like to see the rest of the suite?"

"Why, thank you," Agnes responded, grasping his arm and pulling herself up on shaky legs.

"If you'll excuse us," Damien said, nodding politely at Lorraine and then shooting Maurice a knowing smile. With that he turned, picked up one of the kerosene lamps, and led Agnes off to the bedroom, closing the door behind them.

Maurice could hear giggling and the rustling of either clothes or bedding from behind the closed door. He turned and smiled sheepishly at Lorraine, who averted her eyes slightly. "Would you like some more?" he inquired, indicating her glass.

"I . . . I think not," she replied.

Lorraine leaned forward to place her glass on the table at the same instant that Maurice reached over to take it from her, and his hand brushed against her chest. "Excuse me," he said, pulling back his hand, his eyes fastened on her heaving, ample bosom. "You are very pretty," he whispered, cautiously reaching back and touching the lace at her neckline, just above the swell of her breasts.

"Why, thank you." She looked into his light-brown eyes, then glanced down at his hand, which was gently caressing the lace. She drew in a deep breath, and her breasts swelled, pressing against the palm of his hand. She looked into his eyes again, then said, "I . . . I don't think I should—"

"Of course not. I—I'm sorry," he stammered, quickly pulling back his hand, his gaze still locked on hers.

Suddenly and without warning, Lorraine grabbed Maurice's hand and jammed it between her heaving breasts. She leaped at him, throwing her arms around his neck as her mouth hungrily sought and devoured his. Maurice was thrown backward onto the couch underneath her, and then she rolled sideways and pulled him to the floor on top of her.

"Oh, Mr. Salomon!" she moaned, thrusting her tongue into his mouth, her hands ripping open his shirt studs as she rolled him onto his back and, hiking up her skirt, climbed on top, straddling and gripping him with her thighs.

SAN FRANCISCO

* * *

Rachel Salomon was more than relieved when the *Vigilant* finally pulled into its berth at the Port of New York. The inspection of the ship had been long and exhaustive, and every passenger and crew member had been interrogated privately. When no sign of Aidan McAuliffe had turned up, the ship was finally allowed to head into the port, docking early on the afternoon of the second of June, almost twenty-four hours after pulling into New York Harbor.

"Rachel!" a voice shouted as she started down the gangplank. She looked out among the gathered crowd of well-wishers and saw a young man pushing toward the front.

"Maurice!" she called in reply, waving at her brother. As she continued down the gangplank, she noticed that someone was at Maurice's side—a slightly taller man with blond hair.

"It's so good to see you!" Maurice exclaimed, rushing over to his sister and throwing his arms around her.

"It's wonderful to be home!" she said, embracing him. "Well, halfway home," she added, pushing him away slightly and looking him over. "At least the rest of the way will be on dry land, with a friendly face at my side."

"Rachel, I want you to meet a friend of mine." He turned toward the young gentleman at his side. "Damien Picard, this is my sister Rachel."

"A pleasure to meet you," Damien greeted her warmly, lifting her hand and kissing it lightly.

"You aren't from San Francisco, are you?" she asked.

"New Orleans. Maurice and I met last week in New York." Seeing her questioning expression, he explained, "I am in the city on business—well, more pleasure than business, I must admit. My mother runs a small restaurant that caters to an exclusive clientele. She sent me north to find out what is fashionable in the restaurants of New York. You can say I'm eating my way through the city." He gave a pleasant smile, adding, "Your brother has been kind enough to share my burden."

Maurice grinned. "He's right. I must have put on ten pounds this past week."

113

For a moment Rachel found herself locked in the intense gaze of Damien's cool blue eyes. Then she turned back to her brother and said, "If you've gained any weight, it sits well on you. That suit looks divine." She fingered the lapel of his brown suit.

"Not half as lovely as you," Maurice declared, taking her hand and holding her away so that he could admire her rose, lace-trimmed dress, which was gathered at the waist to complement her figure. "Isn't my sister beautiful?" he asked Damien.

"Even more than you said," he replied.

Maurice took hold of Rachel's arm. "Let's get away from this crowd. We've a carriage waiting, and I've already arranged to have your baggage delivered to the Astor House."

The two men escorted Rachel to a nearby landau, where they directed the driver to take them along the East River and then through Central Park before heading back downtown to the hotel. As they rode, Rachel described her journey, and though she mentioned stopping in Halifax, she said nothing about having met and helped Aidan McAuliffe.

Damien Picard was unusually quiet during the ride. He had known many beautiful women, but few as stunning as Rachel Salomon. As he gazed upon her fiery copper hair and animated green eyes, he could not help but wonder if she shared some of the passionate spirit at times exhibited by her younger brother. But while Maurice was no stranger to the pursuit of pleasure, willingly participating in some of Damien's more perverse pastimes, there was an air of nervous caution about him that annoyed Damien. Rachel, on the other hand, seemed far more certain of herself. And while she appeared to be the very embodiment of the perfect lady, Damien grew increasingly convinced that her capacity for passion, once properly tapped, would far exceed that of most women he had possessed.

As the carriage headed through Central Park and Maurice pointed out the sights of the city, Damien leaned back against his seat and smiled. He knew that Rachel was scheduled to spend several days in New York, and he was determined to use that time to discover just how hot her spirit ran.

When at last the carriage arrived at the Astor House, Maurice suggested that they take an early dinner in the hotel restaurant. He left Damien to escort Rachel to a table, while he went to the front desk to see if any messages had arrived for him or his sister.

As soon as Damien and Rachel were seated at a table near the window, Damien ordered a bottle of fine French wine, then turned to Rachel and said, "I don't mean to sound bold, but Maurice has spoken of you so much this past week that I feel as if we are already friends."

Rachel grinned. "Maurice has many friends—he makes them easily. But I am afraid only a small percentage end up friends of mine, as well."

"You don't approve of them?" Damien asked cautiously.

"Oh, they are fine—for Maurice. A young man should have friends to go out drinking and gambling with. However, I prefer gentlemen with more refined interests than those usually exhibited by Maurice's friends."

"Such as the opera? Mozart's *Don Giovanni* is a particular favorite of mine."

"Then you enjoy the opera?" Rachel asked, a bit surprised.

Damien laughed. "Only *Don Giovanni*. I'm afraid I sleep through everything else." He leaned closer, and in a soft, alluring voice he recited with dramatic feeling:

> *"Chi l'anima mi lacera—*
> *Chi m'agita le viscere!*
> *Che strazio ohimè! Che smania!*
> *Che inferno! Che terror!"*

Sitting back in his chair, Damien smiled and said, "*Don Giovanni*, act two, the final scene."

"How lovely," Rachel commented sincerely. "What does it mean?"

His grin broadened as he translated:

"My heart bursts in my bosom—
The serpents gnaw my vitals!
What tortures! Oh, what madness!
What horror! What despair!''

"And I thought it was something romantic."

"But it is," he insisted. "Romantic . . . and tragic."

Rachel looked at him closely. "You certainly know your *Don Giovanni.*"

"Some say that Mozart's tragic Don Juan is a role I was put on earth to play."

"Then I'm afraid you're a lot like the majority of Maurice's friends."

"Ah, but there is a difference."

"And what is that, Mr. Picard?" she asked, looking into his unwavering blue eyes.

"The only thing those other men care about is the pleasure they expect to receive from a woman. My delight is the pleasure I give."

Rachel stared at him in silence for a long moment, then said, "You are very sure of yourself, Mr. Picard."

"My name is Damien."

"I know that, Mr. Picard."

Damien's smile grew more pensive. "I hope in time you will consider me a friend, Miss Salomon."

"I should think you would first hope I considered you at all," she said flatly, picking up her menu.

Damien had to force himself not to frown. He picked up his own menu and pretended to be reading it as he reviewed the approach he had used and debated what new tack to try. His thoughts were interrupted by Maurice, who pulled out his chair and slumped into it. When Damien and Rachel looked up at him, his face was ashen white.

"What is it?" Rachel quickly asked, putting down her menu and placing a hand on her brother's arm.

"A telegram," he said, raising his hand to reveal a crumpled piece of paper. "From Nina."

"What does she say?" Rachel's voice betrayed her growing concern.

116

"It's Father," he said hollowly. "He has had another heart attack."

"Oh, my God!" Rachel gasped, letting go of Maurice's arm and clasping her hands together.

Maurice seemed to snap out of his own shock, and he leaned across the table and took his sister's hands in his own. "He's still alive," he reassured her. "But Nina says that he's gravely ill. We are to catch the first train home. I checked at the desk, and the next one leaves at nine in the morning."

Rachel looked up at Maurice, then glanced over at Damien. "I . . . I want to go to my room now," she told her brother. "I want to be alone for a while."

"I understand. Your suite is just down the hall from mine. I'll take you up there, then have a dinner tray sent up." He turned to Damien. "I'll be back in a moment."

"Shall I order you something?" Damien asked, trying to sound properly concerned.

"Yes . . . why not. I'll only be a few minutes." He stood and helped his sister from her chair.

"Rachel . . . uh, Miss Salomon," Damien called as she started from the room. When she turned toward him, he gave her a sympathetic smile and said, "I'm sorry . . . about your father."

Without responding, she turned and walked from the room.

Along the waterfront near the pier where the *Vigilant* had recently docked, the front door of the Gold Anchor flew open, and a hulking, surly-looking man in a blue pea jacket staggered into the room. He glanced around disapprovingly at the bare walls, rough-cut tables, and rows of unmarked bottles behind the slab of wood that passed for a bar. Even in an alcoholic haze, Bill Brannon knew that this dockside tavern was little more than a cheap dive that watered down its whiskey and poured any half-finished mugs of beer back into the keg. Just now he did not particularly care. He had but a few dollars in his pocket, and thanks to that prig of a captain, August Toomey, he did not know where his next dollar would come from.

Pushing aside a little man in a wool sailor's cap who was teetering just inside the door, Brannon saw a familiar face at the bar and weaved across the room. "Rubens!" he called, raising a hand.

"Well, Billy boy, come t'share a drink?" the fellow asked, moving to make room at the bar. "Best hurry, though. 'Tis almost time t'be back at the ship."

"Not f'me," Brannon muttered, leaning against the bar and signaling the bartender to pour him a beer.

"But Toomey ordered all hands back by nine."

Brannon glowered at him. "Well, tha' is all right f'you, Mr. Eric Kiss-the-Captain's-Ass Rubens."

"What's your bother?" the shorter man asked, jabbing Brannon's arm with his mug of beer.

Brannon gave a low snort, then picked up his mug of beer and nearly downed it in one gulp. Slapping the glass down on the bar, he turned to his mate. "Tha' cold-hearted bastard of a ship's captain gave me the heave."

"Put you off the *Vigilant*? But why?"

"Said I had three sheets to the wind. Said I ain't steady enough on me feet t'make it round the Horn."

"I've warned you about drinkin' on duty."

"Damn it! I always done me job."

"That may've been enough on a freighter, but we're haulin' respectable passengers now."

"Hell, they get just as pissed as I ever done—only they do it wi' bubbles instead o' brew."

"Maybe so, but they pay f'the pleasure o' drinkin' their way across the Atlantic on a sea o' fine champagne. You and me, Billy boy, get our mug o' rum a day and are expected t'make due till the next port."

"He's still a bastard," Brannon muttered, picking up his mug and draining the rest of its contents.

"So what'll y'do now?"

"Make him sorry he ever crossed the likes o' William Edward Brannon."

"Get off it, man. You know you aren't goin' to—"

"The hell I ain't."

"What can the likes o' you do to a man like Toomey?"

"I'll turn him in to the New York constables."

"What are you talkin' about?"

"For aidin' and abettin' a fugitive from justice, that's what."

"You're daft, man," Rubens said, turning away and draining his mug.

Brannon waved the bartender over and had the man refill their mugs. " 'Tis the truth," Brannon said in a quieter voice as soon as the bartender left. "I saw him wi' me own eyes—slipped over the side in Halifax and swam t'shore."

"You're crazy."

" 'Tis the God's truth. He hit the water as we were pullin' from shore. Jumped from beside the number one starboard quarter boat."

Rubens stared at his mate for a long moment, then seemed to decide he was telling the truth. "Why didn't you say as much when the police were questionin' us? Or to the captain when we were up in Halifax?"

"Up there I figured him for a poor bloke who couldn't afford a ticket, so I kept me mouth shut. And when the police come sniffin' about, I said why should I be the bastard t'put a noose 'round his neck? I got no love for the police—let 'em do their own work." Brannon slurped the foam off the beer, then leaned on the bar and glowered as he added, "And like a fool I thought I was keepin' the *Vigilant* from gettin' in trouble."

"And now you figure t'do your civic duty?" Rubens asked, looking at him askance.

"You're damn right." In several long gulps, Brannon drained the mug, set it down, and pushed it away from him.

"Ah, you're just talk," Rubens declared, waving off Brannon's threat as absurd.

"The hell I am!"

Rubens slipped his hand into the pocket of his jacket and produced a shiny gold coin—an American half eagle, worth five dollars. "I got this eagle says you are."

Brannon checked his pocket, decided he had enough to

cover the wager, and replied, "You're on!" Leaning across the bar, he called, "Barkeep—where's the police station?"

The bartender looked at him curiously, then shrugged his shoulders. "Go left three blocks. It's on the right."

"Thanks, mate." Brannon pushed himself away from the bar, then turned back to his friend. "Well, c'mon. Let's get this done with."

"Are you serious?"

"Just come along and watch."

Brannon pulled the mug out of his friend's hand, dropped it to the bar, and started for the door, dragging Rubens along by the coat collar. Together the two men weaved on unsteady legs into the cool, dark night. They debated a moment which direction was the left, then finally stumbled down the road toward the station house. With some effort, they found the appropriate single-story brick building and made their way inside.

"We've got your man f'you," Brannon called out as he approached the front desk, where a young policeman in a blue coat sat reading a newspaper. When the man glanced up disinterestedly, Brannon went on, "Some o' your mates came out to the *Vigilant* lookin' for a stowaway by the name of Aidan some such thing."

"The *Vigilant*?" the man asked, lowering the paper. "Wouldn't that be the harbor police?"

"The who?"

"If it's something to do with your ship, you want to see the harbor police. This is a city police station."

"We're talkin' about a murderer," Brannon said gravely. "Surely you'll be wantin' t'hear about that."

The man sat up straighter and squinted at the two men. "You fellows been hitting the sauce, haven't you?"

"Wha' d'you expect after weeks at sea? But tha' don't change wha' I seen in Halifax."

"Halifax?"

"Nova Scotia, man," Brannon said a bit testily. "Wha' I'm tryin' t'tell you."

"Well, come on, get out with it," the policeman said in resignation, picking up a pencil and some paper. "I might as well take your statement. I can see you boys aren't likely to make it over to the harbor police still on your feet." He glanced up at the sailors. "Names?"

"Ours?" Rubens asked a bit warily.

"Of course. For the report."

"My mate didn't see nothin'," Brannon put in, to which Rubens quickly nodded. "Just me, William Edward Brannon. That's *B-r-a-n-n-o-n*."

After jotting it down, the policeman asked, "So what did you see?"

"I seen a stowaway jump overboard and swim t'shore when we was leavin' Halifax."

"And you think he was a murderer?"

"Aidan McAuliffe, I think they called him," Eric Rubens interjected.

"Yeah, that's the bloke," Brannon agreed.

"Are you sure?"

"That's wha' Captain Toomey called him."

The policeman looked up at Brannon. "Your captain knew he was on board?"

"Sure as hell did," Brannon said with conviction. "I seen this Aidan fellow give Toomey some money just 'afore he jumped ship. Figured it was t'keep him quiet."

As the policeman wrote down the information, Rubens tugged anxiously at his friend's sleeve, but Brannon shot him a look, warning him to keep quiet.

"Have you told any of this to the harbor police?" the man finally asked.

"I'm 'fraid not," Brannon admitted, looking down at his feet and feigning a sheepish frown. "When they questioned us, I didn't want t'get old man Toomey in trouble. But then I got t'talkin' wi' me mate, here, and he made me realize wha' I had t'do. Ain't tha' right, mate?"

Rubens found both men staring at him, and with a nervous shrug of his shoulders, he said, "It didn't seem right that a murderer should walk free."

The policeman asked Brannon for a few more particulars, which the sailor embellished just enough to make Captain Toomey seem as much a villain as the stowaway murderer.

Brannon concluded by saying that he was thrown off the ship when the captain got wind that he might tell the police what he saw. Then the policeman sent the two men on their way, promising to send a copy of the report to the harbor police.

As soon as they were gone, an older policeman approached the desk from the back room. "What was that all about, Sergeant?" he asked the man at the front desk.

"A couple of drunk sailors claiming to have seen a murderer jump ship at Halifax."

"You'd better report it to the harbor police."

"I'll send them a copy of the report, Lieutenant," the younger man replied. "But I don't put much stock in it."

"Why not?"

"One of those sailors was kicked off the ship, and I think he just wants to get the captain in trouble."

"Include that in your report, Sergeant. It may be as you say, but the harbor police will probably want to inform the authorities in Halifax, just in case."

"Yes, sir." The sergeant picked up his pencil and continued filling out his report.

Outside, Bill Brannon grinned smugly at his friend. "That'll teach Toomey t'be messin' wi' the likes o' me."

"Damn you, man!" Rubens lashed into him as they headed back down the street. "What kind o' stunt were you pullin'? You know the captain had nothin' t'do with that stowaway."

Brannon chuckled. "Let him try t'prove it."

"You're daft, man," Rubens muttered. "They'll never believe a sea bum like you agin the word of a captain. And if they try t'blame old man Toomey, I'll just have to—"

Brannon came to a sudden halt, grabbed his mate by the coat lapels, and swung him against the side of the building they were passing. "You'll keep your mouth shut!" he shouted, shaking the smaller man. "And you'll give me tha' half eagle you promised."

Rubens pulled his coat free from Brannon's grasp. Looking up at the bigger man indignantly, he replied, "Our bet said nothin' about you lyin' about the captain. Man, you could get *me* thrown off the ship, as well.'' He paused a moment and reconsidered the wager. ''No, I'll be payin' no money to the likes o' you.''

Brannon's eyes narrowed, and he hissed menacingly, ''You will give me tha' eagle or answer t'this.'' Suddenly his hand darted out, and something hot tore across the smaller man's forearm.

Looking down, Rubens saw a jagged tear along his coat sleeve and felt a warm, moist trickle of blood running down his arm. Brannon just smiled at him, a small dagger clenched in his fist. Looking up quickly, Rubens gauged the coldness in the big man's eyes. His own eyes started to twitch slightly, and then he shrugged and slipped his hand into his pocket. '' 'Tis only a coin,'' he muttered, glancing nervously up and down the deserted street as he fished around in his coat pocket.

''That's a good boy,'' Brannon said, smiling and slipping the knife into his pocket. ''You don't want t'be called a welcher, now do you?'' Clapping his left hand on the smaller man's shoulder, he held out his right. ''Now give it here.''

With a half smile, Rubens withdrew his hand and jabbed it forward at Brannon's slightly protruding belly. ''You can have it, all right,'' he said, pulling back his hand and jabbing again.

Brannon felt a strange burning sensation across his midsection and for a moment thought only that Rubens had punched him in the belly. But this time when Rubens pulled back his hand, Brannon saw the knife blade. Suddenly his guts seemed to burst into flame, and he dropped to one knee, his hand desperately groping in his pocket. He managed to come up with his dagger, but Rubens had backed out of reach. With a groan, Brannon looked up at the smaller man in shock and surprise. He reached forward, the knife falling from his numbed fingers. His lips tried to fashion a curse, but then he fell forward on the pavement and lay still, the final breath slowly escaping his body.

''You shouldn't have cut me,'' Rubens said nervously, stepping closer. He looked up and down the street, then at the knife in his hand. Kneeling beside the body of the big man, he wiped the blade on Brannon's coat, then dropped the knife back into his pocket. With a grunt, he rolled Brannon onto his back, then quickly searched the pockets of his pea jacket and took the few coins Brannon had in his possession.

Standing, Rubens started to back away from the body, all the while looking around the deserted street. He began to turn away, but then he spun back around, reached into his own pocket, and withdrew the gold half eagle. Tossing it at the body lying on the street, he muttered, "You can't call Eric Rubens a welcher. Use it for a decent funeral." Then he turned and ran off into the night.

After dinner in the restaurant at the Astor House, Maurice left Damien at his suite and went down the hall to check on his sister. A few minutes later he returned to his suite, locking the door behind him. Several lamps were already lit, and as he walked into the sitting room, Damien Picard rose from the coach and approached.

"How is your sister?" he asked, holding out a glass of whiskey for his younger friend.

"She's resting," Maurice replied, taking the glass and downing it in a gulp.

"Take it easy," Damien urged as he slipped an arm around Maurice's back and led him over to the couch. "You've had an awful shock this evening, so just sit down and relax."

Maurice nodded and took a seat beside Damien.

"That's it," Damien said, patting his friend's knee.

"Another drink," Maurice mumbled, holding out the glass.

"I've got something better." He reached into his pocket and produced a small silver box. He pressed the catch on the front, and the lid popped open, revealing a dark, treacly substance not unlike molasses. When Maurice looked up at him curiously, Damien said, *"Chandoo."*

"Opium?" Maurice asked, translating the popular Chinese name for the drug.

"Yes. The finest prepared opium from Patna, India. Compared to Chinese opium, it is like champagne to *vin ordinaire*."

"I don't know. . . ." Maurice hesitated, his gaze locked on the dark paste.

"Your first time? What better way than with a friend?"

Damien stood and offered his hand. As Maurice rose from the couch, Damien took his forearm and led him to the bedroom. There the young man from New Orleans removed the glass chimney from the lamp beside the bed and lit the wick, adjusting it to a low blue flame. He placed the silver box beside the lamp, then produced from his inner coat pocket a long-stemmed pipe and an equally long silver dipper, pointed at one end and flattened at the other.

"Take off your coat and lie down here on your side," Damien directed his younger friend as he piled the pillows near the edge of the bed beside the nightstand.

As soon as Maurice was in position, lying on his side with his head held high on the pillows, Damien handed him the pipe, which had a round upright bowl near the end. Damien then took the pointed end of the dipper and twisted it around in the tarlike substance inside the silver box. Pulling it out, he continued to turn the dipper so that the drop of opium would not fall from the end. Deftly he held the tip of the dipper over the burning wick, turning the dipper as he slowly roasted the opium. When it was sufficiently dry and almost at the flash point, he grasped Maurice's hand, held the bowl of the pipe over the lamp flame, and thrust the roasted ball of opium into the opening at the center of the bowl, quickly removing the empty dipper.

"Inhale," Damien instructed his friend as he held the pipe over the flame.

As Maurice breathed in deeply, the oxygen ignited and vaporized the hot ball of opium. He had to force himself not to cough as the acrid smoke filled his lungs, and then he exhaled slowly and drew in a second deep breath.

"Hold it in," Damien said, pulling the pipe from Maurice's lips. Then leaning close to his friend, he whispered, "Breathe it into my mouth." Placing his mouth against

125

Maurice's, he parted his lips and inhaled the smoke. With a smile, he leaned away, exhaled the smoke, and handed the pipe back to Maurice.

As Maurice finished smoking the remainder of the pellet of opium, Damien roasted another drop over the lamp. He added it to the bowl, but pushed Maurice's hand away when the younger man tried to give him the pipe. "This is your first time," Damien said softly, watching Maurice's eyes half close as he drew in on the pipe. "I'll take my pleasure in other ways."

After Maurice inhaled several more puffs, Damien took the empty pipe from him and laid it on the stand. He slipped the chimney back over the lamp, lowered the flame slightly, and turned back to Maurice, who sat looking up at him through half-closed eyes, a faint smile on his lips.

"It's hot, isn't it?" Damien asked, reaching over and unbuttoning Maurice's shirt.

Maurice reached up, either to help or push Damien away, but then his hands fell loosely at his sides and he just stared up at his friend and smiled.

"Yes, it's so very hot," Damien continued as he undid the last of the buttons and opened the shirt. Kneeling beside the bed, he pulled Maurice's undershirt out of his pants, raising it up over his chest, his left hand sliding down along Maurice's belly and slipping under his waistband.

Maurice shuddered slightly as Damien's hand moved expertly along his groin, and then there was a stab of pain as Damien bit the flesh just under his left nipple. Moaning softly, he stared into the flickering lamp as Damien's hands and teeth and lips guided his body out across the ocean, up among the clouds, where pain and pleasure blended one with the other until there was only sensation—neither good nor bad, yet sublime.

Damien was wearing Maurice's dressing robe when he answered the knock at the front door of the suite. Swinging it open, he nodded at the elderly porter, who was carrying a tray of fruit and champagne.

"Your order, sir," the porter said.

"Yes. I'll take it." When the porter handed him the tray and turned to leave, Damien added, "Could you do me a small favor?"

"What would that be?" the man asked as Damien placed the tray on a table in the entryway.

Slipping his hand into the pocket of the robe, Damien took out a five-dollar bill and handed it to the porter. "Miss Rachel Salomon is just down the hall in Suite 512. Could you tell her that her brother would like to see her?"

The man shifted uncomfortably on his feet. "It is quite late, sir."

Damien handed him a second bill. "This is an emergency of sorts. He isn't at all well and needs to see her at once."

"If you are quite certain . . ." the porter replied hesitantly.

"I am. And thank you." Damien closed the door, taking care to leave it unlocked, then picked up the tray and headed back to the bedroom.

A few minutes later, there was another knock at the door, but this time Damien made no effort to answer. The knocking came again, but still no one answered. Finally the doorknob turned and the door swung open.

"Maurice?" a gentle voice called. When there was no response, Rachel called for her brother a second time and closed the door behind her. Cautiously she entered the sitting room, where a lone lamp was burning quite low beside one of the couches. She was dressed in a long blue nightgown, over which she wore a calf-length robe buttoned down the front and cinched at the waist.

"Maurice?" Rachel called yet again as she crossed the room. At the far end, a door was open slightly, and she could see a light burning in the room beyond.

"Maurice? What's wrong?" she asked as she approached and pushed open the door. "Are you feeling ill—?" The words died in her throat as she saw her younger brother. He lay on his back spread-eagle on the bed, his hands near the headboard posts, his feet near the footboard posts. And he was entirely naked.

As Rachel entered the room, she realized with a shock

that Maurice's hands and feet were tied to the posts with some kind of cord—perhaps from the draperies. He seemed only semiconscious, his eyes half closed, his head lolling from side to side. There was no gag around his mouth, yet he made no sound.

"Maurice! What happened!" she blurted as she approached the bed.

It was not until the bedroom door slammed shut behind her that Rachel realized that she and her brother were not alone. She spun around, focused on the figure standing in front of the door, and whispered, "Damien?"

The young man was smiling as he stepped more fully into the light, wearing nothing more than a dressing robe. "Your little brother is in an opium stupor. He'll be all right."

Rachel stared back and forth between the two men, her head shaking as she tried to comprehend what was going on.

"I wanted you the moment I saw you—even more than I wanted your brother." Damien started across the room toward her. "I would have preferred to take you slowly, but with you leaving so soon, it looks like there isn't the time."

"What the hell are you talking—?"

"Don't be coy," Damien cut her off. "You're no stranger to pleasure—I saw that in your eyes as soon as I met you."

"You filthy bastard," she hissed. She gave a final glance back at her brother, who looked up at her but did not appear to recognize her. Then she stalked toward the door. As she brushed past Damien, he reached out and grabbed her by the arm. "Let go of me," she said calmly but firmly, trying to pull her arm free.

Suddenly Damien's other hand lashed out, and he slapped her across the face. Her free hand shot up to her cheek, and she just stood there, looking at him in shock. Grabbing both of her arms, he pulled her toward him and tried to kiss her full on the mouth, but she struggled and twisted her face to the side. Roughly pushing her away from him, Damien glowered at her a moment, then reached out, took hold of her robe, and tore it down the front, popping the buttons off the material.

Rachel gasped as Damien threw her against the wall and ripped her nightgown from her shoulder, baring one of her breasts. And then finally she realized that he would not be stopped, and she screamed. But her scream was immediately stifled as he slapped her even harder and clapped a hand over her mouth. Jamming her against the wall, he dragged her down onto the floor. With his hand clamped tightly around her jaw, he tore away her nightgown and shoved some of the material into her mouth as a crude gag. She moaned, tried to scream, tried to kick him in the groin, but he held her pinned to the floor as he wrenched her arms up over her head and lashed her wrists together with the sash of her robe.

Rachel tried to scream her brother's name, but she choked on the gag and felt as if she would suffocate. Her struggling only served to arouse Damien all the more, and he cast off his own robe and began to press himself between her thighs. Closing her eyes, she forced herself to breathe through her nose as steadily as possible, fighting not to lose consciousness as he rammed himself into her and cursed with brutal delight.

A few feet away, Maurice heard the strange noises and shook his head to clear the fog. The lamp was glowing more brightly, and it seemed to burn his eyes. He looked away but was frightened by the shadows all around him—especially over on the floor, where strange demonlike forms were struggling in some sort of infernal battle. Again he shook his head, fought to clear his brain and remember where he was and what he had been doing. Slowly it came back to him—Damien, the champagne, the opium. He seemed to recall making love to someone, though the only image that came to mind was that of a naked man taking him like a woman. *But how could that be?* he asked himself.

And then he began to recognize the sounds in the room, and he tried to sit up, but his hands and feet were held fast in place. He twisted his head around, saw the cords around his wrists and ankles, then arched his head and looked across the room. Yes, it was Damien, and he was naked, just like in Maurice's dream. And someone else was lying naked under him—a woman.

Rachel!

He gasped and tried to call her name, but no sound would come. His tongue felt swollen and would not respond to his command. Again and again he tried to call her, but no sound emerged.

Maurice heard Damien give a shuddering groan, then heard Rachel sobbing softly. A few moments later Damien was standing over him, looking down at him and grinning wickedly.

"I was wrong about your sister," Damien said as he pulled on his shirt and began to button it. "She was no better than the rest of them—hardly worth the effort."

Maurice strained against the ropes but could not move. He tried to rise up and speak, but then his head fell back against the pillows.

"Don't be jealous," Damien whispered as he stepped into his pants. "You were far more delectable." He leaned close and kissed Maurice on the lips, thrusting his tongue into the younger man's mouth.

As Damien backed away, Maurice's lips quivered, his eyes squinting with rage. Suddenly he managed to blurt out, "B-bastard!" And then he spit, spraying Damien with saliva.

Damien instinctively raised his hand to strike Maurice, but instead he laughed hollowly and ran his sleeve across his face. "How dramatic," he muttered, standing away from the bed. He glanced to where Rachel was lying curled up on the floor in a near semiconscious state, her wrists lashed together. Then he looked back at Maurice. "If either of you reports this to the police, I will tell the world the real kind of man that Maurice Salomon is."

Picking up his shoes, Damien started to turn away from the bed, then looked back and winked at Maurice. In a mockingly suggestive voice, he whispered, *"Tutto a tue colpe è poco, vieni c'è un mal peggior!"*

With a wicked sneer, he turned and started across the room, pausing a moment to look down at Rachel, who lay sobbing on the floor. With a faint, almost bittersweet smile, he repeated in English what he had recited to Maurice—the final lamentation of the chorus at the close of *Don Giovanni*: "Horror more dire awaits thee, and dread is thy dark doom!"

Damien Picard tossed his head and gave an abrupt, sharp laugh, then turned and stalked out of the room.

EIGHT

CAYLEIGH CABOT LAY IN BED, LOOKING AT HER HUSBAND beside her, thinking about her first husband and the handsome newcomer who was asleep in the guest room down the hall. *You're such a good man*, she thought, her hand reaching to touch the light-brown hair that curled over the back of Scott's pajama collar. Instinctively she pulled her hand back, afraid that she might awaken him, desiring that he would turn, take her in his arms, and awaken that part of her that had not been aroused in so long.

Why do I always want more? she asked herself for what seemed like the thousandth time. *You've given me your home, your name, security, companionship. . . . Why can't I be satisfied with that?* But she knew that she hungered for more, and when she looked at Aidan McAuliffe or thought about her first husband, she felt that secret desire building within her, and she feared that she would drown.

It's right for a woman to want her man to make love to her, she told herself. *How long has it been? Three months? Four? There must be something wrong with me—some reason he finds me unattractive.*

132

Cayleigh turned away from Scott and stared out the window at the lights of Halifax. Her belly felt as if it were burning, and she slipped her hands down along her stomach and thighs, as if to smother the fire.

"I want you," she whispered, thinking of Scott and yet seeing images of her first husband. "I want to love you," she added, uncertain whether she meant sexually or in some more spiritual way.

Turning around, Cayleigh pulled down the quilt and forced herself to touch Scott's back. He stirred slightly, then settled back to sleep. Moving closer, she snuggled against his back and wrapped her right arm around him, caressing his chest. As she leaned closer and kissed his ear, he rolled partway toward her and patted her hand.

"Can't sleep?" he mumbled with a moaning yawn.

Cayleigh's reply was to nibble gently at his ear as she ran her hand down toward his belly.

Scott awakened more fully now, and he turned the rest of the way toward her. "What's the matter?" he asked, opening his eyes to look at her.

"I . . . I'm lonely," she whispered, her hand cautiously moving lower.

Scott seemed to understand her true meaning, for he raised his hand to her cheek and kissed her softly on the lips. She responded with a sense of urgency, her lips parting and her hand slipping inside his pajama pants. Scott rolled her onto her back, his hand squeezing her breasts as he began to kiss her neck. She moaned lightly, all the while her hand working to arouse him more fully. For several minutes she caressed him, alternately roughly and gently, and though he tried to concentrate on the feelings her hand was producing, he did not respond—partly out of fear, partly out of shame at not being able to perform as he expected of himself.

"It's all right," she whispered. "Just touch me. Just hold me close."

"I . . . I can't," he blurted, pulling away from her and looking up at the ceiling.

Cayleigh lay on her side, her hand resting on his shoulder.

"It's all right," she soothed. "You work too hard; you're tense. And you've been ill."

He rolled away from her onto his side. "You deserve more," he muttered. "You deserve a man."

"You are a man," she said, moving closer and curving her body against his. "This will pass."

"I . . ." His voice trailed off, and for a long time they just lay there in silence.

"Maybe if we got away for a while," Cayleigh finally suggested. "Perhaps I could join you when you go to Cape Breton later this week. I miss Bay St. Lawrence—even though I couldn't wait to move away from such a small village. And I haven't seen Finley Orcutt in a year."

"It would be good to see your father-in-law again," Scott agreed, referring to the father of Cayleigh's first husband. "But I'm not sure this is the right time."

"Why not?"

"I wanted you to assist Aidan while I was gone," he explained. "He's only worked a couple of days at the office, and he may need your help."

"But I miss Cape Breton. Please, take me along."

"I . . . I don't know." He paused, then turned toward her and said, "Here's an idea. Why don't I send Aidan to Cape Breton? The route is so well established that it would be simple for him to handle—especially with you along."

"Me?" she asked in surprise.

"Of course. I really think one of us needs to take care of the house and office—but there's no reason for you to miss the opportunity to visit home. You can show Aidan the route and stop off in Bay St. Lawrence for a couple of days to visit Finley."

"But I thought if we could get away together . . ."

"We will. I promise. I'll have to make another journey in a month or so, and by then Aidan will be ready to take care of things in Halifax."

"I . . . I'm not sure." She turned away slightly.

"Come on. It will be fun. And it will give Aidan a chance to learn the business firsthand."

"I'm just not sure it's proper."

134

"Cayleigh," he said, turning her face toward him. "I trust you. And I know Aidan is an honorable man." He chuckled lightly. "Anyway, from what I sensed on the *Vigilant*, he's already preoccupied with another woman."

"Rachel Salomon?"

"I'm certain of it."

"Are you sure you and I can't go together?" she pressed.

"Next time. I promise."

"All right," she said hesitantly, forcing a smile.

"Good. I'll make the arrangements tomorrow. Now let's get some sleep."

He started to turn away, but she reached out and touched his cheek. "Scott?" she whispered.

"Yes?"

"Do you still love me?"

"Don't be silly," he replied, leaning over and lightly kissing her forehead. "Now let's get some sleep."

Scott rolled away and curled up with his back to Cayleigh. For a long while she lay there, looking at him in the faint light that spilled through the window. Then she turned away and stared out the window, her thoughts spinning between Scott, Aidan McAuliffe, and her first husband, her body aching to be held, to be taken, to be loved.

Three days later, on Friday morning the fifth of June, Cayleigh Cabot and Aidan McAuliffe were seated aboard a coach heading east along the southern coastline of Nova Scotia. The first leg of the trip would take them one hundred seventy miles to the small community of Antigonish, a journey taking about twenty hours and requiring three drivers and nine teams of horses.

The macadam road hugged the coastline, circling numerous small inlets and harbors and traversing one picturesque bluff after another. It was well maintained and fairly level, allowing the six-horse team to sustain a pace of about eight miles an hour, with a change of team every twenty miles or so. The coach itself was a big American Concord, purchased following the closing of the overland routes and repainted red from the traditional Wells Fargo green.

The coach had a near-full load of eight passengers, three each on the front and back seats and two sharing the removable center bench. Cayleigh had the choice seat, her back to the driver on the right side of the coach, where the effects of dust and rain were least noticeable. Aidan sat beside her, with the only other woman on the coach at the other window of the rear-facing bench. The center bench was occupied by the woman's two young boys, ages eight and eleven, while the forward-facing bench held three men returning home from business in Halifax.

Though the first day of a journey by coach always seemed the longest, Cayleigh and Aidan passed the time in good humor, sharing stories about their youths with each other and with the young boys. The mother seemed disinterested in joining the conversation, and in time Cayleigh and Aidan learned from her sons that she was a recent widow, heading to Antigonish to live with her parents. The boys did not seem overly depressed about the loss of their father, which Aidan guessed might have something to do with his having been a military man who had spent little time at home.

"But he always brought us home something special," the older boy said, his eyes lighting with enthusiasm as he pulled aside his jacket to reveal a small knife sheathed at his belt.

"Yeah," his younger brother piped in. "Papa killed loads of Indians when he was young. Didn't he, Jimmy?"

The older boy nodded and was about to reply when his mother leaned forward and said somewhat curtly, "Your father never killed anyone. Now stop pestering these folks."

"It's all right," Aidan assured her, but already she had resumed looking out the window. Deciding that it might be best to change the subject, Aidan asked the older boy, "Have you ever been to Antigonish?" He pronounced the name phonetically, with the accent on the second syllable.

"Antigo*nish*," the boy corrected him, clipping and slurring the beginning of the name and accenting the final syllable, so that it came out sounding like annaga-*neesh*. "You speak funny. Where are you from?"

Aidan glanced uncomfortably at Cayleigh. Then he smiled at the boy and told him the story that he and the Cabots had decided upon. "I used to live in Australia. That's a long way from—"

"The other side of the world!" the boy beamed. "What's it like?"

"It's a very rugged land, but the people are just like here in Nova Scotia."

"Are there any Indians there?" the younger boy asked.

"Why, yes. But we call them aborigines."

"Do they scalp white folks?"

"Hush, now!" his mother insisted. "I told you to leave these people alone."

The two boys frowned and turned to look out the windows. Across the aisle, Aidan decided that it was best not to continue talking about himself, and he let the conversation die. He looked past Cayleigh at the small fishing boats gathered in a long, narrow harbor just below the road and said, "It's certainly beautiful along here."

Cayleigh smiled at the sight. "That's Musquodoboit Harbor."

"I'm not even going to attempt saying that," Aidan replied with a chuckle. "I'll just call it Cayleigh's Harbor. That's a much more beautiful name."

"Thank you."

"Does it mean something special?"

"Cayleigh?" she asked, and he nodded. "Actually, my mother changed the spelling from an old Scottish-Gaelic word that's pronounced the same but spelled *c-e-i-l-i-d-h*. It means 'companion' or 'visit' and is the name we give to our daylong singing and dancing festivals."

"Why, yes—*ceilidh*. We have plenty of *ceilidhs* in Scotland—" Suddenly he realized that he was supposed to be from Australia, so he added, "Or so my Scottish relatives tell me. *Ceilidh*. It makes a lovely name."

"My mother changed the spelling so people would know how to pronounce it."

"A wise choice, I daresay."

"And the name Aidan . . . do you know what that means?"

"I'm afraid not," he admitted.

"Ah, but I do." Her eyes brightened. "With the name Aidan, I'm afraid you've got a touch of the Irish in you."

"What if I do?" he asked defensively.

"And I see you are living up to your name, for Aidan means 'little fiery one.' The Irish-Gaelic spelling is *A-o-d-h-a-n.*"

"How did you know that?" he said in wonder.

Her eyes lowered, and her smile grew bittersweet. "My first husband . . ."

"Yes. I had forgotten." He patted her hand, and she looked up at him, tears glistening her eyes. He was about to remove his hand, but she placed her left hand over his and held it in place. He could feel her tremble slightly.

"If I ever have a son, I will name him Aidan," she whispered.

"And if you have a daughter?"

"I promised Scott I would name her Rachel, for all the good things Rachel Salomon has done for him . . . for both of us." Suddenly she looked self-conscious and released his hand. In the faintest of whispers, she said, "That is, if I ever have a child."

"I hope it happens for you just as you desire."

Again she looked away, raising her hand to catch the tear that ran down her right cheek.

The coach stopped for a brief dinner break at the Port Dufferin way station, built on a promontory overlooking Beaver Harbor. Passengers were given but a few minutes to wolf down an ample though unimaginative supply of dry cornbread, overly steamed vegetables, and some sort of beef stew that more closely resembled gravy.

As soon as they had finished eating, Aidan and Cayleigh headed outside to stand near the edge of the promontory and look out across the harbor as the lowering sun washed the clouds in red and orange. The night was brisk, and Cayleigh wrapped her shawl more tightly around her, then moved closer to Aidan and slipped her hand through his arm.

"It *is* cold, isn't it?" he asked, feeling her shiver.

"Aye. But so beautiful."

"It's too bad your husband couldn't be with you now."

"I'm enjoying myself with you," she responded a bit abruptly.

"But we're just friends," he said, adding wistfully, "This is a night for lovers."

"Aye. It is." She let go of his arm. "We'd better get back to the coach."

Nodding, Aidan casually placed his arm around her—like a brother assisting his sister—and led her back to the waiting stagecoach.

A few minutes later the coach was on its way again, passing through East Quoddy, Harrigan Cove, Moosehead, and the curiously named little towns of Necum Teuch and Ecum Secum. Then the road turned north and continued along St. Mary's River to Antigonish, near the northern shore of Nova Scotia. There travelers could transfer to coaches heading west to New Glasgow or east to Cape Breton Island.

Arriving at Antigonish in the middle of the night, Aidan and Cayleigh took rooms at an inn alongside the way station and were able to sleep late before catching an early afternoon coach to Auld Cove, thirty miles away, where they would take the morning ferry across the Strait of Canso.

Sunday morning dawned clear and brisk as Aidan and Cayleigh stood upon the deck of the flat-bottomed ferry *The Bluefin* and watched the approaching hills of Cape Breton Island. Several private carriages lined the deck, though the stagecoach had remained at Auld Cove for the return trip to Antigonish. New stagecoaches would meet passengers at the other side for passage to all points of Cape Breton.

"That's Balache Point." Cayleigh pointed to where the ferry would be landing.

"You're excited, aren't you?" Aidan asked, noting her enthusiasm.

"It's my home."

"And how far to Bay St. Lawrence?"

"Almost one hundred fifty miles, I'm afraid. We'll make the journey in three parts. Today we'll take the stagecoach just a little over fifty miles to Baddeck."

"Yes. I have a list of several places Scott wants us to visit there."

"We should be able to finish our business in the morning. Then we'll hire a private carriage and go about the same distance to Ingonish, stopping at some of the small villages along the way to meet with the local weavers and arrange purchases of their goods. That will leave us only about forty miles by boat to Bay St. Lawrence."

Aidan stepped toward the bow of the ferry and placed his palms on the rail. He stared up into the green hills beyond and felt the warming sun against his face.

"It reminds you of home, too," Cayleigh said, coming up beside him. She swept her arm to take in the hills. "Cape Breton is called the Highlands of Nova Scotia. But these are really the lowlands. Wait until we get to Ingonish." She placed her hand over his on the rail and looked up at him. "You're thinking of her, aren't you?"

"Her?" he asked with a touch of embarrassment as he turned to face Cayleigh.

"Rachel Salomon." She smiled. "It's all right. I understand. I . . . I was thinking of Scott," she lied.

"I suppose I *was* thinking of Rachel," he admitted.

"She's very beautiful."

"And so are you," he replied almost instinctively.

Cayleigh giggled. "This isn't a contest. You can think of Rachel—even think her more beautiful than me. After all, I'm a married woman." Her smile faded.

"And your husband is a very lucky man." He turned to look back at the approaching hills. "But I wasn't just thinking of Rachel. I was remembering home."

She reached up and gently stroked his cheek. "You miss it very much, don't you?"

Aidan suddenly felt uncomfortable, and he took her hand and moved it away from his face. Trying to cover his action, he continued to hold her hand. "Yes, I miss Scotland. But it is very beautiful here, as well. A man could fall in love . . . with this land."

"If he were with the right woman," Cayleigh added. "A woman like Rachel Salomon."

It was Aidan's turn to smile. "You are determined to ferret a confession out of me. Well, my dear little Cayleigh, I'll give you one." He lifted and kissed her hand. "Your suspicions have no basis in fact, but plenty in fantasy. The fact is that nothing untoward happened between Rachel and me during that long trans-Atlantic voyage. The fantasy is that every night I dreamed that it would."

Cayleigh glanced down and frowned. "You're making fun of me."

"Not at all," he asserted, letting go of her hand and raising his chin until she looked at him. "I appreciate your concern, but don't worry so much about me. I found Rachel very attractive, but I will never do anything to compromise her."

"Aidan, do you think me so callous as to question your integrity?" she asked somewhat testily. "After all, what you and Rachel do is your own af—"

"Easy, now, Cayleigh," he declared, raising his palms and grinning. "Let's not argue. We're here to enjoy ourselves."

"I'm sorry." She forced a smile. "Perhaps we should agree not to mention Scott or Rachel again."

"Agreed."

"We can talk about you, instead," she suggested.

"Let's not forget Cayleigh Cabot—a far better topic of conversation."

"Ah, but one that will have to wait," she put in quickly, nodding toward the approaching dock.

Aidan gave a mock pout. "Don't think you're getting off so easily. I expect to hear everything."

"In time, my dear friend. In time," she teased, patting his cheek lightly, then turning and walking toward the gate from which they would disembark.

Two mornings later, Aidan and Cayleigh at last found themselves in Ingonish along the eastern coast of Cape Breton, the farthest point that they could reach by land. They had made the last leg of the journey by hired carriage, stopping along the way to do business with weavers whose products Scott Cabot regularly purchased for export to establishments such as Salomon's Emporium. Now they would have to ar-

range for a fishing boat to take them the rest of the way to
Bay St. Lawrence around the almost-impassable mountains
to the north.

There was a light, warm breeze that Tuesday morning, and
Cayleigh insisted that before leaving for Bay St. Lawrence
they rent a small skiff at the inn where they had spent the
night and sail across North Bay Ingonish to Middle Head, a
narrow peninsula that jutted two miles into the water, separating the bay into twin harbors.

"I'm not a swimmer," Aidan pointed out with trepidation
as Cayleigh led him down to the small dock beside the inn.

"Don't be afraid," she told him, taking his hand and pulling him out onto the dock. "The innkeeper assured me that
there are life vests under the seat. And I haven't lost a ship
yet."

"Have you ever sailed one?" he asked as she prodded him
into the small, single-masted boat, which was barely big
enough for the two of them.

"Of course," she replied a bit indignantly. "I was a fisherman's wife, remember?"

"Yes, but—"

"Don't be so fussy," she said, climbing into the weathered
boat and raising the single spritsail. It immediately caught
the wind, and the boat began to strain against the rope that
held it to the dock. "Release the line," she directed, poking
him when he was slow to react.

With excessive caution, Aidan leaned out over the dock,
unleashed the rope, and pushed against the dock. The boat
moved forward with a lurch, and Aidan had to drop to his
knees to keep from tumbling out. Cayleigh laughed as she
worked the rudder and expertly turned the boat out across
the bay. The sail billowed and filled, and the boat leaned
away from the wind and glided across the water, shuddering
with every slap of the waves. It seemed only a few minutes
before they were halfway across to the long finger of land
known as Middle Head.

"That's where we'll put in," Cayleigh called, pointing to
a low notch about halfway out the steep-sided peninsula. "It's

a meadow used by fishermen to clean their catches of mackerel. The rest of the cliffs are too steep to climb."

Staying low in the boat, Aidan gave a tenuous smile.

A few minutes later, Cayleigh had the boat nestled among the large rock formations at the shoreline and securely tied to a granite boulder veined with pink quartz. Taking Aidan's hand, she led him up a gravelly incline to the broad meadow about fifty feet above the water. The meadow, which sat like a saddle in the middle of the higher, fingerlike peninsula, was only about one hundred feet wide and afforded views of the coastline to the north and south.

"This way," Cayleigh said, letting go of Aidan's hand as she started to run through the knee-high grass toward a small footpath that led out to the point of Middle Head.

Pausing to pick a sprig of the yellow wildflowers that dotted the meadow, Aidan hurried after her up the footpath, which wound through the scrub pine that covered the rest of the ever-widening peninsula. The small trees were so thick that they blocked all but fleeting glimpses of the coastline until the couple reached the clearing at the head of the peninsula. Suddenly the trees came to an abrupt end, and Aidan found himself standing in a wide, grassy field, bordered by steep, jagged cliffs, more than a hundred feet above the Atlantic Ocean.

"My God!" he breathed with awe as he came alongside Cayleigh and stood looking out across the ocean.

"Are those for me?" she asked coyly, looking down at the sprig of flowers, which Aidan was still clutching tightly in his hands.

Looking down, he realized that he was crushing the flowers. Relaxing his grip, he straightened the drooping stems and sheepishly held them forth. "For you," he pronounced, handing them to her. "For bringing me here."

"Come!" she blurted as she snatched away the flowers and went racing toward the cliff.

Aidan held back for a moment as she ran up to the very edge of the cliff and threw the flowers out over the ocean. When she spun around and again called to him, he advanced cautiously. Coming up beside her, he glanced down the sheer embankment at the waves crashing against the giant rock formations along the base of the cliff.

"Why did you do that?" he asked as the flowers spiraled down and were swept up in the swirling white foam.

"It's for luck . . . and for love," she said, her tone somewhat bittersweet as she stared down at the crashing waves far below.

"Let's move back a little," he softly urged, taking her arm to lead her away from the cliff.

Cayleigh started to move, but then she stopped and turned to Aidan. Her eyes were misty, but she threw back her head and laughed lightly. "Afraid of heights as well as sailing?" she teased, taking a step closer to the edge.

"Be careful," he said, gripping her arm more tightly. "Scott would kill me if—"

"Shhh," she whispered, moving closer and touching the hand on her forearm. "Don't speak of Scott just now." Holding his hand in place, she turned and leaned back against him, so that he was holding her from behind as they looked out over the water. "It's so beautiful . . . and so romantic." She sighed.

"It must remind you of . . . of—"

"Aidan Orcutt, my husband." Her voice faltered slightly. "Aye, I miss him. It was here that he asked me to marry him."

Aidan looked around the grassy clearing at the point of Middle Head and remembered the story Cayleigh had told him about her first husband pretending to jump from the cliffs when she said that she would not marry him. "It was here?" he asked.

"Right over there." She pointed across the clearing to the north-facing cliff.

"I'm sorry."

Cayleigh turned in his arms and looked up at him. "What are you sorry about?"

"That you lost him."

"Not forever. Someday I'll return here to Cape Breton, and we'll be together again."

"Do you really believe that?"

"With all my heart." So saying, she leaned up and kissed Aidan lightly on the cheek. He seemed taken aback and touched the spot she kissed, uncertain how to react. She sensed his discomfort and lowered her head. Moving close against him, she whispered, "I miss him so."

Aidan wrapped his arms around Cayleigh. Though he could not hear her crying, he felt her body shake as she sobbed ever so gently. He reached up and touched her soft brown hair, pulling her head against his chest. "It's all right," he whispered. "I understand."

She shook her head. "You can't," she murmured. "You have no idea how I feel."

"I know it hurts. I just wish Scott could be here to be with—"

Cayleigh stiffened and pulled away slightly. In an almost scolding tone she said, "I told you not to speak of Scott."

"I'm sorry. I only meant—"

"You have no idea, do you?"

He looked at her curiously. "I don't understand."

Suddenly her eyes welled up with tears. "I . . . I just need . . . to be held." Her lips quivered, and her hand raised toward his cheek, then pulled back. "By you," she added, her voice dropping to the faintest whisper.

Cayleigh started to look down, but Aidan lifted her chin and gazed into her soft brown eyes. Slowly their lips came together, and they kissed ever so delicately. Aidan's hand caressed her cheek, and then he slipped it around her neck and pulled her closer. Her lips opened, and their tongues touched hesitantly at first, then with increasing hunger as Cayleigh wrapped her arms around him and pressed her body tight against his.

"Aidan," she whispered, her lips moving along his cheek to his ear as she breathed the name over and over. She moved into him as he backed away from the cliff and then lowered himself onto the grass, pulling her down on top of him. His hands reached to open the buttons at the neck of her dress, and then he hesitated. His eyes betrayed his concern, and he opened his mouth to speak, but she pressed her finger to his lips.

"Don't be afraid. Don't think of anything," she breathed, taking his hand and placing it against her breast, then moving it down along her belly to her thigh. Leaving it there, she began to raise her skirt with one hand as she slid her other hand up along his leg to his groin, stroking him as she whispered, "I just need to be held."

Pressing herself against him, Cayleigh brought her lips down hard upon his mouth, her hand searching and releasing the buttons at his waist, her body shuddering with excitement as his fingers slipped beneath her panties and began to caress her.

NINE

NINA SALOMON WAS DRESSED IN THE SOMBER BLACK OF mourning, her face shadowed behind a half-veil that hung from a pillbox hat, her shoulders covered with a dramatic black sable wrap, as she swept into the hospital room where her daughter lay recuperating from the paralyzing injury to her right arm. Phoebe was awake and alert, but when she saw her mother, she seemed to sink deeper into the pillows, and her eyes closed partway. Her jaw tensed, and her left hand clutched the coarse woolen blanket that covered her.

Nina glanced at her daughter and then turned away, as if distressed by the sight. She gave an involuntary shudder and then crossed to the window and raised it a few inches.

"It's so stuffy in here. I don't know how you stand it." Nina headed back across the room and pulled a chair beside the left side of the bed, Phoebe's good side. Sitting down, she faced her daughter, but she could not look into her eyes for more than a moment, so she lowered her head and gazed down at the bed. "Stop doing that," she suddenly said, reaching toward where Phoebe was clutching the blanket but then pulling away before their hands met.

Phoebe looked up at her mother; her lips moved as if she was about to speak, but no sound came.

"What is it?" Nina asked. She glanced down at herself and seemed to read the unvoiced question in her daughter's mind. "Oh, my dear, no. Your father is still alive. I just didn't feel it appropriate to wear anything more gay, given the circumstances."

Phoebe relaxed slightly but still did not speak.

"They told you about his heart attack?" she asked, and Phoebe nodded. "Good. I asked them to. I know I should have told you myself, but it's been so trying this past week. I . . . I really could not bring myself to come back here to this awful place. And I had to take care of your father. You understand, don't you?" she beseeched, like a young child eager for approval.

Phoebe looked away from her mother but nodded that she understood. Gripping the blanket even more tightly, she said in a thin, reedy voice, "How . . . how is he?"

"Charles?" Nina asked almost offhandedly. "Not at all good. The doctor says he suffered a stroke during the attack. It's affected his faculties, I'm afraid. All he does is lie in bed and look at the ceiling." Seeing that her daughter was growing more agitated, she added, "I don't mean to be morbid, but we must face the truth. Your father may not make it."

Phoebe broke into tears.

"There now," Nina soothed, leaning closer and almost patting her hand. "The doctor says there's nothing we can do but keep him comfortable—and make sure he does not suffer any more upsets. Time will have to take its course."

"I . . . I'm s-sorry," Phoebe stammered. "It's all my f-fault."

Nina looked momentarily unsettled. "Enough of that," she finally said. "After today we're not going to talk about this dreadful . . . accident of yours ever again—or about your unfortunate condition. When you get home—"

"But don't you see?" Phoebe cried aloud. "It's all my fault. Nothing would have happened to Father if he weren't so upset about me."

"We don't know that," Nina insisted. "Certainly he was upset, and of course it could have affected his heart, but we just don't know, so there's no point in dwelling on it."

Her words did little to soothe Phoebe. On the contrary, she broke down sobbing, burying her face in her hand. Nina just sat there, unable to reach out and comfort her daughter, not knowing what else to do. Finally she pulled out a handkerchief and held it toward Phoebe. "Here, get hold of yourself."

Phoebe took the handkerchief and patted her eyes as she slowly regained her composure.

"That's better. Crying will solve nothing. What we have to do is figure a way out of this mess." She waited as Phoebe sniffled and blew her nose. "Now, I told you that I'd come up with something, and I have."

Phoebe looked up at her anxiously.

"And for once you're just going to have to trust me. Your father and I discussed the whole thing before he was stricken, and we are in complete agreement."

"What about?" Phoebe asked in a faint voice.

"I said you'll have to trust me. Will you do that?"

Phoebe stared at Nina a long while, then slowly nodded.

"That's the spirit." Nina stood from the chair. "I've discussed everything with the doctor, and he has agreed to let you come home now—provided you stay under the care of a personal physician."

"Dr. Kates?" Phoebe asked.

"No, not our family doctor. Your father and I have a special doctor in mind—one who knows how to take care of someone in your condition."

"My condition?" Phoebe asked a bit dubiously.

"You know. Your arm and . . . and all." Nina turned away abruptly. "Enough talk now; we have to be going. I brought along that lovely brown crinoline outfit I bought you in New York. I'll send in the nurse to help you get dressed, while I wait out in the carriage."

Phoebe watched as Nina walked from the room without even a glance back. She tried to reach out with her right arm toward her mother but remembered that it would not move at her command. Yet she was certain that she could feel her hand, and she imagined herself flexing the fingers and tightening them into a fist, then slamming the fist down against the bed, against air, against nothing at all.

It was growing dark as the big phaeton, its top raised against the evening chill, made its way across town in the gathering fog. Phoebe Salomon paid little attention to where she was being taken. If she had, she might have thought it peculiar that they were heading so deep into the less-than-reputable district south of Market Street. Instead she merely leaned back against the soft leather seat and enjoyed the cool evening air that flowed through the open window.

Phoebe listened to the clatter of the phaeton's wheels and the clop of the horse's shoes against the pavement. She saw streetlamps whizzing by and the oil headlamps of other vehicles rolling past. In the distance she heard the wail of a foghorn somewhere out upon the bay. It was a typically brisk June night in San Francisco, unique among American cities in growing cooler as summer set in and then heating up again when September came around.

And it was a beautiful June night. One Phoebe would have missed had she succeeded in taking her own life.

I've been so foolish, she told herself. Sliding her left arm under the sling that held her paralyzed right one, she felt the growing swell of her abdomen. *There's still life within me. Still reason to be alive . . . even if Eaton Hallinger won't have me.* She slipped her left hand inside the sling and rubbed her bandaged right arm. It no longer hurt, but she could not even feel it being touched, as if her injured arm belonged to some other person. *And Eaton won't have me,* she knew. *Not the way I am now.* She lowered her head and cried softly.

"What is it now?" Nina asked, leaning across the aisle from her place on the opposite seat. "I thought we'd settled everything and you weren't going to cry anymore."

"I'm sorry," Phoebe muttered, sniffing back her tears.

"That's better." Nina settled back on her seat. "We're

almost to the doctor's, and when we get there, I want you to let me do the talking."

"What doctor is it?" Phoebe asked.

"He comes highly recommended."

Just then the carriage pulled up in front of a small brick building. A doctor's shingle hung outside, the painted letters flaking with age. The lantern at the door was not lit, but a streetlamp halfway down the block cast enough flickering light for Phoebe to make out the name of Dr. Trevor Danin.

"Wait for us here, Michael," Nina told the family coachman as he helped the women from the carriage. She turned to her daughter. "Let's hurry along. The doctor is expecting us."

Phoebe held back, frowning as she looked up at the dilapidated shingle that hung in front of the small brick building. Nina waited a moment, then stepped closer and took her left arm, leading up the stoop to the front door.

The elderly man who answered the door seemed too nervous and distracted to be a physician. He was fairly short and balding, with an uneasy grin that did little to put Phoebe's fears to rest. "So this is the patient?" he asked in a birdlike voice, locking the door behind them and leading them into a waiting room poorly lit by a single kerosene lamp. Apparently it was after usual calling hours; there was neither a nurse nor secretary on hand.

Danin stepped back and rubbed his chin as he looked Phoebe up and down. "Got herself in all kinds of trouble, she has?" he said, more a statement than a question.

"You can help her, can't you?" Nina asked.

"I should think so." He chuckled humorlessly. "Of course, I can't give her back use of her arm; only the good Lord can see to that. But about the wee one, yes, I can set things right."

Phoebe looked over at her mother uncomfortably. "What is he—?"

"The doctor will need to examine you," Nina cut in.

"Right in that room over there," he said, pointing to a

door on the right side of the waiting room. "If you'll come along now."

"What's he going to do?" Phoebe asked in growing fear.

"He just needs to examine you."

"He's not going to—"

"He just wants to make sure everything's all right," Nina assured her. "Now come along." She led the way over to the examining-room door, and Phoebe reluctantly followed the doctor inside.

"You can wait out here," Dr. Danin told Nina. "We won't be but a minute."

Nodding, Nina took a last look at her daughter climbing up onto the examination table as the doctor closed the door. Then she began to pace back and forth across the floor.

A half hour later, Nina glanced up at the wall clock for perhaps the hundredth time and noted that it was taking far longer than a minute. The doctor had assured her that the abortion would be a quick, painless affair—"As quick and painless as the affair that brought her to this sorry state," he had snickered when Nina had come the day before to make the arrangements and pay his exorbitant fee. At least Phoebe was no longer crying, Nina noted with some measure of relief. For the first few minutes in the examining room, Phoebe had moaned piteously but then had stopped abruptly—undoubtedly due to the ether Nina could still smell drifting under the doorway.

"I only hope that old idiot hasn't drugged *himself* to sleep," Nina muttered to herself.

The doctor had promised to put Phoebe to sleep so that she would not know that she was undergoing an abortion. Afterward, the doctor would make up a story about complications during the examination, which led to a spontaneous miscarriage.

Nina was just approaching the examining-room door when she heard a sharp cry—perhaps from her daughter but sounding far too high and weak. It was followed by a series of gagging sounds, as if someone—or something—were dying on the other side of the door. Nina raced over and reached for the doorknob, then held back. Again the noises came, this time the unmistakable first cries of a newborn baby.

Nina burst through the door, and Dr. Danin spun around, looking as shocked as Nina as he held forth a blood-splattered, crying infant. Behind him, Phoebe lay unconscious on the table, her feet up in stirrups, her dress raised above her waist, her legs smeared with blood.

"A . . . a b-boy," the doctor stammered, shrugging and forcing a sheepish smile.

"But . . . but how—?"

"You didn't tell me she was so far along. She was near term. I couldn't help it. It just . . . came out alive."

"That's impossible," Nina exclaimed, coming closer. "She was just a few months . . ."

"Did she tell you that?" he asked as he picked up a square of cloth from the side table and wrapped it around the infant, who immediately began to calm down.

"No, but I assumed . . . I mean, she didn't even look—"

"Many young women don't—especially with the first child." He approached and held forth the bundled infant.

"No," she said, waving him away. "I can't."

"It's your grandson," he said matter-of factly.

"No!" she protested. "Never! Not that bastard."

"Quiet down," he chided, nodding toward Phoebe. "You'll awaken her. I only administered a small dose of ether." Still holding the infant, he headed out into the waiting room, then glanced back at Nina. "Well, come on."

Forcing herself to turn away from her daughter, Nina joined the doctor in the other room, closing the examining-room door behind her. Her expression darkened even further as she glared at the sleeping baby. "This just won't do," she declared, waving a hand at the infant. "You were supposed to get rid of that . . . that thing."

"It wasn't my fault," he proclaimed with a shrug. "I had hardly begun examining her when she went into labor. I gave her the ether, but it didn't stop things. She gave birth, and here's the baby. What do you expect me to do?"

Nina glowered at him.

"I won't be a party to murder," he added quickly, reading the rage in her eyes. "Aborting a helpless fetus is one thing, but now? That would be murder."

"Take care of this baby for me, and I'll double your fee," Nina said emotionlessly.

"Take care . . . ?"

"Do whatever must be done, but get rid of it. I don't want to know. Just tell my daughter that she gave birth and that the baby was stillborn."

"Double the fee?" the doctor said cautiously, weighing the risks involved.

"Triple."

Danin eyed the baby sleeping in his arms. "Done!" he agreed, looking back up at Nina. "Just wait here." He crossed to a door at the far left side of the room, pulled it open, and disappeared inside. A moment later he came back out, the bundle gone from his hands.

"The baby?" Nina asked as he locked the door and approached.

"I'll take care of it as soon as you and your daughter are gone. I'll bring it to a foundling home and say it was found on my steps; they'll assume it's just another prostitute getting rid of her burden."

"I don't want our name—"

"No one will ever know. I promise."

"What about Phoebe?"

"I'll go clean her up. She should be awakening any—"

His words were cut off by a piercing wail, followed by a series of high-pitched shrieks. Nina and the doctor spun around toward the examining room and heard a crashing noise and then the sound of Phoebe staggering across the room, all the while shrieking in terror.

Nina gasped as she raced toward the door. But it was flung open from inside, and Phoebe staggered out, nearly bowling her mother over. The young woman moved on stiff legs, her left hand raised and covered with blood, her right one no longer in the sling but hanging loosely at her side.

"My baby!" she wailed, waving her arm first at her mother, then the doctor. "What have you done to my baby?"

"Nothing," the doctor said as calmly as possible. He took a few steps toward Phoebe, but she backed away, so he held his ground.

"Where's my baby?" she asked her mother, her voice desperate with fear.

"I . . . I'm so sorry." Nina tried to keep her voice gentle and soothing. "You went into labor. The baby was stillborn."

Phoebe backed toward the examining room, shaking her head with disbelief. "That can't be. . . . I—I heard it. I'm certain I heard it."

"You were under the ether," the doctor explained, taking a cautious step toward her. "It was a dream."

"No!" She raised her good hand to stop him. "I heard my baby cry!"

As if on command, the faint whimper of an infant sounded from the far end of the room. Phoebe's eyes widened as she turned toward the closed door. "My baby!" she shouted, staggering across the room.

"No!" Nina yelled, racing up behind her daughter and pulling at her shoulders, forgetting completely that she was touching Phoebe's crippled right arm.

"That's from the next apartment," the doctor insisted, hurrying around to block Phoebe's path.

"My baby!" Phoebe shouted again, jerking her shoulders free and barreling past the doctor. From beyond the closed door, the infant began to cry more forcefully, and Phoebe hurried over and yanked at the knob. "Let me in!" she screamed when the knob would not turn. She pounded on the door with her fist. "Let me have my baby!"

"Your baby is dead!" Nina declared as she came up behind Phoebe and tried to turn her around. The doctor joined her, and together they were able to pull Phoebe away from the locked door.

"No!" Phoebe shrieked as the infant cried louder. "I

want my child!'' She raised her hand to her mouth but allowed herself to be led partway across the room.

"It's all right," Nina tried to console her.

"Oh, my God! No!" Phoebe wailed as the infant screamed at the top of its lungs from the next room.

Suddenly the baby fell silent, almost as if it really had died. Phoebe's eyes went wide, her mouth dropping open in horror. She began to shake, slowly at first, then in convulsive waves that shuddered through her body, causing her arms—her paralyzed one included—to flail about wildly. Nina pulled away and stared in shock as Phoebe's legs buckled and she fell to the floor, her body jerking spasmodically, her eyes rolling back in her head.

The doctor grabbed something off a nearby table and dropped to the floor beside Phoebe. She was drooling profusely as Danin tried in vain to force open her mouth and shove a magazine between her teeth. But the convulsion grew more intense, and her mouth began to bleed as she bit through her lips. Her body gave a final severe jerk and went limp so abruptly that the doctor jumped back in surprise. He looked a long moment at her motionless form, her eyes staring vacantly toward the ceiling, her chest no longer rising or falling, the color draining rapidly from her cheeks. Then he pressed his fingers against her neck and stood up, slowly shaking his head.

"Phoebe!" Nina gasped. She began to drop to her knees beside her daughter, but the doctor grabbed her arms and pulled her away. "Phoebe?" she asked hesitantly, staring into the doctor's eyes and seeing the dreaded reply.

In the next room, the infant boy again started to cry. Sudden tears welled up in Nina's eyes. "My baby," she sobbed, reaching out her hand toward her daughter. "My poor little baby!"

Nina Salomon's fur-trimmed wrap slid off her shoulders and rolled down the marble stairs as she ever so slowly made her way up to her bedroom. She paused at the door, her hand hovering over the knob, her shoulders drooping. She wanted to go inside and curl up under the covers.

She wanted to hide there in the blanketing warmth until it all disappeared and everything was back the way it had been . . . the way it could never be again. But she knew that she must tell Charles, even if he was unable to comprehend what she was talking about. Perhaps that was a blessing. She could confess the truth and would not have to look into his disapproving eyes or hear his silent reproach.

Turning from her door, Nina continued down the hall to her husband's room. The door was open; inside was only silence and the faint light of a low-trimmed table lamp.

As Nina entered the room and approached the bed, she saw her husband's thin, emaciated form, looking as if it had aged ten years within the past few days. She tried to detect some sign that he was still alive. His chest barely moved under the blanket that was drawn up to his neck, and his breathing was so shallow that it could not be heard even as Nina leaned over him and delicately kissed his cheek. As she stood and stared down at him, the only discernible sign that he was still alive was the occasional flutter of his open eyelids. Otherwise, his fixed upward stare could be that of a corpse.

"Something has happened," Nina tentatively began, turning away so that she would not have to look at him as she spoke. "Something terrible has happened to Phoebe."

Charles's eyes widened; the lids began to flutter more rapidly. Still he did not move his head or shift his gaze from the center of the ceiling overhead.

Nina took a deep breath and let it out slowly, then forced herself to continue. "I . . . I took her to a doctor. A special doctor who knows how to get rid of unwanted babies." She started to turn toward her husband, then stopped and crossed over to the window. "I had to do it. I simply couldn't let her have that—that bastard child." Her voice cracked with emotion. She pulled the curtain aside and glanced down off Nob Hill at the city lights below, then let the curtain fall back in place.

Nina returned to the bedside but still would not look directly at her husband. "I had no choice. Her . . . her so-called accident was bad enough. Who would marry a cripple? And then to have a bastard child. She'd be laughed out of decent society. We all would." Nina glanced at her husband, then quickly looked away. She never saw the tears that were pooling atop his eyes, unable to fall as he stared directly upward.

"I didn't do it just for Phoebe but for the other children, as well." She sat on the edge of the bed with her back to Charles. "It would have destroyed everything we've worked so hard to build up for them. Now they need never know. No one need know what Phoebe did . . . what I did." She began to sob but quickly wiped away the tears.

Slowly regaining her composure, Nina went on in an exceedingly faint voice, "How was I to know the baby would be born alive? I thought Phoebe was only a few months along, but the baby . . . the baby . . ." She fought the tears with a forced smile. "But we needn't worry, for the doctor has promised to find it a respectable home. No one—not even our other children—will ever know that it is the child of our shame."

Nina abruptly stood up from the bed and, keeping her back to her husband, gripped the post at the corner of the footboard. "I'm afraid there's more," she said, her voice surprisingly steady, as if she had steeled it from some inner reserve of strength. "Following the operation, something went wrong. Phoebe didn't make it." She gave a hollow, bitter laugh. "Our daughter didn't make it, but her bastard child did."

Nina thought that she heard a moan from the bed, but she could not bring herself to turn around. "Forgive me for what I've done . . . but she's at peace now. No one will make fun of her. No one need ever know."

Nina could no longer fight the tears as she lowered and shook her head. "Dear God, please forgive me. I had no other choice. I had to do it. For Phoebe's sake. For the sake of our entire family." Sobbing, she went running from the room.

SAN FRANCISCO

Alone on the bed, Charles continued to stare at the ceiling. The tears pooled heavier upon his eyes, until the fluttering lids washed them over the sides and sent them streaming down his cheeks. The only other movement was the quivering of his lips as they parted slightly and tried to fashion a word . . . a name: Phoebe.

TEN

AIDAN MCAULIFFE AND CAYLEIGH CABOT SHARED A BENCH at the stern of the small sailing boat they had hired to take them around the rugged coastline from Ingonish to Bay St. Lawrence, where Cayleigh had lived during her first marriage. Because of the presence of the captain, who stood at the wheel on a small raised bridge near the center of the ship, and the two crewmen who worked the lines, the couple took care not to make a show of affection and kept their conversation to generalities. But the presence of others was not the only inhibiting factor, for they had begun to withdraw from each other even as they sailed alone from Middle Head back to their inn at Ingonish. It was an inhibition caused by the knowledge that they had betrayed someone they cared deeply about.

For her part, Cayleigh did not regret what she had done. Neither was she ashamed at having succumbed to her yearning to be held and caressed and loved. But she felt a deep sorrow at knowing that as yet she had been unable to share the same depth of feelings with her husband—and at knowing that even as she and Aidan sat together on the sailing ship, he was slipping away from her and soon would be gone.

Noticing that the crewmen were working up near the bow, Cayleigh again gave in to her feelings and moved closer to Aidan. She slipped her hand through his arm, and though he turned to her and smiled, his body stiffened, and she knew that she had lost him . . . that she had never really had him at all. She clutched his arm all the more tightly, drawing what strength she could before she would have to return home to a man she cared for but did not fully love.

"It's very beautiful," Aidan commented, nodding toward the coastline, a seemingly unending bank of dark mountains that rose from the ocean into a cloudless sky.

"Aye," Cayleigh replied without taking her gaze from Aidan. Again they fell into awkward silence, until Cayleigh squeezed his arm and asked, "Are you sorry?" When he looked at her questioningly, she added, "Don't be. I wanted us to be together."

Aidan hesitated. "I shouldn't have. It was my f—"

"No one is to blame. We both were lonely, that's all."

"Yes, but you're a married woman. I shouldn't have—"

"I'm a *woman*," she cut in. "With the feelings of a woman. Marriage has nothing to do with it."

"Yes, but I . . ." He stopped as he saw one of the crewmen coming along the starboard rail.

Cayleigh slipped her hand from Aidan's arm, and they sat again in silence, looking at the scenery and smiling politely. When the man had finally finished what he was doing and returned to the bow, Cayleigh leaned toward Aidan and whispered, "I wanted it to happen. You're not to blame."

"But we mustn't let it happen again, as much as I might want to. I can't offer you—"

"I don't want anything from you," she said curtly. "Only your friendship."

"You have that."

"I know." She tried to smile, then turned away.

"Tell me about your home," he said to change the subject.

"Bay St. Lawrence? It's a small town at the northern tip

of Cape Breton. A tiny inlet between the cliffs leads into a small, protected harbor, where the sailors keep their ships. That's where we'll find my father-in-law.''

''Finley Orcutt,'' Aidan put in, remembering the name she had told him earlier.

''Finley is a fisherman, like my Aidan was. He has a small house—a shack really—on a hill overlooking the sea. I lived there for a time following my husband's death. That's where I met Scott.'' Her smile was genuine now. ''He was so different from Aidan. Perhaps that's what appealed to me.'' She turned and looked up at Aidan. ''I had been alone—without a man—for three years. I didn't even look at another man but kept myself busy with my weaving and with taking care of Finley.'' She laughed lightly. ''I suppose I should say that Finley was taking care of me. But then Scott came along on his first buying trip, and he purchased all the sweaters I had made that winter. I still remember the way he smelled—of Halifax . . . of the city. There was nothing of fishing about him. Just a friendly smile and a shoulder to lean upon. We were married two months later.''

''You fell in love very quickly.''

''No, not quickly at all,'' she confided, looking away. ''Scott is a very generous man, and when he fell in love with me and wanted to take me back to Halifax, I didn't want to disappoint him. And I didn't want to be alone anymore.''

''Do you love him at all?''

''Aye . . . in my own fashion. But not the way that I loved my first husband. Not with all that I am capable.''

''Perhaps in time . . .''

''It's been almost three years. Things have merely settled into place.'' She gazed along the coastline. ''He is like a brother to me.''

''There are worse things than that.''

''And better,'' she said wistfully. She turned back to Aidan and smiled. ''But that isn't your concern. Things will work out; I'm certain of it.''

''I hope so.''

''They will. I'll make them.'' She touched his arm with

one hand and pointed up the coast to where the mountains came to an abrupt halt. "There it is."

"Bay St. Lawrence?"

"Not quite, but just around the bend from there. A couple of hours and we'll be there."

The captain locked his wheel and came to the back of the bridge. "Ye folks like t'try a hand at some fishin'?" he called down to them. "There's been salmon along these banks o' late—even a tuna or two. Ye can set a dragline off the stern while we push on t'Bay St. Lawrence."

"Would you like to try?" Cayleigh asked, grabbing Aidan's arm eagerly.

"I've not done much fishing," he warned.

"Any fish ye'll be catchin' will be novices at the game, as well," the captain assured him with a grin.

Aidan looked from Cayleigh to the captain and finally shrugged his shoulders and smiled. "All right. Why not?"

"I'm sure the fish can come up wi' a thousand reasons why not," the captain said. "But in the meanwhile, I'll have the boys rig a line and set some bait." He walked across the bridge and called down instructions to the two crewmen at the bow.

"I hope I don't end up looking ridiculous," Aidan whispered to Cayleigh.

"What makes you think you don't already?" she teased. "Just take off your coat and roll up your sleeves." When Aidan hesitated, she prodded, "Come on. It'll be fun."

"Whatever you say, ma'am," he replied, unbuttoning his jacket and tossing it onto the bench.

As Aidan rolled up his sleeves, Cayleigh looked at him with a touch of longing. "You look handsome that way," she proclaimed. "Like another Aidan I once knew."

"And you're one of the most attractive women I've ever known."

"As attractive as that Barbara Eastmann you once were in love with?"

"Even more."

"And what about your first love?"

"Deborah Ilene?" he asked, and when she nodded, he

adopted a mournful frown. "I'm sorry, but no one's ever as beautiful as a first love."

"I know," Cayleigh said wistfully as she walked over to the rail and looked out at the cliffs of Cape Breton Island. "How well I know."

Evening was settling over the Cape Breton hills as the captain guided his fishing boat through the inlet that led into the sheltered harbor of Bay St. Lawrence. Though Cayleigh had sent a cable telling Finley Orcutt that she would be coming, she had not been able to give him the exact date, so she did not expect him to be on hand at her arrival. Upon docking alongside the other fishing boats and disembarking, she spoke to a couple of seamen on the pier and found out that her father-in-law had not yet returned with his day's catch. She left a message with them that she and her friend would be waiting at Finley's cabin. Then she hired a man with a small cart to take them there.

The unpainted, weather-beaten cabin was as unassuming as Cayleigh had warned. It stood at a slight angle—several angles at the same time, really—on the headland overlooking the ocean. From the outside it seemed as if it could contain little more than a single room. And from the stacked lobster traps and the trawling net hung over a rickety porch rail, there was no mistaking that this was the home of a fisherman.

After paying the man with the cart and sending him on his way, Cayleigh and Aidan picked up their bags and headed inside. The poor condition of the exterior was a sharp contrast to the neat, orderly interior. As Cayleigh gave a quick tour of the premises, Aidan was surprised at the cheerful though simple decor. There was a main room that served as both living room and kitchen. The far wall was dominated by a huge bay window, which was decorated with unusual shells and even a few delicate bird's nests and which afforded a spectacular view of the beach and ocean some fifty feet below. Aidan would have assumed the upholstered couch and easy chair had been purchased from a fine furniture maker until Cayleigh told him that Finley had made each by hand. The intricately carved table and matching chairs that separated the kitchen and living area were his work, as well, and showed an acute attention to detail. The flowered curtains, made by Cayleigh when she lived with Finley following her first husband's death, exhibited the same quality of craftsmanship.

There proved to be three rooms in the unexpectedly spacious cabin. Just off the kitchen was a small bedroom that contained little more than an iron bed, a dresser, and a cedar wardrobe. Off the living room, also with a view of the ocean, was Finley's library.

Entering the library alone, Aidan discovered that it was the most surprising room of all. A small mahogany desk stood facing the window, while the other three walls were lined with shelves of books. And unusual books they were. One entire section was devoted to botany, oceanography, and the natural sciences. Another featured history and political treatises. Almost one whole wall contained great works of literature, such as the plays of Shakespeare and collections of British and American poets.

Aidan was about to leave the library when he caught sight of a particular volume that sat about eye level on the far wall. It was a work he had studied at the university by the philosopher Paracelsus, a sixteenth-century alchemist and physician. Aidan walked over and pulled out the book, *Secrets of Physick and Philosophy*. As he skimmed through the familiar pages, he recalled how intrigued he had been by Paracelsus's espousal of such esoteric concepts as reincarnation and the search for the philosopher's stone, said to give the finder not only the secret of transmuting base metals into gold but the cure for all disease and the means to prolong life indefinitely.

Aidan was more than intrigued to find such a volume in the home of a Nova Scotia fisherman. As he replaced it on the shelf, he realized that the surrounding books on three shelves dealt with similar topics. There was Madame Blavatsky's *The Secret Doctrine*, Ignatius Donnelly's *Atlantis: The Antediluvian World*, and the famous treatise on mysticism by Saint John of the Cross, *The Dark Night of the Soul*.

The spine of one curious little volume that caught his eye was beautifully engraved in Chinese ideograms, and he pulled it out to see the English translation. But the front cover had the same Chinese lettering, and when he opened the book he was surprised to discover that it was entirely in Chinese.

"Ye be a student of Chinese?" a gruff voice called, and Aidan spun around to see a short, squat man standing in the doorway. He had a full head of thick gray hair with a matching beard but no mustache. Behind him, Cayleigh stood smiling at Aidan. "Aye, I'm Finley Orcutt," the man said, entering the room. "And ye must be the friend Cayleigh wrote me about."

"Aidan—"

"McAuliffe," Finley cut in, not giving Aidan a chance to use the pseudonym he had adopted. "Aye, and I know all about ye, so we'll not keep any pretenses 'atween us. If ye be a friend o' Cayleigh's, ye be welcome in me house."

Finley crossed the room and held out his hand; his grip was as firm as Aidan had expected.

"The *I Ching*," Finley said, tapping the book in Aidan's hand. When Aidan looked up at him in confusion, he added, "*The Book of Changes*. From ancient China. It predates the Bible." He took the book from Aidan's hand, patted it lovingly, and replaced it on the shelf. "Have ye an interest in such matters?"

"I . . . I read a little Paracelsus when I was at the university."

Finley nodded and touched the spine of the book by Paracelsus. "His real name was Philippus Aureolus Theophrastus Bombast von Hohenheim, though I suppose I'd change it, too, if I was saddled wi' a name like tha' one." He looked at Aidan closely. "There comes a time when a man has t'choose his own name . . . his own destiny."

Finley walked back to the doorway. "Well, come on, son. Ye must be as hungry as me, and I want t'hear all about England." He turned and gently touched Cayleigh's cheek. "And about your life in Halifax."

* * *

That night Cayleigh slept in Finley's bedroom, while the two men shared places in the living room—Aidan on the couch and Finley, at his own insistence, on blankets on the floor. Cayleigh had been in bed for quite some time but unable to sleep when she heard what sounded like humming outside the window, which faced the front porch.

After a few more restless minutes, Cayleigh got up, donned a robe, and walked quietly into the kitchen area of the main room. She glanced across the room, and in the moonlight streaming through the bay window, she saw Aidan sleeping on the couch. The bed set up on the floor was empty, however, so she quietly opened the front door and slipped outside.

A glowing kerosene lantern hung on one of the upright posts at the far end of the porch. Beneath it, Finley was seated on a small stool, smoking a pipe as he repaired holes in the trawling net that hung over the rail. He had been humming, but he stopped when he saw Cayleigh come out.

"Aye, and wha' are ye doin' awake, lassie?" he asked as she approached and knelt beside his stool. "Did I keep ye awake wi' me singin'?"

"No. I just couldn't sleep."

"Too much on your mind, I daresay," he said, and she nodded. "Would ye like t'talk of it?"

"It's nothing," she insisted.

"It's Aidan," he declared.

"Aidan?" She looked up at him in surprise.

"Aye." He grinned and tousled her dark-brown hair. "And I dinna mean me own Aidan Orcutt. I'm talkin' about tha' tall, handsome fellow in there." He waggled his pipe toward the cabin behind him.

"What about Aidan?" she asked.

"Dinna be so coy wi' me, young woman. I know ye so well I can practically read wha' ye be thinkin'."

Cayleigh narrowed her eyes. "Which is?"

"Tha' ye care for this Aidan more than a married woman should be allowed."

Cayleigh opened her mouth to object, but then she sighed

and shrugged her shoulders. "I never could keep a secret from you."

"Aye, ye can, me little one. It's your eyes tha' always give ye away."

"Am I that transparent?"

Finley patted her head and pulled it against his lap. "And wha is wrong wi' that? Light is transparent. Ye kinna see it unless it strikes upon somethin', and then it illuminates the world."

"I don't want him to know," she said firmly.

"Tha' ye love him?" he asked, and she nodded. "If it be love—o' which I'm not so sure."

"Why do you say that?"

"I see the way ye look at him when he kinna see. But there's somethin' else there—somethin' else in your eyes."

"What do you mean?"

"I think ye be in love wi' a memory—a memory ye kinna shake no matter how hard ye try." He waited until Cayleigh looked up at him, then continued, "A memory ye should'na have t'shake."

"Aidan," she whispered, and the way she said the name, it was clear that she meant her first husband.

"Aye. It's always been Aidan for ye."

"But I'm remarried. I should—"

"Ye kinna tell your heart wha' t'feel."

"And I feel something for Aidan McAuliffe. Not just because he reminds me . . ." Her voice trailed off.

"Aye." He softly caressed her cheek. "We all feel things we dinna fully understand. But wha' will ye do about it, me Cayleigh?"

"He loves another woman."

"Did he tell ye?"

Cayleigh smiled up at him. "His eyes give him away."

"See? Lads can be just as transparent as the lassies." He chuckled lightly.

"But what should I do?"

"Wha' d'ye want t'do?"

"I want to be with him," she admitted.

"Ye kinna keep a man who loves another woman."

"So what should I do?"

"Ye will have t'follow your heart. If he really loves another, dinna try t'hold him by trickery. Ye will only hurt yourself in the bargain."

"I know that," she muttered dejectedly.

"And wha' about Scott Cabot?"

Cayleigh looked down and frowned. "I don't want to hurt him, either."

"People dinna hurt other people, only themselves. And I think ye are hurtin' yourself right now, because ye dinna really know how ye feel or wha' ye want t'do. Ye dinna know if it's this Aidan ye really love or the memory o' the one who was taken away before ye was ready t'say goodbye."

Cayleigh rubbed away a tear that ran down her cheek. She stood and tenderly kissed Finley's forehead. "I'll be all right," she assured him. "I'll give it time."

"Aye, time is wha' it needs. Time . . . and enough light to illuminate wha' as yet ye kinna see." He stood up and rested his pipe on the stool. Wrapping his arm around Cayleigh, he led her back to the door. "Now get some sleep. I promise not t'keep ye awake wi' me infernal singin'."

Cayleigh smiled and kissed him again, then pulled open the door and slipped inside, quietly closing it behind her.

Finley walked back to the stool and picked up his pipe. Clenching it between his teeth, he stepped from the porch and walked to the small footpath that led down to the ocean.

"Aye," he whispered as he started down toward the beach. "Enough time and light is all ye need."

Rachel Salomon allowed her brother to hold her arm lightly as he led her through New York's Grand Central Station toward the track where the train was already boarding passengers bound for Chicago and points west. As they reached the gate, Rachel suddenly pulled up short and stood staring at the crowd filing onto the train.

"What is it?" Maurice asked in concern as he let go of her arm. "Are you all right?"

"I . . . I'm not sure I'm ready."

"But our baggage is already aboard. It's been a week since we were supposed to leave. I can't keep wiring Nina that you're sick. She'll get suspicious."

"I know." She sniffled and pulled out a handkerchief, which she dabbed at her nose. "I'm just not ready." She glanced back down the platform; the crowd was thinning as the conductor called for everyone to finish boarding. "There are so many people."

"I've arranged for us to have a private room. You needn't talk to anyone."

The conductor called for final boarding, and Maurice reached for his sister's arm. Instinctively she drew away from him.

"I'm sorry," he whispered. "I just want to help."

"I know. I can do it myself."

"Are you sure?"

"Yes." She forced a smile, which immediately faded.

"We have to hurry," he said, raising an arm to signal the conductor that they were coming.

"Yes, I know. I'm ready."

She started down the platform. When Maurice came up beside her and cautiously took her arm, she stiffened but continued out along the platform.

"Car seven, room three," Maurice called to the gray-haired conductor as they came up alongside him. The man nodded and led them to the next car in line.

Maurice helped his sister onto the car and down the aisle to the second door on the right, which was marked with the number three. Opening the door, he ushered her into the compartment, which contained two plush benches facing each other. Rachel removed her brown woolen wrap and took a seat by the window facing forward, while Maurice closed the door and sat across from her.

The very moment they were seated, the train began to pull out of the station. They rode in silence, watching the city roll past, each uncertain of what to say. A few minutes later the conductor entered, took their tickets, and explained how to find their sleeping berths—numbers eleven and twelve—in the next car forward. As soon as he was gone,

Maurice and Rachel became silent again, lost in their private thoughts. Twice Maurice tried to exchange pleasantries about the scenery or weather, but Rachel seemed disinterested in small talk. And whenever his knees accidentally touched hers, she cringed and turned to the side.

In the end they fell into a steady silence—much as they had spent the past week, with Rachel in her bed at the Astor House and an agitated Maurice fetching her meals and rebooking their reservations from day to day. During that time Damien Picard had disappeared into thin air, having checked out of the lodgings he had been keeping at a small uptown hotel.

It was Rachel who finally broke the silence, catching Maurice by surprise when in a faint, somewhat frightened voice she muttered, "We have to talk about what happened."

Maurice tried to face her, then bowed his head, unable to look her in the eyes.

"Did you know?" she asked.

"What he would do?" he asked sharply, turning to the window. "You can't believe that."

"What else can I think?"

"You can think better of your brother."

"Can I? What was going on in that room before I came in?" she pressed. When he said nothing but continued to stare through the window, she leaned forward and said, "Look at me, Maurice. If we don't talk about it now, we may never talk again."

"I had no idea what he was like," Maurice blurted, turning to look at Rachel, his eyes misting with tears. "I didn't know what he'd do. He got me drunk. He—"

"He gave you opium, didn't he?"

"No! I mean, I . . . he . . ."

"I saw it on the nightstand. You smoked opium, didn't you?"

Crestfallen, Maurice closed his eyes and nodded.

"It wasn't your first time, was it?"

"Yes, it was. I swear it!"

"And after you smoked the opium . . . ?"

"I . . . I don't know what happened."

"Yes, you do."

"No!" Maurice cried, burying his face in his hands.

"You know," she repeated. "What he did to me, and what he first did to you."

Maurice began to sob. "I—I'm sorry. I d-didn't know. I didn't know what he was like."

"I think you did, Maurice," she said as he shook his head in denial. "You never suspected what he would do to me, but you knew what he was like."

Maurice broke down completely, his body racked with sobs. "I-I'm so s-sorry," he stammered. "I d-didn't mean for it to happen."

Rachel almost reached out for him, but then she drew back and wiped the tears that coursed down her own cheeks. "I know you didn't," she said at last. "But it happened."

Maurice gradually calmed down. Steadying his voice, he asked, "What are you going to do?"

"If I were going to go to the police, I would have done so already." She shook her head and looked out the window. "No, there's no point in that. He would only drag you into it, and I couldn't bear that." She took a deep breath. "I can live with it. I only hope that you've learned a lesson from all this."

"What do you mean?" he asked tenuously.

"I can't protect you forever," she declared. "This isn't the first time I've kept quiet to cover up your little escapades. There was that time—"

"I know. . . . I know," he cut her off, looking away again.

"Isn't it about time you took stock of yourself? You're young, intelligent. You can't spend your life drifting from one adventure to the next."

"Forgive me," he beseeched, his voice pathetically weak.

"It's not enough for me to forgive you. You have to forgive yourself . . . and start changing your ways."

"I . . . I've tried."

"You have to want to change."

Maurice nodded but did not reply. He leaned back in his

seat and stared blankly through the window. After a few moments he whispered, "I'm sorry."

"I know you are," she told him. "But sometimes being sorry isn't enough."

"I know." Falling silent once again, he sat for several minutes just staring out the window, and then he stood and looked down at his older sister. "I'm very tired. I'd like to take a nap." When Rachel nodded, he added, "I'll be in my berth."

Leaning over, he kissed Rachel's cheek with such tenderness that she was taken aback. She looked up at him and smiled. "I know you're sorry, Maurice. And I forgive you. We won't speak of it again."

"Thank you." He pulled open the door and started into the aisle, then looked back and said, "I love you, Rachel."

"I know you do," she replied.

Maurice slowly closed the door, and Rachel heard him walking down the hallway to the next car, where their sleeping berths were located.

Rachel leaned back and sighed, trying to put the events of New York out of her mind. She found herself thinking of Aidan McAuliffe, and she looked down at the ring on her finger. "Perhaps I should have told him . . ." she whispered, then shook off the concern. "If he comes to the United States, he'll visit me," she told herself, convinced that more than friendship had blossomed between them. That would be the time to explain she was not married. Until then, it would be inconsiderate to put him in a position where he might jeopardize his safety to be with her.

For the next half hour, Rachel sat alone looking out the window at the passing countryside. It lulled her, and as she watched New York receding into the distance, she felt the pain of what Damien Picard had done to her receding as well. Soon she found herself growing weary, and though it was only late morning, she decided that a nap before lunch might be just the thing to help her forget the recent nightmare and move forward with her life.

Leaving her wrap in the berth, Rachel headed down the hallway. Passing across the outside platform, she entered the sleeping car and made her way down the aisle, which was on the left side of the car between the windows and the row of double-decker berths. The berths were set perpendicular to the aisle, with a small, closed entryway leading to each group of four.

Finding the sign for berths nine through twelve, Rachel opened the door and stepped into the tiny entryway, at the far end of which was a narrow window that flooded the area with light. There were numbers on each berth, and hers was the lower one on the left. As she pulled aside the curtain and looked into the narrow compartment, she heard the heavy breathing of her brother in the upper berth. He seemed to be sound asleep, and Rachel took care not to awaken him as she removed her shoes and climbed into the berth. She did not change out of her clothes or even climb under the blankets but merely closed the curtain and lay against the pillow on the thin mattress, shutting her eyes and feeling the roll of the train.

The clatter of the wheels was strangely lulling, and soon Rachel felt herself drifting into a light sleep. It was almost as if she were back on the *Vigilant*, feeling the sway of the ship, the swell of the ocean below. She was in Aidan McAuliffe's arms, their bodies moving slowly, rhythmically, their moist lips touching and exploring each other.

Rachel could hear her heartbeat grow louder, pounding ever more forcefully, like a mallet drumming incessantly against her chest. She felt the pressure weighing down on her, and her body tensed in fear as she envisioned her father's heart bulging, bursting in his chest. Even in her half-asleep state, she tried to calm her breathing and steady the beating of her heart. But it grew louder, almost as if a giant faucet were dripping on her chest.

Suddenly something wet struck her cheek, and Rachel jerked up from the pillow. Her eyes opened, and in the darkness she was momentarily uncertain of her surroundings. Again something splattered against her face, and she rolled quickly to the side and raised her hand to touch her cheek. It was moist and warm, and as she remembered where she was and recalled that her brother was sleeping above, she muttered in disgust, "Whiskey."

Sitting pressed against the wall, Rachel could hear the liquid dripping beside her on the blanket as she raised her wet fingers to her nose and sniffed, expecting to discern the pungent aroma of alcohol. But it was odorless; apparently Maurice had not fallen asleep with an open flask in his hands. And as Rachel rubbed her fingers together, she realized that the liquid was strangely sticky.

Leaning across the berth, she yanked open the heavy curtain. Her eyes were briefly blinded by the light pouring in from the entryway, but as she blinked and regained her focus, she saw that the curtain was smeared red where she had grasped it. She looked at her hands, then at the bodice of her dress. She was covered with blood, which continued to drip on her from where it had pooled on the underside of the berth above.

Rachel gasped and recoiled against the wall. The blood dripped steadily on the blanket, turning the blue material a sickly purple. For a moment she could not breathe as she stared down at her blood-drenched dress and hands. Then she touched her wet cheeks and began to shriek hysterically, uncontrollably, unable to stop.

Someone must have been in the aisle of the sleeping car, because doors started slamming and a voice shouted, "What is it? Where are you?" Finally the door to Rachel's berth flew open, and a burly, black conductor rushed in front of the open curtain and looked in on her.

Upon seeing him, Rachel managed to stop shrieking but continued to cry as she held out her bloody hands. When he started to lean into the berth, she shook her head and waved him off, pointing up. It was then that he saw the blood dripping from above.

Rachel watched as the man straightened himself and opened the curtain of the upper berth, then stepped onto the edge of her bed to reach into Maurice's cubicle. She could hear movement, as if he was shaking her brother. A moment later the conductor climbed down and peered in at her. His expression was bleak as he told her, "He's still alive, but barely. You've got to help me."

Rachel could not bring herself to move. Her hands trembled, and she shook her head with fear.

Reaching in and grasping her arm, the man said in a deep, calming voice, "You can do it."

She felt herself being pulled from the berth, and she winced as another drop of blood struck her. Avoiding the spot from which it was dripping, she quickly climbed out into the entryway. Her legs nearly gave way, and the conductor had to help her stand.

"Are you all right?" he asked, and when she nodded, he let go of her and again stepped onto the lower berth so that he could reach into the upper one. A moment later he pulled Maurice out, lifting his thin, pale body as easily as if it were a rag doll. Climbing down carefully, he lowered Maurice onto the floor.

Rachel backed into the corner near the door as she looked down at her brother. His white shirtfront was completely red with blood, and for a moment she thought that someone had shot him in the chest. But then the conductor lifted Maurice's limp right hand, and Rachel saw the blood oozing slowly from a slash at his wrist. The other wrist was slashed, as well, and the conductor wrapped his hands around each of them and pressed against the wounds.

"Come down here," he ordered, and Rachel hesitantly complied, kneeling awkwardly in the cramped quarters on the opposite side of her brother.

"Grab his wrists and squeeze—as tightly as you can. There's a doctor in the forward coach; I'll get him."

The conductor held Maurice's hands toward Rachel, and she reached out, then pulled back.

"He needs you," the big man said calmly, holding Maurice's hands closer to her.

Rachel took a deep breath and took first one wrist and then the other. She cringed at the slimy feel of the bloody skin, but she forced herself not to gag as she pressed her palms against the jagged slashes and began to squeeze.

"That's it," the conductor said. "With as much pressure

as you can. I'll be right back.'' He stood, stepped across Maurice, and disappeared through the doorway.

Rachel could hear the man running down the aisle as she stared at her younger brother and continued to press against his wrists. Maurice looked so white, as if all the blood had already drained from his body. But she could see his chest shallowly rising and falling.

''Why, Maurice?'' she wept as she squeezed his wrists and pressed them against her chest. She looked at his ashen face and began to cry. ''Oh, dear God, don't let him die.''

Aidan and Cayleigh joined Finley Orcutt at the wheel of his fishing boat as he sailed them around the coast from Bay St. Lawrence to Ingonish, where they would hire a coach for the return journey home. It was a warm, balmy morning—a perfect day for fishing—but Finley had insisted upon taking them back in his own boat.

''Why not try a hand at the wheel,'' Finley told Cayleigh, stepping aside so that she could take charge of the ship. ''Just keep her steady as she goes,'' he said, walking forward toward the bow. He spoke briefly with the young sailor who was working the lines, then returned to where Aidan and Cayleigh were standing.

''Wha' are your plans once ye return t'Halifax?'' Finley asked Aidan.

''I'm not sure. Scott would like me to continue working for him, but I don't know if that's a good idea.'' He gave Cayleigh an awkward glance.

''Strange work for a physician,'' Finley commented.

''I'm afraid that for now I can't practice my usual trade,'' Aidan said somewhat dejectedly.

Finley nodded. ''Ye'll be needin' to establish a new life for yourself. Usin' a false name may not be good enough, unless ye can prove who ye are.''

''I know, but if I stay in Halifax—''

''Ye may find tha' not possible. If the police get wind ye were on the *Vigilant*, they may track ye t'Halifax, and tha' could put Cayleigh and her husband in jeopardy.''

''I've been thinking the same thing.''

"But if ye try t'leave, ye may not get far without proper identification." Finley patted Aidan on the shoulder. "Lad, I have somethin' I want ye t'take." He reached into his jacket pocket and pulled out a sheaf of papers tied with a string. "These are the documents o' me son, Aidan Orcutt—birth certificate, confirmation papers, and the like. He was buried at sea, and the only record of his death is in the local church, where it will'na soon be found. Our little community is hard t'reach, and no one is likely t'come lookin'. But if they write to inquire, I'll back up ye story." He held out the packet.

Aidan looked at him closely. "Are you saying . . . ?"

"I want ye to use me son's name."

"Aidan Orcutt," Aidan said, reaching out and touching the papers.

Finley slipped them into Aidan's hand, then gripped Aidan's forearm. " 'Twill do me proud t'know tha' me son could be of help."

"I . . . I don't know what to say."

"Just say tha' ye will'na shame the Orcutt name," Finley declared with a smile.

"I'll do my best."

"Aye, tha' ye will."

"And I'll send these back to you just as soon as I am able to clear my own name."

Nodding, Finley returned to the wheel and took over from Cayleigh.

"Thank you, Finley," she whispered, leaning up and kissing his cheek, her eyes moist with tears.

"I thought our Aidan would'na mind."

"I'm certain he wouldn't," she said, kissing him again.

It was early afternoon when the boat pulled into Ingonish. Aidan could see a commotion on the dock and a tall man pointing toward their ship, and for a moment he feared that someone was on hand to arrest him. But then Cayleigh gave a cry and shouted, "Scott!" Aidan squinted, and sure enough there was Scott Cabot standing on the dock, grinning and waving at them.

Finley brought the ship to a halt beside the dock, and as he and his crewman secured the lines, Cayleigh and Aidan clambered onto the dock to greet Scott.

"What are you doing here?" Aidan asked as Cayleigh embraced her husband.

"I just arrived and was arranging for a boat to bring me to Bay St. Lawrence."

"But why?" Cayleigh asked.

Just then Finley stepped down from the boat and shook Scott's hand. He immediately sensed that all was not right, and he said, " 'Tis about Aidan, isn't it?"

"Yes." Scott's smile faded as he turned to Aidan. "A couple of days after you left, I was visited by the local police. They had received word from New York that a stowaway had slipped off the *Vigilant* in Halifax, and they suspected him to be a convict named Aidan McAuliffe. They knew that I had hired a new man and had already confirmed from others who saw you in town that you match the description of the wanted man." He shook his head. "There was nothing I could do."

"What do you mean?" Cayleigh asked, pulling on his arm.

"They had a photograph. I had to admit that it was the same man I hired."

"My God!" Cayleigh gasped.

"They didn't arrest you, did they?" Aidan asked.

"No. I said that you followed me after I left the *Vigilant*, and that we got friendly. I told them you admitted being a stowaway but that I had no idea who you really were and assumed you were simply too poor to pay for passage." Seeing a look of disappointment in Cayleigh's eyes, he added, "I had to do it, Cayleigh—not only to protect us but to protect Rachel Salomon. If they ever found out she hid Aidan aboard ship—"

"You did the right thing," Aidan assured him.

"There's more," Scott continued. "I claimed that we had a falling out and that you left town, bound for New Brunswick. I think they believed me, but I didn't want to risk sending you a telegram, in case it was intercepted. So I boarded a coach and have been on the road ever since.''

''Are you sure you weren't followed?'' Cayleigh asked.

''Yes. But we may have some questions to answer when we get back.''

''What, about Aidan?'' Cayleigh's voice betrayed her fear and concern.

''I can't return with you,'' Aidan pronounced.

''No, that is out of the question,'' Scott agreed.

''But what will you do? Where will you go?''

''He will come wi' me,'' Finley put in, stepping closer.

''With you?'' Aidan asked.

''Aye.'' Finley smiled. '' 'Tis a lovely day for ye t'do some lobsterin'—tomorrow, as well. And when the hull is filled up wi' enough o' them pesky creatures, I think we may get a better price at the Boston wharfs.''

''Boston?'' Aidan said incredulously.

''Aye. We'll take the whole load o' them down the coast and sell them to the Boston Fish Bureau.'' He grinned at Aidan. ''And then I think I'll be so sick o' seein' your sorry face tha' I'll have t'throw ye off me crew and let ye fend for yourself—whether ye be me son or no.''

''Your son?'' Scott asked in confusion.

Aidan patted his pocket. ''Finley gave me his son's official papers.''

''They should do the trick wi' customs. Workin' a Nova Scotia fishin' boat, they will'na question ye too closely.''

Aidan began to nod in agreement. ''Yes, that just might work.''

''But what will you do in Boston?'' Cayleigh asked him.

''I don't know. First I'll need to earn some money to repay Rachel the loan she gave me.''

''Speaking of which . . .'' Scott pulled his wallet out of his coat pocket and removed several large bills, which he held out to Aidan. ''It's for the work you've already put in at Cabot Export.'' Seeing Aidan's reluctance to accept the money, he said, ''Go on, take it. You've earned it.''

''No, I haven't. I'll take it only as a loan.''

"Whatever you wish," Scott said, handing him the bills. "But don't worry about repaying me—at least until you've taken care of your other problems."

"Will you stay in Boston?" Cayleigh asked.

"I don't know—but I'll get a message to you once I've settled somewhere." He paused, then added, "I'd like to go to San Francisco . . . to thank Rachel for all she did." He grinned ruefully. "But I don't suppose her husband would—"

"Husband?" Scott said in surprise. "Rachel has no husband."

"But she was wearing a ring. She told me—"

"She always wears a ring when she travels—it's safer for a young woman alone. But trust me, she isn't married."

"But why would she . . . ?" Aidan's voice trailed off as he realized that she had probably kept up the ruse not only to protect herself but to protect him.

"Then it's decided?" Finley declared, clapping his hands. "If so, we'd best be on our way."

"Cayleigh and I, as well," Scott said. "I rented that carriage in Baddeck." He pointed to a covered, single-horse buggy that stood on the shore near the end of the dock. "If we start back now, we can return it in time to catch the morning coach."

Finley shook hands with Scott and embraced Cayleigh, who whispered her thanks for all that he had done to help both her and Aidan. Meanwhile, Scott retrieved Cayleigh's bag from the boat, then said good-bye to Aidan and started toward the buggy. Finley quickly reboarded the boat, leaving Cayleigh and Aidan alone for a moment.

"I'll miss you," Cayleigh told him, reaching out and touching his arm.

"I won't forget you."

"You should try to," she replied, forcing back a tear.

"Never."

"Then you are as foolish as you are handsome." Stepping closer, she kissed him lightly on the cheek. "Good-bye, Aidan McAuliffe," she said, her voice breaking. She turned and hurried away along the dock.

Aidan stood alone, watching as Cayleigh took her husband's hand and stepped up into the buggy. Scott climbed in beside her, picked up the reins, and slapped them against the horse's back.

"I won't forget you, Cayleigh," Aidan whispered as the buggy jerked and clattered away down the narrow dirt road.

ELEVEN

"SALOMON'S EMPORIUM," THE STOCKY, DISTINGUISHED-looking young man called up to the driver as he pulled open the door of the gurney cab and climbed inside.

"Yes, Mr. Salomon," the driver replied, straightening in his seat and picking up the reins. It had been several months since Jacob Salomon had been in San Francisco, but the cabbie had often transported him about town and had recognized him at once, despite the beard he had grown.

Jacob leaned back in the seat as the closed carriage pulled away from the wharf and started across town toward Union Square, just off Market Street. He paid little attention to the familiar sights of the city, instead taking a small notebook from his leather valise and jotting down a few notes below the last entry.

"Three P.M., Thursday, June eleven, eighteen ninety-six," he recited as he wrote. "Disembarked at pier forty-one. Arranged for delivery of goods to Salomon's. Sent luggage to my house. Took gurney to Salomon's."

After returning the notebook to his valise, Jacob glanced outside. He caught a glimpse of his own image in the polished-chrome window edging and noted that he looked some-what thin and tired following the long ocean voyage from Japan. Even his usually bright and expressive gray eyes seemed puffy and lusterless.

"An old man," he muttered, reaching up and running a hand across his balding head. He was only twenty-seven, yet he was beginning to feel as if his youth had passed him by. He looked back at his reflection and touched his trim brown beard, wondering if it made him look older and what his family would think when they saw it.

The ship had arrived a day early, and his family would not be expecting him, just as Jacob preferred. He would report to his father at the store, then go directly to his small town house at the foot of Nob Hill, several blocks from his parents' home, where he could relax and get a good night's sleep before facing Nina in the morning.

As the cab turned off Market onto Geary Street, Jacob leaned his head out the window to catch his first sight of Salomon's Emporium, which dominated the corner of Geary and Stockton, just a block ahead. It was an imposing four-story structure, elegant in its simplicity, created with three shades of brick laid out in precise geometric patterns. The windows and front doors were brass, set in the same black, highly polished marble that had been used throughout the Salomon mansion on Nob Hill. Just under the black-slate mansard roof, six flagpoles stood perpendicular to the brick wall, each one bearing a long banner on which was painted the store's initials in ten-foot-long cursive letters.

"Home," Jacob breathed, leaning back against the plush leather seat and smiling, for the store truly had become a home to him—a refuge of sorts from the growing rift that had been developing between his mother and him. Though Nina relied on her eldest son to assume increasing responsibility for the operation of the business as his father's health declined, she was reluctant to relinquish any control herself. This inevitably created conflict, for she could not make Jacob jump at her command the way Charles did. In fact it was largely because of this growing friction between them that Jacob had purchased his own home.

Jacob took a deep breath as the gurney pulled up in front of the store. Opening the door himself, he stepped down onto the sidewalk and whispered, "Please, don't let her be here," referring to the periodic unannounced visits Nina made to Salomon's, striking fear into the hearts of the employees, who never knew whether they would find themselves on the receiving end of her legendary though infrequent largess or equally legendary and far-more-customary wrath.

After paying the cabbie, Jacob approached the brass double doors in the marble entranceway. One of the doors was immediately opened by the liveried doorman, an elderly black man who had been with Salomon's for the past twenty years, becoming a fixture in downtown San Francisco. As Jacob turned to greet him, the man said in a surprisingly subdued tone, "Good to have you home, Mr. Salomon."

Thinking the doorman must have had a tiring day, Jacob replied, "Good day, Powell," then passed inside without further conversation.

The door closed behind him, and Jacob stood for a moment and looked around. The main floor was two stories high and half a city block in each direction. In the center of the room was a raised, eight-sided patio, at each corner of which stood a free-standing Corinthian column, forming an open-topped pavilion of sorts. Between each pair of columns were steps, which led down to eight gold walkways that radiated out like a sunburst, dividing the room into equal sections like so many pieces of pie. In the ceiling high above the pavilion was a shallow, recessed dome, lit by a ring of gold chandeliers and painted with a trompe l'oeil depiction of mythical fairies and angels.

As Jacob turned left and circled the perimeter of the store, he noted with pride that it was bustling with well-dressed men and women being attended to by the large, well-trained staff. He made his way to the elevator along the east wall and caught the eye of a number of the salespeople. While a few gave a polite hello, he was surprised that many of the others turned away quickly, almost as if they did not wish to see him.

The elevator was already on the first floor, its door open

and the young operator seated inside. "Hello, Dwyer," Jacob said as he stepped inside.

"Uh, hello, Mr. Salomon," the teenager replied, quickly standing and closing the outer door and inner gate.

Seeing how nervous Dwyer seemed as he pulled back the lever in line with the word *Up,* Jacob asked, "Is something wrong? The place seems like a morgue."

"Uh, y-yes, Mr. Salomon," the boy stammered.

Jacob, suspecting that Nina was either on hand or had recently made one of her infamous inspections, decided not to pursue the topic but to wait until he saw his father.

When the elevator reached the top floor, where the offices were located, Jacob bid Dwyer good day and headed down the hall to his father's suite. He came to an abrupt halt when he saw that the outer door was closed. It disconcerted Jacob, for he could not remember ever having seen it shut during office hours. He knocked, then turned the knob. His shock multiplied when he discovered that the suite was locked. Immediately he knew something was wrong, for Charles never locked the office, even at night.

"Mr. Salomon," a thin, high-pitched voice called from behind him. "We didn't expect you back today."

Jacob spun around to see his father's elderly assistant, David Gelde, rising from a desk in the office directly across the hall, where the clerks usually worked. Gelde's own desk was in the outer room of Charles's office.

"What's the meaning of this?" Jacob asked, jiggling the locked doorknob as Gelde came out into the hall.

Gelde ran a nervous hand through his white hair. "Mrs. Salomon ordered the office closed and locked. She had me move across the hall."

"But why? Has something happened to my father?" When the older man did not respond but shifted uncomfortably on his feet, Jacob said, "What is it, Mr. Gelde? Has he died?"

"You haven't been home?" Gelde asked hesitantly.

"I came straight from the ship. Tell me what's happened."

"He . . . he hasn't died," Gelde began, and Jacob gave an audible sigh. "But he's had another attack—and a stroke, I'm afraid."

Jacob just stood there, stunned, his mouth gaping open. Turning slowly, he pressed his hands against the closed office door. After a moment he looked back at the older man and said in a controlled voice, "Have you seen him?"

"Your mother says that he cannot have visitors."

"Is he . . . is he still in command of his faculties?"

"I really don't know. But he isn't taking any work, and I've been told to close his office and keep it that way until your mother instructs me otherwise. But of course I can open it if you'd—"

"No," Jacob cut in. "I should go straight to my parents' house." He turned to start back down the hall. "Thank you, Mr. Gelde."

"Mr. Salomon . . ." the older man called, and when Jacob looked back, he added, "I'm afraid that isn't all."

Jacob stared at him curiously. "What do you mean?"

Unable to face him, Gelde bowed his head and said, "There has been a tragic accident. Your youngest sister, Phoebe . . . she was struck by a cable car. She badly injured her arm and seemed to be recuperating just fine, but soon after the hospital released her, infection set in and she . . . and she . . ."

"Dead?" Jacob muttered, his voice hollow and faint. "Phoebe is dead?" His hands clenched, his body stiffening as Gelde nodded. "Dear God," Jacob gasped. He turned and walked woodenly down the hall.

Jacob Salomon stared vacantly out the window of the gurney cab, seemingly unaware of his surroundings until the vehicle turned into the circular drive in front of his parents' large home atop Nob Hill. When the cab came to a halt, he got out, paid the driver, and looked up at the gray edifice with its towers and turrets and gargoyles. He felt himself shudder and wanted nothing more than to turn and walk away. But his father was lying inside, possibly suffering, probably helpless.

Mounting the stairs, Jacob pressed the bell push. A few moments later the door swung open and the butler exclaimed, "Mr. Salomon! How good to have you home!"

"Good afternoon, Cameron," Jacob said without enthusiasm, walking in and removing his outer coat. "Is my mother at home?" he asked as Cameron took the coat.

"She's resting upstairs," the butler said, but just then a voice called Jacob's name, and the two men turned to see Nina descending the stairs in a floor-length dressing robe and slippers, looking far older than her forty-five years. It was apparent she had been crying; she wore no makeup, yet her face was streaked with lines, and her long brunette hair hung loose and unbrushed upon her shoulders.

"Oh, Jacob, I'm so glad you're home." She hurried across the polished marble floor and fairly threw herself into the arms of her eldest son. He was taken aback and touched at the same time.

"It's all right," he consoled her. "I've already heard about Father . . . and Phoebe."

"It's been such a tragedy," she moaned. "Maurice and Rachel are still on their way home from New York. They don't even know about Phoebe. I had to bury her all alone."

"You've already had the funeral?" he asked, leading her toward the parlor.

She shook her head. "It seemed pointless with no one here and your father so sick. I wasn't up to attending a ceremony, so the doctor took care of all the arrangements."

"I understand," Jacob assured her, easing her onto a small sofa and sitting beside her. "How is Father?"

She looked down and wrung her hands together. "Not good. Not at all good."

"I want to see him," he said, standing.

She clutched at his sleeve. "He won't recognize you. He just sleeps or stares at the ceiling."

"It doesn't matter."

"He's in his bed," she told him. "You won't tire him, will you?"

"No. I just want to see him. Will you be all right down here?"

She nodded. As he started to walk from the room, she called, "Jacob . . ." and he looked back at her. "You . . . you aren't going to keep that beard, are you?"

Jacob just stared at her, uncertain if she was being serious, amazed that she would think about his beard at a time like this. Shaking his head, though not as a reply to her question, he turned and continued from the room.

Jacob mounted the stairs and headed down the hall to his father's room. The door was open, and he entered the room and approached the bed. Charles lay unmoving in the center of the wide bed, his eyes closed, his breathing shallow but regular. He was thinner and paler than Jacob had ever seen him. While Jacob had been away, Charles had become an old man . . . an old, dying man.

Jacob moved closer and stood beside the bed. He reached to take his father's frail, bony hand, but then he held back, not wanting to awaken him. He stood there looking at him in the soft light that filtered through the curtains, then turned and walked from the room.

Returning to the parlor, Jacob found his mother standing by the fireplace, looking somewhat more composed.

"I didn't realize he would be so frail," Jacob said as he walked over and leaned against the marble mantel.

Nina turned away and said in a hushed tone, "It would be a blessing if God saw fit to take him."

"Don't speak like that," Jacob blurted.

"I can't help it. I've lived with it for nearly two weeks, and I can't bear to look at him like that any longer. He's unable to move, to speak . . . even to think."

"Where there's life, there's—"

"I don't believe any of that," she said bitterly. "There's just an old man lying on a bed waiting for death. We'll all be better off when his suffering has ended."

Jacob approached his mother and reached to put an arm around her, but she pulled back and walked stiffly toward the window.

"It must be very hard on you," he said softly.

"I don't want to talk about it anymore." She stood facing the window, breathing deeply as if gathering strength. Suddenly she turned toward Jacob and gave a half smile. "Tell me about your trip."

"That can wait."

"I want to hear all about it. How was Japan?"

"It was very . . . exotic."

"Did you bring anything back for me?" Her smile grew more animated, like a child anticipating a present.

"Of course. But you'll have to wait until I get home and unpack my bags."

"And what about your purchases for the store?"

"I did better than we had hoped. Everything is being off-loaded from the ship."

"Delightful!" She clasped her hands together. "Oriental goods have become quite the rage, and I want to make sure Salomon's is in a position to profit."

"Let's not talk about the store just now," Jacob said distractedly as he crossed to the sofa and sat down. He withdrew a cigar from a walnut box on the side table and absently began to roll it between his fingers.

"Yes, I understand." Nina took a seat on the chair beside the sofa. "You must be tired from your journey. And what with this business about your father, I don't want to burden you with problems about the store."

"What do you mean?" Jacob asked offhandedly, only half listening to her.

"Oh, I've had such trouble over there since your father—"

"Trouble?" He looked at her more closely now.

"Thieves, that's all they are. And your father's trusted assistant, that odious Mr. Gelde, he's the most untrustworthy of all. The moment your father takes ill, he and his cronies use it as an excuse to rob us blind."

"David Gelde?" He looked incredulous. "I hardly think him capable—"

"I caught him paying the employees without proper authorization from anyone in the family."

"But Father had taken ill, and we were all away. I'm certain he just didn't want to burden you with—"

"That's precisely right. He didn't want to burden us. In fact, he wanted to *unburden* us . . . of our hard-earned profits. The way he keeps books, there's no untangling what he may be doing behind our backs."

Jacob sighed. "Don't worry about Mr. Gelde. I'll go over the books myself, and I'm certain they'll prove to be in order."

"The others are just as bad. I've received reports that they've been taking lengthened lunches and have been dressing in the most scandalously casual attire. Why, Mrs. Reukauff told me that she saw one of our floorwalkers in a skirt at her calves. It's a wonder we haven't lost all our customers in the past week."

Jacob suppressed the urge to say that such a spectacle would probably draw in more customers than it drove away. Instead he calmly replied, "I was there just a little while ago, and everyone seemed to be doing his job as usual. You're overreacting."

Nina threw her hands in the air. "Someone around here has to. If I left it to Charles, he'd have the employees coming in and out whenever they wished, clad in any old hand-me-down, and the customers paying whatever they could afford." She leaned toward Jacob. "If it weren't for my *overreacting*, as you call it, there'd be no Salomon's Emporium. Your father would have let the customers walk off with it." She leaned back and folded her arms, her lips turned down in a pout.

Jacob knew that his mother was partly right. Nina's father, Isidore Salomon, had created and built up the business, but it was Nina's driving energy that had sustained it since his death fifteen years ago. Charles was a capable administrator and was beloved by his employees, but he lacked the hard edge sometimes needed to make a business successful. It was that softness, that amiableness, that had led him to agree to Isidore's request that he give up his own surname, Roth, and take the name Salomon when he married Isidore's only child so that the Salomon name would be carried on and the name of the store would be ensured for the future. Yet in many ways Jacob's father was the heart and spirit of what Salomon's had become—an establishment devoted to meeting the needs of its customers. And should Charles die, Jacob feared that spirit might be crushed, as well.

"Will you be going back to work tomorrow?" Nina finally said.

"I really don't want to talk about that just now," he replied a bit testily.

"I'm sorry. You must be upset. . . ."

After a long, awkward silence, Jacob lowered his head and murmured, "I can't believe she's gone."

"I know. I enter her room, and I expect her to be there."

"How exactly did it happen? They said it was an accident . . . a cable car?"

"Yes." She hesitated, then whispered, "Such a tragedy."

"But how? What happened?"

"It . . . it doesn't matter." She waved her hand in the air.

"It does to me. Phoebe was my sister."

Nina turned to her eldest son, saw that his eyes were filling with tears, and quickly looked away. "She was out walking. It was after dark, and somehow she stumbled in front of a cable car, and . . . and it mangled her arm."

"Walking? But where? With whom?"

"Down on California Street. She was alone."

"Alone? But why?"

"I don't know!" Nina shot back, her voice edged with pain. "We were having a dinner party. I thought she was upstairs, but she must have taken it in her foolish head to go out alone."

"Don't speak like that," he chided.

"But she *was* foolish. She always was. And now look where it got her!" Nina buried her face in her hands.

"Don't cry," he pleaded. "I just want to make some sense out of it all."

"There is no sense. Just tragedy . . . foolish youth and tragedy."

Jacob wiped a tear from his cheek. He waited until his mother calmed down, and then he ventured, "Surely she must have said where she was going. It's not like her to go out alone at night—and on foot."

"She was upset," Nina admitted, glancing over at Jacob. She started to speak again but thought better of it and looked back down at her hands.

"What was it? What was bothering her?" Jacob pressed.

"Just an argument . . . with Charles. He insisted she come down to the party and be civil to Carl Emrich."

"Father? That doesn't sound like him."

"But it sounds like *me*. Is that what you're saying?"

"Let's not argue, Nina," he protested. "I just want to know about Phoebe."

"There was a disagreement, she refused to come down, and then she ran off in the middle of the night without even putting on a coat. How do I know what was bothering her? She's dead—isn't that enough?"

Nina stood and dramatically draped an arm across her brow. "This talk has given me a headache." As she walked toward the door, she called back, "Stay as long as you wish, but I simply must lie down."

Jacob sat watching through the doorway as his mother crossed the foyer to the marble staircase and made her way upstairs. Looking down, he noticed that he was still holding the unlit cigar and had crushed it at the center, so he dropped it into an ashtray on the side table and stood to leave. At the front door he was met by the butler, who held out his coat for him.

"May I speak with you in confidence, Cameron?" Jacob asked, taking the coat.

"But of course, Mr. Salomon."

"You were here the night of my sister's accident?"

"Why, certainly."

"Did you see her leave?"

"I'm afraid I was attending to the guests at that time."

"Then you don't know what her mood was?"

"I do know that she was quite upset that evening. If I may speak openly . . ." He paused, and when Jacob nodded for him to proceed, he went on, "She had quite a row with her mother before the party."

"Just as I suspected. Do you know what it was about?"

"No. They were up in Phoebe's room. I only know that they argued because I could hear their voices down on the second floor."

"Thank you, Cameron."

"Shall I send the carriage around to take you home?"

"Not tonight. I feel like walking." Jacob started to put on his coat, then stopped and said, "On second thought, I'd like to visit Phoebe's room first."

Cameron nodded and took the coat from Jacob, who quickly mounted the stairs to the second floor, moving quietly so that he would not disturb his parents as he continued up to the third floor.

Entering Phoebe's room, Jacob stood looking around, wondering why he felt like an intruder. Nothing had been moved since the night of Phoebe's accident. Even her toiletries were still laid out at the dressing table, and several of the bottles were uncapped. Jacob lifted an open bottle of French perfume to his nose, and as he closed his eyes, he saw Phoebe standing before him, smiling and laughing in her timid yet alluring way. He picked up the glass stopper and pressed it into the neck of the bottle, then set the bottle back on the table.

Circling the room, Jacob stopped in front of one of the shelves and examined Phoebe's collection of porcelain dolls, each from a different country that one of the Salomons had visited. He gave a bittersweet smile as he thought of the delicate little geisha doll that had just made the return journey with him from Japan, wrapped ever so carefully in a cerulean silk scarf that he had chosen to match Phoebe's soft blue eyes.

Glancing across the room, Jacob saw Phoebe's diary on the writing desk beside her bed. The clasp was unlocked, and the small silver key rested next to it. Jacob recalled how jealously Phoebe had guarded that key when they were children, and he was surprised that she would have left the book unlocked with the key in plain sight. Perhaps it was because Phoebe had been distraught the night of her accident or because Rachel and Maurice were away. Yet it was not her siblings but Nina from whose prying eyes she protected it.

Jacob stood beside the desk and started to open the book. He hesitated, wondering if Phoebe would understand, and then he realized that a diary was a daily chronicle meant to cast light upon the true nature of a person's life. Surely Phoebe would want those truths to be understood now that she was gone, or else she would have kept them hidden within her thoughts and carried them to her grave.

Opening the book almost with an air of reverence, Jacob riffled the pages until he came to the final entry. As he began to read, his expression darkened, and he found himself reading more rapidly. He worked his way back in time, entry by entry, watching his sister's life unfold in reverse, sensing Phoebe's fear and frustration as she tried to figure out what was happening to her body. Flipping page after page, he finally came to the entry the previous autumn that made it undeniably clear who the father had been.

Jacob slammed shut the diary and let it slip through his fingers to the floor. He left it lying there as he turned and walked stiffly into the hall and down the stairs to his mother's room. Pounding on her door, he did not wait for a response but turned the knob and pushed his way in.

Nina was at her dressing table running a silver brush through her long brown hair when Jacob stormed into the room. "What—?" she started to say, catching her breath as she looked in the mirror and saw the expression in his eyes.

"I know," he said ominously.

"Whatever are you talking about?" She turned toward him on the seat.

"Phoebe was pregnant."

"Good God! Are you certain?"

"Don't play games with me!" he hissed, stalking around the bed toward her. "I read her diary. The last entry was just before she went out the night of the party—*after* she told you about her condition. That's what was bothering her, wasn't it? Not Carl Emrich. And not a *disagreement* with Father."

Nina stared up at him a long moment, then said in a cold, emotionless tone, "Yes, she was pregnant." She turned back toward the mirror and continued to brush her hair.

Stepping closer, Jacob grabbed hold of her wrist and locked it in place. "How could you?" he declared.

"How could I what?" She wrenched her hand free and dropped the brush onto the table.

"How could you be so cold to her?"

"What are you talking about?" she asked.

"I read the entry. You made her feel as if she had shamed the family."

"Well, she did! But I told her I'd take care of it. If she hadn't acted so rashly . . ."

"Then you know that, as well?" he asked. "She didn't fall in front of a cable car. She jumped!"

"You don't know that!"

"It doesn't take a genius to read her diary and know that she was suicidal. If only you had shown her some compassion instead of making her feel like a leper!"

"You're wrong," Nina seethed, her words sharp and grating. "You weren't there. I tried to help . . . and if she hadn't run off and pulled that stunt, I would have."

"I'll bet you would."

"What's that supposed to mean?" she demanded, standing to confront him.

"You'd have helped her get rid of the baby! Anything to make sure that no scandal touched the Salomon name."

"I was concerned about your sister—about her reputation."

"You were concerned about yourself!"

"Get out of here!" Nina flared, turning her back on her son. "Just get the hell out of here!"

"With pleasure!" He turned and strode from the room.

In the dressing-table mirror, Nina saw Jacob turn down the hallway. She stood there a moment, her hands clenched, her body trembling in anger. Then she snatched up the silver brush and ran out into the hall. Jacob was just starting down the stairs, and she raced over to the railing, waving the brush as she shouted, "Go ahead, blame me—like you always do! Or have you forgotten Eaton Hallinger?"

"He only got her pregnant. It took a mother to kill her!"

"You bastard!" she screamed, flinging the brush down the stairs at him. "Get the hell out!"

Jacob Salomon walked past his own unassuming, two-story town house and continued to California Street, where he stood on the sidewalk and watched the cable cars roll past, their bells clanging harshly as they neared each corner. They came in an unending, relentless stream, their speed and path unchanging, their fate in the hands of the operators who worked the levers that detached the cars from the continuously moving underground cable and set the brakes.

Any one of the cars that clattered past Jacob could be the vehicle of death, he realized. Perhaps the brakeman had not seen her standing there; perhaps she had jumped under the wheels at the last instant. Or could it really have been an accident, as Nina wanted everyone to believe?

Jacob knew that he had been cruel to his mother. He did not doubt that Nina had handled the entire situation poorly, but Phoebe should have been used to that by age nineteen. No, it was not their mother who drove her to take her own life. Nina was right; if anyone was to blame, it was the man who got Phoebe pregnant.

"Eaton Hallinger," Jacob muttered disdainfully as he turned away from the cable cars and headed down the street.

Jacob knew Abraham Hallinger's only son quite well. They had been in the same grade at school and had once considered themselves friends, though neither had ever dared bring the other boy home, so aware were they of the enmity that existed between their parents. But they had not been friends for many years. As far as Jacob was concerned, Eaton had never grown up, despite being a few months older than Jacob. In many ways Eaton reminded him of his own younger brother, Maurice, whose only passions in life seemed to be women, liquor, and horses. But Maurice was only twenty-one and might still mature. Eaton was nearly twenty-eight and showed no signs of reforming.

Jacob knew that Phoebe had found Eaton attractive in a dashing, irresponsible way, and he had assumed it was because of Eaton's similarity to Maurice, with whom she was particularly close. But Jacob had no inkling that things had gone farther than a few chance meetings and perhaps a dance or two at parties thrown by mutual acquaintances. It had come as quite a shock to read in Phoebe's diary that she and Eaton had met secretly on several occasions, the last of which had led to her unfortunate pregnancy.

That Eaton apparently had not known of Phoebe's condition did not excuse what he had done. Phoebe had been a gentle, delicate creature, a young woman who did not have the sophistication to ward off the advances of an experienced man such as Eaton Hallinger. It was clear from what she had written that she had neither planned nor expected what had taken place in the back of his carriage that day in Golden Gate Park. Neither could she have foreseen the tragic consequences that would ensue.

Jacob found himself wandering aimlessly along what was known as the "cocktail route"—a string of restaurants and clubs that were the heart of San Francisco night life. It was a place of loud music and raucous laughter where men such as Eaton Hallinger spent most of their evenings, boozing and carousing until all hours of the night. Following the route, Jacob passed many a club he once regularly patronized and still occasionally visited, when the emptiness of living alone grew too great a burden. Glancing through the windows, he recognized the manufactured smiles and dissipated expressions of the young revelers in their polished shoes and fine evening jackets. These were places populated by the respectable sons of privilege. Women on the premises cared little about respectability; they had come to earn money, not spend it.

Continuing up the street, Jacob halted in front of Les Grenouilles, a newly opened dinner club that had become the rage among the more affluent set. Only slightly more respectable than most of the other establishments along the cocktail route, here the patrons sat around tables set with fine linen and silver as they drank overpriced champagne or underaged wine and enjoyed a light repast of Terrapin à la Maryland or Frog Legs à la Poulette. A prime attraction was the huge glass tank in the window, which contained hundreds of live turtles and frogs, from which the patrons could choose their dinners.

Jacob was about to move on when he saw someone he recognized at one of the tables. It was another former schoolmate named Marcus Tasher, a thoroughly dissolute young man who was known to be a drinking companion of Eaton Hallinger's. Tasher was holding court at a table with three other men, and from the way he was waving his champagne glass and pontificating, Jacob guessed that he was already quite inebriated. Though he could not see the faces of all Tasher's companions, he could tell that Eaton Hallinger was not among them.

Jacob nearly walked on, but then almost without thinking he turned and opened the front door. As soon as he entered the restaurant, he heard Tasher's booming voice proclaiming, "Three times that night! And three different fillies! Each more eager than the last!" The young man tilted his glass and drained it in a gulp, then reached for the open bottle of champagne.

Jacob waved off the maître d'hôtel and headed for Marcus Tasher's table, uncertain of what he would say. The problem was solved by Tasher, who was just putting down the bottle when he saw Jacob approaching. His eyes widened, and then he grinned broadly and exclaimed, "Jacob Salomon! Back from the Orient already? Come join us, good fellow, and tell us all about those lovely geisha girls!"

The other three men turned to greet Jacob, who recognized two of them by sight but not name. As he nodded and forced a smile, he saw Tasher start to pull over a chair from another table, and he waved him off, saying, "I can't stay. I'm looking for Eaton Hallinger."

"Eaton?" Tasher asked. "Whatever for?"

"I've some business to discuss," Jacob replied in an undertone. "Have you seen him?"

"Not today. But surely business can wait until morning. The evening's just begun, so sit down and have a glass of champagne. I was just telling my friends about a party I attended at the Clinton Arms the other night."

Jacob's smile faded. "I'm sorry, but I'm not in the mood to drink."

Suddenly one of the other men leaned toward Tasher and whispered something. Tasher immediately slapped his hand on the table and said to Jacob, "Good God, man, I'd totally forgotten. I'm so sorry about your sister. That was such a tragedy."

"Yes," Jacob muttered, turning to leave.

"Shall I give Eaton a message if I see him?"

"No, that won't be necessary." Jacob started toward the door, then abruptly halted as it swung open and a tall, slender man with wavy blond hair and a pencil-thin mustache entered, his overcoat slung over his left arm, a derby in his right hand.

"Why, Jacob Salomon," the man said, smiling as he came over to where Jacob was standing. "I didn't know you were back." He shifted the hat to his left hand and held out his right to shake Jacob's. With a look of genuine concern, he said, "I was so sorry to hear about Phoebe. If there's anything I can do for you or your family . . ."

Just then Tasher stood and called, "Why, Eaton, you old fox. Jacob's come here looking for you."

"You did?" Eaton asked, lowering his hand when it became clear that Jacob was not about to shake it. "Whatever for?"

For a time Jacob just stood staring at the other man. Finally he said in a voice as thin as a reed, "I just wanted to see the man who murdered my sister."

Eaton's face went ashen with shock. Tilting his head slightly, he said, "Whatever are you talking about?"

"I'm talking about my sister Phoebe," Jacob replied, his voice slightly louder though still quiet enough so that others would not hear. "I'm talking about a man who took advantage of an innocent young girl—a girl who knew no other way out of her trouble than to take her own life."

"Phoebe? But I thought it was an acci—"

"I know what you thought," Jacob cut in, "but the truth is that you destroyed her honor and walked away without looking back. She didn't tell you she was pregnant because she wanted to protect you. . . . God knows why."

"Look, Jacob," Eaton said, raising one hand, "I don't know what's bothering you, but I had nothing to do with—"

"The hell you didn't!" Jacob blared, loud enough now to attract the attention of patrons at nearby tables. "You killed her, as surely as if you had stabbed her with a knife!"

"You're crazy, Jacob! I never took advantage of your sister," Eaton insisted indignantly. "And if she claimed otherwise, she was lying."

"You filthy bastard!" Jacob shouted, lunging forward and grabbing Eaton by the collar. Eaton dropped his coat and hat and tried to yank his collar free, but Jacob was far bigger and more burly, and he twisted the material cruelly as he swung Eaton around and forced him to his knees.

Eaton was choking and gasping for air as Tasher and his friends surrounded Jacob, taking hold of his arms and trying to wrest his grip from Eaton's neck. They dragged him back toward the front door, until finally his fingers slipped from Eaton's collar, and Eaton went sprawling against one of the chairs.

"Bastard!" Jacob yelled as he tried to pull himself free. But Tasher and the others crowded between him and Eaton, who was scrambling to his feet.

"You're crazy!" Eaton blurted as the other man forced Jacob toward the door. "Your whole family's crazy!"

"I'll see you in hell!" Jacob raved, pointing a finger at Eaton as he was pushed out into the street. "I'll damn well see you in hell!"

TWELVE

MAURICE FELT AS THOUGH HE WERE FLOATING SOMEWHERE among the clouds, unwilling to come down yet still tethered to the earth far below. He could see only blue sky and sun, and a part of him wanted to cut the line tugging gently from below and fly free into that warm, white light. But a gentle, soothing voice reached up to him, seducing him with the beauty of its song. He felt himself being drawn back, spinning ever so softly into and through that music, back toward the earth and away from the light. He heard his own voice rising in harmony, felt himself shudder with expectation and pleasure, saw his body lying so peacefully below, connected only by a faint silver cord. And as the cord retracted, he fell toward his body, into the fog, until the white light was but a memory, a dream.

"Maurice," the alluring voice called. "Do you hear me, Maurice?"

He felt something caressing his hand, and slowly the fog lifted and the image of a woman—a Madonna—came into focus hovering overhead, aglow in the flickering lamplight. Her face was delicate and thin, with high cheekbones and full, soft lips, set in a halo of long, silken brown hair. It was her eyes that captivated him, so cool and green, so open and filled with light.

Those emerald eyes reminded him of another woman, and in a hoarse whisper, he stammered, "R-R-Rachel . . . ?"

"No. My name is Merribelle."

As Maurice's head continued to clear, he remembered that he had been boarding a train somewhere. He tilted his head slightly and saw that he was in a white room with black curtains, and he wondered if he could still be at the station. He blinked, tried to focus, and saw a white table laid out with bottles of medicine. He tried to raise his hands but did not have the strength. When he looked down at them, he noticed that both wrists were heavily wrapped in gauze. And then he became conscious of the cloying chemical smell, and he knew for certain that he was in a hospital.

"What h-happened?" he asked weakly.

"Don't you remember?" the woman asked.

Maurice shook his head. "Who are you?"

"Merribelle Knowles, but everyone calls me Belle. I'm a nurse." The young woman's voice had a lilting beauty that for a moment Maurice could not place, but then he realized that she spoke with the hint of a Southern accent.

"What happened?" He tried to lift his head off the pillow, but Belle quickly placed a comforting hand on his forehead and eased him back down.

"You must rest, Maurice. You lost a considerable amount of blood."

"But how? What hap—?" He swallowed the words, and his eyes opened wide as he remembered the train, the berth in the sleeping car, the straight razor. "My God," he muttered. "What have I done?"

"It's all right, Maurice," Belle soothed, stroking his forehead. "You are going to be fine."

"Rachel?" he asked abruptly, looking toward the closed door.

"She's sleeping in the next room; it's the middle of the night. I'll go get her."

"Wait," Maurice said as she started to rise from her chair beside the bed.

"What is it?" She reached out and touched his shoulder.

"Could you . . . could you just hold my hand for a moment? I . . . I'm not ready yet."

She smiled so genuinely that Maurice felt a flood of warmth course through him. And when she picked up his left hand and held it between her two hands, a shiver ran through him, and he thought he would start to cry.

"Everything's going to be all right," she whispered. "You'll see."

Maurice blinked back the tears, his lips quivering as he said, "I don't know if I can face her—after what I did."

"She's your sister. She loves you."

"She'll never be able to forgive me."

"She already has. She only worries that you won't forgive yourself. That you'll . . ."

"Try it again?" he asked, and she looked down. "Perhaps everyone would be better off—"

"Don't talk like that," she cut him off, squeezing his hand. "You've been given a gift—a second chance. You can't squander it in self-pity."

Maurice sighed. "You just don't understand." He closed his eyes and turned away.

"Maybe I do . . . better than you think."

"How can you? You don't know anything about me."

"But I understand self-pity." Letting go of his hand, she touched his cheek, turning his face toward her. "I know the depths to which it can bring a person." She raised her left sleeve and held her wrist out for him to see a wide, jagged scar. "And I know that it can be battled and overcome."

He looked from the scar on her wrist to Belle's warm, compassionate eyes, and suddenly he began to cry, slowly at first, then building in intensity. He tried to turn his face away, but she held it in place, caressing his forehead and cheeks.

"It's all right," she murmured. "You'll see. Everything will be fine."

"I . . . I'm s-so embarrassed," Maurice sobbed. "I've been such a f-fool."

"And so have I." Belle gave a short, deprecating laugh. "Good Lord, so have I. So have we all. It's what we make out of our foolishness that's the measure of a man."

"I'm no man . . . just an idiot. I deserve to die."

"And you will. I promise you. But not before your time."

"My time was back there on that train," he declared, his tone hardening.

"No it wasn't, Maurice," she replied firmly.

"How do you know?" he asked, looking back at her.

"Because you're here. Because you're alive."

"I'm not sure I want to be."

"At least that's a start," she told him.

"What do you mean?"

"You're not sure about living, whereas yesterday you were certain that you wanted to die. Give yourself time, Maurice. Just give yourself a bit of time." She stood and looked down at him. "Are you ready to see your sister? She's been very worried about you."

Maurice drew in a deep breath. Letting it out, he gave Belle a faint smile and nodded. She grinned back at him, and as she turned to leave, he said, "Thanks for sitting with me, Merribelle."

"My friends call me Belle," she reminded him, and then she walked over to the door and disappeared outside.

"Belle . . ." he called softly after her, turning his face against the pillow and closing his eyes.

A few minutes later, Rachel sat down in the chair beside the bed and kissed her brother's cheek. As he opened his eyes, she smiled. "I was afraid I'd lose you."

"I . . . I'm so sorry," he said, his voice quavering, his eyes fluttering open and closed.

"Shhh . . ."

She touched a finger to his lips, but he moved his head and went on, "I've been such a fool. And what happened to you . . . I can never—"

"It wasn't your fault. We won't speak of it again."

"But I have to. If it weren't for the irresponsible way I've been carrying on, none of this would have happened."

205

"That's all past," she told him. "What matters now is the future—getting you better and getting back home."

"Where are we?" he asked abruptly, raising his head slightly and looking around.

"We're still in New York—in Albany."

He leaned against the pillow, his eyes closing as the fatigue washed over him. "They know, don't they?" He sighed.

"Who?"

"Our family."

"No, Maurice. I haven't told them. I just sent a telegram saying that I'd taken ill again and that we had to get off the train in Albany. I didn't tell them where we are, so no one will bother us. You can rest, and when you're feeling up to it, we'll continue home."

"Home . . ." His eyes opened halfway, and he said, "I'm going to change. You'll see."

She patted his hand lovingly.

"I'm going to try, Rachel."

"I know you will," she replied. "Now get some rest."

His eyes closed, and he smiled. The smile faded as he drifted back to sleep.

"I know you'll try," she whispered as a tear ran down her cheek.

"Aye, ye may come aboard!" Finley Orcutt shouted as the harbor cruiser approached his fishing boat.

The cruiser was a sleek, steam-powered vessel, manned by several officers of the Boston harbor police. As it pulled alongside, a gangplank was lowered to the deck of the fishing boat, and two of the officers came across.

Near the stern of the fishing boat, Aidan McAuliffe stood coiling some rope, trying his best to appear nonchalant. Beside him, Finley's young deckhand gave Aidan a nod of encouragement.

"Your business in Boston?" the older officer said.

"Been lobsterin'." Finley crossed to one of the hatches just behind the bridge and lifted it to show the catch of lobsters in the hold.

"And you've come all the way to Boston?" the other man asked as he looked down into the hold. "Why not Halifax?"

"Ye'll be seein' more of us the next few days," Finley said, his voice calm and casual. "The Halifax price has been cut in half, and we'll be bringin' them to the mainland until they let it rise again."

As the younger officer closed the hatch, his senior partner said, "We'll need to check your papers."

Finley already had them out, and he handed over his ship's registry and his maritime identification papers. Meanwhile the younger officer walked over to where the two crewmen were standing and held out his hand for their papers. When they handed them over, he read both and started to return them, but then he held back and looked more closely at Aidan's. Squinting at it slightly, he brought it to the other officer.

"This name sound familiar?" he asked, showing him Aidan's identification.

"Aidan Orcutt," the older man read. "Why, yes." He nodded toward Finley. "This fellow's name is Orcutt, too."

"He's me son," Finley declared with pride.

"No," the young officer said. "Aidan . . . it sounds familiar."

"Of course." The senior officer reached into his pocket and pulled out a small pad. Flipping through the notes he had jotted down, he found the one he was looking for and read, "Aidan McAuliffe—a convict from England. New York traced him to Halifax, but he's left there and is said to be on the way to New Brunswick." The two officers turned and stared at Aidan, who put down the rope he had been coiling and smiled.

"Aidan!" Finley called. "Come on over here."

As Aidan approached, the senior officer scanned Aidan's maritime papers and noted that he was about the right age and pretty well matched the physical description.

"I dinna know about no English convict," Finley said with a grin. "This here is me own Aidan Orcutt—a Cape Breton Scotsman through and through—and some day master o' this vessel."

Putting on a thick brogue, Aidan said, " 'Tis a pleasure t'meet ye.'' He touched his woolen sailor's cap and nodded.

The officer glanced at the papers again. "It says that you're from Bay St. Lawrence. I think I've been there."

"Ye'd remember it if ye had," Aidan told him. " 'Tis at the northern tip o' Cape Breton and kinna be reached too well by land. There's a narrow inlet, tricky when the waves are up, which leads into a sheltered harbor—as round and gentle as a lake."

"Yes, I was there once as a merchant sailor." The man smiled at the memory. "Beautiful country. Rugged but magnificent."

"Aye, tha' it is," Finley put in. "But a wee bit isolated for most folks . . . though not for me and me lad."

"It has to be in your blood, I suppose." He turned to his younger partner. "We'd best get going. These men have work to do." When the other man looked at him uncertainly, he added, "There are plenty of Aidans in Nova Scotia—Great Britain, too. But I doubt an English convict could ever find his way to Bay St. Lawrence." He grinned at Finley.

"I hope ye get your man," Finley told them.

The officer shrugged his shoulders. "It's not really our concern. Apparently he's on land in New Brunswick. It's one for the Canadian police, now."

The officers walked over to the gangplank. As the younger one started up to the cruiser, the other man turned back to Finley and asked, "How long will you be ashore?"

"We'll be catchin' the mornin' tide."

The man nodded. "Enjoy your stay in America."

"Aye, tha' we will." He wrapped his arm around Aidan's shoulder, and they stood watching as the officers crossed to their own ship and the gangplank was raised. As soon as the harbor cruiser pulled away, Finley clapped Aidan on the back and said, "Ye make a fine Scotsman, me lad."

"I *am* Scottish, remember? Born in Edinburgh."

"Aye, but raised in too many o' them fancy schools. They've beaten the brogue out o' ye."

Aidan chuckled. "I've heard some of the thickest brogues on people who've never set foot in Scotland."

Finley shook his head disapprovingly. "Some day, me lad, ye'll learn tha' Scotland is not a place but a state o' mind!" He headed back to the wheel and nodded for his young assistant to set the sail. "But enough o' tha'," he called to Aidan as he steered the boat into the inner harbor and headed toward the docks at the Boston waterfront. "Right now 'tis not the right state o' mind we've got t'get ye into, but the state o' Massachusetts!"

An hour later, Finley Orcutt docked the boat at T Wharf beside the Boston Fish Bureau, one of the largest fish markets in the entire United States. It took another hour for the lobsters to be unloaded and weighed and for Finley to be paid for the catch. Then, holding forth a portion of the receipts, he walked over to the foot of the wharf, where Aidan was standing with his suitcase at his feet.

"No," Aidan said emphatically, raising a palm.

"But ye earned it."

"I was working my passage." He patted his pocket. "And I have plenty, thanks to the generosity of friends."

"Aye, a friend is worth his weight in gold." Finley pocketed all of the money but one bill, which he pressed into Aidan's hand. "Now I'll hear nothin' more about it," he declared. " 'Tis for ye t'take tha' friend o' yours out to the finest restaurant when ye reach San Francisco."

"You knew I was going there?"

"But o' course. There's nothin' for ye in Boston; ye may as well go west." He placed a hand on Aidan's forearm. "But keep an eye over your shoulder, me friend. If they tracked ye t'Halifax, they might make the connection to your friend in San Francisco."

"Don't worry, Finley. I'll be careful." He shook the older man's hand.

"Aye, and there's somethin' else I have for ye, I'd almost forgotten." He reached into the big outer pocket of his jacket and pulled out a book, which he handed to Aidan.

"The *I Ching*?" Aidan said, looking down at it.

"Then ye remember the title?—'cause ye sure as hell kinna

read it.'' He chuckled as he nodded toward the Chinese ideograms on the cover of the book.

"But why are you giving it to me?"

" 'Twas a gift t'me a long time ago, but I kinna read a word of it, either. But wi' all the Chinese in San Francisco, it may do ye a lot more good than me.''

"I shouldn't—"

"Go on, keep it. Never turn down a gift given in friendship.''

Aidan looked into Finley's sincere gray eyes and smiled. "Thank you. I'll treasure it always.''

"Just until ye see fit t'pass it along to someone who can make better use of it than ye.''

Again the two men shook hands.

"So ye be off to the train depot, I suppose?" Finley asked.

"Yes."

"Then may the saints guide ye . . . and may the sinners never know when ye pass!''

"Thank you, Finley. And I want you to thank Scott and Cayleigh for all their kindnesses.''

"Tha' I will.''

"And tell Cayleigh I had a wonderful time in Cape Breton.''

Finley saw Aidan's bittersweet smile, and he nodded but remained silent.

"I suppose I'd best be off," Aidan finally said. "I hope we meet again someday.''

"And a brighter day 'twill be," Finley replied. "Ye can count on that.''

Aidan picked up his suitcase and headed up the street, which was busy with fishermen and merchants, boys pushing carts of produce, women carrying sacks of goods they had purchased. Reaching the corner of Atlantic Avenue, Aidan turned to look back. He raised his hand to wave but saw that Finley had already climbed aboard the boat and was busy working on the lines.

"Good-bye, Finley," he intoned. Then he turned and disappeared into the crowd.

* * *

Maurice Salomon still felt quite unsteady as he and his sister boarded a train in Albany to continue their journey to San Francisco four days after his near-fatal suicide attempt. Entering their private compartment, he slumped down onto the cushioned bench and pouted at his sister, who took the seat opposite him. "You didn't have to hire a nurse for me," he grumped.

"You're still quite weak, and there's the possibility of infection."

"I'm not a baby."

"The doctor didn't want to release you so soon. He agreed only on the condition that a nurse accompany us."

"I don't want to have to sit and make small talk with some old—"

"You haven't even met her yet."

"I don't like nurses."

"You seemed to like that Miss Knowles."

"She was different—not the usual nurse at all."

"And just what is the usual nurse?"

"An old lady with thick hands, foul breath, and a face that would stagger a horse. Why do you think people get better at hospitals? Anything to get away from those nurses."

"Is that what you think of us?" came a soft, feminine voice, and Maurice turned in shock to see Merribelle Knowles standing in the open doorway, dressed in an elegant blue traveling outfit with a lace-trimmed parasol in hand.

"What are you doing here?" he asked in surprise as his sister giggled across the aisle.

"I've come to see if there are any horses that need staggering." She arched her eyebrows, then smiled. "I'm the nurse who's accompanying you to San Francisco."

"You? But . . ."

"Is there a problem? Aren't my hands thick enough? And I've been chewing garlic all morning to make my breath properly foul."

"I . . . I didn't mean . . ."

The two women burst into laughter. Entering the compartment, Belle sat down beside Maurice. "It's all right. I also heard you say that I'm not the usual nurse."

"I should say not," Maurice agreed, feigning a frown. "But I never said whether you were better or worse."

"That all depends upon the patient," Belle declared.

The coach gave a gentle lurch, and the train started out of the station. "I'll be glad to leave Albany behind," Rachel said as the train picked up speed.

"I'm afraid you didn't see our city under the best of circumstances."

"You're not originally from Albany, are you?" Rachel asked.

Belle smiled. "My accent gives me away, I suppose. My family lives in Louisville, Kentucky."

"That's thoroughbred country." Maurice's expression brightened; he took no note of his sister's disapproving frown.

"My family has raised racing horses for three generations. My grandfather owned Connie's Folly, and my father's first horse was Painted Wind."

"Painted Wind? Didn't he set a record for the mile and a half?"

"It held for ten years."

"And what brought you to Albany?" Rachel asked in an attempt to turn the subject away from horse racing.

"I wanted to be a nurse."

"But surely there are hospitals in Kentucky."

Belle stared into the distance, as if remembering a distant sorrow. As she spoke, she rubbed her left wrist, which was covered by the long sleeve of her blue dress. "My parents had a different future in mind for me. I'm afraid I didn't live up to their expectations."

It was Maurice, seeing the pain in her eyes, who now changed the subject. "Have you ever been to San Francisco?"

"No, but I've always wanted to visit California."

"Will you have to turn right around and go back to Albany?"

"Your sister has been kind enough to offer a week's hotel stay in addition to the train fare."

Maurice smiled at Rachel. "I thought that's what we give

the *usual* nurses. Surely in this case we should be offering two weeks.''

Rachel started to speak, but Belle cut in, saying, ''That's really quite generous, but I don't think my employers would appreciate my taking off so much time.''

''We'll just have to make sure you see all the sights within a week, won't we, Rachel?''

''The respectable ones, at least,'' she replied.

''But of course,'' Maurice agreed, grinning mischievously. ''We'll leave the unrespectable ones for your next visit.''

Seeing the way Maurice and Belle were looking at each other, Rachel stood and said, ''I think I'll go down to the dining car and examine their dinner menu.''

''Would you like me to go with you?'' Belle asked, but Rachel waved off her offer.

''The doctor would want you to stay with the patient. He looks a little pale.'' She opened the door, saying casually as she walked out, ''I may be a while. I hear they have an observation car.''

''Take your time,'' Maurice assured her with a surreptitious smile. ''We'll be all right.''

''I'm certain you will,'' Rachel replied, closing the door and heading down the aisle.

During the next couple of days, Rachel became a frequent visitor to the dining and observation cars as she found numerous excuses to leave Belle and her brother alone in the private compartment. Rachel was quite taken with Belle, whose inner strength and deep compassion belied her somewhat fragile Southern exterior. And Belle was certainly having a remarkable effect on Maurice. He seemed genuinely smitten with the young woman from Louisville, and Rachel could not remember that ever having happened before.

On the afternoon that the train was crossing Nebraska, Maurice and Belle sat alone across from each other as she changed the bandages on his wrists. Finishing, she put her supplies into her medical bag and turned to watch the sweep of the high plains as the flat prairie land began to buckle and rise into the foothills of the Rocky Mountains. She was about to comment on the beauty of the scenery when she noticed that Maurice was staring at her rather than out the window. She blushed slightly as their eyes met and locked.

"It was very nice of you to agree to this journey," he said to put her at ease.

"It really was my pleasure. When Rachel asked me to accompany you, I jumped at the chance. As I said, I've always wanted to see San Francisco, and . . ." Her voice trailed off.

"Yes?"

"And I like you . . . both of you."

"You don't really know me," Maurice commented, his smile fading somewhat.

"I know enough to see that you're a good person. Quite entertaining, as well—and witty."

He grinned. "I think Rachel would say that I'm a little too entertaining for my own good. Look where it's got me." He held up his hands, and the sleeves fell back enough to reveal the gauze bandages.

"What happened to you has nothing to do with being entertaining. It comes from self-pity, plain and simple."

"I'm not so sure about that. I'd say it comes from self-doubt."

"There really isn't that much difference between the two. Self-pity is when you react to your doubts in a negative way."

"And how does one react positively?" he asked.

"By doing something about it. By taking action."

He stared down at his wrists. "I took action."

"Against yourself. That's not what I mean. You have to stop dwelling on missed opportunities and start seizing new ones."

"But it seems that whenever I try to seize an opportunity, I fail, and that just adds to the doubts."

"Give me an example," she requested.

"Our business, for instance. I'm not very good with numbers—and my mother says that I haven't the backbone to close a business deal to our advantage. I'm afraid that whenever I try to get more deeply involved, it ends up costing us money.

That's why my father's been grooming my brother to take over.''

"Isn't your brother older?"

"Yes. Jacob's twenty-seven."

"And you're twenty-one, right?" she asked, and he nodded. "And what was Jacob doing when he was twenty-one?"

"Oh, I don't know. Let's see—I was about fifteen." Maurice scratched his head, then chuckled. "Actually, I remember what happened on his twenty-first birthday. My parents had planned a small surprise party—just us and a few family friends. Jacob had no idea what was going on and figured he'd been forgotten. Well, the guests had arrived, and we were all waiting for him to come home when a cabbie drove up with a note from Jacob saying that he was working late at the store. Nina sent my father to get him, and Father let me go along." He laughed somewhat louder.

"What happened?" Belle asked eagerly.

"Father and I arrived at the store to discover that Jacob had invited a couple of dozen of his friends and thrown his own party, complete with music and dancing girls—and plenty of champagne."

"Oh, dear," she said with a giggle. "What did your father do?"

"He sent the carriage back with a note for Nina saying that there was a serious problem at the store and that regrettably we would be detained. When we finally made it home, my mother's guests had departed and she was furious. Of course, the situation wasn't helped by the fact that the three of us were drunk." He glanced out the window. "Nina didn't speak to Father—to any of us—for a week. But it was worth it—and Father told Nina as much. That's one of the only times I remember him standing up to her."

"You make your mother sound awful."

"No, she isn't. She's just very strong-willed. Sort of like my brother, Jacob."

"He doesn't sound that different from you."

"Believe me, he is. He's got my mother's backbone—and business sense. I'm afraid I've got too much of my father."

"You have both of your parents within you, Maurice. And

215

you can learn to draw upon both: your father's compassion, your mother's strength of will."

"Right now I'm afraid I've got my father's weakness and my mother's lack of sense."

"I don't think so," she said flatly. "You're only twenty-one. Look what Jacob was doing when he was your age. I don't see you throwing any wild parties for yourself."

"How do you know?" he asked, his tone somber. "I've had my share of parties. They may have been on a smaller scale, but they've been just as wild." Again he raised his wrists. "Too wild, perhaps."

Belle leaned across the aisle and took hold of his hands. "Again you're dwelling on the past."

"How can I avoid it?"

"By concentrating on the present—and looking forward."

"To what?"

"That's up to you." She turned his hands over so that the wrists faced upward. "It's up to you whether you learn and grow from this experience or are doomed to repeat it."

"You . . . you just don't understand." His voice quavered. "You don't know what goes on inside of me. If you ever really took a deep look inside, you might be disgusted by what you found."

"I'd find a lonely young man searching for a way to obliterate the pain."

"But you don't know the things I've done—"

"It doesn't matter," she assured him. "What matters are the things you are going to do."

"Like what?"

"What do you want to do?" She let go of his hands.

"I'm not sure. I'd kind of like to give the store another try. I've never been good with the ledgers, but I enjoyed working with the employees and customers."

"Then maybe you should start working regularly at Salomon's Emporium."

"If my parents will let me. And my brother's always thought me a bit irresponsible."

Belle grinned. "You'll just have to remind him of his twenty-first birthday party."

"Are you kidding? He swears it never happened."

"Oh, I'm sure he remembers it more fondly than you'd think. Just prove to him that your twenty-first birthday is over and you're ready to go to work."

"But how?"

"By taking action. By rolling up your sleeves and getting down to business."

When she mentioned his sleeves, he looked down at his wrists and frowned. "I'm not sure I have it in me. If I roll up my sleeves, it'll just prove what an ass I've been."

"I think you're wrong, Maurice. I think you can do anything to which you set your mind." Again taking his hands, she gently touched the bandages covering his wrists. "As far as I'm concerned, you succeeded that day in killing Maurice Salomon—the old Maurice Salomon. Now it's up to you who the new Maurice will be."

Maurice gripped Belle's hands and sat looking into her eyes. Sliding forward, he dropped to one knee in front of her and began to kiss the palms of her hands gently. She took hold of his face and turned it upward, and their lips met in a delicate kiss.

"Merribelle," he whispered as their lips parted. "I know this sounds foolish, but . . . would you marry me?"

"M-Marry . . . ?" Her voice cracked, and her eyes widened with surprise. "But . . . but we've only just met."

He looked down. "It was crazy of me to ask, but—"

"It's not crazy—it's flattering." She turned his head and cradled it in her lap. "But you hardly know me."

"I know who you are," he said, staring up into her green eyes again. "I don't need to know about your past."

"Yes, but . . . marriage. I don't know what to say. It's so sudden."

"I'm sorry." He forced a smile as he rose from the floor and returned to his seat. "It was wrong of me to speak so forwardly. Please forgive me. We'll pretend I wasn't serious."

"There's nothing to forgive, Maurice. I'm honored that you would ask me to be your wife, and I take your proposal quite seriously. But I have to think about it—and we have to get to know each other better." She stood and pointed at the seat beside him. "Is anyone occupying that seat?" she asked coyly.

"Why, no," he replied, standing and offering his hand.

As they sat down together, Belle slipped her arm through Maurice's and took hold of his hand. "Thank you, Maurice," she whispered. "No one has ever asked me to marry him before."

"They're fools," he declared.

"But I thought you said that you're the foolish one."

"I would be if I let you slip away." He turned toward Belle, and again they kissed, this time longer and fuller.

Just outside the compartment, Rachel stood in the aisle, her hand hovering over the doorknob as she watched them through the glass. With a smile and a sigh, she lowered her hand and tiptoed away.

THIRTEEN

UPON ARRIVING AT OAKLAND, JUST ACROSS THE BAY FROM San Francisco, Rachel Salomon left her brother and Belle Knowles in the lobby of the train station and entered the Western Union office. She approached the counter and waited until the elderly clerk finished jotting some notes in a ledger. After a moment the man looked up, saw her standing there, and said, "Can I be of service, ma'am?"

"I'd like to send a telegram to Halifax, Nova Scotia."

The man placed a slip of paper and a pencil on the counter. "I'll be glad to write it down, if you'd like."

"Thank you. It's to Scott Cabot. That's *C-a-b-o-t*," she spelled. "The address is the Cabot Export Company on Barrington Street. I'd like the telegram to say: Arrived home safely. Thank you for your kindnesses. Is our mutual friend still visiting? Give my regards and invite him to visit me in San Francisco." She waited until he had finished jotting down the message, and then she concluded, "Please sign it Rachel Salomon," and gave her return address.

"I'll send this off at once," he assured her. After consulting a chart on the counter, he glanced up at the wall clock.

"It's four hours later in Nova Scotia. That would make it just after seven at night. If you wish to pay an additional fee, I can arrange for a special night delivery. Otherwise it will be delivered first thing in the morning."

"The morning will be fine," she told him. She paid for the telegram, then returned to the lobby and walked over to where Maurice and Belle were standing.

"Our bags are already being loaded aboard a carriage," Maurice explained as his sister came over.

"We'd better hurry then," she said, and the three of them turned and headed from the station.

Maurice led the women to the carriage that would take them to the ferry slips. The vehicle was little more than a two-horse buckboard wagon, with three rows of hard benches and an open bed in the back for luggage. Painted in red on the side panels were the words *Ferry to San Francisco*.

Maurice checked to make sure that all of their bags had been secured in the back, and then he helped the women up into the vacant rear seat. Two other couples already occupied the middle seat, and a pair of gentlemen were seated beside the driver. As soon as everyone was aboard and had paid the twenty-cent fare, the driver released the brake, picked up the reins, and slapped the horses into motion.

It took nearly fifteen minutes for the journey from the center of town to the steel-trestle piers that had been built onto the bay to handle the almost unending stream of ferryboats that plowed the waters between San Francisco and the East Bay communities. The *Glencoe,* a two-story, flat-bottomed steamer, was taking on passengers, and the carriage rode out onto the pier and deposited its passengers at the ticket gate beside the vessel. For an additional ten cents, the driver took care of loading the bags aboard the ship, while Maurice purchased three fares at twenty-five cents apiece.

At precisely three-thirty the ship left the pier and began the fifteen-minute ride across the bay. Maurice and the two women spent the entire journey at the front rail of the upper deck so that Belle could enjoy her first real look at San Francisco. The city comprised forty-seven square miles of the northern tip of a peninsula that marked the western edge of the bay. A similar peninsula jutted down from the north, and the mile-wide channel between the two was known as the Golden Gate, the entrance to San Francisco Bay.

San Francisco had an impressive skyline, made up in large part of one- and two-story buildings that were given added height by the numerous hills—seven by some counts, forty-two by others, depending on how one defined a hill. The largest such hill, Mount Davidson, was just over nine hundred feet high, while the deepest "valley" was at the corner of Fifth and Berry streets, almost six feet below sea level. As the boat approached the Ferry Building at the foot of Market Street, Belle was better able to discern the varying levels of the land.

"There are some three hundred thousand people jammed onto those hills," Maurice commented as they pulled toward one of the ferry slips. "Germans, Irish, Spanish, Chinese, Japanese. We've got them all. A few Americans, as well."

"Indians, you mean?" Belle asked.

Maurice shook his head and smiled. "In San Francisco, an American is anyone who speaks English without an accent."

"What are those buildings up there?" Belle pointed well beyond the Ferry Building to a pair of particularly tall structures that towered above the rest of the buildings on Market Street.

"Why, those are San Francisco's first skyscrapers," Rachel said enthusiastically, using the term that had been growing increasingly popular during the previous decade.

"The eighteen-story one with the pointed roof is the *Call* Building," Maurice explained. "It's the tallest building in the city and is just two years old. Across the street is the *Chronicle* Building. It's only eleven stories high but was built four years earlier."

"Competitive journalism," Rachel commented with a smile.

"And why not?" Maurice asked. "Wasn't it when the Emporium began making plans to open on Market Street that Nina insisted we construct our new building first?"

"The Emporium?" Belle looked somewhat confused. "I thought *your* store was the Emporium."

Maurice grinned. "There was a time when almost every corner store in San Francisco was an emporium. But there's a new store called simply the Emporium that opened only last month in a seven-story building downtown, and already it looks to be one of our chief competitors. When they chose the single name Emporium, Father wanted to fight them in court, but Nina would hear nothing of it. She thinks Emporium makes them sound like a common five-and-dime, whereas Salomon's Emporium is an establishment for finer clientele. It really shouldn't create much of a problem, since most everyone refers to us simply as Salomon's."

"In fact," Rachel put in, "my brother Jacob urged that we drop the word Emporium when we moved into our new building last fall."

"Why didn't you?"

"Nina, of course," Maurice replied with a sneer.

"She didn't want to change the name her father had created," Rachel added.

"We'd best get downstairs," Maurice said as the boat pulled into one of the slips at the Ferry Building. "There's a lot of construction; it may be slow disembarking."

"What is all that?" Belle asked, nodding toward the men and machinery at work all around the building.

"They've broken ground for the new Ferry Building," Maurice explained. "It will be twice as big and will even be able to unload boats from both decks at once."

"And it will become just as obsolete as this one if they ever build a bridge across the bay," Rachel commented.

"That's just a pipe dream," Maurice said. "Such a bridge would have to be seven or eight miles long."

"One day it will happen," Rachel insisted. "Mark my words."

"Impossible."

Maurice turned from the rail and held out his arms. As each woman slipped a hand through one, he led the way across the deck toward the stairway. By the time they reached the main deck, the boat was fully berthed and the gate was open. Walking ashore, they followed the crowd into the long, low-roofed building, where they would pick up their baggage and hire a carriage to take them home.

The Ferry Building was little more than a cavernous garage fronted by a bank of twelve open bay doors, through which cable cars and carriages entered to pick up or unload passengers. Departing passengers purchased tickets at a long row of ticket booths and passed through turnstiles to the ferry boarding area, while passengers just arriving from Oakland were ushered through a bank of one-way gates to the turntable platforms, where the cable cars reversed direction for the return trip up Market Street.

Entering the building, Maurice led the women to the baggage counter, where their travel bags would be brought from the boat. As Maurice handed in his baggage stubs and arranged for a porter to load them aboard a coach for hire, Belle stood gaping in amazement at the unceasing activity all around them. Most of the other passengers from their boat had already gone through the gates and were gathering around the various cable cars, each a brightly painted red or green with the name of the line lettered across the top. The cars were lined up on the turntables just inside the eight left-hand bay doors. A double track led up to each turntable, which allowed the car to be rotated from the entering left-hand track to the departing right-hand one. Most of the cars were already loading passengers, while a few were still being rotated.

"The new building will handle twice as much traffic," Maurice said with pride as he came up beside Belle.

"It's a wonder anyone finds his way home," she marveled.

"We'll have no problem there. We'll be taking one of those." He pointed toward the four bays to the right, which served private carriages, as well as the numerous cabs and coaches for hire. "We'll be going just as soon as the porter has all our bags."

Belle glanced toward the baggage counter and saw a young man in a red uniform loading their luggage onto a low cart, which could be pulled through the gates to where the carriages were lined up.

Rachel came over and touched Belle's arm. "Maurice and I would like you to come to our home for dinner before we arrange for your hotel room."

"But I couldn't impose like that. Your mother isn't expecting me, and—"

"There's always enough for an extra guest," Rachel insisted. "And Nina would never forgive us if we didn't invite you."

"If you're certain . . . ."

"Then it's decided," Rachel proclaimed.

Belle looked at Maurice, who smiled and nodded. Looking back at Rachel, she said, "I'd be honored."

"Rachel!" a voice suddenly called through the crowd. "Maurice!"

All three of them turned to see a husky, bearded man in a gray suit and bowler hat pushing through one of the turnstiles and hurrying toward them.

"Jacob!" Rachel gasped in surprise. She raced toward him.

Maurice quickly turned to the porter, who was just finishing loading the baggage, and said, "Wait here a moment." Then he took Belle's arm and led her toward where Rachel and Jacob were hugging each other. "It's my older brother," he explained as they approached.

"Maurice!" Jacob said with a broad grin as the two men clasped hands and then embraced. "You look . . . thinner. But great."

"You've lost some weight yourself," Maurice commented, stepping back to examine his older brother's slightly trimmer form. "Didn't Japanese food agree with you?"

"Raw fish? Give me a Delmonico steak anytime." He looked at Belle and smiled, then glanced back at his brother, waiting for an introduction.

"Jacob, I'd like you to meet a friend of ours, Merribelle Knowles." Turning to Belle, Maurice continued, "Belle, this is my brother, Jacob Salomon."

Jacob took Belle's hand, raised it slightly, and said, "Delighted to meet you, Miss Knowles."

"Belle is visiting San Francisco for the first time," Rachel put in, not mentioning that she had been hired as a nurse, since it had been agreed among the three of them that nothing would be said of Maurice's suicide attempt. "She comes from Louisville, Kentucky."

"Beautiful country," Jacob remarked.

"You've been there?" Belle asked.

"On my way to Washington three years ago I had the pleasure of visiting the bluegrass country and took in the derby at Churchill Downs. My horse, alas, came in fourth."

"You should have bet on one of her father's horses," Maurice told him.

"Perhaps next time." He tipped his hat slightly toward Belle. When he turned back to his sister and brother, his expression was more somber. "I knew the time your train was due to arrive and took a guess what ferry you'd catch. I've a carriage waiting, so if your baggage is ready . . ."

Maurice motioned for the porter to follow as Jacob turned and led them toward the gate nearest where his carriage was parked.

Sensing a note of concern in her older brother's voice, Rachel slipped her arm through Jacob's and asked, "Is something wrong? Is it Father?"

Jacob feigned a smile. "We can talk on the way home." He glanced back at Maurice, who was escorting Belle. "Perhaps we can drop Miss Knowles at her hotel on the way."

"Belle will be joining us at dinner," Maurice said quickly, his tone cutting off any chance of debate.

"That will be delightful," Jacob said, his words somewhat hollow.

"There *is* something wrong," Rachel whispered as they passed through the gate and approached the family's large phaeton, parked along the circular drive that connected the four open bays. "Has Father . . . ?"

"His condition hasn't changed. We'll . . . we'll discuss it in the carriage."

As they came up to the phaeton, which had its leather top raised, the coachman hopped down and helped the porter stow the luggage under the driver's seat and in the small boot at the rear. Meanwhile, Jacob opened the door and assisted the women as they stepped up into the coach. There were

225

two facing benches, with a leather canopy that rose from the back of each seat and connected in the middle. At the front was a raised open-air seat for the driver, who in rainy weather could attach a smaller canopy.

As soon as the luggage was loaded and the passengers seated, the coachman climbed aboard and started the two-horse team at a brisk walk up Market Street. Belle took a brief look through the window at the bustle of activity along San Francisco's wide, main thoroughfare, but she knew that there would be time enough to see the sights of the city, and so she sat back in the seat beside Maurice, trying to be as inconspicuous as possible as Jacob began to speak.

"I . . . I'm afraid I have . . . sad news," Jacob began, stumbling over the words. "You had already left New York when I returned home to discover that Nina telegraphed you only about Father. I was going to have the railroad pass along a message, but then I learned that Rachel's illness forced you to spend a few days in Albany."

Maurice gave Rachel an uncomfortable look, but neither said anything to correct the story.

"I didn't want to upset you when you were still recovering," Jacob continued.

"My health is back," she reassured him, taking hold of his hand. "What is it, Jacob?"

He looked down and muttered, "It's Phoebe. She . . . I'm afraid she has died."

Rachel gasped, and her hands started shaking. Across the aisle, Maurice stiffened and turned white, as if he had been slapped across the face. Belle, realizing that Jacob was talking about Maurice's younger sister, placed a comforting hand on the back of Maurice's and found it as cold as ice.

"D-Dead?" Maurice stammered. "That's impossible."

"There was an accident," Jacob explained. "She was struck by a cable car, which mangled her arm. Infection set in, and she died."

"I . . . I don't . . ." Rachel tried to speak, but the words caught in her throat. Beside her, Jacob slipped his arm around her shoulder and held her close.

"But when did it happen?" Maurice asked numbly. "Did you see her?"

"I was still at sea. The accident was the day before Father's heart attack, but she died a week or so later."

"Was it news of the accident that led to Father's attack?" Rachel asked haltingly.

"Nina says yes—that Father just couldn't bear the shock. I . . . I myself am not so certain."

"But why?"

"There was more going on. Phoebe was . . ." He hesitated, as if uncertain of how much to say.

"What is it?" Maurice said firmly, leaning forward across the aisle.

Jacob looked into his younger brother's eyes. He tightened his jaw, then took a deep breath and went on, "Phoebe was pregnant."

"Oh, my God," Rachel muttered.

"I read her diary. It seems she told Nina the very night of the accident, and Nina didn't take it well."

"Are you sure it was an accident?" Maurice asked.

Looking down, Jacob slowly shook his head. "I don't believe it was. I think Phoebe jumped—" The words cut off with a choke.

They rode in silence for a while, Rachel crying softly as she rested her head against her older brother's shoulder, Belle holding Maurice's hand. After a time, Jacob began to speak again, describing as calmly as possible the events of the previous week since his return from the Orient. He told of reading the diary and confronting Nina and then coming upon Eaton Hallinger and getting into a fight. He was just concluding with a description of their father's deteriorating condition when the carriage pulled into the circular drive of the Salomon's Nob Hill home.

"There's no point in making a scene with Nina," he cautioned as they prepared to climb out of the carriage. "She may have handled things poorly, but she was all alone and did the best she knew how. I think she's genuinely devastated by everything that's happened."

Maurice and Rachel indicated that they understood, and

then the four of them climbed down and approached the front door. They were met by Cameron, who was understandably subdued in his greeting as he ushered them inside to meet with Nina, who already had been informed of their arrival.

The woman who made her entrance down the grand marble staircase would have been the picture of devastation had it not been for the obvious fastidiousness with which she had prepared for the role. Her silk dressing gown, trailing along the stairs as she descended, was so dramatic in its flared cut and style that it would have been more appropriate at a dinner party. It was a shimmering green, just dark enough to be appropriate for mourning, and was tight enough at the waist and bosom to accentuate her still-youthful figure. Her hair was up in a bun, with a single lock left hanging far too perfectly at her neck, as if she was too distracted to realize it had fallen. And her makeup had been put on with just the right heavy touch to give the impression that she was trying to mask the despair of a woman whose daughter had died and whose husband hovered at the brink.

As she reached the bottom of the stairs and approached across the foyer, it was apparent to Maurice and Rachel that Nina's period of true mourning had come to an end, replaced by the period of receiving condolence calls from sympathetic friends and admirers.

"Oh, Rachel, dear," she cried as she opened her arms to her eldest daughter. "It's been such a trial. I'm so glad you are home. And you, Maurice," she added, embracing her son and accepting his kiss on the cheek. Glancing over his shoulder, she saw the tall, slender brunette standing just inside the front doorway and said in a hushed tone, "And who is this?"

Smiling, Maurice held out an arm toward Belle, who cautiously approached. "This is a friend—Merribelle Knowles. Belle, this is my mother, Nina Salomon."

"Mrs. Salomon," Belle said as she gave a slight curtsy.

Nina eyed Belle suspiciously, then nodded and said, "A pleasure to meet you." Turning to her son, she forced a smile. "You didn't say you were bringing a friend."

Rachel came over beside Belle and said, "Belle was such

a help to me doing the journey, what with my illness and all. She certainly speeded my recovery.''

Nina seemed to relax slightly, and her smile grew more genuine. "I'm so glad you were of assistance to my daughter. Certainly you'll stay for dinner?''

"If it isn't an imposition," Belle replied.

"Of course not. You are a friend of my *daughter*." She emphasized the word, as if wanting to keep as much distance between the stranger and her youngest son as possible.

"How is Father?" Maurice asked, looking up the stairs.

Nina sighed. "He's resting, though it's becoming hard to tell the difference between rest and sleep.''

"I want to see him." Maurice turned to Jacob. "Perhaps you could entertain Belle in the parlor?''

"You can tell me all about Louisville and your father's Thoroughbreds, Miss Knowles," Jacob suggested as he offered Belle his arm.

Hearing the mention of the famous Louisville horse country, Nina eyed Belle more closely and seemed to notice for the first time that the young woman was dressed in the finest traveling outfit and appeared to be of a genteel nature. Her smile began to warm as the young Southern woman took Jacob's arm and started across the foyer to the parlor.

"We'll be down shortly," Rachel told Nina as she and Maurice started toward the stairs.

Nina raised an arm at them. "Please don't tire your father. The doctor says he cannot withstand another shock.''

Rachel nodded, then followed her brother up to the second floor.

The door to Charles's room was open, and Maurice and Rachel stood in the doorway a moment watching as he breathed shallowly, his head propped up on a couple of pillows, his eyes closed. Rachel approached first, coming alongside the bed and touching her father's hand. His eyelids opened at once and began to flutter slightly as she whispered his name and leaned over him so that he could see her face.

"I'm home," she told him. "I love you, Father." She bent down and kissed his cheek. His lips began to quiver, as if he wanted to speak but no sound would come.

"Maurice is with me," Rachel went on, backing slightly and motioning for her brother.

As Maurice came over, his eyes began to mist at the sight of his father lying there so helplessly. "I'm sorry, Father," he said as he sat on the edge of the bed and took Charles's hand. "I should have been here for you."

"It's all right," Rachel told him, touching her brother's arm. "There's nothing you could have done."

"I should have been here," he repeated, looking up at his sister. "But I never have been. Not really . . . not for anyone but myself." The tears started to course down his cheek, as he leaned over his father and their eyes met. "But I'll be here from now on, Father. I promise."

Maurice began to sob softly, and he raised his father's hand and held it to his cheek.

"I'll make up for everything I've done in the past. You'll see." He pressed his father's hand against his lips and lowered his head until it was resting on his father's chest. "I'll make you proud of me. I promise."

Rachel stepped closer and placed one hand on her brother's back, the other against her father's cheek. Charles lay there motionless on the bed, looking up at her, his eyes filling with tears.

FOURTEEN

"WHICH WAY IS SACKVILLE STREET?" THE WELL-DRESSED man in the gray bowler and trim black mustache asked one of the dockmen toting crates off the big passenger steamer that had just arrived in Halifax from England.

The dockman pointed toward the buildings that lined the harbor. "That there's Water Street," he said, indicating the road that ran alongside the docks. "Take it left, and it's the third street on the right."

"Thank you," the man said. Walking away, he reached into the vest pocket of his gray suit and removed a gold pocket watch. He pressed the catch on the side, and the engraved case popped open. Reminding himself that he still had to adjust the watch for local time, he calculated the difference between Atlantic and Greenwich time and determined that it was just after eleven on the morning of the eighteenth of June.

As the young man was about to close the case, he glanced at the inscription from his father: To Jeremy Mayhew on his twenty-first birthday. *Eleven years ago,* he thought, then

231

frowned. *Eleven years, thousands of miles, and a pair of London murders ago.*

Jeremy walked off the dock to where another man stood waiting at the edge of Water Street. This second man did not wear a hat and was dressed in a far more simple, brown wool coat. He appeared to be a good ten years older and was at least half a foot taller and far stockier.

"I took care o' the bags," Nate Gilchrist said when Jeremy Mayhew came up. "Yers 'ave been transferred to the *Shorecrest,* which sets sail at noon. Mine'll be put aboard the *Morgan,* followin' yers later tonight."

"Good," Jeremy replied. "We'll meet as planned at the hotel in Boston. I'd better get going."

"Shall I wait 'ere?" Gilchrist asked.

"Yes." He looked around and saw a small eatery across Water Street. "Have a cup of coffee or something over there. I'll get you when I'm finished."

The big man nodded and turned to cross the street. Stopping, he looked back and said, "Take care o' yerself."

"Don't worry."

Jeremy turned away and headed up Water Street. As he passed the brick and stone buildings that housed numerous small shops and businesses, he pulled a pad from his jacket pocket and flipped it open. The final few pages contained the notes he had made from the police reports his father had been receiving regularly from Scotland Yard. He found the entry regarding Aidan McAuliffe's possible escape to Halifax and double-checked the name and address of the man the local police had questioned. The man was Scott Cabot, owner of a small export company in an alley near the corner of Sackville and Barrington streets.

Looking up, Jeremy saw Sackville Street just ahead, and he quickened his pace. He turned left at the corner and started up the hill. Glancing at his pad, he saw that this Scott Cabot had briefly boarded the *Vigilant* to meet with a business associate named Rachel Salomon, who was a passenger aboard the ship. According to the police, McAuliffe had swum ashore and befriended Cabot. He had even worked for Cabot for a few days, but there had been a falling out, and McAuliffe had left Halifax by land. That had been a few days before the police traced him to Cabot, who apparently had known nothing of his real identity.

After placing Cabot's home and office under surveillance for a time and turning up no sign of the fugitive, the police had accepted Cabot's story. However, Jeremy's father, Gordon Mayhew, was far from convinced that this Scott Cabot fellow had no idea where to find McAuliffe, so Jeremy and Nate Gilchrist had been sent to pay a call on him and use whatever means necessary to extract the truth.

Jeremy tapped the pad against the palm of his hand, then stuffed it back in his pocket. Clenching his jaw with determination, he reminded himself that he had but a short time to learn the whereabouts of Aidan McAuliffe before his boat was due to sail for Boston. If he failed to get the information peaceably, it would be left to Nate Gilchrist to obtain it whatever way he could. If that were to happen, at least Jeremy would be well at sea already and would not come under suspicion—especially since he and Gilchrist had booked separate cabins on the steamer from England and had avoided any contact with each other during the voyage. Unfortunately, Gilchrist might have a trickier time leaving Halifax. He was paid well to take such risks, however.

At the top of the hill, Jeremy came to Barrington Street, the main thoroughfare through the Halifax business district, and stood at the corner looking around for an alley. Just to the left he saw a gap between the buildings halfway to the next corner, so he turned that way and soon found himself in a small alley between a pair of three-story brick buildings. Fifty feet in on the right was a door over which hung the sign for Cabot Export.

Coming up to the door, Jeremy rapped several times and thought he heard a voice calling for him to enter. Turning the knob, he opened the door and stepped into the large single room that was Cabot Export. A half-length counter separated the entryway from the rest of the room, which consisted of little more than a desk and walls of wooden filing cabinets. A young, fair-haired man with wire-rimmed glasses was seated at the desk, and he stood and approached the counter as Jeremy entered.

"Can I help you?" Scott asked, raising his eyebrows slightly and smiling.

"Are you Mr. Cabot?"

"Scott Cabot. Yes."

Adopting an authoritative tone, Jeremy said, "My name is Adler. I'm with the London Metropolitan Police." He reached into his pocket and pulled out a small billfold, which he flipped open on top of the counter. Inside was an impressive-looking identification card for one Detective Kenneth Adler of Scotland Yard, the detective division of the metropolitan police.

"Is something wrong?" Scott asked a bit nervously.

"We're following through on the Aidan McAuliffe investigation. The Canadian authorities reported that the escaped convict spent some time with you in Halifax."

"Yes, that's true. But I haven't seen him for a couple of weeks. I already gave a full report to the police."

"We realize that. But I'm afraid we have some problems with your story. In the report, nowhere does it mention the reason you and McAuliffe had a falling out."

"It . . . it was just a difference in personalities," Scott replied hesitantly. "He was far too brash for me."

"But a man on the run doesn't have the luxury of making enemies of people who help him along the way. Was it something more? He stole money from you, perhaps?"

"Nothing like that. We just didn't get along."

"But why leave a comfortable arrangement like this?" Jeremy waved his hand, indicating the office. "It couldn't be that you're covering up for him? Perhaps you know where he's gone, and—"

"Detective Adler," Scott cut in abrasively. "I don't like your insinuations. This isn't England; I think you should take up your questions with the local police."

"I didn't mean to offend you, Mr. Cabot, but we have to follow every angle. You can appreciate that we're concerned with capturing this murderer. To be honest, the Halifax police just doesn't have the stake in this case that we do."

"I wish I could help you, but I've already given a full report. I've nothing more to add." Scott started to turn from the counter.

"Just a minute, Mr. Cabot," Jeremy called, and Scott stopped and looked back at him. Adopting a friendly smile, he said, "Perhaps you could give me the actual dates he worked for you. It wasn't listed in the report."

Scott stared at him a moment, then shrugged his shoulders and said, "I suppose so. I'll have to look it up." He headed back to his desk and sat down.

As Scott rummaged through his desk drawer, Jeremy came around the open left side of the counter and approached. Scott paid him no attention as he took out a small ledger and opened it to verify the dates in question.

"I'll write down the dates," Scott said, taking up a pen and dipping it into the open inkwell.

Jeremy stood at the corner of the desk, trying to read the ledger upside down. It contained a series of dated entries, but Jeremy would have to examine it closer to see if it gave any clue as to Aidan McAuliffe's current whereabouts. Hunching his shoulders in frustration, he frowned. Likely he would have to let Nate Gilchrist return and ransack the place. Jeremy only hoped that Gilchrist could do it without creating any more casualties.

Jeremy had about given up hope of learning anything useful when a piece of paper caught his eye: a Western Union telegram. It was atop a pile of other papers beside Scott's left arm, and Jeremy had to come around the desk slightly and crane his neck to make out the message.

"There you are," Scott said a moment later, putting down his pen and holding up a piece of paper on which he had written the dates Aidan McAuliffe had spent in Halifax.

"Why, thank you," Jeremy replied, quickly looking away from the telegram and taking the paper from Scott.

"Will that be all?" Scott asked, standing.

"Yes. Thank you." With a perfunctory nod, Jeremy turned and headed from the office.

Standing outside with his back to the office door, Jeremy glanced down at the piece of paper and stuffed it in his pocket.

Paul Block

It was of little use to him, he realized. The telegram was another story, however. Jeremy had been able to read enough of it to know that it was from Rachel Salomon in San Francisco and that it was about a "mutual friend" who was visiting Scott Cabot—a person who undoubtedly was the very man Jeremy Mayhew was seeking.

Jeremy walked back along Barrington Street and turned down Sackville. As he returned to the docks, he smiled with satisfaction, convinced that at last he knew where he would find the man who murdered his sister. Indeed Aidan McAuliffe had left Halifax, probably with Scott Cabot's assistance, and now was likely on his way to seek refuge with the person who had helped him stow away aboard the *Vigilant* in the first place: Rachel Salomon of San Francisco.

Jeremy found Nate Gilchrist waiting outside the café, and the two men wandered over to a secluded spot between a pair of buildings.

" 'Tis almost time f'yer ship t'leave," Gilchrist commented, nodding toward the waterfront across the street.

"Don't worry. You know where to meet me in Boston?"

"Aye. I'll be there. But what about that Scott Cabot fellow?"

"You can forget about him," Jeremy said with obvious relief.

"He give you what y'wanted?" Gilchrist asked in surprise.

"Not exactly. He wouldn't say anything. But I saw a telegram there that gave me a good idea that we can find our man in San Francisco."

"All the way t'California?"

"We can take a train from Boston. That's not a problem, is it?"

"No," Gilchrist replied emphatically. "But I'd 'oped it'd end 'ere in 'alifax."

"I'm afraid we've got one more journey to make. I'll see you in Boston as planned."

"I'll be there."

"Right," Jeremy concluded, turning to leave.

"Are y'sure y'don't want me t'do somethin' about that Cabot fellow?"

"There's no need. I got what I need."

Gilchrist nodded and stood in the small alleyway between the buildings watching as Jeremy Mayhew crossed the street, glanced back once, and headed down along the docks to where the *Shorecrest* was taking on passengers for the run to Boston. Then he stepped out from between the buildings and headed back to the café, where he sat down at one of the curbside tables and ordered a cup of black coffee. When the strong brew arrived, he sat sipping it slowly, all the while watching the dock where the *Shorecrest* was preparing to depart.

Two cups of coffee later, the ship finally gave three sharp blasts of its steam whistle and began to pull away from its berth. Gilchrist waited until it passed from sight beyond the wharfside buildings and headed out through the harbor toward the Atlantic Ocean, and then he paid for his coffee and left the café.

Though the afternoon was warm, Gilchrist pulled up the collar of his brown coat as he walked along Water Street. Pausing at the corner of Sackville Street, he looked around to satisfy himself that no one was paying any attention to him, and then he turned right and walked briskly to the corner of Barrington Street. If the information Jeremy Mayhew had been given was correct, Cabot Export could be found in an alley near this very corner, and sure enough, he spied just such an alley a short distance to the left.

A few moments later, Nate Gilchrist found himself standing in front of Cabot Export. For a second he thought of Jeremy's admonition to forget about Scott Cabot, then rejected it just as quickly. Gilchrist was being paid good money to protect Gordon Mayhew's only son. Surely if this Scott Cabot had any sense and was in league with Aidan McAuliffe, he would guess what Jeremy had been up to and would pass the word along to McAuliffe in San Francisco. That would put McAuliffe on alert and make Jeremy and Gilchrist's job all the more difficult and dangerous. No, it was a foolish, weak-hearted idea to leave this Scott Cabot fellow alive—a mistake that Gilchrist would correct without Jeremy Mayhew ever being the wiser.

Without knocking, Gilchrist pushed open the door and entered the office of Cabot Export. As he closed the door behind him and looked across the counter at the slight, bespectacled man, Gilchrist slipped his hands behind his back and surreptitiously turned the latch above the knob, locking the door.

"Good day," the man at the desk said, rising and approaching the counter.

"I'm lookin' f'Scott Cabot," Gilchrist said, moving away from the door.

"At your service."

"We're startin' a new ferry line across the harbor, and the owners sent me t'do some business with you."

Extending his hand, Scott started around the open side of the counter, saying, "Pleased to meet you, Mr. . . . ?"

"Just call me the ferryman," Gilchrist said with an icy smile.

Meeting Scott beside the counter, Gilchrist reached out and grasped his hand. Locking it in a viselike grip, Gilchrist drew back his left hand and without warning threw a brutal punch into Scott's lower belly, doubling him over. Choking and gasping for air, Scott was so taken by surprise that he made no effort to protect himself as the huge stranger brought up his right knee, connecting solidly with Scott's nose. Scott was thrown back off his feet, blood spurting from his nostrils as he landed on his back.

Gilchrist leaned over the far-smaller man, took hold of his shirtfront with his left hand, and hauled him off the floor as easily as if he were hoisting a rag doll. Scott shook his head to clear it, then grabbed the big man's left wrist and twisted it in an ineffectual attempt to free himself. But Gilchrist merely gripped the shirt tighter as he swung a haymaker with his right hand, which caught Scott on the jaw and snapped his head back. His eyes rolled back, and his arms fell limp at his sides. He was unable to protect himself as Gilchrist followed with a series of vicious jabs to the belly, which knocked the remaining wind out of him. Gilchrist gave a final backhanded blow across Scott's face, then released his shirt and let him fall. His head banged against the side of the counter as he went down, and he was unconscious before he hit the floor.

Gilchrist glanced around the office. He would take the place apart before he left—both to make it look like a robbery and on the chance that he might turn up additional evidence regarding Aidan McAuliffe. But first he would finish with this Cabot fellow.

Crossing to the window beside the front door, Gilchrist reached up and pulled down the shade so that no one could see into the office. Then he returned to where Scott was lying and stooped down, straddling his limp form as he wrapped his long, beefy fingers around the smaller man's neck. Slowly and painstakingly, he began to squeeze, choking off the air supply. Scott gave no resistance, his face turning blue as Gilchrist increased the pressure.

Something rattled behind Gilchrist, and he gave a start, momentarily relaxing his grip on Scott's throat. There was the sound of knocking followed by more rattling, and he shot a glance over his shoulder to see that someone was trying the doorknob. But it was locked; surely whoever was outside would think the office was closed for lunch and would soon go away.

Disregarding the rattling of the doorknob, Gilchrist tightened his grip and bore down on Scott. He did not notice the metallic rasp of the lock being turned by a key and was unaware that the door was being opened and closed until a woman called out, "Why'd you lock the door, Scott? I brought lunch—"

The words cut off abruptly, and Gilchrist spun around to see a petite, attractive woman with dark-brown hair standing against the closed door, a lunch basket hanging from her arm, her mouth open wide as she stared at the two figures on the floor. He guessed that it was Scott Cabot's wife—a woman listed in the police report as Cayleigh.

For a moment Cayleigh did not seem to realize what was happening, but then she took a step forward and gasped, "Scott!" Before she could react to the situation, the huge man leaped off her husband and lunged at her. Instinctively she raised the basket to protect herself, but the man merely reached over it and slapped her full force across the face, throwing her against the door.

''You fool!'' he blurted as he came at her again, grabbing hold of the basket to toss it aside.

Cayleigh held tight to the basket hanging from her arm but could feel it slipping from her grasp. As she tried to keep him from yanking it away, she slipped her right hand under the cloth that covered the contents and groped inside.

With a sudden, violent twist, the huge man wrenched the basket from her hands and threw it across the room. ''Bitch!'' he snarled as he came at her, his hands raised. He glimpsed only the briefest flash of metal near his waist as he wrapped his fingers around her delicate neck. And then, as he began to squeeze, he felt a sharp stab of pain at his belly, a fire that ran up through his chest and down his arms, causing his fingers to stiffen and go numb. He tried to squeeze more tightly, but his fingers seemed nerveless, and they opened of their own accord. He found himself staggering backward, and it was only then that he saw the long kitchen knife in her right hand, its ten-inch blade dripping with blood.

Gilchrist stumbled back against the counter and tried to reach his hands up to his belly. He was gasping for air as he tilted his head down and saw the gash in his coat, the blood already seeping through the wool and dripping onto the floor. He looked up at the woman, who stood immobile against the door with the bloody knife in her hand. Forcing up his arms, he took a faltering step toward her, then a second and a third, and then everything began to swirl around him and he went falling to the floor.

For several moments Cayleigh stood over the huge man's motionless body. Slowly the realization set in that he was dead—that she had killed him. She stared down at the knife in her hand and wanted to cry or scream, but no sound would come. All at once she remembered her husband, who was lying on his back on the floor beside the counter. Letting the knife slip from her fingers, she raced across the room and knelt beside him.

Scott's face was covered with huge welts and bruises and was blue from the loss of oxygen. His eyes were open but had rolled back until they were almost completely white. His chest did not move, and when Cayleigh placed her cheek close to his lips, she could not feel him breathing.

"Scott!" she cried, grabbing hold of his chest and shaking him. "Scott, don't leave me! I love you, Scott. I love you!" She sobbed as she called his name over and over and continued to shake him. The tears ran down her cheeks, and she wiped them with her hands, then took hold of his face and began to pat him, calling his name, begging him to breathe . . . to awaken . . . to live. Finally she leaned close and lifted his head up off the floor, pressing it against her chest. "Don't let him die!" she wailed, her tears coursing down her cheeks. "Oh, dear God, give me a second chance! Don't let him die!"

Suddenly she felt Scott's body spasm, and with a deathly moan, he sucked in a great gasp of air, his body jerking and convulsing as it struggled to breathe. He gave another gurgling gasp and then began to sputter and choke.

With a cry of joy, Cayleigh moved closer to him and tenderly lowered his head and cradled it on her lap. He choked a few more more times and then started breathing more regularly. His eyes closed, and his head lolled from side to side. He was still unconscious—but alive.

"Oh, Scott!" she cried, leaning forward and kissing his cheeks as she sobbed and held him tight. "I love you, Scott. Oh, God, please let me love you!"

FIFTEEN

THREE DAYS AFTER ARRIVING HOME, RACHEL SALOMON WAS
seated beside her father's bed, reading him the Saturday, June
20, edition of the *San Francisco Chronicle* by the afternoon
light that spilled through the half-closed curtains. She did not
know whether he understood what she was saying, but she
noticed that whenever she read to him, his breathing grew
slightly deeper and more calm. Still, despite the long hours
she had spent with him during the past few days, his breathing seemed to be growing increasingly short and raspy, and
he was beginning to develop a dry, hacking cough.

"Would you like me to read you an article about young
Charley Fair's return from France? It says he's brought back
one of those new horseless carriages—a Panhard, it is called—
and some sort of a bicycle with a motor on it called a motorcycle. He tried to take the Panhard for a spin in Golden
Gate Park, but the police told him there's already an ordinance on the books banning automobiles from the park as a
public nuisance." She looked up and shook her head. "Or-
dinances already," she marveled, "and with fewer than a
dozen automobiles in the entire city."

Rachel skimmed some more of the article and laughed lightly. "It seems Charley got the best of those officers in the end. When they refused to let him enter the park, he drove home and returned on his motorcycle. The officers were forced to admit that the ordinance says nothing about motorcycles, and they had to stand aside and let him pass."

Rachel read silently for a moment, then suddenly exclaimed, "Oh, dear—can you imagine that?" She lowered the newspaper slightly and looked over at her father. "It says right here that Mrs. C. C. Moore was seen driving her husband's automobile the other day. They call it a scandal, but I quite like the idea. What would you say if I tried my hand at it?"

"Miss Rachel?" a voice called gently from the hall, and she turned to see the butler standing in the doorway.

"What is it, Cameron?" she asked.

"There's someone on the telephone for you."

"For me?" she asked in surprise. A telephone call itself was a rare occurrence, since only a handful of homes and businesses in San Francisco as yet had telephone service; that the call was for Rachel was even more unusual.

"The gentleman did not give his name but would say only that he met you aboard ship."

"Thank you, Cameron," she told him, masking the excitement in her voice as she turned and said, "I'll be right back, Father."

Rachel felt her heart racing as she folded the paper onto the bedstand and hurried from the room. She went down to the first floor, where the single telephone in the house hung on a wall in the pantry just off the kitchen. Racing through the kitchen and into the small room, she snatched up the earpiece, which had been left hanging by the cord, and quickly adjusted the mouthpiece to her height.

"Hello," she said breathlessly into the mouthpiece. "Is someone there?"

"Rachel Salomon?" a crackling voice asked.

"This is she. Who's calling?"

"It's Aidan," the voice replied, and Rachel's racing heart stopped for an instant.

"Aidan? Is that you?" she asked in disbelief, then without awaiting an answer, she continued, "Where are you calling from?"

"The Hotel Willard—at Golden Gate Park."

Rachel was stunned into silence. When she did not reply, Aidan added, "I'm here in San Francisco, Rachel."

"S-San Francisco! But you sound so far away."

"Too far," he agreed. "I would have called on you in person, but I wanted to let you know I was in town first—in case it isn't wise for me to come to your home."

"Not at all. But stay right there. I'll be over in a few minutes."

"You really don't have to. I can take a cab—"

"I want to," she insisted. "Don't go anywhere, all right?"

"I'll be in the lobby," he told her. "It's at the corner of Fulton Street and Willard North."

"Yes, I know. Good-bye, Aidan."

"Good-bye," he replied.

Rachel hung up the phone and raced out into the foyer, where she almost barreled into Cameron, who was just coming down from her father's room. "My green shawl," she told him breathlessly as she rushed up the stairs. "And have Michael bring 'round the carriage," she called down to him as she gained the first landing and continued to the second floor.

Racing into her father's room and approaching his bed, she said breathlessly, "The most wonderful thing has happened, Father. A friend has come to call on me—"

"What friend?" a voice snapped sharply from behind her, and Rachel spun around to see her mother standing in the shadows beside the bureau.

"I—I didn't see you there," Rachel said in surprise.

"I came to look in on Charles while you were downstairs." Nina took a few steps toward the bed, bringing her more fully into the thin light from the curtained windows. She was dressed in a blue satin dressing robe, and her hair was down and somewhat disheveled, as if she had been napping. "Now what is this about a friend?"

"A gentleman I met aboard ship," she explained, carefully choosing her words.

"A man? What man?"

"Just a gentleman from Halifax." She started toward the door. "I really must go. I'm picking him up at the Hotel Willard, and I'll bring him here to meet you." Without looking directly at Nina, she hurried past her out into the hall.

"The Willard?" Nina exclaimed, her voice dripping with disapproval. "That isn't at all our sort of place." She followed into the hall and saw that Rachel was already descending the stairs. She strode over to the railing overlooking the foyer and said sharply, "You haven't told me his name."

"I'll be back in an hour or so to introduce you," Rachel called up to her mother as she reached the foyer, snatched her shawl from Cameron's waiting hand, and pulled open the front door.

"But I'm not dressed for visitors, and your father—" Her words were cut off by the sound of the front door slamming shut.

"Oh, dear," Nina muttered, shaking her head in dismay. She turned and slowly walked back to her husband's room, where he lay motionless, his breath a rasping wheeze as his lungs struggled for air. Entering only a few feet into the room, she crossed her arms and looked over at the bed. "I don't like this, Charles," she complained. "Not one bit."

"Please wait here, Michael," Rachel told the young coachman as the open-topped phaeton pulled up alongside Golden Gate Park in front of the Hotel Willard, an imposing two-story black house fronted by a portico with four massive gold columns.

The Willard, which looked like a cross between a wealthy man's mansion and a notorious madam's bordello, was an unconventional though respectable establishment run by a colorful matron named Josephine Jeffries. A onetime opera diva, Josephine had retired from the stage to this home, bequeathed to her by a wealthy former lover. Unwilling to settle into quiet obscurity, she had turned it into the Hotel Willard, an inn of sorts that catered to San Francisco's bohemian community. Singers, artists, and writers alike were drawn to the Willard by its moderate prices and by Josephine's reputation as a flamboyant eccentric who loved to regale her dinner guests with famous arias and who thought nothing of spending her own money to promote the careers of friends she considered particularly talented and worthy.

As Rachel stepped down from the phaeton and walked up the short walkway to the hotel, she wondered how Aidan had heard of the Willard. She could only guess that he had been told of it by some fellow traveler who recommended it as a moderately priced, welcome refuge for strangers to the city. But however he had stumbled upon the Hotel Willard, Rachel had to admit that it was the ideal place for someone like Aidan, who could remain inconspicuous among the unusual types who frequented the lodging.

Rachel had just begun to reach for the bell when the door swung open to reveal a short, voluptuous woman with graying brown hair who was dressed to the hilt in a sleek black gown that shimmered with strings of tiny maroon beads. As she gave Rachel a cursory examination, her soft brown eyes sparkled, making her seem far more youthful than her fifty-odd years.

"You must be Rachel," the woman exclaimed, taking her visitor by the arm and leading her across the front hallway and into the parlor, which served as the hotel lobby. "I am Josephine Jeffries, and this"—she dramatically swept her arm through the air—"is your good friend Aidan."

As Josephine stepped back, Rachel looked across the parlor to see Aidan McAuliffe standing beside one of the easy chairs. He was dressed in a particularly smart-looking gray suit with thin black stripes—a style that was becoming the rage among the more fashion-conscious young men, who had begun to refer to it as a "pinstriped" suit.

"Aidan . . ." Rachel's jaw dropped as she gaped at him. "You . . . you look wonderful."

"He looks delicious, doesn't he?" Josephine declared as she stepped toward Aidan and motioned him closer. "That suit was inadvertently left here by an actor friend of mine when he returned to Paris. He and Aidan are a perfect match, and he would have been mortified had I not insisted Aidan make use of it until he returns." As Aidan cautiously approached, Josephine slipped over to him and took his arm, drawing him closer to Rachel. "You must admit, Aidan, that the London outfit you were wearing is a bit dated."

"You look beautiful," Aidan said softly as he came up in front of Rachel.

"That she does," Josephine put in. "So tall and stunning. And such beautiful copper hair."

Rachel smiled demurely at the older woman.

"Ah, but here I am going on about nothing, while you young people would far prefer to be left alone. And so you shall be." Letting go of Aidan's arm, she backed away. "But if you should desire anything at all, please don't hesitate . . ." She turned and disappeared through the front hall.

"Rachel," Aidan whispered, taking hold of her hands. "I've missed you." He raised her left hand with his right and gave it a gentle kiss. Still holding her hand close to his lips, he smiled and said, "I see you've misplaced your wedding ring."

"Oh . . . I . . ." she stammered, looking disconcerted.

She was about to explain further, but Aidan shook his head slightly and said, "It's all right. I already know."

"I'm sorry," she apologized. "I should have told you on the boat."

"Ah, but then you would have found yourself at the mercy of a crazed stowaway who might have stopped at nothing to get what he desired."

"Is that a promise?" she asked, closing her eyes as she leaned toward him. Their first kiss was tentative and delicate, but then they kissed again, slowly and with more feeling. Pulling away at last, Rachel asked in concern, "Is everything all right? I didn't expect to see you so—"

"Everything's fine. I'll tell you all about it over dinner."

"I want to bring you to my house first. On the way you can tell me about Nova Scotia and how you got here."

Rachel led Aidan out to the carriage and asked Michael to drive through the edge of Golden Gate Park before heading for home. As soon as she and Aidan were aboard, Michael snapped the reins and started the carriage west along Fulton Street. At the next corner, Arguello Street, he turned left into Golden Gate Park and followed the winding path to the right, bringing the carriage to the main east-west road through the park. Here he turned the horses left and drove past the beautiful glass Conservatory, a Victorian-style botanical greenhouse that was a replica of the one at Kew Gardens near London.

The carriage headed east through Golden Gate Park and out along the Panhandle, a one-block-wide, eight-block-long swath of grass and trees connected to the eastern edge of the park. As they drove alongside the Panhandle, Aidan told Rachel of his stay in Nova Scotia and how Cayleigh Cabot's father-in-law provided his son's papers and helped Aidan escape to Boston. Rachel described her own journey to San Francisco, confiding in him about her brother's suicide attempt but saying nothing of being attacked by Damien Picard. Similarly, Aidan made no mention of his brief affair with Cayleigh.

After leaving the Panhandle and continuing down Fell Street, the carriage turned left onto the broad boulevard of Market Street. At the corner of Leavenworth Street, the driver prepared to turn left and head up toward Nob Hill, but Rachel tapped the back of his seat and said, "Please take us down Dupont Street to Broadway."

"Are you certain, ma'am?" Michael asked with a hint of trepidation.

"Yes, Michael." Leaning closer to Aidan, she said, "I want to show you Chinatown."

Aidan sat back in his seat and watched the world change before him as the phaeton covered the final few blocks of Market Street and turned north onto Dupont—a street so infamous in reputation that eventually the city fathers would deem it judicious to change the name to Grant Avenue.

Even as they started up the hill toward the district known as Chinatown, Aidan saw dramatic evidence that they had entered an area considered far from respectable by the white community. At the outskirts of the Chinese district, in the block between Bush and Pine streets, were half a dozen shooting galleries, luring young men in search of adventure and marking the entrance to the carnivallike world that lay beyond. Barkers stood at the entrances, urging passersby to enter their establishments and enjoy the pleasures of shooting at moving figures or trying a hand at one of the numerous games of chance.

The block beyond the shooting galleries was little more than a row of buildings with windows half shuttered, from which gaudily painted, scantily dressed white women leaned out and called lewd remarks to the passing men below. This was one of the most conspicuous of San Francisco's red-light districts, serving the whites who frequented the Chinatown area; the Oriental prostitutes just a few blocks farther up the street were not allowed to commune with the Occidentals.

"That's old St. Mary's Church," Rachel said as they passed a brick building that stood off to the right, looking down impassively upon the scene of iniquity. "It was the first Roman Catholic cathedral in San Francisco, before the new St. Mary's was built five years ago," she explained. "Some of the stone came from China, and the bricks were brought around the Horn from Boston."

Aidan grinned as he read the inscription carved in bronze over the clock tower: *Son, observe the time, and fly from evil.*

A block farther up the hill, the phaeton crossed Sacramento Street, and Aidan suddenly found himself in another world. The two- and three-story brick buildings, which had been built by New England merchants, had been given a face-lift of sorts, the bricks painted red, the window frames and lintels enameled a glossy orange or blue. Tiny wrought-iron balconies, crammed with porcelain flowerpots and gaily colored lanterns, hung out over the sidewalks. Banners and signs were suspended everywhere, proclaiming heaven-knew-what in painstakingly lettered Chinese calligraphy.

But what made this tiny world within San Francisco come alive for Aidan were the people. Men dressed in blue denim and conical straw hats padded in straw-topped slippers up and down the street, their shoulders stooped under the weight of enormous baskets of vegetables slung from bamboo poles, their black pigtails swinging rhythmically behind them. Merchants wearing bright silk jackets stood in their doorways or worked feverishly behind their counters, selling cloth or meat or household goods to women dressed in black alpaca trousers and pants, their hair pulled back in tight chignons at the neck.

Rachel pointed to an elderly woman dressed in royal-blue silk who tottered down the street between two young servants. A woman of affluence, her position in the community was assured by the horrible deformity of her feet, which had been bound as a child to make them fashionably tiny and as a sign that she was not a common laborer. Aidan glanced at some of the other women and noticed that they wore awkward wooden slippers set upon a high, single wooden stilt at the center of the arch, giving them a gait similar to the aristocratic woman, whom they emulated.

The butcher shops were the most colorful establishments, for they sold not only meat and fish but chinaware, paper lanterns, and anything else that could be displayed in a window. Most had pictures of firecrackers painted on their window, and Rachel explained that it was at these butcher shops that young white boys would purchase their penny fireworks for the upcoming Fourth of July.

"What's that?" Aidan asked as the coach stopped at the corner of Jackson Street. He pointed to a tiny shop that seemed far more solemn than the others along the street. The inside contained a long wooden counter and walls lined with tiny drawers and shelves of bottles. Several large bottles of colored liquid stood on display in the window.

"The pharmacy," Rachel explained. "That's where the Chinese buy their herbs and medicines."

"Fascinating. What do you think is in those bottles?"

"Would you like to see?" she asked, her mouth quirking into a mischievous smile.

"I suppose so," he answered hesitantly.

Leaning forward, Rachel tapped on the driver's seat and said, "Michael, hold up here a moment. We're getting out."

The young driver turned around in shock but held his tongue. Engaging the brake, he waited until Rachel and Aidan climbed down from the carriage, and then he said, "I'll pull over to the curb just ahead."

"Thank you," she replied, taking Aidan's arm. "We'll only be a moment."

The Orientals passing on the street paid little attention to Rachel and Aidan as they approached the pharmacy window. Aidan was looking around somewhat nervously, but Rachel seemed totally at ease. She squeezed his arm and said, "Don't worry—we are perfectly safe in Chinatown. A woman could walk alone through here, even in the middle of the night, and nothing untoward would happen to her. The Chinese are too aware of the possibility of reprisals to allow violence toward their white visitors."

They came up to the window, and Aidan found himself staring at half a dozen three-foot-high flasks of colored liquid, each filled with objects that were not immediately identifiable until Rachel pointed to one and remarked, "Snakes, said to be good for the heart. And those are sea horses." She indicated a second jar, which was crammed full of the curious-looking little animals. Suddenly Aidan realized that these jars were filled with the preserved carcasses of animals that were considered medicinal to the Chinese. A third jar held some kind of toad, while the contents of the others were completely unknown to him.

"You like see?" a thin, high-pitched voice asked from beside them, and Aidan and Rachel looked over to see an extremely short man standing in the doorway. He could not have been much over four feet tall, and his white hair was tied in a pigtail that fell almost to his knees.

"We were just admiring your shop," Aidan said.

The old Chinaman grinned. "Please, you come in," he said, stepping into the shop and motioning them inside.

Aidan raised his eyebrows at Rachel, who shrugged and said, "Why not?"

As they followed the little man into the shop, he padded around the counter, which was as tall as he was, and climbed up onto a platform that put him almost at their height. Flattening both his palms on the counter, he leaned toward Aidan and squinted one eye. "You a doctor, yes?"

Aidan's jaw dropped open, stunned at the pronouncement. It was left to Rachel to say, "How did you know that?"

The little man's grin broadened. Placing one finger alongside his nose, he explained, "Yarrow sticks foretell a man of great healing will visit my shop. Many white men come stand at window; many times I ask them in. But you are first to come inside." He nodded, as if his logic would be obvious to all. "So you a doctor. Correct?"

"Why, yes," Aidan replied, surprised at his own admission.

"Ah! Then I must give you something." He turned, climbed off the platform, and disappeared through a small curtained doorway that led to a room in the back. When he returned, he held a black lacquer box, beautifully carved with the image of a bird whose plumage was tinged with red lacquer, as if it were ablaze with fire.

"Fêng huang," the man said as he placed the box on the counter in front of his visitors and touched the engraving. "In your language, it is the phoenix—symbol of the life reborn." Opening the box, he reached in and removed a sphere of glass about three inches in diameter. The sphere was perfectly clear except for numerous straight, threadlike needles that ran through it at every angle, as if a thousand strands of silver hair had been encased in the glass.

"I recognize this," Rachel said as the little man held the sphere to the light. "It's polished crystal—rutilated quartz, if I'm not mistaken. Those are strands of the mineral rutile."

"A crystal ball?" Aidan asked, and the Chinese man smiled and placed it in the palm of Aidan's hand. "But why are you giving it to me?"

"Not for me to know," the man replied with a shrug, his high voice taking on an aura of mystery. "This stone given me many years ago in China. Last year it ask to be given you, and the yarrow tell me who you are."

"The yarrow?" Aidan repeated. "What is that?"

The little man's black eyes widened, and in a hush he said, *"I Ching."*

"I know that!" Aidan blurted, recalling the book Finley Orcutt had given him.

"You know *I Ching*?" the Chinaman asked, obviously impressed.

"Someone told me about it. But no, I don't really know what it is."

"You like see?"

"Why, yes, I would."

"Ah, then come!" He took the quartz crystal from Aidan's hand and placed it in the felt-lined box, then closed the box and disappeared with it into the curtained back room. A second later his head popped out, and he beckoned to them and said, "Come! Come!"

Rachel and Aidan followed through the curtain into the small, windowless back room. It was quite bare, containing only a wooden chest against one wall, a straw mat covering the floor, and several embroidered silk cushions.

"You sit," the man said, motioning toward the cushions.

"Go ahead," Rachel whispered to Aidan. "I'll stand."

Leaving Rachel standing in front of the curtain, Aidan approached the mat and placed one of the cushions near the edge. He was about to sit down on it when the man started waving his hand excitedly and said, "Shoes! Shoes!" Aidan looked down and saw that the man had removed his black slippers. With a sheepish glance back at Rachel, Aidan stooped down and untied his shoes. He placed them on the floor beside the mat, then awkwardly sat down in a cross-legged position.

By now the Chinese man had opened the trunk and was removing several objects, which he placed on the mat in front of his cushion directly across from Aidan. The first object was a hand-sewn, coverless book with two large Chinese characters on the front sheet. The top one looked like a four-pane window with little vertical lines in each pane. The lower symbol resembled a curved, elongated capital letter *D*, to the left of which were three parallel, diagonal lines. The two symbols were identical to the ones on the cover of the book Finley had given Aidan.

"*I Ching*," the man intoned as he sat down and pointed to the symbols.

Beside the book was a writing set, consisting of a piece of

paper, a brush, a small stone tablet with a depression in the center, and a black stick that looked like charcoal. The last object was a very small straw mat that was rolled around something. As he unrolled the mat, Aidan saw that it contained a pile of smooth, polished sticks.

"Yarrow stalks," the man said almost reverently as he picked up the sticks and held them horizontally on his open palms. He closed his eyes and sat in motionless silence for a few moments, then grasped the pile in his left hand and carefully removed one stick, which he set beside him on the mat. Opening his eyes, he leaned forward and placed the rest of the pile in front of Aidan, saying, "Divide in two."

Aidan reached out and separated the sticks into two piles. With a nod, the little man took one stick from the right-hand pile and stuck it between the little finger and ring finger of his left hand. He put the entire left-hand pile in his left hand and with his right hand removed groups of four sticks until only one group remained, which he placed between the ring and middle fingers of his left hand. Next he repeated the process with the right-hand pile, placing the final group between his middle finger and forefinger. Finally he removed the sticks from between his fingers and put them on the mat beside the writing set.

Gathering together the yarrow stalks he had discarded in groups of four, the man presented the pile to Aidan and again said, "Divide in two." After it was done, he went through the same ritual and set the resulting sticks beside the pile from the first count. A third division of the discarded sticks was made, and the sticks that remained between his fingers were placed beside the first two piles.

Once the three groups were determined, the little man counted the number of sticks in each group. Then he picked up the charcoal and flaked some of it onto the stone tablet. Wetting the tip of the brush with his tongue, he dabbed it against the powder, turning it into ink, and drew a broken horizontal line near the bottom of the piece of paper.

The entire procedure was repeated again. After counting the three piles, the man drew a single solid line just above the broken line. Four additional times the procedure was carried out, resulting in two more solid lines, a broken line, and a final solid line at the top. Finally he gathered all the yarrow stalks and rolled them up in the small straw mat.

Placing the piece of paper in front of Aidan, the man tapped the six-line figure he had drawn and said, "*Ting*, the Caldron." He nodded with great portent and picked up the hand-sewn book, flipping through the pages until he found one with an identical figure at the top. He read the Chinese words below for several minutes, then nodded again and closed the book.

"The Caldron brings superior man supreme good fortune and success," he declared with a smile. But then he narrowed his eyes slightly and added, "But only to man who enhances his fate by taking correct action. See here . . ." He pointed to the bottom broken line and said, "The legs of the Caldron," then to the three solid lines above and said, "the belly," and finally to the top broken and solid lines and concluded, "the carrying rings and cover. But if not careful, the legs may be upturned. Then the Caldron is cracked and your meal is spoiled. Great misfortune."

"What can I do?" Aidan asked.

The Chinese man looked at him a long moment, then he opened the carved lacquer box and handed Aidan the crystal. "Close eyes," he declared, and Aidan complied. After a few moments, he reached over and took the crystal from Aidan's hands. He gazed into it a few moments, then closed his own eyes. "Legs upturned . . . Caldron cracked . . . meal spilled. In the crystal I see you at great banquet. A table is overturned. An enemy tries to cause you harm. You desire revenge. To avoid misfortune and enhance fate, you must act correctly, without concern for what the outcome will be."

The little man opened his eyes and looked into the crystal again. "That is all," he said and began to lower the crystal, but then he hesitated and added, "except for child." He looked over at Aidan and then up at Rachel. "Is there a child?" When both of them shook their heads, he frowned slightly and said, "Bottom line of the Caldron speaks of concubine who has a son. When a man's wife cannot give him children, it is proper for him to take concubine who has a son.'' He paused, then continued, ''In crystal I see child of a concubine, not a wife. If child is disowned, caldron will burn too hot, contents will be destroyed. Child must be embraced if there is to be good fortune.''

''I don't understand,'' Aidan said. ''There is no child.''

The little man shrugged. ''I see this child. It is not for me to understand.'' He placed the crystal back in the box and handed it to Aidan. Standing, he said, ''That is all. You come back sometime, yes?''

''Yes, thank you,'' Aidan replied, putting on his shoes and standing. He and Rachel walked out into the shop and turned to thank the little man for his hospitality.

''One thing more,'' the man said before they were able to speak. ''In the crystal was child of a second concubine, but it was dark and far away. I do not understand.'' He grinned and shrugged. ''You come back sometime?''

''Yes, we'd like that,'' Rachel told him.

''Thank you,'' Aidan added.

The man bowed slightly and then led them to the door.

As Aidan followed Rachel outside, he turned back to the little man. ''You never told us who you are.''

''I am a *fang shih*,'' he said without explaining the meaning of the term. ''I am called Hsiao Ch'u.''

''And I am Aidan . . . Aidan McAuliffe,'' he replied, using his real surname.

The two men bowed slightly, then Aidan took Rachel's arm and led her down the street to the waiting carriage.

SIXTEEN

SALOMON'S EMPORIUM WAS NEARING CLOSING TIME SATUR-
day evening, and Jacob Salomon was seated alone in his father's office, going through some of the paperwork that had
accumulated following Charles's heart attack. There was a
light rapping, and Jacob looked up to see David Gelde, his
father's elderly assistant, standing in the open doorway of the
outer office.

"There's someone here to see you," Gelde said. "Mr.
Rafael Acuesta."

"Show him in. And Mr. Gelde, there's no reason for you
to stay. I'll be working late; feel free to go home."

"Thank you, sir. I will," Gelde replied, taking Jacob's
suggestion as an order. He turned to the man waiting in the
outer office and said, "Mr. Salomon will see you now, Mr.
Acuesta."

As Gelde moved aside, a handsome, dark-skinned man in
his midforties entered the office, carrying a manila portfolio
tied with a black ribbon. "Good day, Mr. Salomon," he said
as Jacob motioned him toward one of the chairs that faced
the desk. He sat down and placed the portfolio on his lap.

"I didn't expect to see you again so soon," Jacob said.

"My research took far less time than anticipated."

"Yes. Very good." Jacob glanced toward the open doorway. "Just one moment." He stood and circled the desk to the door. In the outer office, Gelde was just putting on his overcoat and hat. "Good night, Mr. Gelde," Jacob said, nodding toward the employee, who smiled back and headed out into the hall, closing the door behind him. Jacob shut the door to the inner office and returned to his seat. "What have you got?"

Acuesta tapped the portfolio. "Proof that Eaton Hallinger has embezzled more than twenty thousand dollars to pay off his gambling debts."

Jacob eyed the man closely. "You didn't manufacture this evidence, did you?"

"No one wants to get rid of that prissy chap more than I do. But no, I didn't . . . because I didn't have to. He's dug his own grave, and I'll be glad to see him lying in it. Then maybe his father won't pass the rest of us over at promotion time."

"You've been with Hallinger's bank for sixteen years, haven't you?" Jacob asked.

"Seventeen this September. And Eaton was made vice president in less than five."

Jacob grinned smugly. "Well, I think it's time the members of your bank's board of directors learn what they're getting for their money when they pay their young vice president his salary every month."

"What do you think his father will do?" the man asked with a note of concern.

"Abraham? I'm certain if he got wind of what you've got there, he'd make sure the funds were paid back before a scandal broke. But I know someone on the board who'll see to it your information gets into the right hands before Abraham can do anything about it." As Acuesta slid the portfolio across the desk, Jacob placed the palms of his hands on top of it and said, "If what you've got in here proves to be all you say it is, I'll arrange for a transfer into your account of that two thousand dollars we discussed."

Acuesta rose from his chair. Fixing Jacob with his dark brown eyes, he said evenly, "I want you to know that I didn't do this for the money. It's just not right for that irresponsible young prig to make the rest of us do his work and then take all the credit while he's lollygagging around the gaming parlors—"

"I understand, Mr. Acuesta. But I'm grateful for your bringing these matters to light, and I'm certain your family will find good use for the token of appreciation you'll be receiving."

"Yes," he admitted, looking down and nodding. "Thank you." He started toward the closed door, then turned and gave Jacob a curious look. "It just doesn't make sense, does it?"

"What doesn't, Mr. Acuesta?"

"Look what he stands to inherit. Why would a chap like that risk it all at the gambling tables, then have to do what he has done to keep his father from finding out?"

Jacob shrugged. "I suppose he likes the danger."

"He's a damn fool, if you ask me."

"I agree completely. Good day."

"Yes. Good day." Rafael Acuesta turned, opened the door, and headed through the outer office.

As soon as the man disappeared out into the hall, Jacob opened the manila portfolio and pulled out the small stack of papers. As he perused the contents, he began to smile broadly. "Yes, Eaton, you're a damn fool," he whispered as he confirmed that he had enough evidence in hand to put Phoebe's murderer behind bars for a long time. "And you're going to learn it was a fool's bet indeed when you wagered against my sister's honor."

After leaving Chinatown, Rachel had the coachman drive Aidan and her to the family home on Nob Hill, where Rachel was surprised to learn that her mother had taken to bed, leaving her regrets that she was not feeling well enough to meet her daughter's friend.

"We'll go up to see my father," Rachel told the butler as

259

they handed him their coats. When Cameron looked at her uncomfortably, she asked, "What is it?"

"Mrs. Salomon said for me to tell you that she preferred Mr. Salomon not be disturbed."

"We'll be quiet," she replied, taking Aidan by the arm and leading him across the foyer toward the stairs.

"Of course, but—"

"I'll take full responsibility," she said a bit brusquely.

"Yes, Miss Salomon." Cameron gave a sheepish nod, then turned and carried away the coats.

As Rachel started up the marble stairway, Aidan held back and said, "Perhaps if your mother prefers—"

"Don't worry about Nina," she chided, tugging at his arm. "She just doesn't think it proper for visitors to see Charles in his condition. But I want you to meet him and give me your opinion about how he's doing."

"I'm not equipped to examine him," Aidan said, starting up the stairs alongside her.

"Just your general impression, that's all."

When they reached the second floor, Rachel brought Aidan down the hall and cautiously opened her father's door, so as not to disturb him if he was asleep. Seeing that his eyes were open, she entered and approached the bed. His breathing was still harsh and raspy, and his chest heaved in short, sharp gasps.

"Hello, Father," Rachel said softly as she looked down at him. His eyes immediately opened wider, and she thought she detected a smile—if not on his lips, then certainly in his eyes. "I've brought a friend—a physician. We met in the East." She turned and motioned Aidan closer. "Father, this is Aidan."

"I'm pleased to meet you," Aidan said, placing himself in the older man's line of vision.

Charles's lips began to quiver, and he opened his mouth as if to speak. His breath grew even more ragged, and suddenly he began to cough.

"It's all right," Rachel soothed, placing a hand on her father's forehead.

"How long has he sounded like this?" Aidan's voice betrayed his concern as he rested a hand on Charles's chest.

"It's been getting worse the past few days. Our family physician says the paralysis is making it difficult for his lungs to work."

Aidan shook his head. "I don't like the sound of it."

"What do you mean?"

"Mr. Salomon," Aidan said, looking down directly into the man's eyes. "Can you hear me?" When Charles made no reply other than to cough again, Aidan suggested, "If you can hear me, blink your eyes once." Instantly the old man's eyelids fluttered, then closed once and opened.

"Father!" Rachel exclaimed. She turned to Aidan. "He knows what we're saying!"

"I thought as much," Aidan replied. "Mr. Salomon," he asked Charles. "I'm going to listen to your chest. Is that all right?"

When Charles blinked a single time, Aidan immediately unbuttoned the man's nightshirt and leaned over, placing his ear directly upon the chest. He listened for quite some time, gauging the lung's abilities as the old man breathed raggedly. After Charles coughed a few times, Aidan lifted his head and said, "Thank you, Mr. Salomon."

"What is it?" Rachel whispered in concern.

Aidan took Rachel's elbow and led her away from the bed. "I'm convinced it isn't the paralysis," he told her.

"But the doctor said—"

"I doubt your doctor examined him very closely, or he would have realized that your father has not lost his faculties, only his ability to move."

"But what is it?" she asked again.

"I can't be certain without a more thorough exam, but I suspect acute pneumonia, brought on by his weakened condition."

Raising her hand to her mouth, Rachel drew in a deep breath. "Will he . . . ?"

"His chances will greatly improve if he's transferred to a hospital at once. He needs round-the-clock attention."

"Yes. I understand," she said in a surprisingly steady voice. "I'll have the carriage made ready."

Rachel headed out into the hall and called down from the head of the stairs for Cameron to have the carriage brought around. A moment later she came back into the room and returned to her father's side.

"Aidan thinks you have pneumonia," she told Charles in as calm a voice as she could muster, "so we have to take you to the hospital. Is that all right?" She paused, and he blinked once. "I love you, Father," she pronounced, leaning over to kiss his cheek as he blinked again.

"Does he have a dressing robe?" Aidan asked, and Rachel pointed across the room to the dressing table. Aidan retrieved the robe, which was folded on the chair in front of the table, and brought it back to the bed. "Let's get him dressed," he said, handing Rachel the robe and coming up alongside Charles's head to lift him from the pillow.

Just as Aidan was helping Charles to a seated position, a voice from the hallway boomed, "What's going on here?"

Rachel and Aidan turned to see Nina standing in the doorway. She was dressed in an elegant blue evening dress, and her long brown hair was carefully coiffed upon her head.

Rachel looked up at her in surprise. "I thought you were rest—"

"I've had enough sleep," Nina declared, striding into the room. "What's the meaning of this?" She pointed at the heavy wool dressing robe in Rachel's hands, then glanced over at Aidan, who eased Charles back against the pillow.

"We're taking Father to the hospital," Rachel proclaimed.

"What are you talking about?" Nina looked back and forth between her daughter and Aidan.

"Mrs. Salomon," Aidan said, rising from the bed and taking a step toward her. "I believe your husband's breathing difficulties are due to pneumonia."

"And who is he?" she asked, her eyes fixed on Aidan.

"I told you about my friend. His name is Aidan Orcutt," Rachel answered, using the alias.

"A friend? And you take the word of this friend, when our own family doctor insists Charles should not be moved?"

"Aidan has studied medicine," Rachel said cautiously, not wanting to give away too much about his background.

"But is he a physician? And what does he know about Charles and our family?"

Aidan took a step forward. "I've heard your husband's cough, and it's not due to paralysis but to the accumulation of fluid that accompanies pneumonia."

"Mr. Orcutt," Nina grated, her voice only just under control, "you'll do me the favor of waiting downstairs. This is for my daughter—"

"No, Nina," Rachel cut in, holding out an arm to make sure Aidan did not leave. "I asked Aidan to examine Father, and I trust his advice. Father will be moved to the hospital at once so that he can be properly examined."

Nina's cheeks flushed with anger. "This is sheer lunacy," she snapped, snatching the robe from Rachel's hands. "You'll do as I say—both of you—before you kill that poor old man."

"No," her daughter replied firmly.

When Rachel reached to retrieve the robe, her mother flung it across the room. "You will not defy me, young woman!" she raged. "Now get out! Both of you!"

"Father is going to the hospital," Rachel declared flatly.

Suddenly Nina lashed out and slapped her eldest daughter across the cheek. Stung more by the action than by the pain, Rachel raised her hand to her cheek and backed up beside Aidan.

"Get out of here!" Nina ordered with a scowl.

Rachel merely shook her head.

Taking another step toward Nina, Aidan said, "Mrs. Salomon, your daughter wants to do what's best for her father. And Mr. Salomon himself has agreed to be taken—"

"Him?" Nina blurted derisively, waving a hand toward Charles, who lay propped against the pillows staring at her, his eyes blinking rapidly, his breath growing increasingly shallow and harsh. "Don't be ridiculous! He couldn't agree to blow his own nose!"

"Mother!" Rachel gasped.

"Face the truth!" Nina lashed out, turning away from the bed and frowning in disgust. "That's not Charles . . . not anymore. He's no longer a man. He's . . . he's nothing.'' It was Rachel who stepped forward now and swung out with her open palm, but Nina caught her wrist before it struck across her cheek. ''He's not your father!'' she shrieked, twisting Rachel's wrist and turning her toward the bed. ''Look at him!'' she raged. ''He's nothing! And if he *does* have pneumonia, maybe it's a blessing in disguise!''

''Don't say that!'' Rachel yelled, yanking her arm free.

''I have to! Someone has to!'' Nina approached the bed and looked down at her husband, who lay gasping for breath, his chest rising and falling shallowly. ''He'd agree with me if he could! He wouldn't want to live like this!''

''He can hear you!'' Rachel insisted, grabbing her mother's arm and pulling her back from the bed.

''He hears nothing! I . . . I wish he were dead!''

''Shut up!'' Rachel shouted, and this time she did strike her mother.

Nina was so shocked that she staggered back from the bed, clutching her cheek as her eyes filled with tears. Her eyes narrowed, and she hissed, ''You little slut! Go ahead—take him! But do us all a favor and don't bother to bring him back!'' She glanced bitterly at Aidan, then turned and ran from the room, slamming the door shut behind her.

Rachel immediately turned to her father, who was struggling for air, his face contorted with pain. ''It's all right,'' she said soothingly as she caressed his cheek. ''Nina didn't mean what she said.''

Aidan grasped Rachel's shoulders and pulled her back from the bed. ''Let me see him,'' he said anxiously.

Realizing that her father was unable to breathe at all, Rachel moved aside to give Aidan room, and he quickly yanked the covers off Charles and grabbed his legs, pulling him toward the foot of the bed until he was flat on his back. He tossed aside the pillows and leaned over the old man, whose body was jerking spasmodically as it fought for breath.

Aidan slipped one hand under Charles's neck and tilted his head back to open the passageway to his lungs. When he was still unable to breathe, Aidan pinched Charles's nostrils and completely covered Charles's open mouth with his own. Aidan tried to exhale into the lungs, but the passage was obstructed, and so he readjusted Charles's neck and exhaled again. This time the old man's chest filled with air. As Aidan lifted his head and drew in a breath, the air came out of Charles with a gurgling sound.

Aidan repeated the process several times, all the while checking the carotid artery to make sure Charles's heart was still beating. After a minute, he stopped and watched. There was a pause, and then Charles drew in a short gasp and let it out. He gasped a few more times, then began to breathe, though still shallow. His eyes were closed, and he seemed unconscious.

"Will he m-make it?" Rachel stammered.

"I don't know." Aidan stood away from the bed. "His heartbeat is faint and irregular. I'm afraid . . ."

Rachel began to cry, and Aidan put his arm around her shoulders and held her close. After a few moments, she pulled away and sat down on the bed beside her father. Resting her head against his cheek, she said, "I love you so much, Father. Please don't go."

She looked up at his face and saw that his eyes had opened slightly. His breath was ever so weak, and it sounded as if he was moaning.

"Rest," she urged him, but he continued to moan, his lips quivering slightly.

"I think he's trying to speak," Aidan said, placing a hand on Rachel's shoulder. She looked up at him, unsure of what to do, and he nodded and said, "Put your ear by his lips. Go on."

Leaning over her father, she said, "What is it?" She placed her ear directly over his lips and listened as he tried to speak. "Yes, I love you, too!" she said excitedly, then glanced up at Aidan. "I heard him!"

Again Rachel leaned close to Charles's lips and struggled to make out what he was saying. From only a few feet away, Aidan could hear nothing but the sound of his wheezing and moaning. Aidan moved a few feet to the side so that he would have a better view of Charles's face, and he saw that his lips were indeed moving slightly.

For almost a full minute Charles spoke, and then abruptly he went silent—totally silent. His chest stopped rising and falling, yet his body did not struggle for air. At first Rachel did not know what had happened, for she whispered, "What was that, Father? I can't hear you." But then she realized that she no longer felt his breath on her cheek, and she pulled back and stared at him. "Father?" she said, looking anxiously at Aidan, who shook his head sadly.

"No," she murmured as Aidan leaned down and placed two fingers against Charles's neck to confirm that his heart had given out. "Oh, God . . . no!" She began to cry.

Aidan took Rachel in his arms and held her tight. He spoke to her soothingly, but she just stood rigid and unresponsive, her head shaking slowly.

"It will be all right," he promised. "You'll see."

"No," she said, looking up at him, her face sheet white. "You don't understand." He looked at her questioningly, and she turned toward her father and said, "He told me . . . about Phoebe."

"He knew that she died?" Aidan asked, remembering that Charles had suffered his heart attack after Phoebe's accident but before her death.

"Yes . . . but not that. About the baby."

"Her unborn child?"

"No," she said forcefully, her face a mask of anger as she turned to face Aidan. "Mother thought he couldn't hear. She told him what really happened." Shuddering, she folded her arms across her chest. "My sister did not die of infection but from an abortion—an abortion she was forced to undergo by Nina." When Aidan started to speak, she cut him off, saying, "That's not all. She was too far along in the pregnancy, and the baby was born alive . . . a boy."

"Are you sure?" he asked incredulously.

She nodded. "Nina arranged for the doctor to get rid of it. For all I know, it may still be alive."

"My God, that's just what Hsiao Ch'u said. Remember? He warned us not to disown a child born out of wedlock."

"I have no intention of disowning my nephew." Rachel shook her head and hissed, "That bitch—she'd do anything to keep the family name from being sullied. But I never thought she'd sink this low.'' As she started across the room, she proclaimed, ''I'll make her tell me where—''

''Just a minute,'' Aidan called, hurrying over and pulling her back by the arm.

''She'll tell me what that doctor did with my nephew, if I have to—''

''Not so fast,'' he urged. ''Think this thing through.''

''What do you mean?'' she asked, hesitating.

''If your mother finds out that you know about the baby—and if she really is intent on making certain it's never discovered—she could arrange for it to disappear forever, if it already hasn't.''

''Believe me, if she tries any—''

''Just hold on a second,'' he cut her off. ''I think I have a better idea.''

''What do you mean?''

''The doctor—the one who signed Phoebe's death certificate. On Monday I can get his name from the certificate and get him to take us to the baby.''

''But how?''

''He's an abortionist—remember?'' Aidan gave a rueful smile. ''I know a thing or two about that subject. I'm certain I can convince him to turn over this particular baby—or face prosecution for his crimes.''

''Are you sure?'' she asked.

''Trust me. He's the one who knows where to find the baby, so we've got to get to him before your mother does.''

Rachel's shoulders slumped slightly, and she nodded. The fire that had been in her eyes but a moment before seemed to lessen, and she turned toward the bed, where her father appeared to be sleeping peacefully. ''She killed him,'' Rachel whispered bitterly. ''And she'll pay.''

Stepping behind her, Aidan gripped her shoulders. ''You mustn't think like that. The end was inevitable, I'm afraid—even if we had gotten him to the hospital.''

Rachel bowed her head and began to cry softly, then turned and fell into Aidan's arms, burying her head against his chest.

Choking back her tears, she stammered, ''J-Just before he d-died, he . . . he said, 'Forgive her. It's my fault that she's become what she has.' He told me that despite it all he loved her . . . and he always would.'' She sobbed more deeply, her tears soaking Aidan's shirtfront. ''I don't understand,'' she muttered. ''I just don't understand.''

SEVENTEEN

A SMALL, PRIVATE FUNERAL SERVICE WAS HELD ON MONDAY afternoon, the twenty-second of June, two days after Charles Salomon's death. It was attended by Jacob, Rachel, and Maurice Salomon, Merribelle Knowles, Aidan McAuliffe, and a few of their closest friends and business associates. One conspicuous absence was Nina Salomon. Upon learning of her husband's death, she had fallen apart completely and had required sedating. When the hour of the service arrived, she was still in bed, far too weak and distraught to attend.

During the service, Rachel noticed the tenderness displayed between Maurice and Belle and wondered if the young woman would actually board the train in two days as planned for her return journey to Albany. She knew that the young couple had spent every day together since their arrival in San Francisco, and Rachel could only marvel at the positive effect Belle seemed to be having upon Maurice. In fact, Jacob had told Rachel that Maurice was talking about coming into the business on a full-time basis and taking a more active role in the future—a prospect that delighted both of Maurice's siblings.

After the brief service was concluded, Aidan took Rachel aside and showed her a copy of Phoebe's death certificate, which he had obtained that morning at City Hall by pretending to be the new assistant to the Salomon family's personal physician. The certificate was signed by Dr. Trevor Danin, whose office was listed at an address just south of Market Street.

Taking leave of the others, Rachel and Aidan hired a cab and went directly to the doctor's office. When they pulled up at the stoop in front of the shabby-looking building on which hung the doctor's dilapidated sign, Aidan suggested that Rachel wait in the carriage, but she refused and accompanied him up the front stairs to the door, leaving the cab to wait for them at the curb.

Without knocking, Aidan and Rachel entered the building and turned to the right into a waiting room just off the front hallway. It was decorated in furniture that was frayed and faded with age, giving the room a dreary appearance that did little to evoke confidence in prospective patients. Perhaps that was why the room was empty, despite there being two hours before closing time.

"Hello?" Aidan called, looking around the room and noting at either end a pair of closed doors, which probably led to an examining room and the dispensary. "Is someone here?"

A second later, the door to the left swung open and a balding, elderly man peered out, his small eyes widening upon seeing the well-dressed couple. "Welcome, friends," he proclaimed in a high, singsongy voice as he entered the waiting room. "May I be of service?"

"Are you Dr. Trevor Danin?" Aidan asked.

"Why, yes. And who might you be?"

"My name is Rachel Salomon," Rachel put in. "I believe you know my mother, Nina Salomon—and my sister, Phoebe."

The man's eyes narrowed, and his voice dropped in pitch slightly as he cautiously replied, "Is there something I can do for you?"

Aidan stepped forward from beside Rachel. "It has come

to our attention that Phoebe did not die as the result of an infection following the injury to her arm." He gave a portentous pause, then added, "In truth, she died in childbirth."

"Don't be preposterous," the doctor blurted, looking away nervously.

"There's no point in denying it," Aidan continued. "Nina Salomon confessed the truth to her husband."

"But she promised—" He cut off abruptly, as if to stop himself from saying too much.

"Then you admit she paid you to falsify the death report?"

"See here . . . I will not stand here and be accused—"

"We are not the law, Dr. Danin," Aidan cut in. "In fact, we have no desire to involve the law in this sordid affair. We only seek the truth."

Danin waved his hand brusquely and began to pace across the room in short, birdlike steps. "Yes, she died in childbirth," he confessed. "The shock of her accident must have brought on labor prematurely, and she was far too weak to survive the ordeal. You're right, her death wasn't due to infection. But I only changed the cause of death to help a grieving mother." He stopped in place and turned to the two of them. "Why, the woman's daughter was dead and her grandchild stillborn. I thought it an act of Christian mercy to help the poor woman protect the only thing her daughter had left—her good name."

"You little liar!" Rachel suddenly raged, advancing toward him.

Aidan quickly grabbed her arm and pulled her back. "Please wait for us outside," he told her firmly. When she held her ground and continued to glower at the physician, he said, "Please, do as I say."

Rachel turned to Aidan and saw the calm determination in his eyes. Clenching her fists in frustration, she nodded slowly, and he released her arm. She immediately spun on her heels and stormed outside to the waiting cab.

"She had no right . . ." the elderly doctor said as soon as Rachel was gone.

"She's very upset—and with good cause," Aidan replied

pointedly. "You see, she happens to be aware that her sister's baby was born alive."

The doctor gasped but did not reply.

"Dr. Danin, let me be blunt with you," Aidan went on. "You and I both know that Phoebe died undergoing an abortion—an abortion carried out by you right here in this office. But the baby was born alive, and so you arranged for it to disappear—to a foundling home, perhaps?"

"You can't prove that!" Danin blustered. "I was examining her. She went into labor and died. That's all."

"I don't have to prove it. Your signature on the death certificate will be proof enough—particularly with Nina Salomon's signed affidavit." He reached into his inner coat pocket and removed a folded piece of paper—in actuality the copy of the death certificate—and waved it in the air as if it were the affidavit, then returned it to his pocket.

"She'd never swear to such a thing," the little man said with increasing agitation. "Why, she's the one . . ." His voice trailed off.

"Then you admit it?"

"I admit nothing of the sort. But even if what you say were true, Nina Salomon would be just as guilty as me. No, she'd never swear to such a thing."

"Nina Salomon realizes she made a grievous mistake in abandoning that poor child, and she wants to set it right. That's why she sent us here." His tone grew more calm and reassuring as he continued, "You see, Dr. Danin, we have no desire to besmirch your good name. All we want is the young infant so it can be raised in the bosom of its family."

The doctor looked at him suspiciously. "I'm not sure I understand."

"If you'll simply help us recover the infant boy, the entire matter will be dropped."

"And if I am unable to assist you?"

"Then we shall be forced to involve the police. Certainly the courts will understand the actions of a distraught woman whose thought was to protect her daughter's name. But will they look so kindly on a doctor who for a hefty fee went along with her obviously hysterical request?"

"You're trying to blackmail me," Danin grated.

"Not at all. I'm merely seeking the return of a child, and if you are unable to assist me, I will be forced to turn to more . . . legal channels."

"Now, that won't be necessary," the doctor proclaimed, adopting a nervous smile. "I'm certain we can resolve this amicably. If you'll just wait here a moment." He turned and passed through the doorway on the left, returning a few moments later with a small slip of paper. "This is the receipt for the child in question," he said, handing it to Aidan. "The agency will have to tell you if it has yet found the infant a home."

Aidan read the receipt, then stuffed it in his pocket. "Good day," he said brusquely as he started from the waiting room.

"You'll keep my name out of this," the elderly man declared as Aidan entered the hall.

With a brief glance over his shoulder, Aidan replied, "Yes . . . if the baby is where you say it is.' He opened the front door and gave it a forceful slam behind him as he hurried down to the waiting carriage.

That same evening, a coach-bodied landau, drawn by a matched pair of gray horses, pulled up in front of the Juan de la Cruz Orphanage and Foundling Home. The coachman, dressed in red livery, pulled on the brake and jumped down to the sidewalk. He opened the door of the covered carriage and stepped back as Jacob Salomon climbed out.

"You'll wait for us here," Jacob said to the coachman of the carriage-for-hire.

Turning, Jacob held out his hand, and Merribelle Knowles took hold of it and stepped out onto the sidewalk. Rachel appeared next, and she was followed by Aidan McAuliffe and Maurice Salomon.

"This is the place?" Jacob asked, looking up with distaste at the two-story brick building in the city's Mission District.

"Juan de la Cruz," Aidan said, reading the austere black lettering over the front door. "Yes, this is it."

As the group started up the walk, Belle held back and said to Maurice, "Perhaps I should wait with the carriage."

Maurice shook his head and took her arm. "Rachel was right to invite us all. This is a family problem—and the fate of Phoebe's child must be a family decision."

"Yes, but I'm not family."

"I'd be glad to change that," he whispered pointedly. "In any case, you're my friend, and I value your opinion." He led her up the walk behind the others.

After being admitted to the foundling home by a young woman in a nurse's uniform, the group was taken to a reception area that looked more like the poorly appointed parlor of a modest home. "If you'll wait here," the young woman said, "the matron will be right with you." She turned and headed down the hall.

Rachel and Belle took seats, while the three men remained standing. There was an uncomfortable silence, which Rachel finally broke by saying, "I hope we're doing the right thing."

"If I've a nephew, he doesn't belong in here," Jacob proclaimed, looking around the room and frowning with disdain. "I don't care if he *is* Eaton Hallinger's son."

"Do you think Eaton will fight for custody of the child?" Maurice asked.

"I would seriously doubt that," Jacob replied.

"Anyhow, we're agreed not to divulge the child's true parentage," Rachel put in. "At least not until a legal adoption is complete." She turned to her older brother and added, "You're certain you want to go through with this?"

"Yes," Jacob stated emphatically. "I'm the one who should adopt. I'm the oldest and most secure financially, and I have my own home. I think we're agreed it would not be wise to raise the child under Nina's roof." Just then footsteps were heard approaching, and Jacob said in a hush, "Remember to let me do the talking."

A moment later, a middle-aged woman in a starched black gown entered the room. Her eyes were coal black, and her dark hair was drawn into a tight bun that was almost as severe as her stiff, slightly crooked smile. "Good day," she said woodenly. "I am Madam Krauss. How may I be of service?" She looked from one person to the other, her smile fixed and rigid.

SAN FRANCISCO

"My name is Jacob Salomon, and this is my sister Rachel and brother Maurice." Jacob indicated his siblings with a wave of his hand, then motioned toward Aidan and Belle. "These are our close friends. We've come about an infant."

"Are you trying to place a child, or have you come seeking one?" she asked.

"We'd like to adopt."

The woman eyed the group suspiciously, taking in their demeanor and the cut of their clothes. It was apparent that she was not used to seeing gentlemen and ladies of their caliber interested in adopting an abandoned or orphaned child. Still, she saw the potential for profit, and she did not want to scare them away to one of the many other such establishments in the city, so she picked her words carefully and said in as light a tone as she could muster, "Certainly all of you are not adopting. Perhaps I could bring the couple in question to meet some of our children."

"That's not necessary," Jacob said, reaching into his pocket and pulling out the slip of paper Aidan had given him in the carriage. "We've come about a particular child. Our family physician, Dr. Trevor Danin, told us about an infant that was left at his office. I believe he turned it over to you two weeks ago." Jacob held out the slip of paper. "He gave us this receipt so that you could identify the infant."

The woman took the paper and perused it carefully, then nodded. "Yes, of course I remember this child. He is our most recent arrival. Would you like to see him?"

"Yes!" Rachel blurted, then controlling her excitement, said more calmly, "Yes, we would like that."

Madam Krauss turned toward the doorway and said, "Virginia." She paused, folded her arms across her chest, then called a bit more testily, "Miss Ghent, please come here." She drummed her fingers on her arm until the young nurse who had let them into the building appeared in the doorway and gave a slight curtsy. "Bring me number eighty-four—that new boy."

"Yes, ma'am," the young woman replied. She hurried down the hall.

Turning back to the group in the reception room, Madam Krauss asked, "Which is the couple that desires to adopt?"

"Couple?" Jacob asked.

"But of course. Our requirements are quite standard and designed for the benefit of the children. All adoptions must be to suitable married couples of sufficient means; that is our one unbending rule."

Jacob glanced frantically at his sister. Not only was he single, he was not even seeing any woman on a regular basis and had no prospects of marriage in the immediate future. "Perhaps we could see the child first," he said awkwardly, hoping to buy time.

"But of course," the woman replied. Just then the young nurse came through the door carrying a bundled baby, which she handed over to Madam Krauss.

"Could I hold him?" Rachel asked, approaching eagerly.

Krauss handed her the child and asked, "Would you like to be alone for a few minutes?"

"Yes, thank you," Rachel said, her eyes fixed on the sleeping infant.

As the woman left the room, the others crowded around Rachel, who pulled back the blanket that half covered the little infant's face. His eyes were closed, but from his fair skin and curly blond ringlets, Rachel guessed that they were blue like Phoebe's. His cheeks were pudgy, yet he had a thin look to him, though he seemed to be in good health.

"He's lovely," Belle said, reaching and stroking his cheek. The baby instinctively turned toward her hand and began to suck at the air, as if searching for a nipple.

"He looks so much like . . . like Phoebe," Maurice stammered, his eyes beginning to mist as he smiled down at the helpless little baby.

"What are we going to do?" Jacob asked. "I can't very well rush out and marry the first person I grab off the street." He looked at Rachel, then over at Aidan. With the hint of a grin, he said, "What about you, Sis? Any hope for a marriage in the near future?"

Rachel and Aidan shared an uncomfortable look, each wondering what they would do if Aidan's situation did not preclude the thought of marriage. "I'm afraid that's not possible," Rachel said at last. "It's . . . it's out of the question. At least for now." She did not elaborate, and Jacob accepted her decision without pressing the matter.

"What about Maurice?" Belle asked, looking from Jacob to Rachel, then turning to smile at Maurice.

"But I'm not—"

"Not yet. But you could be by tomorrow," she said.

"You mean . . . ?" Looking into her eyes, he read the answer for which he had been praying, and tears began to run down his cheeks.

"What's going on?" Jacob said in confusion.

"Belle has just accepted my proposal of marriage," Maurice announced, wrapping his arm around Belle's shoulder.

"I'm so happy for you!" Rachel cried.

"Congratulations!" Jacob declared, slapping his younger brother on the back. "You can stay at my house until we arrange for one of your own."

"But are you certain you want to adopt Phoebe's child?" Rachel asked.

"Yes," Belle said with conviction. "From the moment I first laid eyes upon him." She took a step toward Rachel and held out her arms. There were tears in both women's eyes as Rachel handed her the child, who whimpered once, then settled back to sleep.

At that moment, Madam Krauss appeared in the doorway. "I see that you and the child have gotten acquainted," she said, entering the room. "Have you made a decision?"

"Yes," Maurice replied as he looked down at his sister's son. "Belle and I will be adopting the child."

"Then it isn't you?" the woman asked Jacob in some surprise.

"Oh, no," he said matter-of-factly, as if that had never been his intention. "It's my brother, Maurice, for whom I was speaking. If I seemed perturbed, it was because he and Belle are not yet married."

"Oh, dear me." She frowned. "But our policy is very strict. There can be no adoption—"

"I know," Jacob cut her off. "But that has all been resolved. They are to be married tomorrow. And if we can take care of the paperwork right now, they'd like to pick up the child immediately after the ceremony."

"This is quite irregular, but I suppose it can be arranged, provided your references check out."

"They will," Jacob said plainly. "Maurice is an executive of our family business, Salomon's Emporium."

"Why, yes, you said your name is Salomon," she noted, obviously impressed. "I'm certain there will be no delay." She paused, then added cautiously, "You realize there will be an adoption fee. . . ."

"I understand. But Maurice and I would prefer to discuss the particulars in private."

"Of course. If you gentlemen will come with me, I will draw up the papers, and we can finalize the arrangements." She started from the room, then turned back and said, "Perhaps while we're gone, the future mother can give some thought as to a name for the infant. We will need it for the papers."

"I already have a name—if it's all right with you, Maurice."

"What is it?" he asked.

"Charles . . . Charles Salomon. Do you think your father would have minded?"

"I think he'd have been delighted," Maurice said, choking back the tears as he turned and followed Jacob and Madam Krauss down the hall.

"Charles," Belle repeated, leaning down to kiss the baby's forehead. "My little, precious Charles."

At the other end of the continent, it was just after ten o'clock in the evening when a loud knocking brought Cayleigh Cabot out from the kitchen to answer the front door. She swung it open to find a short, squat man with a gray beard standing on the stoop.

"Finley!" she cried, rushing into the arms of her first husband's father.

"I came as quick as I could," he told her as he held her

close and felt her body tremble. "How's the lad?" he asked, tilting her chin so that he could see her face.

"Scott is asleep upstairs," she said, leading him into the hallway and closing the door. Arm in arm, they entered the small parlor and sat together on the sofa.

"Then he's come out o' the coma?" Finley asked.

"Yesterday. He had a good night's sleep last night and looked much better today."

"He was beat up bad, I daresay."

"Almost killed. I . . . I didn't think he'd make it." She sniffled, and a tear ran down one cheek.

"He's a strong lad, ye'll see. He'll be up and about in no time."

"I know," she said, drying her cheek. "And he does seem better today. Yesterday he didn't say much—he hardly remembered what happened. But today it started coming back to him, and he was able to talk about it."

"Did he know the bloke who jumped him?"

"No. The police said he came off one of the ships from England, but his identification turned out to be false."

"Tha' was a brave thin' ye done, Cayleigh."

She shook her head. "I was only trying to survive."

"Aye, but ye did'na lose your head. Ye did wha' ye had t'do."

"I don't want to think about that horrible man," she said.

"I'm sorry, lass. But it's strange tha' he's such a mystery."

"Scott thinks he came with that London detective."

"Who?" Finley asked.

"Today Scott told me that another man came earlier that afternoon and said he was from Scotland Yard, though Scott now doubts he was telling the truth."

"Wha' did he want?"

"Aidan, of course," she said flatly. "Scott refused to give him any information."

"And he thinks tha' men sent his partner t'beat the truth out o' him?"

"If so, it didn't work."

"Aye. Tha' is the truth of it."

"Just to be safe, Scott had me send a telegram to San

Francisco this evening with a description of the man from Scotland Yard, so that Aidan can be on the lookout for him.''

"Tha' makes sense.''

"Would you like to go up and see Scott?'' she asked, taking Finley's hand in her own.

"Not if he's restin'. There'll be plenty o' time tomorrow for tha'. Actually, right now I could use a bit o' grub and a good night's sleep.''

"I'm sorry. I should have offered you something to eat.'' She started to stand. "I'll fix you something—''

"Not so quick,'' he said, pulling her back down onto the sofa. "The food can wait until ye tell me how things are goin' wi' ye.''

"Things are all right,'' she muttered, looking down.

"Is tha' true?'' he asked, turning her face toward him. "Those pretty brown eyes kinna tell a lie, and they seem t'be sayin' tha' somethin' is botherin' ye, and more than this trouble wi' your husband.''

Cayleigh stared into Finley's piercing gray eyes and tried to mask what she was feeling, but she was unable to keep the tears from welling up and overflowing. Finally she turned away and mumbled, "It's nothing, really.''

"Aye, but it is,'' he said, patting her hand. "Now why dinna ye tell Finley wha' else is upsettin' ye?''

She looked up at him again and suddenly broke down in loud, mournful sobs. "Oh, Finley!'' she wailed, throwing herself into his arms. "What am I going to do?''

Upon hearing Cayleigh's voice as she greeted Finley downstairs at the front door, Scott stood on shaky legs and slipped his arms into the sleeves of his bathrobe. Pulling tight the sash at his waist, he stepped into his slippers and walked to the dressing table, where he raised the wick of the kerosene lantern and examined his reflection in the mirror. He looked bruised and haggard, but not so bad for having spent the better part of a week unconscious in bed.

Making his way across the room, he pulled open the door and walked down the hall to the landing at the top of the stairs, where he stood listening to the people downstairs in the parlor. A few minutes before, when the knocking at the front door had awakened him, he had immediately recognized Finley's voice, but even now, from his place at the top of the stairs, he was unable to discern what they were saying. Probably Cayleigh was describing Scott's injuries and the progress he had been making. And what better way to dramatize that progress, he thought, than to surprise them by making an appearance in the parlor?

Padding softly down the stairs, he approached the open parlor door at the end of the hallway. The voices grew more distinct, and he heard Finley ask Cayleigh what was upsetting her and then heard Cayleigh begin to cry. When Cayleigh asked, "What am I going to do?" and sobbed all the louder, Scott suddenly felt like an intruder.

With a twinge of guilt, he turned to sneak back upstairs, but then he froze in place as Finley said softly but clearly, "Ye are pregnant, aren't ye?"

Scott tried to move, but his legs would not respond. He felt the breath go out of him when Cayleigh choked back her tears and stammered, "How d-did you know?"

"I sensed as much when ye came t'visit me home in Bay St. Lawrence."

"But that's impossible," Scott heard his wife reply. "I had no idea then. It was . . . too soon."

"Aye, but I could already sense the change within ye—the glow o' new life."

Scott tried to pull himself away—to race back down the hall and up the stairs. But he could not move—could not breathe—could only listen as Finley continued, "Have ye told Scott?"

"Not yet," Cayleigh replied in a near whisper, like a child confessing a terrible sin.

"Aye, I did'na think so," Finley continued. "Because Aidan McAuliffe is the father."

Scott did not have to hear his wife's response to know that it was true. He was painfully aware that they had not made love in far too long a time for him to be the father.

Scott felt a heavy, chilling fog settle over him. He only vaguely heard Finley ask Cayleigh what she would do and her reply that she did not know but that she was certain she wanted to keep the child. Then Finley asked something about her feelings for Scott, and Scott waited for the knife that would cut through him when she admitted that she could no longer spend her life with a man she did not love.

"I *do* love him," she said softly but with a sure, steady voice—a voice that cut through him not like a knife but like a warming beam of light. "I didn't realize it before," she went on. "I kept thinking about my Aidan, and then I fantasized that Aidan McAuliffe was him come back from the grave. I never saw how brave and selfless Scott really is. Aye, it's true—I love him. But . . ."

"But what?" Finley asked.

"I'm afraid he no longer loves me . . . or wants me. He . . . he has hardly touched me these past months, and when he finds out about this child, I fear he'll never touch me again."

Scott heard her sobbing softly and Finley soothing her with gentle words. He realized that he, too, was crying. A part of him wanted to take Cayleigh in his arms and tell her that everything would be all right, while another part wanted nothing more than to lash out and strike her down. He stood motionless for a few more moments, and then his legs started to move, almost of their own accord.

Scott felt the cold fog dissipating as he headed slowly up the stairs and returned to his room, where he sat down in his chair and stared at the lantern, waiting, wondering what he would feel when he looked into Cayleigh's eyes.

It was perhaps an hour that he sat like that, watching the light and only vaguely aware of the sounds from below as Cayleigh helped Finley settle into the guest room for the night. And then she was there, standing in the doorway, looking in surprise at her husband seated in the chair.

"I . . . I thought you were asleep," she said.

"I only just woke up," he lied, his voice more faint than he expected it would be.

"You should be lying down," she said distractedly, approaching and holding out her hand to help him up.

When Scott felt her hand touch his, a warm shudder ran

through him. He grasped her hand and held it tight. "I'm sorry," he said softly, pausing slightly before continuing, "for the distance I've allowed to come between us."

"No," she murmured, and her eyes began to fill with tears. "It was me—"

"Shhh," he hushed, rising from the chair. He took both her hands and squeezed them gently. "It was my fault. I should have seen that you were unhappy. I should have let you know that I love you."

Cayleigh looked down at the floor. "I . . . I don't deserve your love. I've made a terrible mistake, and I'll understand if you no longer want me."

Scott pulled her close to him. "If you're talking about Aidan, it doesn't matter. I know how attractive he must have seemed—especially after the way I had been neglecting you. No, it's *you* who should not want *me*."

Looking up at her husband, Cayleigh started to say, "There's more—" but Scott pressed a finger to her lips.

"The only thing more that needs to be said is that I love you." He leaned down and kissed the tears from her cheeks. "I want us to be together. As husband and wife." He led her toward the bed as his right hand rose along her spine and began to undo the hooks at the back of her dress. "And I want us to have a child—our child—right here and right now." He kissed her neck, his left hand moving up along her side.

Cayleigh drew in a sharp breath as his hand began to caress her breast. She tried to speak—to confess what she had done—but he cut her off with a deep, passionate kiss. As their lips parted, he whispered, "Don't say anything more. Just let me show you how much I love you." He pulled her dress down off her shoulders, then stooped down slightly and slipped his hands up under her skirt, gripping her around the buttocks and lifting her off the floor. She felt herself falling back onto the bed, and then he was on top of her, kissing her shoulders and breasts, his hands pressing and kneading her thighs.

"I love you, Cayleigh," he breathed into her ear as he raised himself up over her. She felt his fingers touching, searching her, felt the passion building within her, and she slid her hands along his waist and tugged at the sash of his robe, pulling it open wide. "I love you," he repeated. "And I'll make it right. You'll see. Everything will be right. . . ."

His lips came down upon hers, their tongues 'meeting as he entered her. Feeling him deep within her, she realized that somehow he knew that she was pregnant, yet he loved her all the same. And as she gave herself to him fully and felt him giving himself in return, she knew that with this act of love he was claiming her child as his own.

EIGHTEEN

"Do you, Maurice Salomon, take this woman, Merribelle Knowles, to be your lawfully wedded wife, to love and to honor, in sickness and in health, until death do you part?"

"I do," Maurice said, his voice quavering with emotion.

"And do you, Merribelle Knowles, take this man, Maurice Salomon, to be your lawfully wedded husband, to love and to honor, in sickness and in health, until death do you part?"

"Yes, I do," Belle replied, smiling as she looked up into Maurice's light-brown eyes.

"Then by the power vested in me by the State of California, I now pronounce you man and wife."

Jacob and Aidan cheered in unison and Rachel clapped as Maurice took Belle in his arms and they kissed.

The bespectacled little man who had read the abbreviated ceremony stood grinning at the other side of the counter in the office of the justice of the peace at City Hall. He waited a moment before saying, "If you'll just sign here . . ." He pushed a document across the counter and held out a pen.

Maurice signed first, then Belle. "It is official now," the man announced, and again the young couple kissed.

Thanking the man, Maurice and Belle walked arm-in-arm to where the others were standing. Jacob was beaming with delight as he slapped his younger brother on the back and said, "Congratulations! And how about a kiss from the bride?" They embraced and kissed on each cheek.

After Aidan and Rachel congratulated the newlyweds, Rachel said, "This calls for a celebration. Why don't we all go out for dinner?"

"A splendid idea!" Jacob proclaimed. "There is a superb new restaurant on Columbus Avenue I'd love to take you to. It's called Il Calderone."

"That sounds delightful," Rachel said.

"Then it's decided." Jacob motioned the others toward the door.

As they headed through the lobby of City Hall, then through the big brass front doors and down the wide stairs to the street, Maurice spoke quietly with Belle. When they reached the sidewalk, he stopped and said, "There's something Belle and I would like to do before any celebration." He waited until he had their full attention, then continued, "We feel there is no point in putting off the inevitable, so we'd first like to stop at home and tell Nina of our marriage."

When he paused, Belle added, "And about our baby, too."

"Are you certain?" Rachel asked.

"Yes," Maurice said with determination. "The point in not telling her before was to make certain she could take no action to delay our marriage or forestall the adoption. Now that those things have been accomplished, there's no point in delaying. There's nothing left she can do."

"We'd like to stop at the orphanage on the way," Belle added. She looked up at her husband. "Maurice and I won't feel comfortable until we have little Charles in our hands."

"I think you've made a wise decision," Jacob agreed. He stepped to the curb and signaled for the coach, which he had hired earlier in the afternoon and was now parked farther down the street.

As soon as the two-horse, coach-bodied laudau came to a halt at the curb, Jacob opened the door and ushered the others into the covered compartment. Before stepping in himself, he looked up at the driver on the raised seat in front and said, "The Juan de la Cruz Orphanage on Valencia Street." He stepped inside and closed the door, and the coach pulled away and clattered down the road.

An hour later, after a stop at the foundling home, the coach halted in front of the Salomon mansion on Nob Hill. It had been decided that Maurice and Belle would go inside alone first, while Jacob, Rachel, and Aidan remained in the coach with the baby. They would give the newlyweds a few minutes to break the news to Nina, and then they would bring little Charles in to meet his grandmother.

Jacob climbed out of the coach and graciously held the door for his brother and new sister-in-law. He stood watching from the curb as the young couple headed up the walk and were greeted at the front door by the butler, who spoke briefly with them.

The door closed for a moment, but then it opened again and Cameron came outside and approached the coach. Rachel and Aidan were sitting inside the coach beside the open door, and when Rachel greeted Cameron, he glanced briefly at the baby sleeping on her lap and then said, "I am sorry to bother you, Miss Salomon, but this telegram arrived for you earlier in the day, and I thought you might want it immediately." He held out an envelope, which she took.

"Thank you, Cameron," she said, opening the envelope as the butler turned and headed back to the house.

Rachel saw at once that it was from Scott Cabot in Nova Scotia and had been transmitted the previous evening. As she read the message, her expression darkened, but she said nothing and merely folded it back up.

"Bad news?" Jacob asked, looking through the door.

"Not really," she replied, putting on a smile. "It's from Scott Cabot in Nova Scotia. You remember Scott."

"Of course, though we've never met. A business problem?"

"No. He was a bit under the weather but is better now. He just wanted to know if Aidan arrived all right."

When Jacob turned away from the door, Rachel handed the telegram to Aidan and signaled him to look at it. As he read about the assault on Scott and the description of both the attacker and the man who claimed to be from Scotland Yard, he frowned and slowly shook his head. Slipping the telegram into his coat pocket, he looked up at Rachel, who shrugged her shoulders. He gave her a reassuring smile.

"Shall we give them a few more minutes?" Jacob asked, looking back inside the coach.

"Yes," Rachel replied. "Though I doubt it will help."

Inside the mansion, Nina Salomon ushered Maurice and Belle to one of the sofas in the parlor to the right of the foyer. Maurice could tell that she was distracted and obviously still distraught over the death of her husband, but he was pleased to see her up from bed and dressed. She wore a modest gray gown with black lace trim and had even applied some rouge and powder to her face. Her hair was pulled back in a chignon at the nape of her neck. She hardly glanced at Belle but sat in a chair across from the young couple, nervously clutching a small handkerchief.

"You did not stay here last night," Nina commented, her tone brusque but civil.

"Jacob has given me a room at his town house."

"And . . . your friend?" She waved the handkerchief toward Belle but looked away.

"She still has a room at the hotel," Maurice began. He took a deep breath and plunged ahead. "That's what we've come to talk with you about." He took Belle's hand in his own. "Merribelle and I decided to get married."

Nina's head swung around, and she raised one eyebrow. "But that is out of the question," she said flatly.

"Why?"

"You hardly know the girl," she replied, almost as if Belle were not in the room.

"I am in love with her."

"And I love your son," Belle added, her voice soft but steady.

"*Love . . .*" She said the word as if it were distasteful to her. "What do you youngsters know of love?"

"You were younger than I am when you married."

"That was different. Your father was older—and far more settled than you, Maurice." She paused, then shook her head and said, "No, a marriage is out of the question. Perhaps after a suitable period of courtship—"

"I'm sorry, Nina," Maurice cut in. Gripping Belle's hand more tightly, he went on, "The marriage has already taken place—at City Hall this afternoon."

The handkerchief slipped from Nina's fingers. Her eyes widened as she stared at her son, then looked for the first time at her new daughter-in-law. "What?" she gasped.

"That's right—we're already married." He began to smile. "I'd like to introduce Mrs. Maurice Salomon."

Nina's lower lip started to quiver, and her right hand clenched into a fist. Squinting one eye, she fixed her gaze on her son and grated, "How could you do this to me?"

"I wasn't doing anything to you. We just—"

"How dare you! This . . . this marriage must be annulled. It simply cannot be!"

"But it already is."

"Never! Not like this!"

"We are in love, and we are now man and wife. That's all there is to it," Maurice stated with conviction.

Looking back and forth between the two of them, Nina forced herself to take a deep, calming breath. "You could have told me before," she said, her voice lowering a pitch. "If this . . . this marriage had to be, the least you could have done was to wait a respectful time after your father's death and allow me to arrange a suitable wedding for someone of our station. But now—what am I supposed to do? It's too late for announcements, and a reception would be unseemly so soon after your father's—"

"There wasn't time," Maurice interrupted. "The wedding had to be today."

Suddenly Nina's jaw dropped, and she turned to Belle and eyed her closely, her gaze moving up and down her body and finally settling at her waist. "If you're trying to say that circumstances have forced a hasty marriage . . ." Her words trailed off as she looked up into Belle's eyes.

Realizing what Nina was thinking, Belle met her gaze and said firmly, "I am not pregnant, Mrs. Salomon."

"No—nothing like that," Maurice assured his mother. "In fact . . ." He hesitated, but Belle patted his hand and nodded for him to continue. "Well, the fact is that we already have a child. Not our own—" he quickly added. "But a child we adopted this very afternoon. That's why we hurried the wedding, so that we would be eligible to adopt."

"This is ridiculous," Nina blurted, standing from her chair.

"No, it isn't," Maurice replied. "Please sit down, for there is more."

Numbly, Nina took her seat, her hands wringing together in her lap as she waited for him to speak . . . as she waited for him to say the very thing she most deeply feared.

"We found out about Phoebe's child," Maurice said bluntly. "Jacob, Rachel, and I. We agreed that we couldn't let the baby be raised by strangers—not when he's the only link we have left to our sister."

Nina looked up to see Rachel standing with Jacob and Aidan at the entrance to the parlor, the infant bundled in her arms. "You—you mean you adopted that . . . that little bastard boy?" she stammered in shock as she raised a hand toward the doorway.

"Yes," Rachel declared as she approached with the child. "But he has a name now."

"We've named him Charles," Belle said expectantly, hoping that Nina would be touched by what they had done and would accept Belle and the child into the family.

"Blasphemy!" Nina suddenly screamed, standing and shaking a fist at the infant. "You can't name a . . . a *bastard* after my beloved husband!"

"He's your grandson," Rachel said, holding out the child.

"Father would have been pleased. He's the one who told us about Phoebe's baby and—"

"Lies!" Nina screeched, throwing her hands over her ears and turning away from them. "Your father died a help-less cripple! Thank God he never lived to see the shame you've brought upon this household!"

"There is no shame," Maurice said, reaching for his mother's arm. But she pulled away and walked across the room. "The only shame is in your heart."

"How could you do this to me?" Nina cried, turning to face the group. "Don't you care about our good name?"

"If that's your only concern, you can stop worrying," Maurice told her. "No one knows that this is Phoebe's child. He's simply a little boy whom Belle and I adopted. No one need ever know the truth."

"What about him?" she shot back, pointing at Aidan. "And who knows who else you've told!"

"If you'll just look at the child," Maurice pleaded. "Just hold it for a minute—"

"I'll be damned if I'm going to play grandmother to that . . . that little bastard!" she raged, storming across the room toward the foyer. "I want you out of here! All of you!" She turned toward them, and when they did not move, she yelled, "Right now! Get out of my house!"

"Come on," Jacob told the others as he strode past his mother and headed for the front door, with Rachel and Ai-dan following close behind.

Maurice and Belle rose from the sofa and started across the room. Pausing in front of his mother, Maurice said, "I'm sorry—"

"Get out!" she shrieked, pointing at the front door. "And don't ever bring that bastard back into this house!"

Maurice took Belle's arm and led her through the foyer and out the front door. When they caught up to the others at the coach, Rachel handed little Charles to his mother.

"Don't worry about Nina," Rachel said reassuringly. "Give her time; she'll come around."

"I'm not so sure," Maurice said.

"You did the right thing, Maurice," Jacob said. "I was proud of you in there."

"Thank you," Maurice replied, smiling at his older brother.

"Let's not allow this to ruin our celebration," Jacob continued. "We're still going out to dine, aren't we?"

"Of course we are," Rachel said enthusiastically.

"Then let's get aboard." Jacob held the door open for the others, then called up to the driver, "Il Calderone on Columbus Avenue. And keep those horses stepping lively!"

As soon as the coach door closed behind Jacob, the driver snatched up the whip and snapped it over the horses' heads, setting the animals off at a trot down the drive.

So quickly did the coach pull onto the street and head down Nob Hill that the occupants were unaware of the man who sat in a hansom cab just across the street from the driveway entrance. The man was well aware of them, however, for he had been watching the house for several hours and had seen them arrive a short time before.

Putting down the opera glasses that he had used to identify the occupants of the coach, the man rapped on the back of the seat, then leaned out the window to call up to the driver on his raised perch behind the passenger compartment. "Follow that landau," he said in a voice that betrayed his English heritage.

As the hansom cab started down the hill after the coach, Jeremy Mayhew leaned back and smiled ruefully. Having only arrived in San Francisco that very afternoon, he had not expected to find Aidan McAuliffe so quickly. He had taken up his position across the street from the house, which he had found using the return address from Rachel Salomon's telegram, with the hope that he would be able to identify Rachel and that eventually she would lead him to Aidan. But when the coach had arrived, he had been surprised to see Aidan among the group. Jeremy had recognized him at once; Aidan's image was burned in his consciousness from the long hours of the trial that had led to the conviction of his sister's killer.

Jeremy patted his side and felt the small revolver nestled in his pocket. He thought briefly of Nate Gilchrist, who would have been quick to use the gun on Aidan McAuliffe, and he muttered, "The stupid fool." Jeremy had waited in Boston only to learn about Gilchrist's mysterious death from one of the seamen aboard the ship Gilchrist had planned to take from Halifax. Apparently he had gone against Jeremy's orders and had gotten himself killed in the process. If he were alive now, he would probably urge Jeremy to put an end to this whole affair with a single bullet to Aidan McAuliffe's head.

"No," Jeremy whispered. Killing Aidan would be far too simple and quick, and it would not give Jeremy's father the satisfaction of seeing his daughter's murderer brought to final justice. No, Jeremy would not kill him, though his heart cried out for revenge. Instead he would find the right place to take him into custody and turn him over to the police for extradition to England, where the sentence of the court would at last be fulfilled.

As Jeremy watched the coach through the front window of the hansom cab, his smile faded. It had been a long journey to San Francisco, a journey that soon would be at an end. Suddenly he felt very hollow inside, and he wondered if he would finally feel at peace when this entire business was concluded. But then he remembered the sickening feeling of thrusting a knife into the belly of an innocent man, and he realized that he may have been seeking one measure of peace only to discover an eternity of hell.

Feeling totally alone in her empty mansion, Nina wandered aimlessly from floor to floor, passing through each of the children's rooms on the third floor and then heading down to her late husband's bedroom, where she stood looking at the empty bed.

"Oh, Charles," she moaned. "Why?"

She touched the pillow, then sat down on the bed and placed her cheek where her husband's head had rested.

"What have I done?" she whispered. "I didn't want to

throw them out. I . . . I just couldn't look at that baby. Not after what happened to Phoebe.''

She began to cry, then looked at the pillow and said, ''You forgive me, don't you, Charles? You know that it's for the best—that I did what I had to do—for Phoebe's sake.'' She sobbed more loudly.

''Oh, Phoebe!'' she wailed. ''Don't hate me! I'm so sorry!''

Nina lay sobbing into the pillow for several minutes. As she began to regain her composure, she heard the butler call her name from the hallway. Standing from the bed, she wiped her cheeks and said, ''Yes?''

''There is a visitor, madam,'' Cameron told her through the closed door.

''Who is it?''

''A friend of Maurice's. His name is—''

''I . . . I don't want to see anyone.''

''Yes, madam.''

''Wait a minute,'' she called, crossing the room and opening the door. ''Tell him to wait in the parlor. I'll be right down.''

''As you wish.'' Cameron turned and headed downstairs.

Nina hurried over to the dressing table and looked in the mirror. She frowned at her image and sat down to touch up her hair and smooth away the streaks that ran down her cheeks.

''I'll make it up to them, Charles,'' she said aloud as she worked on herself. ''You'll see. I'll find them and tell them I didn't mean what I said.'' She patted her hair into place and sat checking her handiwork. ''Perhaps this friend of Maurice's knows where they've gone and can take me to them.'' She nodded approvingly at her reflection, then stood up from the table and turned toward the bed. ''You'll see. They won't hate me anymore.''

Nina left the room and headed down the stairs to the foyer. Straightening her skirt, she approached the parlor entrance and spied a tall, blond-haired man in a light-brown suit standing by the fireplace. As he turned to face her, she saw that he was devastatingly handsome, with piercing blue eyes, a firm jaw, and full, sensuous lips.

The butler was standing just inside the parlor, and he nodded respectfully to Nina and announced, "Mrs. Charles Salomon, may I present Mr.—"

"Damien Picard," the young man interjected with a slight bow. "Delighted to make your acquaintance, Mrs. Salomon." He approached and held out his hand. As Nina offered hers, he raised it to his lips and gently kissed the back of her hand. He lowered it but did not let it go.

Turning to the butler, Nina said, "Thank you, Cameron. That will be all."

Cameron nodded again, then departed through the foyer.

"You and Maurice are friends, Mr. Picard?" Nina asked.

"Please call me Damien," he insisted. "Yes, we are, Mrs. Salomon."

With a demure smile, she said, "That is far too formal for a friend of Maurice's. You must call me Nina."

"Of course, Nina." He again raised her hand to his lips, then finally released it. "If I seem at all taken aback, it's because Maurice never mentioned having a sister-in-law— and one as attractive as you."

"Sister . . . ?" Suddenly Nina giggled. "Would that I were his sister. I am Maurice's mother."

"Impossible."

"But true. And thank you for the compliment."

"Your husband is a very lucky man."

"My husband, alas, has recently passed away." She adopted a suitably remorseful expression. "A sudden heart attack. He never recovered."

"I am sorry, ma'am."

"Nina . . . please," she insisted, smiling again.

"Yes, of course."

"Your accent—it sounds . . . French?"

"Creole. My family is from New Orleans."

"Is that where you and Maurice met?"

"Actually, we met in New York. He invited me to visit if ever I came to San Francisco."

"I'm afraid you just missed him." She crossed the room

to a small table beside the sofa. "Would you like a brandy?" she asked, lifting a decanter.

"That would be delightful," he replied, coming over as she poured the drink and handed it to him.

"It seems that Maurice has gone out and gotten himself married," Nina said plainly, smiling ruefully at the handsome young man.

Damien nearly choked on the brandy. "Maurice?" he exclaimed. "I only just saw him . . ."

"I'm afraid it's the truth. A young woman he met during the journey home."

"Isn't that kind of impulsive?"

With a slight frown, she said regretfully, "I have given up being surprised by the actions of my youngest son."

Damien nodded knowingly. "Sons can be a burden. Just ask my father." He gave a self-deprecating grin. Swirling the brandy in his glass, he continued, "I didn't mean to impose upon your time. Do you expect Maurice back soon?"

"I don't know when he will return. I'm afraid we had some words, and . . . and he left."

"I'm sorry. Perhaps I can leave the name of my hotel."

"Please don't rush off just yet. It's nice to have a visitor. Would you like to see the rest of our house?"

"Why, yes, I would. Thank you."

Damien placed the brandy on the table and held out his arm. Taking it, Nina led the way back through the foyer to the cavernous reception hall. As she showed him the view of San Francisco through the arched windows that lined the hall, he could not help but marvel at the kind of money required to own and maintain a home such as this.

"Maurice told me that your family owns an emporium," Damien mentioned casually as she brought him through the hall to an enormous living room, perhaps fifty feet square, that was tastefully decorated in an almost Oriental style. In the center of the room was an intricately woven Chinese rug with a floral pattern, each petal shaved at the edges to create a three-dimensional effect. The floral motif was picked up in the four sofas and dozen or so chairs and was also used to trim the massive green drapes. The tables and furniture were all of polished mahogany, with sweeping, graceful lines that were reminiscent of peaked temple roofs.

"Salomon's Emporium was started by my father," Nina explained as they walked through the room. "It is the largest retail establishment in California—indeed, west of the Mississippi River."

"Its reputation has even reached New Orleans."

"Perhaps I can offer you a tour of the store during your stay in San Francisco," she suggested.

"That would be most gracious of you. But I wouldn't want to impose—particularly during your time of mourning."

"One cannot mourn forever," she sighed as she stopped in the middle of the living room. "Many another mother has lost her husband and daughter."

"Daughter?" he asked.

"Oh, didn't you know? My youngest daughter, Phoebe, was in a fatal accident. I'm afraid the shock precipitated my husband's heart attack."

"Maurice never mentioned it."

"He didn't know until he returned home. There was nothing anyone could do."

"I'm so sorry," Damien said in a consoling voice as he took Nina's hand and gripped it soothingly.

"Thank you," she replied, her voice faltering slightly. "You've been so kind."

"And so have you, to open your home to me like this. Perhaps there's some kindness I might offer in return?"

Nina looked into his clear blue eyes for a long moment. "Perhaps there is one thing."

"What is it?" he asked eagerly.

"I mentioned that Maurice and I had words. I'm afraid it runs deeper than that. We argued over his hasty marriage—and over an infant boy he adopted."

"A baby?" Damien asked incredulously.

"I know it sounds preposterous, but it's the truth. He and his new wife decided to adopt some foundling and then rushed into this thing without any real thought . . . without even considering that to others it might look as if he and this woman had to get married.''

"But he didn't, of course," Damien quickly put in.

"Of course not. But the woman is not from around here, and there will be those who think this child is hers and that Maurice was forced into the marriage by circumstance."

"What can I do?"

"Speak with him," she begged. "Convince him that he's made a mistake, before it's too late to undo what's been done." Her eyes suddenly filled with tears, and she had to dab at her cheek with the back of her hand.

"Is something else wrong?" he asked, taking out a handkerchief and handing it to her.

"I'm sorry," she murmured, wiping her eyes with the cloth. "It's just—first my husband and daughter, and now this thing with Maurice. I'm afraid I spoke quite harshly to him. I'm not certain he'll ever forgive me."

"I'll speak with him," Damien promised. "I don't know if he'll listen to me, but I'll see what I can do."

"Thank you," she said in a barely audible whimper as she clutched the handkerchief in her hand.

"You just try to relax and not worry about things." Stepping closer, Damien boldly placed an arm around her shoulder. "I'm sure this has all been quite a shock to you. Not just losing your husband, but your daughter, as well. They say that the loss of a child is the hardest burden for a mother to bear."

She sniffled and raised the handkerchief to her nose. "I love Phoebe very much."

"And it hurts to have lost her."

"No one understands," she mumbled, looking down and shaking her head. "I never wanted to hurt her. I only want what's best for her."

"I believe you, Nina," Damien declared, looking at her askance and wondering what exactly she was talking about.

"Thank you, Damien." Pulling away from him, Nina wiped her eyes a final time and handed him the handkerchief.

Accepting it, he raised her hand and kissed it for the third time. "I'll do all that I can to help you, Nina."

"Thank you." As she withdrew her hand, she added, "You're not at all like Maurice's other friends."

"Am I a disappointment?"

"Not in the least. So many young men today are coarse and unrefined. You are a delightful change."

"And you are unlike any mother I have ever met. You restore my faith in motherhood." He grinned almost suggestively, and Nina blushed.

"I wish I were a better mother," she admitted.

"You mustn't be so hard on yourself. If you love your children, they will feel it. The rest is unimportant."

"If only that were true," she muttered. Then her expression brightened, and she said, "But I mustn't bore you with my troubles. You've already been so generous."

"I hope you will let me be more generous in the future," he responded in a soft yet assertive voice.

Realizing that she was blushing, Nina looked away and took Damien by the arm, leading him from the living room back through the smaller parlor and out into the foyer. "It's been so nice to have you visit," she told him.

"You'll tell Maurice that I called?" he asked. "He can find me at the Baldwin Hotel."

"Yes, I'll tell him," she assured him.

The butler came forth just then and presented Damien his brown derby hat and silver-knobbed cane. When Cameron moved toward the door, Nina signaled him away, and he departed through the cloakroom.

"Thank you again, Damien." Nina took the young man's hand. "You've been so kind to listen to a mother's troubles."

Damien started to lift her hand yet again, but she pulled it away, as if a bit uncomfortable, and walked to the door. She opened it, and he bowed respectfully and started through. At the last moment, he paused and turned to her. "You are a unique woman, Nina," he said, tipping his hat. "I hope your children realize just how remarkable you are."

"Thank you," she replied, her voice quavering. She

watched him turn and start down the walk, and then she swung the door shut and leaned back against it, breathing hard.

This Damien Picard was certainly a handsome and personable young man, she thought, but now that he was gone she felt even more alone than before. His visit had stirred memories that she had been struggling to contain, and now they assailed her with the force of a whirlwind.

"What have I done?" she breathed. "Oh, my dear little baby, what have I done to you?"

Nina could hear Phoebe's voice calling from within her, begging for her help—begging to be released. "I . . . I had to," she stammered. "'There was no other hope for you."

A sudden wave of fear washed over her. She saw Phoebe alive though far from well—moaning and suffering, lying senseless in a stupor in a cold prison cell, sentenced by her own mother to an eternity in hell.

"No!" she exclaimed, her piercing cry bringing Cameron at a run. "I have to find out . . ."

"What is it, madam?" he asked in concern as he came into the foyer.

Gripping her arms, Nina forced herself not to shiver as she stood away from the door. "Have Michael bring the buggy around. There is somewhere I have to go."

Cameron stared at her a moment, then said, "Perhaps you'd prefer him to drive you in the carriage."

"The buggy!" she shouted. "I must go alone!"

"Yes, madam," he replied, bowing and hurrying away.

"I must . . ." she repeated as she strode across the foyer to the cloakroom to retrieve her evening shawl. "For once and for all . . . I have to find out."

Outside, Damien reached the gate at the end of the driveway and turned to see that Nina had closed the front door. He stood there a moment, his hands resting firmly on the knob of his cane as he took in the splendor—and the power—of the Salomon's Nob Hill mansion.

"Maurice, you're a sly dog," he whispered. "I knew you were loaded, but I had no idea . . ."

Damien cocked his hat slightly on his head. "You've done the right thing coming here, old boy," he told himself as he pushed open the gate and started down the sidewalk. "There's money to be made here—and plenty of it."

Just now that sounded very good to Damien Picard. His pockets were so close to being empty that he could last but a few nights at the expensive Baldwin Hotel and did not dare waste funds on a cab. But soon all that would change— if not with Maurice's help, then with Nina Salomon's.

Swinging the cane jauntily, he began to whistle as he walked sprightly down the road.

NINETEEN

THE LARGE COACH-BODY LANDAU PULLED TO A HALT IN front of a newly erected brick building on Columbus Avenue near the corner of Beach Street, which ran along the waterfront. Though it was already getting quite dark, the moon was bright enough to reveal the long row of small, sleek Mediterranean feluccas with their henna-colored lateen sails, the craft of choice for the Italian fishermen who dominated the North Bay wharf area.

Before climbing out of the coach, Jacob pointed to the waterfront and said, "It's like a bit of Italy here, and you're about to eat in one of the finest Italian restaurants west of Sicily: Il Calderone. It's famous for its steaming pots of *branchio cioppino* and *calamari picata,* which is why it's named Il Calderone—The Caldron."

Aidan shot a look of surprise at Rachel, who also recalled the name from the reading of the *I Ching* by Hsiao Ch'u. They shared a cautious smile.

"Shall we go?" Jacob asked as the coachman opened the door.

"Jacob," Maurice said hesitantly as his older brother

302

stepped out to the sidewalk. "Belle and I have been thinking it over, and though we appreciate what you're doing, we'd prefer to forgo the celebration." He looked at his wife beside him and the tiny child sleeping in her arms. "We'd like some time alone with our son."

Jacob looked at each of them, then grinned broadly. "Of course. This is your honeymoon, isn't it?" He reached into his pocket and removed a set of keys, which he handed to his brother. "The driver will take you to my house. You'll find everything in order; I had the store deliver all the needed supplies for little Charles." He turned to Rachel and Aidan. "It looks as though we'll be celebrating alone. Shall we?"

With a smile, Rachel took his hand and stepped from the coach. She was followed by Aidan.

Looking back through the doorway, Jacob said, "Now you two hurry along and enjoy yourselves." With a grin, he added, "And don't wait up for me. I have it in mind to spend the night at a hotel downtown."

Maurice grinned back at him. "Thank you, Jacob."

"Now get going!" Jacob declared, slamming shut the door and stepping back on the sidewalk.

From inside the coach, Maurice and Belle watched the threesome standing in front of the restaurant. They heard Jacob call the address of his town house up to the driver, and then with a lurch the coach pulled away from the curb and made a wide turn to head back up Columbus Avenue.

Maurice turned to his bride and felt the tears welling up in his eyes. She looked so very beautiful holding Phoebe's baby—their little child—in her arms. He knew that he did not deserve such happiness, and he took a silent oath to make up for his past profligate ways.

"I love you, Merribelle Salomon," he whispered as he reached over and stroked her cheek.

"And I love you," she replied, easing a hand out from under the baby and pressing his palm against her lips.

"I'll try to be the husband you deserve."

"I know you will."

"And I'll make up for the mistakes of the past. You'll see I will."

"Don't worry about the past," she soothed. "We are starting a new life together. The past need never come between us, for ours is the present and the future."

Belle lifted the baby slightly and held it forth, and Maurice moved closer and took his wife and his son in his arms. "I love you," he repeated as their lips met in a soft, prolonged kiss.

Across the street from Il Calderone, Jeremy Mayhew watched Aidan McAuliffe and his two friends enter the restaurant. "The perfect place," he said aloud as he returned the small pair of opera glasses to his left coat pocket and stroked his black mustache. "In public, with no way to escape."

Patting the revolver in his right pocket, Jeremy sat looking at the restaurant, fighting the urge to pull the gun and finish things once and for all. But now that he had reached the end of his journey, he would handle things within the law; he wanted to give his father the pleasure of seeing Aidan McAuliffe stretch a hemp rope on the gallows of Millbank Penitentiary.

Jeremy could try to take Aidan alone, but he worried that people might mistake Jeremy for an armed robber and help the real criminal escape. Instead he would take the more conservative approach and arrange for Aidan to be apprehended by an officer of the law. Then there would be no one to help Aidan—no chance of escape.

Jeremy opened the door of the hansom cab and stepped out to the street. "Where's the nearest constabulary?" he called up to the driver.

"The what?" the man said, rubbing his chin.

"Constabulary," Jeremy repeated. "Police station."

"Ahh," the driver exclaimed with a nod. "It's that gray building up there." He pointed to a small stone building a block up Columbus Avenue. "Want me to take you?"

"No. I'll walk." He reached into his inner pocket and produced his wallet. "What do I owe you?" he asked, removing some bills.

"Let's see . . . it's been near four hours. . . ."

"Will this cover it?" Jeremy asked, handing the man twenty dollars.

"Why, yes. Very generous of you, sir." He stuffed the money in his pocket. Looking back at Jeremy, he asked, "What about your bags?" He nodded down at the boot below his seat, where Jeremy Mayhew's luggage had been stored ever since hiring the cab at the Ferry Building earlier that day.

"Deliver them to the Palace Hotel and tell them to hold them for my arrival. My name is on the baggage."

"Shall I come back for you?"

"That won't be necessary. I'll hire another cab when I'm ready."

"As you wish, sir." He nodded and picked up the reins.

As the hansom cab headed back up Columbus Avenue, Jeremy glanced over at the restaurant, then reached into his pocket and took out a folded piece of paper. Opening it, he looked at the photograph of Aidan McAuliffe on the wanted poster. A policeman would have no difficulty recognizing Aidan from the photo, and though the poster listed him as an escaped convict from England, it gave notice that the American and Canadian governments had authorized his apprehension and extradition.

Returning the poster to his pocket, Jeremy started up the street toward the police station. Soon it would be over, and then perhaps he would be able to find a way to make up for the terrible things he had been forced by circumstance—and by Nate Gilchrist—to do. Perhaps he would at last put to rest the terrors that assailed him—the demons that threatened him on every side.

Seated alone in her buggy, Nina Salomon felt as if she were being chased by the furies, and she slapped the reins harder against the back of the old brown mare, urging it to greater speed. Still, it lumbered along at barely a trot as the buggy traversed the rising ridge of land that led from Nob Hill out to the Presidio, with its magnificent views of the Golden Gate. But just now she was not interested in the twinkling lights of Sausalito across the bay or the hills of evergreen and eucalyptus that rolled down to the cliffs at the water's edge. Her attention was on the forbidding black edifice that loomed just ahead near the end of Pacific Avenue, across the street from the Presidio.

Nina pulled the buggy to a halt in front of the tall double gate at the center of the black iron fence that surrounded the grounds of the imposing building. Engaging the brake, she wrapped her shawl tighter around her and climbed down from the buggy. She could see that the gate was padlocked, but beside it in the fence was a small door, which allowed admittance by pedestrians. Turning the latch, she found it unlocked, and she slipped through onto the grounds.

Making her way up the lamplit walk beside the wide, circular drive, Nina felt the cold fog stinging her face, and she wiped away the moisture that had collected on her cheeks. She moved more quickly, afraid that if she stopped going forward, she might turn and run and never come back.

At last she reached the massive front door and reached for the bell push, then withdrew her hand without pressing the button, unable to face what she might find on the other side of that door. She took a few steps back and looked up at the archway, illuminated by the flickering light of the lamps that lined the walk, and read the wrought-iron letters: *Presidio Asylum for Incurables*.

"No . . ." she whispered, backing away from the door as she stared up at the sign. "I can't. . . ."

She felt tears welling up in her eyes, and she turned and hurried back down the walk. Halfway to the street, she stopped abruptly under one of the kerosene lamps, her shoulders hunched as she sobbed quietly into her hands.

"Nina . . ." an exceedingly gentle voice called.

Catching her breath, Nina looked up through a veil of tears to see someone approaching through the door in the fence. She wiped at her eyes, and the vision cleared until she recognized the tall figure of Damien Picard.

"Nina," he repeated, holding out his arms as he came up to where she was standing. "It's all right."

"Wh-What are you doing here?" she asked, her body going rigid as he grasped her shoulders.

"I'm sorry . . . I had to come. You seemed upset when I left. And then I saw you drive away so quickly in the buggy. A cabbie was passing, and I had him follow you."

"You had no right," she said, though without conviction.

"I had to. I was worried about you."

Nina stared into his cool blue eyes. She started to speak, but her lips trembled, and she broke down sobbing. Pulling her close, Damien comforted her, whispering that everything would be all right. When she began to calm, he tilted her chin until she faced him.

"Why did you come to such a place?" he asked ever so softly. Again she opened her mouth but was unable to speak. "Don't worry," he whispered, lowering her head against his shoulder. "You don't have to speak. I understand."

"How . . . how c-could you?" she stammered, closing her eyes. "No one can understand."

"It's Phoebe, isn't it?" he asked guardedly. "That is why you've come."

Nina pulled away from him, her eyes narrowing with suspicion. "How did you know?" she demanded weakly.

"From the way you spoke about her," he explained. "As if she were alive." He paused, gripping her shoulders more tightly, then added, "She *is* alive, isn't she, Nina?"

The older woman's entire body began to tremble now, and as she slowly nodded, she let out a deep, mournful wail. Damien gathered her into his arms, pulling her close and whispering soft, soothing words. After a few minutes, she began to calm, and he led her to a small bench that sat beside the walk. As they sat down, he took her hands and said, "You can tell me the truth, Nina. I'm your friend. I will tell no one—not even Maurice."

Sniffling, she nodded and wiped at her tears with a handkerchief until she regained her composure enough to speak. "It was horrible," she began, her voice low and weak but building in strength as she told him the full story of her daughter's suicide attempt and the subsequent botched abortion, which led to Phoebe's seizure in the doctor's office. "At first we thought she was dead," Nina explained. "But when the doctor went to cover her with a blanket, she suddenly drew in a gulp of air and began to breathe. But she was not the same. She . . . she was . . ."

"What is it?" he urged.

Nina looked up at him. "She no longer responded. Not to anything. She could only stare straight ahead . . . unable to move . . . hopelessly insane." She began to cry again, and Damien held her until she was able to continue. "The doctor examined her, but there was nothing he could do. Nothing anyone could do."

"And so you had her brought here?" Damien asked, nodding toward the building.

"He said they could give her the special care she needed. He promised that she'd want for nothing that money could provide, so I gave him enough for the best private room, and he made all the arrangements." She drew in a deep breath, then went on, "Of course I was mortified at the thought—but what else could I do? My husband had just suffered a stroke, and the other children were away. Someone had to make the decision, and no one else would have had the strength to do what had to be done."

"But you said she had died. Do the others know?"

She shook her head. "I didn't want them to suffer the guilt or the shame. And I wanted them to remember Phoebe the way she had been—not how she had become. So I paid the doctor to draw up a death certificate and bring her here under a false name." She grasped his hand and pulled it close, her tone almost beseeching as she said, "It was for Phoebe's own good, don't you see? She has nothing left but her good name. I won't let anyone take that away."

"Why have you come here?" Damien asked in a calm yet firm voice.

"I . . . I was worried about her. At first I hoped she might get better—before her sister and brothers came home. But I've received regular reports, and there's been no improvement—indeed, they tell me there's no hope at all."

"Then why come now? I don't understand."

"I wanted to see for myself . . . to make sure I made the right decision. For Phoebe. For the entire family." She glanced back at the building and shuddered. "But I can't. I just can't look at her the way she is . . . like a corpse."

"You did the right thing—I'm sure of it," he told her. "And if you'd like, I'll go in there and check on her condition. I'll make sure she's getting the proper care."

"Would you?" she asked, looking up at him expectantly.

"Of course, Nina." He stood and helped her to her feet. "I want you to wait in the buggy," he said as he led her back down the walk. "I won't be long, and then I'll drive you home."

Reaching the street, he helped her into the buggy and found out the name under which Phoebe had been admitted. Then he walked over to the cab he had hired and retrieved his cane from the seat. Paying the driver, he sent him on his way, then headed back up the walk, cane in hand.

Damien did not hesitate at the door. He pressed the bell push and stood patiently until a little viewing port in the door swung inward to reveal a portly, unshaven man.

"What d'ya want?" the man squawked, obviously annoyed at being bothered after hours.

"I've come to see one of the patients."

"Impossible. Come back in the mornin'."

"Surely there is someone on duty who can authorize a visit?" Damien asked politely.

The man was about to reply when he saw a folded ten-dollar bill in Damien's hand. "A visit, you say? This is most irregular."

Damien produced a second ten-dollar bill and added it to the first. "I would be most grateful. . . ."

The viewing port popped shut, and a moment later Damien heard the rasping sound of the lock sliding open, and then the big door swung outward.

"Hurry in," the squat little man ordered, looking around the grounds nervously as he snatched away the money and ushered Damien inside. The man was dressed in a drab gray orderly's uniform, which was as disheveled as his rumpled features and thinning black hair. He took Damien to a cage-like office just off the main corridor and asked for the name of the patient, which he looked up on a grimy chart pasted to the wall. Snatching up a small wooden cudgel and a pair of lanterns, he handed one of the lanterns to Damien and said, "She's down this way."

The little man showed Damien down the dimly lit main corridor to a locked gate that led to the patient wards. Pulling a large brass key ring from his coat pocket, he found the appropriate key and fit it into the lock, then swung the gate open and motioned Damien through. After closing the gate behind them and making sure it was locked, he turned left down a dark and narrow hall.

A piercing cry cut the dank, musty air from the distant reaches of the asylum, nearly causing Damien to drop his lantern. The cry was followed by a series of low, moaning wails, sounding like eerie foghorns on a distant harbor. The little man paid no attention to the sounds but continued down the hall, which was lined on either side with heavy padlocked doors, each with a fading number painted on a small, eye-level trapdoor. As they passed one, Damien heard a muffled shriek, answered at the next door by a high-pitched, unearthly laugh.

The night attendant pulled up short in front of one of the doors and looked at the number, saying, "She oughta be in here." He slid a bolt on the trapdoor, opened it a crack, and peered inside, raising the lantern so that some of the light would spill into the interior. "That's her. I remember the arm," he declared, shutting and locking the trapdoor. He turned and eyed Damien's cane and well-cut suit. "Her family must be plenty wealthy; she's got herself a private room."

"Can I see her . . . alone?" Damien asked.

The man eyed him closely, then grinned and said, "But only a few minutes." He rummaged through the keys on the ring and slid one of them into the big padlock on the door. It popped open, and he removed it and yanked open the door a crack. "Go on," he said, motioning Damien inside. "But be quick about it."

Pulling the door open wider, Damien lifted his lantern and looked inside. The room resembled a prison cell, with a cot against the right-hand wall and a small table and chair under the one-by-two-foot barred port that served as a window. A woman was seated at the table facing the bed, but she did not look up as Damien eased into the room and cautiously approached. She continued to stare vacantly at the table, her blond hair hanging in loose, dirty ringlets, her face as ashen as her coarse muslin skirt and blouse.

Damien walked to the cot—a straw mattress on a wooden frame with a single threadbare blanket thrown haphazardly across it. As he held the lantern over it, he saw a number of large black bugs wiggle away from the light through holes in the mattress, and he decided against sitting down. Instead he turned to the table and looked down at the seated figure, who was remarkably attractive despite her pale color and dirt-grimed cheeks. As he stared at her, he noticed that her right arm was hanging limp at her side.

The young woman looked up casually at Damien. She did not smile, yet somehow she seemed at peace.

"Phoebe?" he asked, and her eyes widened slightly.

"Do I know you?" the woman asked in a gentle voice that thoroughly disarmed Damien.

"You can speak?" he blurted, and she cocked her head slightly, as if surprised that he should ask.

"Who are you?" she inquired after a moment's silence.

"A friend of your family's," Damien answered.

Her expression brightened. "You've come to take me home?"

"I've come to see how you're being treated."

"But I don't belong here. I'm not like the others." There was a distant shriek, and Phoebe shivered, her left hand grasping her limp right arm. "You've got to get me out of here," she implored, looking up at him. "Tell them I'm all right now."

Something caught Damien's eye, and he glanced at the floor to see a large gray rat scurry out from under the table and disappear beneath the cot only a few inches from his feet. He jumped slightly and backed toward the door.

"Please go to my father," Phoebe begged, rising now from her chair. "Tell him—"

"Your father is dead," Damien said bluntly. "His heart finally gave out."

Phoebe gasped, her eyes widening with shock and fear as Damien moved closer to the door. Raising her good arm, she took a step toward him. "My mother . . . Tell her I didn't mean to get pregnant. Tell her I know my baby is dead and that I'm all right now."

Damien kept backing away, lifting his cane in front of him and shaking his head as if afraid that she might touch and infect him.

"I want to go home," she cried, moving closer, her fingers groping toward him. "Please, take me home!"

Suddenly Damien dashed through the open doorway and slammed the door, pressing his back against it and shutting his eyes as Phoebe banged away on the other side, moaning and wailing, begging him to set her free.

Damien heard a rasping, metallic sound and opened his eyes to see the night attendant snapping shut the padlock. "Had enough, have you?" the man said with a sly grin.

"Get me out of here," Damien hissed, pushing away from the door and walking ahead down the corridor. Behind him, the sound of Phoebe's knocking was picked up, one by one, from other doors along the corridor, until the entire building reverberated like the pounding of drums.

Ten minutes later, following a brief meeting with the night attendant at his small office, Damien emerged from the Presidio Asylum for Incurables. He had recovered sufficiently from his visit to the wards to offer the attendant a pleasant good night as he tipped his hat and started down the walk.

Damien slowed his pace as he approached the buggy. With an audible sigh, he climbed aboard and sat down beside Nina, who sat stiffly under her heavy woolen shawl.

"How is she?" Nina asked in a steely, almost emotionless voice.

"It was good that you didn't go inside."

"Why?" She lowered the shawl from her face and turned to look at him. "How is Phoebe?"

"I'm sorry," he said, his tone dripping with feigned sincerity. "There's no hope for her. She is as good as dead."

Nina choked back a cry. Breathing deeply and composing herself, she asked, "Did she say anything?"

"Nothing at all. She can only stare—she doesn't hear or speak."

Rubbing her hands together, Nina nodded woodenly.

Turning to her, Damien took Nina's hands in his own. "The important thing now is to know that you did the right thing for Phoebe. She is getting the best of care. You can rest easy knowing that she will be comfortable . . . for the time she has left."

Nina lowered her head and nodded. "I had to do it; the others wouldn't have had the courage," she whispered. "It's a mother's cross to bear."

Damien gently squeezed her hands and raised them to his lips. Gaining her full attention, he said, "I did something for Phoebe . . . I hope you will approve." When she looked at him questioningly, he went on, "Though her accommodations were adequate, she wasn't getting the best they can offer. I had her moved to a larger room, where she'll be more comfortable and receive the maximum care. I thought you'd want that for her."

"Oh, yes," Nina said eagerly, leaning toward him and kissing his cheek. "You've been so helpful."

"I'm afraid it will cost a little more."

"Cost is nothing," she replied, waving off his concern.

"I'll take care of everything," he continued. "There's no need for you to involve that doctor any longer or risk direct contact with this place. You can provide me the funds, and I'll see to it the bills are paid."

"You'd do that for me?"

"Of course. And I'll make sure she always gets the very best of care."

"Yes, I know you will." Nina smiled weakly at him and felt her eyes filling again with tears. "Please take me home," she asked, looking down. "I want to get away from this place."

Damien picked up the reins and was about to release the brake when Nina stopped him by placing her hand over his. "What's wrong?" he asked.

"Everyone has left me and I . . . I'd rather not be alone. Do you have to return to your hotel? Perhaps you could stay at my house tonight."

"I'd like that," he replied with the most sensitive of smiles. "I'd like that very much." He disengaged the brake lever and slapped the reins against the horse's back. The animal stepped out briskly, and the buggy clattered down the road, carrying Damien and Nina into the gathering darkness.

Behind them, the evening fog curled through the neatly manicured grounds of the Presidio Asylum for Incurables, muffling the moans and dreadful cries from within.

TWENTY

"*Signor* Bonissone!" Jacob Salomon called as he led his sister and Aidan McAuliffe into Il Calderone.

"Ah, *Signor* Salomon," replied a tall, husky man in a black suit as he came through the salonlike entrance of the restaurant. "So good to have you with us."

"I'd like to introduce my sister, Rachel, and a friend of hers from Nova Scotia, Aidan Orcutt," Jacob said. Turning to them, he continued, "This is Paolo Bonissone, owner of Il Calderone."

"Such a pleasure to meet you," Bonissone greeted them, lightly kissing the back of Rachel's hand. "You have come for dinner, no?" he asked Jacob.

"But of course. My sister recently returned from the Continent, and I insisted her first dinner out on the town be at Il Calderone."

"*Grazie!*" Bonissone declared, clapping his hands. "You will have your usual table, and I will personally see to it everything you order is *delizioso e sodisfacente*." He raised his fingers to his lips as if to kiss them.

Aidan helped Rachel remove her black wool outer coat,

which he handed through a small window to the attendant
in the cloakroom just off the salon. He and Jacob were not
wearing outer coats, and so they turned to follow Bonissone
into the dining room. The big man led them through an
open doorway covered with a lace curtain and into the large
main room, which consisted of a dozen tables tastefully laid
out with an abundance of silver and crystal atop white linen
edged with ruffled silver lace. The straight-backed chairs
were upholstered in a ribboned, royal-blue felt, which
matched the floor-to-ceiling draperies. The entire room
glowed in the flickering light of four enormous crystal chandeliers, each adorned with several dozen porcelain gas jets
in the shape of candles.

Most of the tables were filled with well-dressed young
men and women, and as Paolo Bonissone led the party to a
square table at the rear, several of the patrons smiled at
Jacob and Rachel and received a nod or smile in reply.

"Do you have a claret you'd recommend?" Jacob asked
as they took their seats at the table, leaving empty the chair
with its back to the room.

"I have a pleasantly dry, eighty-seven Bordeaux that is
soft and light on the palate."

"Excellent."

"If you'll excuse me." Bonissone bowed and walked off
toward the kitchen in back.

"You'll see," Jacob said quietly as he looked back and
forth between Rachel and Aidan, who sat on either side of
him. "This will be the finest meal since our vacation in
Venice when we were youngsters."

"All I remember is being sick the whole time we were
there."

"That's because little Maurice kept rocking the gondo-
las," Jacob replied with a chuckle.

"That's true," Rachel told Aidan. "In fact, he fell into
one of the canals, and Father had to rescue him."

"Nina threw a fit," Jacob added. "When Father dove
over the side of the boat, the whole vessel nearly capsized,
and her favorite hat went overboard—the one with all those
silk flowers and little feathered birds."

Rachel giggled. "I remember that monstrosity. It was all we could do to keep from cheering as it slowly sank below the surface and disappeared into the murky depths."

"But Maurice was all right, I trust," Aidan said.

"He was fine—until Nina got him back to the hotel," Rachel explained. "She made him pay for every silk petal and ostrich feather out of the money he had saved up to purchase mementos of the journey." She giggled again. "Of course, Father slipped the money back to him when Nina wasn't around."

"You must have loved your father very much," Aidan commented.

"He was a wonderful man," Rachel said wistfully.

"And well respected, if a bit weak," Jacob put in. "He always had a soft spot where Nina was concerned. Whatever foolish thing she did, he forgave and accepted, as if he were somehow responsible for her every action. I never understood it myself." He glanced to the side and saw the proprietor returning with an open bottle of wine and three glasses. Jacob waited as the wine was poured, and then when they were alone again, he raised his glass and said, "To Father, may he finally rest in peace."

Rachel and Aidan raised their glasses, and they drank.

"I'd like to propose another toast," Jacob said as they lowered their glasses. Raising his again, he intoned, "To Phoebe, and to the young child who has come to bring joy out of despair."

"To Phoebe and little Charles," Rachel said, tipping her glass and drinking.

"And to Belle and Maurice," Aidan offered, his sentiment echoed by the others.

Putting down his glass, Jacob suggested, "I suppose we should take a look at the menu and decide what . . ." His words trailed off at the sound of a commotion at the front of the restaurant in the curtained-off entryway.

There was a sudden crash, as if a chair had been upset, and then the scraping sound of furniture being moved. All heads turned toward the salon, and the room grew quiet as the patrons strained to hear what was going on. Just then the curtain over the doorway was thrust aside, and a tall, slender man with wavy blond hair and a pencil-thin mustache pushed his way into the dining room. He was well dressed in a fashionable black cutaway suit, but it was somewhat disheveled. And he was staggering—possibly drunk—and swinging his arms around wildly as he weaved his way among the tables, smiling and nodding at the guests as if in greeting.

"Ahh! Jacob! So good to see you!" the fellow proclaimed as he stumbled toward the table in the back.

Jacob gripped his glass more tightly and frowned. He opened his mouth to speak, then decided to remain silent.

"Having dinner with . . . with your lovely sister," the man declared as he came to an unsteady halt a few feet away. "And . . . and with this . . ." He waved a hand toward Aidan and hunched his shoulders, as if at a loss for words.

"What are you doing here, Eaton?" Rachel asked.

"What am *I* doing here?" Eaton Hallinger asked. "You mean, why aren't I in jail?" He laughed coarsely. "The wonders of the modern judicial system. They call it bail."

"What are you talking about?" she asked.

"Don't you know?" Resting one hand against the back of the unoccupied chair, he leaned toward her. "Didn't your big brother tell you?"

Rachel looked questioningly at Jacob, but he merely glowered at Eaton and remained silent.

"Why, I was arrested this very morning. Something about some missing bank funds. Isn't that true, Jacob?"

"I don't know what you're talking about," he seethed.

"Of course you do, because you're the one who had me arrested. Aren't you, Jacob Salomon?"

"You're making a fool of yourself," Jacob said, keeping his voice low. "Go on home and sober up."

"Hah!" Eaton chortled. He stood up straight and waved his arm around the room, taking in the other patrons. "Embezzling, that's the charge. From my own bank, no less! And all handed to the police on a silver platter by good Mr.

Jacob Salomon of Salomon's Emporium.'' He spun back around and pointed a fist at Jacob. ''Isn't that right?''

Just then Paolo Bonissone, having heard the commotion, came through the back door. ''What's going on here?'' he demanded, approaching the inebriated man.

''Just came to have a word with our friend here. I knew I'd find him at his favorite restaurant—Il Calderone!''

''Well, you've found him now, so it's time to go home and get some sleep.'' Bonissone reached for Eaton's arm, but the younger man pulled away.

''Not so quick,'' Eaton protested. ''I've got a few more things to say to my good friend here.''

''I think you've said enough,'' the big man replied, again reaching for Eaton's arm.

''Not until that bastard admits that he's the one who ruined me.''

''That's enough—''

''Just a minute,'' Jacob cut in, waving Bonissone back. He turned to Eaton, who stood rocking back and forth on unsteady legs, and pointed an accusing finger as he said, ''The only one who ruined Eaton Hallinger was himself. It was your own greed and stupidity that brought you down, and I'm glad to have been able to help in some small way.''

''You *are* a bastard, aren't you,'' Eaton hissed, his voice more in control now. ''Just because of what happened to your sister, you decided to become judge and jury. I would have made the losses good, but now it's too late—because of you!''

Without warning, Eaton reached into his pocket and pulled out a revolver, which he waved at Bonissone, forcing him back. Several women screamed, and then people began to scatter toward the front door as Eaton backed away from the table a few feet and swung the gun toward Jacob.

''Eaton!'' Rachel gasped, her eyes wide with horror.

''I—I'm sorry . . . about Phoebe,'' he stammered, looking at Rachel. ''She never told me she was pregnant. I . . . I would have done the right thing, if only I had known.''

''Please . . .'' she whispered, raising her hand, begging him to lower the gun.

Eaton waggled the gun at Jacob, his eyes burning with rage. "But you'll never believe it, will you? You're determined to see me in hell! But not before I see you there first!"

Eaton jerked the trigger just as Aidan McAuliffe leaped sideways from his seat, crashing into Jacob and knocking over the table. As they went tumbling to the floor, Aidan felt a burning stab of pain at his left shoulder, and he realized he had taken the bullet in his upper arm. He paid no attention to it but reached up and yanked Rachel down behind the overturned table.

On the other side of the table, Eaton saw Jacob go down and thought for a moment that his shot had been true. But then he saw the tear on the other man's jacket and the red stain spreading down the sleeve. Immediately he raised the gun again and pointed it at the figures on the floor, trying to get a shot that would find its intended mark.

"Hold it!" a voice shouted from behind him, and Eaton spun around to see two men pushing their way into the dining room through the press of people scrambling to get out. One was a uniformed policeman, and the other wore a dark-brown suit and had black hair and a mustache. The policeman seemed surprised to see a man holding a smoking revolver, and he clawed for the gun at his side.

"No!" Eaton shouted, but when the policeman did not stop, Eaton raised his gun and pulled the trigger twice, and the policeman clutched his belly and went down. Eaton then saw the second man drawing a revolver from his jacket pocket, and he swung his gun on the man and fired again, striking the man in the chest and knocking the gun from his hand as he spun around and fell facedown on the floor.

Eaton turned in circles, waving the gun at the few remaining patrons who had taken shelter behind tables. Then he stopped in place and looked beyond the overturned table to where Rachel was huddled with her brother. Eaton appeared to have forgotten Jacob completely as he raised the gun and muttered, "I'm sorry, Rachel. I didn't mean to do it. . . ." His eyes sought Rachel's for a final time, as if beseeching her forgiveness. And then he pointed the barrel into his own mouth and pulled the trigger.

Rachel screamed as the explosion thundered through the restaurant, followed by the dull thud of a body hitting the floor. Then all was a hush—but only for a moment, until people realized that it was finally over and men and women alike began to cry and comfort one another.

As Paolo Bonissone helped some of his patrons toward the fresh air outside, Rachel crawled over to Aidan and threw her arms around him. Feeling a wetness on her hand, she pulled back and saw that his upper arm was bleeding.

"It's all right," he said when she gasped at the sight. "Just a crease," he assured her, grabbing a cloth napkin and tying it around his arm.

Jacob had pulled himself to his feet, and he helped his sister up from the floor. As they stood looking at the chaos around them, Aidan circled the overturned table and walked over to where Eaton Hallinger lay in a pool of blood, the back of his head blown away. Aidan did not need a closer examination to confirm that the young man was dead.

Leaving the body where it lay, Aidan hurried over to the two other victims near the door. He knelt first beside the policeman and felt his pulse. He, too, was dead, having taken a bullet to the abdomen and a fatal shot to the neck, severing the jugular vein.

Moving to the third victim, who lay facedown on the floor, Aidan detected a rising and falling of his back and pressed his fingers to the man's neck. There was a pulse, strong but somewhat irregular. "Help me!" he called to the restaurant owner, who was just coming in from outside, and together the two men rolled the victim onto his back. The man moaned once, then slipped again into unconsciousness.

Aidan saw at once that the man had sustained a serious gunshot wound to the chest, and he began to unbutton the jacket and shirt to better examine the area. It was when he was pulling open the shirt and baring the man's chest that he first looked at his face. Just then the man groaned, and his eyes fluttered open. He stared up in surprise at Aidan, as if in recognition.

"It's all right. I'm a doctor," Aidan told him, but the man just shook his head, his eyes widening in fear. As Aidan stared down at him, he had the curious feeling that they had met before. And then suddenly he knew where he had seen that face before—at his own trial. This was the son of Gordon Mayhew, who had engineered Aidan McAuliffe's arrest and conviction. It was the very man Scott Cabot had described in his telegram of warning.

Aidan glanced down at the gaping hole in Jeremy Mayhew's chest. He knew that there was no time to transfer him to a hospital; he would have to operate at once if the man were to have any chance of survival. *But why?* he asked himself. *If I do nothing, he'll die and take the knowledge of my whereabouts to his grave.*

Aidan turned away from the wounded man and shook his head at Bonissone, who assumed he meant that there was no hope. Rising, Aidan started to walk back toward the overturned table where Rachel and Jacob were standing. But then he halted and found himself staring at the table, and the words of the old Chinese fortune-teller sounded within him as clearly as if Hsiao Ch'u were standing beside him, whispering in his ear:

"I see you at great banquet. A table is overturned. An enemy tries to cause you harm. You desire revenge. To avoid misfortune and enhance fate, you must act correctly, without concern for what the outcome will be."

"Il Calderone," Aidan whispered aloud, looking around him at the restaurant, his gaze locking on the body of his adversary lying near the front door. "The Caldron."

"What is it?" Jacob asked, coming around the table to where Aidan was standing.

"I have to operate," he announced, still looking at Jeremy Mayhew. "At once."

"What are you talking about?"

Aidan turned to Jacob. "I am a physician. My real name is Aidan McAuliffe."

Jacob looked at him curiously, then turned to Rachel, who came forward and said, "He's telling the truth."

"I don't understand."

"It doesn't matter," Aidan said. "But I must operate on that man at once, or he'll die."

"What can we do?" Rachel asked, touching his arm.

"I need surgical instruments." As he walked back to where Jeremy Mayhew was lying, he grabbed some of the unused linen napkins from the tables. Kneeling down, he pressed several of them against the man's chest to help stanch the flow of blood. Turning to Bonissone, he said, "Bring me several knives of different lengths—the sharpest and narrowest ones you have. Also several long-handled spoons and a pair of metal tongs—the kind you'd use to lift a jar out of water. Boil everything for several minutes, then wrap them in clean linen. Understand?" When Bonissone just stared at him, he added, "I'm a surgeon. I'm going to operate."

Nodding, Bonissone stood and hurried to the kitchen.

As Aidan pressed the cloth against the wound, Jeremy Mayhew tried to raise his head. "Rest easy," Aidan told him. "I'm not going to hurt you."

Jeremy reached up and grabbed Aidan's wrist, squeezing it weakly. He tried to speak but made only a sputtering sound.

"You must be quiet," Aidan urged him, removing the hand from his wrist and placing it at Jeremy's side. "I have to operate if you are going to survive."

"D-Don't . . ." Jeremy managed to stammer. "P-Please don't k-kill me." His head fell back against the floor.

"I'm not going to hurt you. I'm a physician," Aidan replied, but Jeremy had slipped into unconsciousness again.

Looking up to see Rachel and Jacob standing over him, Aidan said, "Rachel, I want you to stay here and help me. Jacob, see if you can find a doctor with a surgical kit. And send for an ambulance."

As Jacob hurried from the restaurant, Aidan motioned for Rachel to kneel beside him and take hold of the cloth that he was pressing against the wound. As soon as Rachel was providing sufficient pressure, Aidan stood and quickly removed his suit jacket. "I'll be right back," he said, dashing off to the kitchen to wash his hands and make sure Bonissone had obtained the right implements. A few minutes later he returned with a pan of water, a pile of folded cloth napkins, and a long metal skewer that was pointed at one end and bent into a small circle at the other.

"We can't wait any longer," he said, kneeling beside the victim. He spread a napkin on the floor and placed the pan and the other napkins on top of it. Quickly checking Jeremy's pulse, he nodded and said, "You can let up now."

As she pulled away the blood-soaked cloth, he dropped several napkins into the water, removed one, and used it to wipe the surface of the wound, cleaning the area and revealing the nearly inch-in-diameter hole made by the bullet near the base of the ribs.

"I've got to get the bullet out first," he explained as he lifted the skewer and began to insert the point into the wound, following the opening between the ribs and guiding it carefully along the track of the bullet just below the left lung. As he worked, Paolo Bonissone appeared from the kitchen with a large tray that contained a number of objects wrapped in a linen tablecloth.

Just as Bonissone was placing the tray on the floor beside Aidan, a pair of policemen came rushing in from the street, stopping abruptly upon seeing Aidan pressing the skewer into the man's chest. "What's going on here?" one of them shouted, reaching for his gun.

"Stay back!" Bonissone ordered. "This man is a physician. He's removing a bullet."

The policemen seemed acquainted with Bonissone, and they nodded that they understood. "Over there," one of them said to the other, pointing across the room to Eaton Hallinger's body.

"Damn, it's Barth!" the other one exclaimed, grabbing his partner's sleeve and nodding toward the body of their fellow officer nearby.

"They're both dead," Bonissone said as the policemen went to confirm the obvious.

"Make sure you keep everyone back," Aidan called to the officers without looking up from his work. He gave the skewer a final push, then smiled and said, "I feel the bullet.'' Glancing at Bonissone, he asked, ''Do you have the other skewer I gave you?'' When Bonissone nodded, Aidan said, ''Take it out and hand it to me, but hold it only near the point; don't touch the eyelet at the other end.''

Bonissone knelt beside the tray and unwrapped the table-cloth, which contained the sterilized knives and spoons, as well as the skewer Aidan had added to the boiling water in the kitchen. Picking it up by the point, the restaurant owner held it toward Aidan, who transferred the other skewer to his left hand but left it sticking several inches into Jeremy's chest. Taking the new skewer by the pointed end, Aidan slid the reverse end down along the first skewer and slowly inserted the eyelet into the wound. He wiggled it slightly as he moved it along the shaft of the first skewer, following it to where the bullet was lodged.

''Hold him steady,'' Aidan said when Jeremy shifted slightly. Bonissone quickly grasped the man's shoulders and held them in place.

''I almost have it,'' Aidan whispered as he tried to slip the second skewer under the bullet and cradle it in the eye-let. As he jiggled it slightly, blood gurgled up out of the wound, and he said, ''Wipe it away.'' Rachel quickly complied, using one of the napkins Aidan had left soaking in the pan of water.

After a few moments, Aidan said, ''There,'' and began to pull up on the two skewers, using the pointed end of the first one to keep the bullet pressed against the eyelet of the second. The skewers slipped once, and he had to wriggle them slightly to trap the slug again, but then he drew the bullet the rest of the way out as easily as if he were lifting a large pea with a pair of chopsticks.

Aidan paid no attention to the cheers from the spectators, who now included many patrons who had ventured back inside to see what was going on. Instead he dropped the skewers to the floor and immediately turned to examine the other supplies.

''Bring over some more light,'' he told Bonissone as he picked up the pair of metal tongs. He held the tongs closed over the wound and shook his head. ''The ends are too big.

I'll have to make an incision.'' He picked up one of the smaller knives and inserted it into the wound, then made a small cut to widen the opening. ''Wipe the area,'' he directed Rachel, who dabbed at the blood with the wet cloth.

''That's about right,'' he said, removing the knife. He picked up the tongs again and inserted the closed, flat ends into the enlarged opening. He worked the tongs between the ribs, then grasped the handles with both hands and began to pull them apart. Like a pair of scissors, the ends of the tongs spread open and stretched the ribs apart.

When Bonissone returned with a lantern, Aidan directed him to kneel and hold it over the wound. Keeping the tongs spread with one hand, Aidan worked the handle of a spoon down into the wound and pressed back against the tissue to examine the extent of damage.

''I'm afraid he needs to be sewn internally,'' he said, removing the handle of the spoon. ''But I don't have the right tools.''

''I may have a needle and some thread,'' Bonissone offered, but Aidan shook his head.

''I have to work too deep. It requires a needle holder and the proper ligature.''

''How about this?'' a deep voice boomed, and Aidan looked toward the doorway to see Jacob pushing through the crowd. In his hand was a medical bag, and close on his heels was an elderly man with a confused expression on his face. ''I found Dr. Wertheim's office up the street, and he offered his services. Didn't you, Doctor?'' he asked, pushing the little man forward.

''Why, yes, but I'm not really a surgeon.''

''Do you have a needle holder?'' Aidan asked.

''There's a Hagedorn kit in there,'' the older man replied as Jacob placed the medical bag on the floor beside Aidan. ''And plenty of catgut ligature.''

''A retractor and clamps?''

''Why, yes.''

''Get them out and douse them with some antiseptic solution. You have some, don't you?''

''Carbolic lotion.''

"Fine." When the man did not respond fast enough, Aidan said, "Hurry! We haven't much time."

The physician stooped down and opened his bag. After uncapping the bottle of carbolic lotion, he held the retractor and some clamps over the pan of water and doused them with the lotion, then handed the retractor to Aidan, who inserted it into the wound in place of the tongs. Meanwhile, the older man found the needle holder and fitted a flat-shafted Hagedorn needle into the tip, then poured the lotion over the whole apparatus. Finally he threaded some of the catgut ligature and handed the device to Aidan.

"Hold the retractor," Aidan directed the doctor as he took the needle holder in one hand and one of the clamps in the other. "That's right," he said, showing the man how wide he wanted the wound opened. "Bring the light closer," he told Bonissone. Then he leaned over and inserted the clamp into the wound.

Working quickly and expertly, Aidan closed off the bleeding vessels one by one and sewed them up with the catgut ligature. Then he sewed together each layer of muscle and tissue, until at last the doctor removed the retractor and Aidan sewed together the top layers of skin.

As Aidan finally put down the surgical instruments and wiped his sweating forehead, the older physician pressed his fingers to Jeremy Mayhew's neck and said, "His pulse is regular and strong. I think he'll make it."

Several of the spectators applauded, and a few cheered, but Aidan paid no attention, instead looking up at Jacob and asking, "Is the ambulance on its way?"

"It's right outside," Jacob replied.

Aidan noticed a couple of men standing near the door holding a closed canvas stretcher, and he called to them, "Let's get this man moved right away."

The two men brought over the stretcher and spread apart the poles, laying it on the floor on the far side of the unconscious man. Under Aidan's direction, they carefully lifted him up and placed him on the canvas. Letting his shirttails and jacket flaps hang off the sides, they grasped the poles and lifted the stretcher. As they moved through the salon and out to the street, Aidan walked alongside, holding a clean piece of cloth against Jeremy's wound.

"I'll ride in back," Aidan said as the two men placed the stretcher on a floor-level bed in the back of the closed wagon. Overhead, two lanterns hung from the wagon roof, illuminating the interior of the ambulance. "Just get us to the hospital as quickly as you can," he added, and the two men climbed out and hurried around to the front.

As Aidan took a position beside the wounded man, he looked out through the open back of the wagon and saw Rachel and Jacob standing there. Rachel was holding the jacket Aidan had taken off before performing the operation.

"I'm coming with you," she announced, reaching up to climb in.

Aidan stared at her uncertainly for a moment, then leaned over and held out his hand. She grasped his wrist, and he pulled her aboard. As she knelt beside him, the wagon gave a jerk and started to move.

"Be careful," Jacob called to them.

"We'll be all right," Rachel shouted back. "We'll see you tomorrow!"

The wagon was already traveling at a fast clip up Columbus Avenue, one man driving while the other clanged the large bell, warning other vehicles of their approach.

"Will he live?" Rachel asked, looking in concern at the wounded man.

"I'm afraid so," Aidan muttered.

"What do you mean?"

"I told you about Gordon Mayhew, the man who maneuvered my arrest. This is his son—the very man Scott Cabot warned us was posing as a Scotland Yard detective."

"Oh, my God," she gasped, raising her hand to her mouth as she realized the wounded man lying on the stretcher perfectly fit the description Scott had telegraphed to them. "What will you do?"

"I don't know. I'm tired of running. Maybe I ought to go back."

''You can't. They'll—''

''I don't want to live my life looking over my shoulder. Perhaps this is for the best.''

Closing his eyes, Aidan sat back against the side of the jouncing ambulance wagon, and Rachel moved close beside him and rested her head on his shoulder.

TWENTY-ONE

THE PORTLY NIGHT ATTENDANT OF THE PRESIDIO ASYLUM for Incurables picked up his cudgel and kerosene lantern and started down the hall from his cramped little office. Unlocking the gate that separated the front hall from the patient wards, he swung it open, passed through, and locked it behind him. Whistling, he turned left down the first corridor and returned to the cell that had been visited a short time before by the well-heeled visitor with the silver-knobbed cane.

Without bothering to look in the viewing window, the little man unlocked and removed the padlock, then grasped the handle and gave it a hard yank, swinging the heavy door outward. The light from the lantern he was carrying revealed the figure of a woman sitting curled up in a fetal position on the bed, sobbing softly into her left hand, her right arm hanging loosely at her side.

"Up with you," the man barked as he entered the cell, and the woman glanced at him but did not respond. "You heard me. Get up—you're gettin' out of here."

Choking back her tears, Phoebe Salomon lowered her feet to the floor and rose from the filthy straw mattress. "L-Leaving?"

she asked, her voice edged with hope. "That man who came here . . . he arranged for me to leave?"

The fat little man laughed mockingly. "Yeah, he arranged, all right. Now come on—your new room's awaitin' you."

"New room?"

"You're bein' moved to the general ward—where you'll make lots of new friends."

"I . . . I don't . . ."

"Don't understand, do you? It's plain and simple. Your family ain't willin' to pay the fee no more for a private room. That's why they sent that gent out here tonight—to arrange for you to be moved down the hall, where we keep 'em packed in like sweet little sardines." With a cackling laugh, he raised his cudgel and approached.

"You're lying!" Phoebe blurted, backing away from him into the corner. "They wouldn't do that to me!"

"Wouldn't, would they?" He waved his club menacingly. "Your own family put you in here in the first place. Now they decided they don't want to spend the money to keep you in this . . . this luxury." He waved his cudgel, indicating the room. "So let's get goin'."

The man placed his lantern on the wooden table and, raising his club, advanced toward Phoebe, who stood in the corner shaking her head and whimpering. Roughly grabbing her good left arm, the man swung her away from the wall, stepped behind her, and brought the cudgel in front of her chest. Still holding her good arm with one hand, he drew the cudgel tight against her neck with the other and hissed, "Be a good little girl, and you won't get hurt—leastways, not yet. What they do to a pretty filly like you in the general ward is up to them."

Phoebe felt her air being cut off, and she squirmed in an effort to free herself. But the powerful little man had too tight a grip on her left arm. He started to drag her back across the cell, but she reached out with her foot and hooked it around the leg of the table, nearly upsetting the lantern. She tried to pull her left arm free, but to no avail. All she could do was hang on to the table with her leg and try to keep from being dragged away.

The man jerked harder on the cudgel, causing Phoebe to gag. On the verge of passing out, she summoned her remaining strength in a last-ditch effort to free herself from his grasp. But the only part of her that was not being held in place was her right arm, and it was crippled and virtually useless. Still, she focused all her concentration on that arm, imploring it to move, to respond to her command. She could feel nothing, but then in amazement she saw it lift, ever so slowly, the hand rising toward the table. She saw but did not feel as the fingers straightened and flexed, reaching outward to the lantern on the tabletop.

Phoebe's leg was giving way from around the table as the man yanked harder. With a final act of will, she drew in her stomach and threw her body forward—and she felt something bang against her hand—the hand that had felt nothing but pain for over three weeks. With a shock, she saw that she had gripped the handle of the lantern, and she forced her fingers to tighten around it. She drew back her arm and, closing her eyes, swung the lantern in a wild, jerking arc that brought it behind her head. As the glass smashed, she heard a dull thud, and then the pressure at her neck let up, and the man released her left arm. Phoebe went stumbling forward into the table, her hand still clutching the broken lantern, which incredibly was still lit.

Behind her, the man staggered and went down on his knees, moaning piteously as he grabbed at the side of his head where the lantern chimney had smashed, leaving a deep gash across his face.

"You bitch!" he screeched, wiping his face and pulling back his hand to see it covered with blood.

Setting down the lantern, Phoebe spun around and saw that the man was on all fours and trying to stand. She was about to grab the lantern again when she saw the cudgel lying at her feet. Without thinking, she reached with her right hand and picked it up. Remembering that it was her bad hand, she grasped the handle with both hands and swung the cudgel through the air.

The man, who was just rising, looked up to see the cudgel come crashing against his face. He groaned, blood spurting from his crushed nose as he fell backward, then rolled onto his side and tried to push up against the floor. But again Phoebe swung the cudgel, striking him on the top of the head and knocking him facedown on the floor. Again and again she brought down the heavy oaken club, cracking his skull, until the spasmodic jerking of his arms and legs ceased entirely and he was dead.

Phoebe looked down at the motionless body, then at the bloody cudgel in her hands. She began to sob, the cudgel slipping from her fingers and falling to the floor. For several minutes she just stood there crying, staring at the body of the dead man, then looking around at the small cell that had been her prison.

Forcing herself to calm down, she wiped her eyes and stepped to the open door, glancing up and down the hall. All was quiet and dark, save for the occasional distant mournful cry that had become so familiar to her. Crossing back to where the dead man lay, she knelt down and felt inside his pockets with her left hand until she found the ring of keys that she had heard him use when he visited their rooms.

Clutching the key ring, Phoebe picked up the broken lantern and started quickly toward the hall. But then she turned back and knelt, placing the objects on the floor beside the man's body. Straddling him, she struggled to roll him over. She could not move him with her left arm alone, but she found that it was becoming ever easier to use her right one. Once she had him on his side, she unbuttoned his coat and pulled it free of his arm. Then she rolled him back onto his stomach and removed the coat from his other arm.

Donning the heavy gray garment, she felt some pieces of paper inside one of the pockets and pulled them out to discover a pair of ten-dollar bills. She stuffed them back in the pocket, picked up the lantern and key ring, and slipped out into the hall. As she pushed the door closed, she eased the padlock back into place and locked it. Then she hurried down the hall to the main corridor.

Turning right, she came upon the closed gate. It took a minute of fumbling with the keys to find the right one, but then the gate swung open, and she passed through and pulled it shut behind her. The lock on the front door did not require a key, and a moment later she was outside in the cold, foggy air, the coat pulled tight around her as she looked out beyond the Presidio across San Francisco Bay.

Where will I go? she asked herself as she staggered down the walkway. Halfway to the street she turned, looked back at the dark, imposing edifice, and shuddered. Suddenly she realized that she was still carrying the key ring and lighted lantern. She blew out the flame and tossed both objects under a bush. Then she turned her back on the asylum and went racing down the walk.

Slipping through the door in the gate, Phoebe found herself standing on the street, uncertain of which direction to go. "Home . . ." she breathed, but then she shook her head. There was nothing at home for her. Her father and little baby were dead, and she did not even know if her sister or brothers had returned from their travels. Only Nina would be waiting, and she was the one who had committed Phoebe in the first place. She might contact the asylum and have her returned. And Phoebe would not go back there—never again.

Phoebe turned to stare a final time at the building across the street from the Presidio. Hidden there in her own cell was the body of a man, dead at her hands. "I have killed a man," she muttered. No, she could not allow herself to be captured—for if they ever caught her, if they ever brought her back, she would face a fate far worse than even the general ward could provide.

I have to get away, she told herself as her hand reached into the coat pocket and touched the pair of bills. *Only twenty dollars, but it's a start. Somehow I'll get away from here. And then . . . maybe one day . . . I will be able to return home.*

Phoebe pulled the coat tighter and crossed the street into the dark woods of the Presidio, following the hills down toward the banks of the Golden Gate—toward her only hope of freedom.

* * *

Across town at a small hospital near the waterfront, Aidan McAuliffe came out of one of the examining rooms and approached Rachel Salomon, who stood waiting in the hall. His left shirt sleeve had been cut away, and his upper arm was wrapped in a properly dressed bandage.

"How is it?" Rachel asked, clutching his suit jacket as she came over to him.

"Fine. It was only a scratch."

"What about Jeremy Mayhew?" Her expression darkened.

"The doctor expects him to recover, barring complications. He's recuperating just down the hall."

"We'd better get you back to your hotel," she said, opening his jacket and draping it over his shoulders.

"There's something I want to do first." He glanced down the hall toward the patients' ward.

"Do you think it wise?"

"At this point, I don't see how it can hurt."

"I'm coming with you," Rachel declared, taking his arm as they headed down the hall.

Aidan asked the nurse on duty where he could find Jeremy Mayhew and was directed to a private room at the far end of the hall. The door was open, so Aidan and Rachel went in and quietly approached the bed, where the wounded man seemed to be sleeping.

"Perhaps we should come back—" Rachel started to say, but at the sound of her words, Jeremy Mayhew's eyes opened and looked up at them.

Recognizing Aidan, Jeremy started to lift himself off the pillow, but Aidan stepped up to the bed and said, "Rest easy," then placed a hand on his shoulder and eased him back against the mattress.

"The doctor . . . he told me what you did," Jeremy said in a tired, pained voice.

"I did what I had to do," Aidan said without emotion.

"But . . . but why?"

"What do you mean?"

"You could have . . . killed me. You could have let me die."

335

"No, I couldn't."

"But I know who you are."

"That doesn't matter. You were wounded. There was nothing else I could do."

Jeremy reached up and grabbed Aidan's shirtfront. "But why . . . why did you save my life?"

"You just don't understand," Aidan replied, shaking his head. "I'm a physician. I have taken an oath to save lives, not take them."

"But my sister . . ."

"I know what you think, but you're wrong. I was telling the truth at my trial. Your sister had already undergone an abortion when she was brought to me. I tried to save her, but it was too late."

"But the witnesses . . . that other doctor . . ."

"Your father must have hired them. Didn't you know?"

Letting go of Aidan's shirt, Jeremy closed his eyes and sighed. "I suspected. But I was so convinced you killed her. . . . I didn't care what it took to see you hang."

Rachel came over now and touched Jeremy's hand. "Mr. Mayhew," she said softly. "Surely you see that Aidan is not a murderer—or an abortionist. He saved your life when he could have saved his own by letting you die."

Jeremy slowly opened his eyes and looked at Rachel, then over at Aidan. His mouth quirked into the faintest of smiles, and he whispered, "There's still time."

"What do you mean?" Aidan asked.

"It's in my pocket." He nodded toward his jacket, which hung on one of the footposts. "Look in my jacket pocket."

Aidan reached into the pocket and pulled out a pair of opera glasses and a folded piece of paper.

"Open it," Jeremy instructed.

Putting back the opera glasses, Aidan unfolded the paper and saw his own picture on a wanted poster.

"I only showed it to that one policeman, and he's dead. Tear it up. No one will ever know."

"What about your father?" Aidan asked.

"He doesn't know I'm here. When I return to London, I'll

explain everything to him. I'll see that your name is cleared. I promise.''

Aidan stared at the poster for a long moment, and then he smiled and tore it lengthwise in half.

Jeremy gave a deep sigh as he leaned back and closed his eyes.

"Thank you," Aidan said, gripping the man's forearm.

Opening his eyes halfway, Jeremy looked up at Aidan and said, "Forgive me."

"You didn't know. You thought I was guilty."

"Please . . . forgive me," Jeremy repeated, his voice growing weaker.

"Yes, I do," Aidan said, but he saw that Jeremy had drifted to sleep, his breath shallow but steady.

"I forgive you," Aidan whispered, placing a hand on Jeremy's forehead. "Sleep now. You're going to be all right."

A half hour later, Aidan and Rachel rode in a hansom cab down Fulton Street toward Golden Gate Park. As the cab pulled up in front of the Hotel Willard, Rachel tenderly took hold of Aidan's hand and said, "May I come in for a few minutes?"

"I'd like that," he replied, stepping out and helping her down from the cab. He paid the driver the fare from the hospital and asked him to wait for a while and then take Rachel home. Then the couple walked arm in arm to the front door of the big, black building.

Despite the late hour, Josephine Jeffries was awake and seated in the parlor when Rachel and Aidan entered. She stood to greet them, but when she saw the torn sleeve of Aidan's jacket and the bandage on his upper arm, she came hurrying over, exclaiming, "Oh, my poor dear, whatever happened?"

"It's nothing," Aidan insisted, smiling uncomfortably.

"Nothing! But there's blood all over the front of your shirt, and—"

"It isn't his," Rachel said, then grinned mischievously and added, "You should see the other fellow."

"Well, I hope you got the best of him," Josephine declared. "I warned you that parts of this town are not fit for ladies and gentlemen."

"Next time I'll be more careful," Aidan promised, his eyes locked on Rachel's.

Seeing the way the two young people were staring at each other, Josephine started to back away and said, "I was just going to bed. I'll just turn off a few of the lights and then leave you to yourselves." She circled the parlor and lowered all the lamps but one beside the sofa. "Good night, now. And please, Miss Salomon, stay as long as you'd like." She gave a knowing smile and sashayed from the room.

"Would you like to sit down?" Aidan asked a bit awkwardly once they were alone.

"Not just yet," Rachel replied, turning to him and resting her hands on his shoulders. "Were you very angry when you found out that I lied about being married?"

"Yes, I was—but not at you."

"What do you mean?"

"I was angry at myself . . . for letting a little gold ring keep me from doing what I had wanted to do from the moment I first saw you."

"Which is . . . ?"

Aidan reached around Rachel's waist and pulled her close, their lips meeting in a soft, tentative kiss that grew longer and more full as their lips parted and their tongues touched and explored. Rachel felt her breath being drawn out of her, and she pulled away slightly and leaned back in his arms, feeling his lips kissing her neck, his hands moving up along her back and caressing her hair.

"Do I have to leave?" she murmured into his ear, and he answered with a long, passionate kiss as he lifted her off her feet and carried her past the sofa, pausing only to blow into the lantern chimney and put out the flame. She clutched him tightly around the neck, whispering gently in his ear as he carried her through the parlor and up the long, winding staircase that led to his room.

Outside, the cabbie slouched down in his high perch at the back of the hansom cab and grinned as he watched the hotel lights going out, first in the downstairs lobby, then at the top of the stairs.

"They said to wait," he muttered to himself, his smile widening as he put his feet upon the roof of the passenger compartment and made himself comfortable. "At five dollars an hour, this could be my lucky night, indeed!"

EPILOGUE

SEATED ALONE IN THE BACK ROOM OF HIS SHOP, HSIAO CH'U gathered the yarrow stalks and rolled them up in a small grass mat. He envisioned the young man and woman who had visited his shop a few days before, when the Caldron had warned them of impending danger and the need to take proper action, regardless of the consequences. Wondering what the *I Ching* would foretell for them now, he lifted to the lantern light a piece of paper and examined the six-line figure, composed of two solid and four broken lines, that he had drawn as a result of casting the yarrow stalks.

Nodding his head sagely, the little Chinese man intoned, *"Ming I,"* then repeated the name of the oracle in English: "Darkening of the Light." In Chinese, he recited from memory a part of the prophecy: "A light that shines too brightly will climb to heaven, then plunge into the depths of the earth." Lowering the piece of paper, he gazed into the light and continued, "Thus the superior man veils his light, yet still it shines."

Hsiao Ch'u saw fleeting images in the flickering lantern light. The young couple was coming together; someone else was running away. He tried to make out the various figures that formed and transformed in the dancing flame, but a veil of fog seemed to descend in front of his eyes, until even the burning wick could no longer be discerned. Leaning forward and reaching toward the warmth, he cupped the air above the lantern and blew down into the chimney, snuffing the flame and darkening the light.

About the author

After graduating from the State University of New York in 1973, Paul Block moved to San Francisco and parlayed his creative-writing degree into a series of jobs as a cappuccino cook, apartment manager, and fish cleaner at California's largest retail fish market. In time he found himself working first as a typist, then copy editor and columnist, at the same newspaper in which he previously had wrapped mackerel and cod. A two-year stint followed as assistant city editor of the evening newspaper in Albany, New York, after which he became an editor for Book Creations, Inc., a book production company located in the Berkshires of upstate New York.

Paul has written five westerns published under various pseudonyms, but SAN FRANSISCO is the first novel to appear under his own name. He currently lives with his family in the Albany area, where he writes and edits novels.

Look for DARKENING OF THE LIGHT, book two in the San Francisco Series, coming soon to a bookstore near you.